The Hall Tree

The Hall Tree 2002

The Hall Tree

An American Family History

The Halls of South Carolina, Georgia, Arkansas, etc.

Wesley E. Hall

Writers Club Press
San Jose New York Lincoln Shanghai

The Hall Tree
An American Family History

All Rights Reserved © 2002 by Wesley E. Hall

Writers Club Press
an imprint of iUniverse, Inc.

For information address:
iUniverse, Inc.
5220 S. 16th St., Suite 200
Lincoln, NE 68512
www.iuniverse.com

ISBN: 0-595-21750-8

Printed in the United States of America

William Newton Hall (1831-1923) - Susan Elizabeth Woods (1851-1918)
[ca. 1915]

To the memory of my mother

Mallie Rue (Carr) Hall
(1882-1971)

Contents

LIST OF ILLUSTRATIONS

PHOTOGRAPHS

FAMILY CRESTS

FAMILY CHARTS

FOREWORD

This family history begins with a branch of the Hall family that was living near Charleston, South Carolina, shortly before the American colonies rebelled against the British. Almost nothing is known about the John (b. 1769) and Mary (b. 1770) Hall, who had a son named Hiram (b. 1795) that moved to Carroll County, Georgia, around 1820. However unremarkable the beginning of this tree, in a single century it moved from South Carolina to Georgia to Alabama and Arkansas and Texas Then it really began to spread out! It suffered through the Civil War in Georgia and the Great Depression and the Dust Bowl in Oklahoma and Texas; and in the years since the beginning of the Twentieth Century it has put down roots in almost all the states in the western half of the United States.

From that first couple, whose name was Norman-English and whose bloodline was just as assuredly Anglo-Saxon, we have moved westward across the country, mingling our blood with that of Native Americans, Latin-Americans, Irish-Americans, Scotch-Americans, German-Americans, Dutch-Americans, French-Americans, Spanish-Americans, Armenian-Americans, and Italian-Americans; and our name, which began as *Hall*, is now Herron, Knuckles, Johnson, Pearson, Hanson, Allred, Prestwich, Van Wagoner, Anderson, Holinsworth, Smith, Lloyd, Wright, Gragg, Hales, Hoenshell, Hendrickson, Domyan, Nelson, Helton, Browne, Lanphear, Beard, Peak, Landers, Cardona, Ramsey, Schornick, Kandarian, Papagni, Swann, Potter, Finley, Terrill, Sheppard, Holmes, Bernard, Ceccarelli, Williams, Patterson, French, Mellow, Randolph, Robinson, Aquilar, Bell, Lawyer, McKay, Brown, FitzPatrick, Cannon, Harris, Hyder, Burney, Crisler, Dawson, Sisemore, Rainey, Hines, Thomas, Rogers, and Tobias.

We are the Halls that planted tobacco in South Carolina, cotton in Georgia, corn in Arkansas, and peanuts in Oklahoma. We are law-abiding, most of us, honest to a fault (some of us), and religious (especially prior to the Twentieth Century).

Down through the years, some Hall men have been hard drinkers, hard workers, high-tempered, quick to fight. But the typical Hall is calm, even-tempered, religious, middle of the road. He shuns vulgar display and loud noises, and he means what he says; and if he is willing to shake hands on a thing, it is a contract sealed in blood. His greatest strength (Some detractors will tell you it is just dumb *luck*) has always been his ability to choose a good woman to be his wife. Hall women, like women the world over, differ from each other in every possible way; and yet these lovely creatures who have selected some hapless, down-on-his-luck Hall male to honor and obey and serve until death separates them, are patient, understanding, creative, strong-willed, and forgiving.

PREFACE

Hall, is a Norman surname. In Latin documents, the surname *Hall,* was usually rendered, *De Aula,* in the official documents.

From such books and printed manuscripts as the *Domesday Book* (compiled in 1086 by William the Conqueror), the *Ragman Rolls,* the Wace poem, the *Honour Roll of the Battel Abbey,* the *Pipe Rolls,* the *Falaise Roll,* tax records, baptismals, family genealogies, and local parish and church records historians have concluded that the first record of the name *Hall* was found in Lincolnshire [England] , where this family was granted lands after the Norman Conquest in 1066.

The Normans were commonly believed to be of French origin but, more accurately, they were of Viking origin. The Vikings landed in the Orkneys and Northern Scotland about the year 870 AD, under their king, Stirgud the Stout. Later, under their Jarl, Thorfinn Rollo, they invaded France about 940 AD. The French king, Charles the Simple, after Duke Rollo laid siege to Paris, finally conceded defeat and granted northern France to Rollo. Thus Normandy. Duke William who invaded England in 1066, was a descendant of the first Duke Rollo of Normandy. After distributing the estates of the vanquished Saxons, many nobles were dissatisfied with their lot, and they rebelled. Duke William then took an army north, and wasted the northern counties. Many Norman nobles fled north and were granted lands over the border in 1070 by King Malcolm Canmore of Scotland.

Upon entering England with the Norman Conquest, the Halls, who were at that time called *FitsWilliams,* settled in Greatford Hall in Lincolnshire, since they were directly descended from Wentworth, Earl FitzWilliam. The younger son of this noble house, Arthur FitzWilliam, was called *Hall*, to distinguish him from his senior brother. Hence Arthur Hall would be the first Hall of record, dating from about the year 1090 AD.

ACKNOWLEDGEMENTS

My special thanks go to the following family members, who went beyond the call of duty to help out with this rather large family tree project: Linda Lamanucci, who found my long lost niece, Sydney McKay, and later tied up the loose ends of the Goff/Kandarian/Papagni/Lamanucci Clan; Myrna Ceccarelli, who has always been there for me from the beginning and who is doing a Bernard Family Tree almost singlehandedly; Clara Swann, who patiently kept at me until I finally corrected most of the errors in her branch of the family; Debbie Hall, who straightened out the kinks in the Luther/Luke/Smith mysteries and even did some footwork on the Karrs and the Keowns for me; L. A. Smith, who saw to it that I had a copy of the Hunter Family Tree, which is one important root of the Smith Clan, and was always there when I had a question about his large and active family; Dave Terrill, who, with his brother, Mark, went to Family Tree Heaven (Salt Lake City) and found a ream of information that helped point me in the right direction; Cecil F. Hall, who visited me when I was living on Dragon Fly Cove with inspiring stories of graveyard searches and the raising of tombstones over unmarked graves (It was he who established the location of the grave site of William Newton Hall); Nelson Gragg, Jr., a grandson of Birtha (Hall) and Ed Gragg and a grandson of Archie Brooklyn Hall, who introduced me to a branch of the family tree I had never heard of before, the descendants of Archie and Nancy's Birtha (After we became good friends he admitted that he had dabbled a bit himself in song writing, that he had published three songs, that Hank Williams, Jr., had kept one of his songs for a month, and another had been played by a Nashville radio station); Jim Gragg, whose father married Pearl Ellen, Birtha's sister and Nelson's aunt, who contributed valuable information about the Gragg family (and who will be remembered for his kind remarks about my little book *The River Bend*, a collection of anecdotes about my childhood).

Finally, I want to give credit to that special group of genealogists (members of our family and/or very closely tied to it) who, by way of the Internet and, yes, expensive Snail Mail, donated their time and expertise to make this project as complete as it is: Trudy Ellen (Smith) Tobias, who died unexpectedly in 1999, heads this list (Trudy, I will not forget your contributions to this Hall tree project); Verla Giolas, the great-grandniece of Sarah Elender Bradley and Green B. Hall, convinced me finally that William Newton Hall was, indeed, the son of Hiram and Charity Hall. This, in turn, led me to discover John Hall (b. 1769) and Mary (b. 1770), his wife, of South Carolina, who turned out to be my farthest-back ancestors (And although neither she nor I have been able to substantiate it, we are convinced that Hiram Hall had a sister named Precilla (b. 1794), who married Wyatt Williams, of Harralson County. Their son, Wyatt N. (b. 1814), who became a well-known judge in Haralson County. In 1850 Precilla was fifty-six and married to Nathan Gann. Verla lives only twenty miles from the Archives of the Latter-Day Saints and the largest family history library in the world, and she leaves no stone unturned in her pursuit of the truth). Another careful recorder of family history who, coincidentally, lives in that same area of Utah, is Richard Van Wagoner, the husband of Tricia Danette Pearson, a direct descendant of Hiram and Charity, John and Nancy (Hamilton), Robert Jefferson and Sara Jane Brewer (Richard shared with me all the generations of John and Nancy Hall down to Barbara Joy Hall and Charles Bradley's children and grandchildren). Phyllis Hall, who has spent most her life within a stone's throw of that same genealogical Mecca, lives with her husband, Vic, on ten wooded acres *near a wide space in the road called Cahone, Colorado*. She has amassed an incredible amount of information about her husband's family, and she has not hesitated to share this storehouse with me. Vic is the son of Carlos Mentril and Winnifred Lorena (Rogers) Hall, the grandson of

Thomas Cleveland and Margie Rena (Roberts) Hall, and the great-grandson of Robert Jefferson and Sara Jane Brewer. A truly indispensable source of information about the Archie Brooklyn and Nancy Caroline McDougal branch of the tree is Jackie Heckathorn, who lives in Green Valley, Arizona, with her husband, Gene, a retired U. S. Navy captain. She was born Jessie Mae Hall, one of Jesse Newton Hall's daughters, and it has been particularly difficult for her to dig out the details of her own large family. Billie Minugh, who put me onto Jessie, has been supplying me with information for the better part of two years. She is a granddaughter of Annie Donna Hall and a great-granddaughter of Archie and Nancy. She lives in Springdale, Arkansas, and has access to the family archives of the Latter-Day Saints; and she is another bloodhound when it comes to chasing down the details of the family history. Finally, I must mention Dennis Herron (b. January 29, 1951, in Fairfield, Alabama), who has contributed some very important information about the Herron branch of the family that left Georgia before the Civil War and moved to Walker County, Alabama. I refer, of course, to the descendants of Arminda Hall (1823-1915), who married Thomas S. Herron (1812-1899).

There were many others who helped out in one way or another, who gave unselfishly of their time by relaying information to me by phone and snail mail, or tolerated my obsession for meddling in other people's business. Under this heading the first to come to mind is my wife, Sharon, the Patient Griselda of my life, who never once said to me, "Enough is enough, now change the subject!"

INTRODUCTION

The origin of *Hall* is English, of course; but the English people of today began as Angles, Saxons, Jutes, and Normans, as well as a few other kinds of marauders that came down from Norse land. Early English history tells us that our clan did not arrive in England with these first three Germanic tribes, who began to show up in large numbers along the east coast of England in 449 A. D. Our ancestors arrived in England with that fourth group, the Normans; but they were distant relatives of the Angles, Saxons, and Jutes (All of whom were *Germanic* in origin). By the time the French Normans got around to invading England (in 1066) they had spent so much time in northern France they thought of themselves as Frenchmen. Indeed, our kinfolks, descendants of the ancient *Danes*, arrived in France sometime around 940 A. D. and convinced Charles the Simple, the first French King, to turn over to them the entire northern one-third of France. This became known as Normandy, and in time the head Dane was knighted and given the title *Duke of Normandy*. Over one hundred years later, in 1066, the Duke of the moment, whose name happened to be William, decided to cross the English Channel and become an English king. That is why he picked up the sobriquet *William the Conqueror*.

Up until the Normans showed up in England the common people of that little island had had no need of surnames. Each villager had but one name, generally something out of the Bible, such as *John* or *Ezekial* or *Ruth*. Of course, when and if a commoner ever visited another village, he had to attach the name of his own village to his given name, to keep the records straight. Apparently, back in those days, care was taken not to name a new baby after somebody else in the village, because of the confusion it would cause.

When the Normans arrived with their accountants and clerks and secretaries, there quickly developed a need for an additional name to keep all the Johns and Roberts from the different villages separated (on the books, for taxation purposes). As a result, it became customary for men to be given surnames that described the work they did, where they worked, what their fathers were called, or for some strength or weakness or skill or obsession. (Girls, who did not work outside the house, did not need two names, since no one but relatives ever referred to them.)

A man's surname, which in time became not only a necessity but a rallying cry, was quite often the father's given name plus *son*, a reference to some peculiarity or defect in a man's anatomical make-up, or what he did for a living : *Johnson, Gray, Short, Hickenbottom, Smith*. Quite often in a small village, to distinguish between two men with the same name, one of them would be given a descriptive additional name: *Long Sam, Littlejohn, Beetlebreath*.

Hall began, then, as a common word meaning a building made out of stone, a big impressive structure just short of castle. When it was written down, there being no standard spelling system or a desire to have one, it took a variety of forms, as mentioned above. One very popular spelling of our name in those days was *Halle*, because it looked more Norman than Saxon.

Among the Normans, who weren't Frenchmen at all but civilized Vikings dressed up like Frenchmen, there were a number of clans that were referred to by their place of residence or for some atrocity or accomplishment associated with them. One such clan, or group of families, was called *Hall*, to distinguish between the younger and the older sons of the noble house (family) of Arthur FitzWilliam. Arthur Hall, who was born Arthur FitzWilliam the Younger, became the first *Hall* of record, which dates back to about 1090 A. D. Quite often he was referred to as *Arthur of Hall*.

This first Hall family resided in (moved about in) the Border Lands, between England and Scotland. Eventually, when the King of England

and the King of Scotland agreed to abolish these badlands (by renaming them *shires*), the Halls moved on into Scotland and Ireland. Until this day there is a *Hall Shire* in central Scotland.

Sometime during the Middle English Period (1066-1485), well before the time of Shakespeare certainly, a man by the name of John Hall committed an act of extreme bravery in the service of his sovereign, the king. He must have stepped out of his role of commoner, disobeyed the rules of his caste (Perhaps he flung himself in front of the Royal Person, his *liege lord*, just as some zealot discharged an arrow from his crossbow that was meant for him. Whatever transpired, there is no doubt that this John Hall did something quite spectacular.

Because he was knighted.

Kneeling before his king, he was tapped lightly on each shoulder and the top of the head with a sword and told to rise *Sir John Hall*. His official title was *Esquire to the King*, and he was granted the privilege of designing his own coat-of-arms. Henceforth, he would be granted a regular stipend from the King, to keep him from having to work for a living! And he would be called *Sir John*.

The coat-of-arms that this first John Hall worked out was an enormous shield made of burnished copper with the following crest: "Three black Talbot's (a species of hound) heads on a silver background

At the top a defiant Talbot hound, with open mouth (and a long tongue lolled out threateningly), and below, in the center of the shield, three similar Talbots' heads (also with mouths open and tongues lolled out)." Beneath all of this there was a scroll with the words *Sauviter sed Fortiter*. Translated from the Latin, this motto said, Agreeably but powerfully.

In the Seventeenth Century another John Hall, this one a surgeon and an esquire, wooed and married Susan Shakespeare, the only daughter of the famous English poet and playwright. He was a direct descendant of the other Sir John Hall, and since Susan was the only surviving child of Sir William and Anne (Hathaway) Shakespeare, whose only male heir, Hamnet, had died at the age of fourteen, it was thought meet and proper that their coats-of-arms should be a combination of the two. After a great deal of mulling and sketching, they settled upon the following:

"At the top a wolf's head (that looked less threatening than a Talbot with lolling tongue) gazing ambiguously northward. Below, surrounding the crest, post oak leaves, these separating a knight's throat armor from a crest of three smiling lambs' heads (with mouths open and tongues lolled out slightly). These protected by nine iron crosses in an azure field."

The motto remained the same.

Most family names in the United States originated in some other country; and almost without exception, it would seem, those that came from England can be traced back to royalty in some form. It is therefore not surprising that a number of thriving enterprises exist today that are engaged in the manufacture and sales of plaques, flags, dinnerware, glassware, goblets, tumblers, tankard mugs, rings, tie tacks, pendants, solid brass door knockers, scroll prints, T-shirts, sweatshirts, blazer patches, all with a family coat-of-arms on them. One such company, which also sells a two-volume *World Book of Halls*, is Halbert's, 3687 Ira Road, P. O. Box 5000, Bath, Ohio 44210-5000.

Since it is rather likely that our ancestors descended directly from some Hall of England (though perhaps not Susan and John), the search backward might begin with England. Incredibly, family information was not recorded and stored by the Engllish government until 1837 (Our National Census began in 1790). Prior to that time baptisms, burials, and marriages were kept by churches and parishes. The address to contact is General Register Office, St. Catherines House, 10 Kingsway, London WC2B 6JP, England.

The largest library collection of family information in the United States is located in Salt Lake City. The address is The Family History Library of the Church of Latter Day Saints, 35 N. West Temple Street, Salt Lake City, Utah 84150. The telephone number is 801-240-2331. This organization can be reached by email, but nothing short of a field trip to Salt Lake City will bring forth serious genealogical information.

For ship's passenger lists from England to this country (The Halls almost certainly migrated sometime in the early Seventeenth Century), write to The National Archives, General Services Administration, Washington, D. C. 20408; and The Washington National Record Center, Washington, D. C., 20509. These lists date mostly from about 1820 to 1900.

There is a Regional Federal Archives and Record Center in Muskogee, Oklahoma, that contains a great deal of information about Southerners and is especially valuable as a place to research Civil War records, from both sides.

In Volume One of the *World Book of Halls*, a John Hall arrived in Charles Town, South Carolina, in 1719 (Coldham, Peter Wilson. *Bonded Passengers to America*. Balt: Gene. Publ. Co., Inc., 1983, Vol. 3, page 31). Another John Hall (b. 1792) arrived in Charleston, South Carolina, in 1820. He was 28. (United States Dept. of State, *Letters from Sec'y of State, List of Passengers....* Baltimore: Genealogical publishing Co., 1967, page 30). A William Hall (b. 1775) arrived in Charleston, South Carolina, in 1804 (Holcomb, Brent H., *South Carolina Naturalizations, 1783-1850*. Baltimore: Genealogical Pub. Co., 1985, page 14). A William B. Hall (b. 1791) arrived in Charleston, South Carolina, in 1823 (U. S. Dept. of State, *Passengers Who Arrived U. S., Sept. 1821óDec. 1823...* Baltimore: Magna Carta Book Co., 1969, page 203). A John Hall (b. 1785), his wife Susannah, and five children arrived in Charleston, South Carolina, in 1824 (Holcomb, Brent H., *South Carolina Naturalizations, 1783-1850*. Baltimore: Genealogical Pub. Co., 1985, page 116).

Seventeen Halls, ranging in age from three to thirty-nine, arrived in Charleston, South Carolina, in 1767. There were three Williams and three

Johns, and this would seem to be about the time our family came to this country.

Our single best source of family information is probably the National Archives in Washington, D. C., where the census records are stored; but these go back only as far as 1790. And at that time only the father's name was listed, along with the ages and genders of the various members of the family. Because most other types of records are quite often unreliable, unreadable, and difficult to locate, tracing the family tree can be quite frustrating at times. Add to this the fact that our family is from Georgia, which was devastated by General Sherman in 1864. County courthouses and state office buildings were special targets of his; therefore, many of the vital records of our family have been lost forever.

Tracing a family name back in time is a most difficult thing to do, even with the help of computers. This is especially so if the name is a common one, like ours, and if most of the ancestors have not been shakers and movers. The job is made easier by the fact that most families tend to name their children after aunts and uncles and cousins. In the Eighteenth Century, we begin with the most common of first and last names: *John and Mary Hall.* And the going at first was slow because practically every Hall family in the South had at least one John and one Mary).

Our John and Mary named their sons *Hiram* and *Green Berry*, not at all common. Hiram and Charity named their children *Armindy, John, Nancy, William Newton, Emeline, Tyre [Tyree], Green Berry, Elander, Charity,* and *Parthena.* Green Berry and Charity named their children *Nancy, John Wesley, James, Mary Anne, Charity, Froni R., Isom R.,* and *Green Berry.* Thus a pattern was established for the researchers. Throughout that century and into the next the names *Green, Tyree, Charity, John Wesley,* and *Nancy* kept appearing from one generation to the next. *Green* was most often attached to *Berry*, but it was also attached to *Tee, Tree, and Briar.* Once it was followed by the initial *M.* The speculation has been that such names were (are) of American-Indian origin, perhaps Cherokee; if this is true, then the Indian blood must go back to the generation of John and Mary, our farthest-back kinfolk, who named their second son *Green Berry*. It is also quite possible that William Newton's wife, Susan Elizabeth Woods (whose last name seems to have become *Owens* in her later life), was part Indian. The only extant picture of her suggests strongly that she had Indian blood in her.

During most of the Nineteenth Century our family lived in Carroll County, Georgia [In 1857 that part of Carroll in which they lived became Haralson County]; but even before the Civil War Hiram and Charity's children began leaving the state. Their eldest daughter, Armindy, married Thomas Herron and moved to Alabama [ca. 1860]; and John, their eldest son, married Nancy Hamilton and moved to Missouri even earlier than that [ca. 1851]. Later, most of their family settled in Childress, Texas.

After the Civil War, three of Hiram and Charity's sons, all of whom were married in Haralson County and two of whom had children, moved to Madison County, Arkansas [ca. 1873]. Apparently, William Newton and Susan Woods made the move first, pausing in Waldron, Scott County, Arkansas, long enough to have their first and second sons, Archie Brooklyn and Dock Walter. Tyree and Arcenia Meritt, with six children, and Green B. and Sarah Bradley, with three children, followed later, going directly to Madison County, Arkansas.

Around the turn of the Twentieth Century these five children and their families began to settle in Alabama, Texas, and Oklahoma. Arminda and Thomas Herron had moved to Walker County, Alabama, between 1857 and 1860, losing all but three of the children during the trip. They located in the area of Carbon Hill and Eldridge. Armindy and Thomas are buried in Pisgaugh Cemetery in Carbon Hill.

In 1851 John and Nancy Hamilton moved with one or more of John's brothers (and families) to Searcy County, Arkansas. There Madison Monroe was born. By 1854 they were living in Frederickstown, Madison County, Missouri, where Richard LaFeyette and the rest of the children were born. Eventually, sometime after the Civil War, they moved to Springtown, Texas.

William and Susan's children and their families began to move into Oklahoma around the turn of the century, and some of them continued on to California even before the Great Depression of the 1930's. In 1900 Greeley Teeman, the third son, eloped with Mallie Rue Karr, who was from Wesley, Madison County, Arkansas, going by horseback to Welling, Indian Territory; and in 1907, when Oklahoma became the forty-third state of the Union, they moved by covered wagon to Cherokee County, near where they had been married.

Archie Brooklyn and Caroline McDougal had all of their children in Arkansas, mostly Madison County; but eventually they settled in Nowata County, Oklahoma. They were, indeed, one of the earliest white families to settle in that area.

Dock Walter, the second son, and Kate Elsey first moved to a farming area near Huntsville, Arkansas, about 1910, where they had three children. After the third child, Cecile, they moved to another farming region near Konawa, Oklahoma, where Jewell, a girl, was born on September 19, 1915. Their last two children, Dovie and Oma, were also born in that area. In March of 1936, in the heart of the Great Depression and the Dust Bowl they moved to Dinuba, California.

The third son, Greeley Teeman, and Mallie Rue Karr had their first three children, Ezra Marion and Gradie and Ollie, in Madison County. Their fourth child, Ruth, was born in Cherokee County, Oklahoma. From then until 1917 they sharecropped across and down the state to Seminole County, having three children along the way: Clara Mable in 1910, Clifford Cleborn in 1912, Delsie Dale in 1914, and Luther Leonard in 1917. Their *permanent* home became the River Bend of Seminole County, near the little town of Konawa. There their ninth, tenth, and eleventh children were born: Vernon, Zack Oberon, and Wesley Elmo. Near the end of the Great Depression, when most of the displaced Okies were settled in California, this family began to travel Route 66 on a regular basis, leaving their farm in the hands of Ezra, the eldest.

Ulysses S. Grant and Vane Pennington remained in Madison County, Arkansas, until their first two children were born, Viola Helen in 1900 and Willie in 1901. Sometime before the spring of 1903, when Albert was born, they moved to Sallisaw, in the Cookson Hills (later to become famous as the birthplace of Pretty Boy Floyd). Shortly after that they moved back to Madison County, where their other three children were born. In time they, too, would move on to California.

There is not much information available about the fifth son, Sidney William. It is known that he married Cordelia Eubanks in Kingston, Madison County, Arkansas, on August 30, 1902. She was fifteen and he was nineteen. They settled in Cherokee County (when and where exactly is not known) and had four children: Melvin (Red), Clint, Nadine, and Orville (?-1940). Nadine married a man named McKissick, a physician, and they moved to Tulsa. She died in 1999. Clint was in a nursing home in 1987. Orville has four children, all of whom live in the Tahlequah, Oklahoma, area.

The sixth child was Cordelia Mae. Delia, as she was called, married Logan Sisemore and they had seven children. Logan and Delia made the trip to California in 1935 and lived in Madera, San Jose, and Mountain View before moving to Lodi in 1958. In 1978 Logan died, and soon afterward Delia moved to Moss Landing. She died in 1982 and was buried in Cherokee Memorial Gardens, Lodi, California, next to Logan.

The seventh child was Charity, about whom very little is known. But unlike the other children, she and her husband, Lee Rogers, did not make the trip to California. I visited them in 1962, just a year before they both died. They were living in a shack near Japton, in Madison County, Arkansas, and she was bedridden. However, it was Lee who went first, in December of 1963. She died a month later. They had two children, both of whom married and had children.

The last child of the William Newton and Susan Elizabeth (Woods) Hall family was Green T., who married Nanny Eversole. They sharecropped in Oklahoma, beginning about a decade after Greel and Mallie and ending up in Seminole County, near the River Bend. And since Uncle Green's initials were the same as Greel's, there was a great deal of confusion over who should get mail addressed to G. T. Hall. Greeley Teeman solved the problem by changing his name to Horace Greel Hall.

Green T. [Tyree] and Nanny had all eight of their children in Oklahoma, beginning with their first in 1911. Sometime in the early 'Thirties they made the trip to California, settling near Lodi, where Delia and Logan Sisemore were living. On December 20, 1945, Nanny died in Fayetteville, Arkansas, while they were on a trip back to see her folk. She was buried in Cherokee Memorial in Lodi, California. Green T. died in 1967 of natural causes. He was buried in Woodbridge Cemetery, near Lodi, California.

*   *   *

One grows up believing he is a Hall, or a Gragg, or perhaps even a Smith or a Jones. Then one day he learns that what is really in his veins is the blood of thousands (perhaps millions) of people who go by names other than his. In our culture we cling to the name of our fathers, but in other parts of the world it is the mother's name that counts.

A family history, of necessity, as well as custom and tradition, focuses upon the male side of the family. This means that from our earliest ancestors down to the present generation we are excluding the very people who gave birth to us all. Our farthest-back ancestors are John and Mary Hall, of South Carolina; but we do not even know Mary's last name or, indeed, anything at all about her. John, of course, was only fifty percent Hall, and we do not know what name that other fifty percent was going by. Perhaps his mother's surname was Hugensnapper or perhaps Gravelsnort. Then, to be perfectly truthful, all of us would be as much Hugensnapper or Gravelsnort as we are Hall. Well, almost as much.

A family tree maker begins with the living generations then, while trying to keep up with what's going on from day-to-day, heads backward into the generations that have gone before. With each generation that comes along we must add new names, each one of which has a history and is potentially the beginning of another tree.

The problem we face when we try to answer the question of just who are we is an algebraic one: With each generation the number of donors to our make-up (blood, brains, DNA, etc.) doubles. We are the direct product of two people, our parents, who were the direct products of four people, who were the products of sixteen, and so on. (Of course, if we are really serious about just how much Hall or some other bloodline we have in us, we must calculate the number of generations we have come and divide that number into *one* (to arrive at a percentage). Let us assume that Adam and Eve were the beginning of the human race, as we know it, and that Adam's last name was Hall (or Gragg, or even Smith or Jones). To simplify things, let us further assume that only one hundred generations have gone before us. That would mean that only one percent of us is Hall, while ninety-nine percent is something else. And with each succeeding generation the Hall blood will be diluted at an ever increasing rate!)

My point is that none of us is what we think we are. We place way too much importance in the name that was passed down to us by our fathers and grandfathers. Regardless of how noble or miserly it has been, its weight on our shoulders is hardly calculable.

Let me illustrate my point with an example of just how ridiculous some of us become about our last name.

I grew up in a remote corner of Seminole County, Oklahoma, a place called the *River Bend*. My ten older siblings attended the local one-room school, *Bugscuffle*, ahead of me, establishing a reputation that was sometimes difficult to follow. Usually, but not always, I could avoid a fistfight by name-dropping; but always I knew I had to stand up and face the music when I was challenged. *I had to keep up the Hall name.* In Konawa, the little town seven miles north of our farm, my family name and the names of several other families in the Bend, such as the Thomases and the Grants and the Riggses, were household words. And I never ceased to be amazed when some townsperson would inform me without preliminary that quite obviously I was a Hall, because of my red hair and the set of my jaw. Perfect strangers would say to me, "You're one of the Hall boys from the Bend."

When I returned home from the Pacific at the end of World War Two, I discovered that one of my nephews, Alton, the son of my oldest brother, Ezra, was attempting to establish himself as a fistfighter. To me he said proudly, "Well, after all I am a Hall." The truth was that neither one of us was a Hall. I positively did not like to fight, and he could not fight his way out of a paper sack.

Although we must carry a surname around with us, I think we should not assume that it is our defining feature. Each of us must stand as an individual, unique and different from all others who carried the same name. I am proud to be a Hall because the Halls I have known, with a few exceptions, have been peacemakers and honest to a fault.

Who Am I?

Hiram Hall
Charity
Wm Newton Hall
Susan's father
Susan Eliz. Woods
Susan's mother
Greel Hall
Wesley Hall
Henry's father
Mallie Carr
Henry Allan Carr
Henry's mother
Alice Howard
Alice's father
Alice's mother

I am the result of countless generations, one line of which had the name Hall!

THE OLD FOLKS

Our branch of the Hall family came from South Carolina. They were living in that area when it was a British colony, and they were there during and following the American Revolution. For a time after they disembarked from the ship that had brought them from England they lived in or near the village of Charlestown. It is possible that one or more of our kinfolk built or helped to build one or more of the grand mansions that still line Church Street in Charleston. One such *Grand Model* was built by a John Hall for Ann Peacock, a wealthy widow from St. George's Parish, Dorchester.

Our farthest-back ancestor was also a John Hall, though probably not the same one. He was born in 1769 near Charleston; and he married a girl named Mary, also from Charleston, who was born there the following year, when Charlestown was re-named *Charleston*. They raised a family but we know (with certainty) the name of just one of their children, Hiram. It is very possible that Hiram had a sister named Precilla. In the census records of Carroll County a woman named Precilla Hall, born in or near Charleston, South Carolina, about 1794, was listed as the wife of Wyatt Williams. Their son, Wyatt N. Williams, became a well-known judge in Carroll County. In a later census Precilla was listed as the wife of Nathan Gann. It is also possible that Hiram had a younger brother named Green Berry. The similarities between these two are striking.

Hiram was born in 1795 near Charleston. When he was still a very young man and unmarried, he went to Carroll County, Georgia, where he met and later married a local girl named Charity. It was 1820. Charity was eighteen and Hiram was twenty-five, and they were among the very earliest residents of that eastern Georgia county. The nearest town was Buchanan.

Hiram and Charity had eleven children, all born in Carroll County before the northern one-third of that county was re-named *Haralson County* in 1858: Arminda (Armindy) (1823-1915), John (1824-1898), Nancy (1829-), William Newton (1831-1923), Emeline (Eveline) (1836-), Tyra (Tyre, Tyree) (1838-), Green (Green B., Green Berry) (1842-), Elander (Ailey, Ailsy) (1843-), Claracy (Charity) (1847-), Parthena (1848-). [In the Carroll County census of 1840, Green B. was born in 1844, a year after Ailsy; but on his tombstone in Ledbetter Cemetery, Madison County, Arkansas, he was born in 1842.]

This much is known about Hiram up to the time he began to raise a family: Sometime before 1820, when he was in his early twenties and his younger brother, Green Berry, was just a baby, he began to work his way up the state of South Carolina to and beyond York County. Apparently, he did not stay long in any one place because by 1820 he had been in Carroll County, Georgia, long enough to court and marry Charity.

Many unanswered questions come to mind: Why did Hiram leave home? Was he merely a wanderer who just happened to end up in Carroll County, Georgia? Quite literally he traveled the entire length of South Carolina from south to north, probably angling toward the northwest corner (York County), and then the entire length of Georgia from east to west. Did he know someone in Carroll County?

Green B. Hall remained in South Carolina until about 1840. It is very likely that he and Hiram corresponded, or in some way kept in touch with each other. Sometime in the early 1840's Green B. married a South Carolina girl named Charity, who was born in 1815 (eight years older than him) near Charleston; and shortly afterward they moved to Georgia, settling in Lumpkin County, not far from Carroll, before 1843. In that year their first child, Nancy, was born in that county. This remained their home until about 1850, because John Wesley was born there in 1844, James in 1845, Mary Ann in 1847, and Charity in 1848. Their next three children were born in Dawson County: The twins, Isom R. and Froni R. (1852) (Froni apparently died before 1860), and Green B. (1854).

It must be admitted at this point that no tangible proof has been found that links these two Halls, Hiram and Green Berry, to the same parents. That they were born in the same part of South Carolina, that they moved to the same general area of Georgia, that both married women named Charity and that the younger tended to name his children after the elder strongly suggests that they were closely related. Perhaps they were cousins or uncle and nephew. They were not father and son because Hiram named his last son Green B.

At any rate, our research has led us to the conclusion that Green Berry Hall (the first of that name, born in 1823) and Charity and their descendants either remained in Georgia after the Civil War or were victims of Sherman's looting and killing, for we have found no trace of them in other parts of the country.

Before the Civil War two of Hiram and Charity's children married and moved to other parts of the United States. Arminda, their first child, married Thomas Herron in 1847; and although they remained in Carroll County for about ten years, sometime before 1860 they moved to Walker County, Alabama. James (1848-1935), Hiram (1850-1909), Charity (1852-1857) and D. F. (1854-1857) were born in Carroll County. That year (1857) the northern part of that county became Haralson County. Jane was born that year; and, apparently soon afterward, they left for Alabama. According to Dennis Herron, the great-great-grandson of Hiram Herron, only three of their children born up to that time survived the trip. Pierce (1860-1902), Green (1862-1925), and Missouria (1864-1945) were born in Walker County, Alabama. Armindy and Thomas are buried in Carbon Hill, Alabama.

Hiram and Charity's second child, Murry John Hall (1824-1898), married Nancy Hamilton in 1848 and they had two children before leaving the county: Emiline (1848-) and Robert Jefferson (1850-1944). In 1848 they moved to Searcy, Arkansas, where Madison Monroe (1852-1928)

4 • The Hall Tree

was born. From there they moved to Frederickstown, Missouri, where the rest of their children were born: Richard Lafeyette (1854-), Janette Ardelia (1856-), Mary Ann (1858-), Nancy Lanore (1859-), Margret Charity (1861-1936), and Maty Ann (1866). It wasn't until after the Civil War that they moved to Springtown, Texas.

John and Nancy's children scattered across Texas, Missouri, and Oklahoma. Robert spent most of his life in Missouri but lived the last twelve near Broken Arrow, Tulsa County, Oklahoma. He died in a convalescent home there. Madison Monroe, named after the county where he was born, lived in Fredericksburg, Missouri, most of his life but moved to a farm six miles northeast of Gainesville about 1902 and was still living there when he died. Nancy Lanore settled in Childress, Texas.

The Civil War, called by various other names in the South, was disastrous for the entire Confederacy; but historians agree that Georgia suffered most, primarily because of one Yankee general, whose name became a curse word in our family. Three of Hiram and Charity's sons fought with the Confederacy, two of them in the infantry and one in the cavalry.

Green B. volunteered in Haralson County on March 4, 1862, as a private in Company G, the Fortieth Georgia Infantry Regiment. He was twenty years old. This unit was called the *Haralson Defenders*. On July 4, 1863, he was captured in Vicksburg, Mississippi. Two days later he was *paroled*, according to his record, with no reason given. The only other notation in his record was that of an AWOL, absence without leave from November 23 to December 31, 1863.

Tyree was drafted in Haralson County a month after Green B., and was apparently a member of the *Haralson Defenders*. After Vicksburg he failed to rejoin his unit (which probably did not exist) and was picked up as a deserter near Dallas, Georgia, on October 26, 1864. On May 12, 1865, at war's end, he was released with the following notation in his records: "Claims to have been loyal. Was conscripted into Confederate Army. Deserted to avail himself of amnesty proclamation."

Tyree, who was twenty-three when the war began, had married a Dawson County girl named Arseeney Merett back on January 20, 1859; and by the time the war began they were already parents. Their first child, David, was born in 1860, in Haralson County, and Lenoria, their first daughter, was born there in 1862. Green B. remained single until April 15, 1866, when he married a Haralson County girl named Sarah Elvira Bradley.

The war story of William Newton Hall is far more complicated than those of his two younger brothers. For one thing, what is available (what was not destroyed by the war) does not agree in some important ways with the testimonials of one of his daughters, Cordelia Mae (1884-1973), who had a great deal to say about her father. Most of what she told the author and numerous other members of the family has been substantiated by reliable sources, while some of it remains myth and legend.

Aunt Delia, as Cordelia Mae, was called by those who knew and loved her, said that *her father was a well-educated man who hobnobbed with the wealthy class, back before the war. He owned land and slaves and was married and had a family.*

No record of this marriage has been found. In the Dawson County (Georgia) census of 1860, Barretts District, there is a William Hall, born in 1830 in Florida, married to Darcas, born in 1836 in Georgia, with four daughters: Sarah (9), Susan (7), Mary (4), and Margaret (2). William Newton was born in 1831 in Haralson County, Georgia.

He used to disappear for a month or more at a time after the family first moved to Arkansas, and I was the only one he ever told about those trips he was making back to Georgia. He was looking for his lost Sid, of that previous marriage.

Census takers were not infallible back in rural Georgia in the mid-1800's. Some of them made inexcusable mistakes in the spelling of names and in the recording of dates and ages. It is quite possible that the William of the Dawson County census was indeed our William N. His lost Sid that Aunt Delia spoke of so convincingly could have been born in 1860 after the census was taken or in 1861, after William N. went off to war.

He was in the Georgia cavalry and on at least two occasions he tried to cross the lines and give himself up to the Blue Bellies. But they almost killed him each time. So he moved in with a family in Atlanta and sat out the war dressed like a woman, in a' dress and a bonnet. That family was named Woods, and they had a young daughter named Susan Elizabeth. She was my mother.

William Newton *did* join the Georgia Cavalry, and he *did* marry a girl of seventeen named Susan Elizabeth Woods, of Atlanta (after the war). The first is confirmed by his Civil War Service Record, on file in the Bureau of Archives, Washington, D. C.; and the second is confirmed by two documents on file in the Haralson County Courthouse: *A List of Marriage Licenses Issued 1856-1882* - Haralson County, Georgia (cf. p. 2) - William N. Hall and Susan Wood - October 17, 1868; and a copy of the actual marriage license issued on that date in Buchanan, Haralson County, Georgia.

However, that William Newton attempted to give himself up and failing that he deserted and lived in the Woods' house until the end of the war is difficult to believe, especially if we can believe his war record. According to that document, he enlisted as a second lieutenant in the Georgia Cavalry at Camp Rose, near Savannah, on October 10, 1861. He was enlisted by Lt. Col. W. S. Rockwell for a period of one year, agreeing to furnish his own horse.

His salary, to be paid in Confederate paper money, was $90 a month, plus 30 cents a month for furnishing his own horse. (Later in the war this increased to 4 cents a day.) By Christmas of 1863 he was a first lieutenant and, according to a letter in his service record, he was planning to dispose of his *negroes* the following year. The following is a facsimile copy of that letter, which is on file in the National Archives in Washington, D. C.:

Brig. Genl. Thomas Jordon
Chief of Staff
Dept So. Ca., Ga. & Fla. *Genl*

I have the honor respectfully to apply for twelve (12) days leave to visit my home in Bulloch Co. Geo. for the purpose of seeing my Father who has my business in charge, and my negroes will be at his place on the 25th of this Month, and I must make arrangements to dispose of them next year. Also to exchange a horse that I have with me for one I have that is more able for service.

Bivouac Near Green Ponds } I have the honor to be
Dec. 17. 1863 } Genl. your obt Servt
No officer absent from my W. N. Heall 1st Lt
Company } "C" Troop 5th Reg Geo Cavalry

The handwriting and the remark about his father and his slaves would seem to confirm at least part of Aunt Delia's myth that William N. was indeed a man of education and substance. However, it must be noted that the ownership of slaves by successful (but not necessarily wealthy) farmers was not out of the ordinary up to the time of the Civil War.

Again according to his service record, William Newton remained in the cavalry throughout the war. Capt. Hendryîs Company, Bullock Troop, in which he enlisted, subsequently became Company C, 2nd Battalion, Georgia Cavalry; and on January 20, 1863, this unit was consolidated with the 1st Battallion, Georgia Cavalry, by S. O. No. 20, Headquarters District of Georgia, South Carolina, and Florida to form the 5th Regiment, Georgia Cavalry.]

On August 10, 1863, he was promoted to first lieutenant, and on December 4, 1864, he was promoted to the rank of captain and given the command of his company, the former company commander, a Capt. Best, having been killed.

From the records, then, at the end of the Civil War, April 9, 1865, Capt. William Newton Hall was Commanding Officer of Company E, 2nd Battallion, 5th Regiment, Georgia Cavalry.

Some hard questions: If this is indeed the service record of our William N. Hall, where did Aunt Delia get the story about the dress and the bonnet? If our William N. Hall already had a family in Dawson County before the war, what happened to them afterward? Why did our Haralson County forebear ride his horse all the way to Camp Rose, near Savannah, to enlist? What happened to William Newton's land and livestock after the war?

On October 17, 1868, three years after the war ended, William Newton Hall, thirty-seven, married Susan Elizabeth Woods, seventeen, in Haralson County. We can only speculate what he and his two brothers were doing for a living and planning to do in the future, but apparently the three of them continued to live in that county for several years, having to deal with carpetbaggers and tax collectors. It was a difficult time for all Southerners, and the stories about great opportunities to the west, especially across the Mississippi River, must have been difficult to ignore.

At any rate, it was William Newton who made the move westward first. Almost assuredly William N. and Susan joined a wagon train, but all we know with certainty is that they moved to Arkansas in a wagon shortly before the year 1871. Indeed, their first child, Archie Brooklyn, was born April 25, 1871, in the little town of Waldron (Scott County), Arkansas. They were still there on December 22, 1873, when Dock Walter was born [There has been some confusion about Dock's middle name. Some family genealogists have mistakenly written it Waldron, after the name of the county in which he was born.]

When, exactly, William N. and Susan moved to the Japton and Drakes Creek area of Madison County, Arkansas, it is impossible to say; but on August 24, 1877, their third son, Greeley Teeman, was born there.

Hiram and Charity's other two sons who had served in the Confederate Army during the war moved to Arkansas a year or two after William N. and Susan did, but Tyree and Green B. went directly to the Drakes Creek, Japton area of Madison County. Indeed, it would seem that William Newton and Susan and their two children moved from Waldron, Arkansas, to that area because of them.

Using the census records as a guide, it is possible to place the move of Tyree and Arcenia and their six children and Green B. and Sarah and their two children as during or slightly before the year 1873.

Tyree and Arcenia had the following children in Haralson County, Georgia: David (b. 1860), Lenoria (b. 1862), Charity E. (b. 1867), Mary A. (b. 1870), James W. (b. 1871), and Lucy A. (b. 1872). They had the remainder of their family in Madison County, Arkansas: Maggie (b. 1875), Arcenia (b. 1878), and George K. (b. 1879).

Green B. and Sarah had the following children in Haralson County, Georgia: William (b. 1867) and Mary E. (b. 1869). The remainder of their children were born in Madison County, Arkansas: Elizabeth A. (b. 1873), Jessica (b. 1878), Angus (b. 1883), Rena (b. 1887), Green M. (b. 1888), Hyram (b. 1892), and Olga (b. 1895).

Whatever William Newton Hall's past had been, farmer and cavalryman and possibly bigamist, he settled into the Japton area to raise a family. With his own hands he built a large log cabin on a sizable parcel of land, and there he and Susan remained until well into the Twentieth Century. The cabin remains there today, an example of how to build a log structure, with the log ends fitted into beveled grooves so snugly no caulking or mortar was necessary. Nearby (gone now) was the only blacksmith shop for miles, where Uncle Will taught his sons the skill and art of blacksmithing. [Cf. *A Visit to Japton and Drakes Creek* in the *Stories and Legends* chapter.]

The fourth son of this family, another boy, was named after the Northern general who, next to Sherman, was most disliked and feared in the South, *Ulysses S. Grant.* Why William Newton, who almost certainly had no help from the mother, would do a thing like that is one of the great mysteries family researchers have pondered. Aunt Delia had said again and again, while she was still alive, that *her father had tried to desert and go to the other side.* Indeed, she made it sound as if *he wanted to switch sides, become a turncoat.*

Grant was born in 1880, and he was followed by Sidney William (another Sid?), who was born in 1882, Cordelia Mae, who was born in 1884 (but swore she was born in 1889), Charity, who was born in 1885, and, finally, Green Tyree (Green T.), who was born in 1887.

Like the other descendants of Hiram and Charity, William Newton and Susan Elizabeth's children began to scatter westward even before the turn of the century. Archie and Nancy would eventually settle in Nowata County, Indian Territory. Grant and Vane remained in Madison County until 1901, when their third child, Willie was born; but in 1903 they moved to Cookson Hills in Indian Territory . Shortly after that they returned to Madison County; but, in time, they would join the others on Route 66 and go to California. Greeley Teeman and Mallie eloped to Welling, Indian Territory in 1900 and, in 1907, when that area west of Arkansas became the forty-third state in the Union, they moved there in a covered wagon. By 1917 they had found their "permanent" home in the River Bend of Seminole County, Oklahoma. Dock and Kate first moved to Huntsville, Arkansas, where three of their children were born before they returned (sometime between 1908 and 1915) to Madison County. Later, they would make the trip to California, where they would settle [cf. *Grant Goes to California,* in *Legends and Stories.*]

The fifth son, Sidney William, and his wife, Cordelia, moved to the Tahlequah, Cherokee County, Oklahoma, area, where all four of their children were born. Cordelia and Logan Sisemore, after all seven of their children were born, moved to the northern San Joaquin Valley of

California and bought a house in Lodi. Charity and Lee Rogers married in Madison County, as the others had done, had their two children there, as most of the others had done, and remained there until their deaths, which none of the others did. Green T. and Nanny sharecropped across Oklahoma, as Greeley Teeman and Mallie had done; but they did not put down roots. Sometime in the early 'Thirties they moved to the San Joaquin Valley of California, settling near Cordelia and Logan.

STORIES AND LEGENDS

Hiram and Charity's Family

Apparently, most of the descendants of Hiram and Charity Hall remained in Georgia after the Civil War. However, the two oldest children, Arminda, who married Thomas Herron, and John, who married Nancy Hamilton, went to Alabama and Texas, respectively. Arminda and Thomas moved to Walker County, Alabama, after their fifth child, who was born in 1857. John and Nancy moved, probably at about that same time, to Childress, Texas. Similarly, most of the descendants of Green Berry and Charity Hall evidently remained in Georgia after the war. The three oldest children, however, moved by covered wagon to Madison County, Arkansas.

Westward, Ho!

The Hall family, rooted but apparently not settled in the wilderness of Madison County, Arkansas, during the last decades of the Nineteenth Century, began to move West even before the turn of the century. Archie and Nancy settled near Nowata, Oklahoma, ignoring the call of the Gold Coast altogether. Dock and Kate (Elsey) moved to the Huntsville, Arkansas, area, where they stayed until after their third child, Cecile, was born; then they moved to Seminole County, Oklahoma, to sharecrop. There on September 19, 1915, near Konawa, Jewell was born. Grant married Vane Pennington on October 12, 1899, and on August 7,1900, they had their first child, Viola Helen. They were still in Madison County in October, 1901, when Willie was born; but in the spring of 1903 their third child, Albert, was born near Sallisaw, in the Cookson Hills of

Oklahoma (It was still the Indian Territory). Shortly after that they returned to Madison County, Arkansas, where their other three children were born. In time they would move on to California.

My parents began sharecropping north of Tahlequah, but after ten years working their way down across the new state, they settled in the River Bend (until the 'Thirties). Cordelia, who married Logan Sisemore, made the trip to California and settled in the upper San Joaquin Valley, of California. Sidney made his home near Tahlequah and Wagoner.

One story handed down about the migration westward concerns Uncle Grand and Aunt Vane.

Grant Goes to California

In March of 1936 three families set out in two vehicles from Madison County, Arkansas, for California to find jobs in fruit harvesting and in the factories. One vehicle, driven by Ulysses Grant Hall, was a converted 1929 Ford Coupe. Next to him was his wife, Vane. In the vehicle also were their daughter Lucy and her husband, John Davis, Ralph C. Cannon, his wife Viola (Hall) Cannon, and their only child, Ralph Junior.

Originally, this had been a sporty coupè; but Ralph had converted it in to a pickup truck by sawing off the rumble seat! Their maximum cruising speed was twenty to twenty-five miles an hour.

A second vehicle in the caravan was a *bona fide* pickup truck driven by Toy Hyder, another son-in-law of Grant and Vane. In it with him were his wife, Mary Elizabeth (Hall) Hyder, their two boys, Jesse Raymond and Jerry, and a third boy that they were raising, Charles Harris (the baby of Maggie Lee, Mary Elizabeth's sister, who had died the previous February).

When this determined group of pioneers reached Arizona, Vane (Pennington) Hall was so ill it was necessary for them to find a place and stop. In a motel in Buckeye on March 11, Vane died of cancer aggravated by a case of pneumonia. She was buried in Phoenix.

Two years later Toy Hyder and his part of the caravan had had enough and returned to Spiro, Oklahoma. But Grant and Vane and the rest stayed on, making California their permanent home.

A Conversation with Earl Hall
by Trudy Tobias

In the late winter of 1995-1996, Trudy Tobias (also Trudy Ellen Smith) and Marti Hyder, practicing genealogists in the family, decided to pay a visit to the home of one of the most colorful Hall characters still alive at that time: Earl Hall. Here is Trudy's account of that visit:

"Just before lunch on February 2, 1996, Marti Hyder and I, Trudy Tobias, ventured out from Tipton [California] to Dinuba [California] for a first-time visit with Earl Hall, Doc Waldron's [Dock Walter's] son. Earl's birthdate was December 19, 1903. He didn't know his home address but gave us directions once we made it to Dinuba.

"His directions led us astray. After trying and failing to get Earl by phone, we called his sister, Jewel. It occurred to us that he might be waiting outside his house for our arrival and couldn't hear the phone. Jewel, who was eighty years old, did know her address but was vague on directions. But after two tries, we made it. She was elated to meet us and greeted us with hugs. Her place was old and small, but well maintained and quite immaculate.

"We chatted with her for awhile then called Earl again. No answer, so the three of us set out to find his place. Jewel had Marti take a wrong turn but we quickly figured it out and, believe it or not, when we found the place, Earl was standing outside by the gate. He had been there for at least an hour. He was tickled to see us. Mind you, although he had never seen us before, he knew we were family.

"Jewel and Earl then began to share stories and names and dates of their family. Marti and I were on a natural high because of all the information we were getting about the family history. I took a video of them and recorded our conversations. They were the nicest people ever.

"Earl was living at 41339 Road 124, in Cutler, California. He told us his father was Doctor Waldron Hall, born in Waldron, Arkansas, on December 22, 1873. Earl was born December 19, 1903. He married Stella Scoggins on July 10, 1926, and they had six children, all born in Konawa, Oklahoma. Stella died in her kitchen after complaining of chest pains. This was around 1994-1995, in Orosi, California. Earl was ninety-two years old. He was dressed very well and really looked good and spiffy. And he was very likable. I left there impressed by his appearance and sharpness.

"Jewel Hall-Beard was born September 19, 1915, in Ada, Oklahoma, the daughter of Doctor Waldron Hall and Kate Elsey-Hall. She had one child, Billy Ray Beard, born April 17, 19??, in Kerman, California. A Dr. Drake delivered him. He married Cathy Stuckey, who died of cancer in Visalia, California. Billy Ray works as a body and fender technician in Dinuba. His youngest son, Keith Beard, works with him. The other son, Gregory Beard, works at the Fresno Airport. Both sons are still single.

"Jewel is a very slender and active person. She takes long walks every-day. Her mind is very sharp, and I was impressed with her.

"Here are some notes I took during this visit:

"Ulysses Grant Hall was born at Drakes Creek, Arkansas, March 31, 1880. He married Sylvania Pennington on October 12, 1899. He died July 9, 1964, in Tulare, California. He was 62 when he did his birth cer-tificate. He had eleven kids. His father-in-law was Aaron Pennington.

"Sylvania (Vane) Pennington's parents were Aaron Pennington and Mary Sisemore. She was born February 25, 1880, and died March 11, 1936. She and Aaron got married December 4, 1862. She was born in Whitesburg, Uker County, Kentucky.

"Their children Viola Helen (August 7, 1900-January 31, 1982, who married Ralph C. Cannon on June 16, 1917. Willie, who was born October 3, 1901, and died December 6, 1906. Albert, who was born in

Salisaw, Oklahoma, on May 26, 1903, and died April 19, 1916. He was buried in Mt. Comfort Cemetery, Oklahoma. Maggie Lee, who was born February 14, 1905, and died February 27, 1935. She married Floyd Harris and they had five children. A baby boy and a baby girl died, but three boys survived. Lowell and Fay Clifton were raised by Ella and Clyde Crisler. Charles was raised by Mary E. Hyder. Maggie died in Blaine Bottoms, Star County, Oklahoma. Mary Elizabeth, who was born September 19, 1906, and died October 6, 1989. She married Toy Hyder. James Arnold, who was born June 8, 1908, married Bessie Crumm on September 10, 1932. Ellar Zona, who was born May 9, 1911, and died May 10, 1990, married Clyde Crisler. She is buried in the Woodville Cemetery.

"Goldie May, who was born December 10, 1913, and died of measles at B. A. Rudolph's place on April 20, 1916, was buried in Mt. Comfort Cemetery. Lucy Florence, who was born in Fayetteville, Arkansas, on March 6, 1915, married John Davis and Guy Dawson. She was living in Arizona in 1995. Iva Alice, who was born May 2, 1916, died of measles in Wesley, Arkansas, at her grandparents' place, Aaron and Mary Pennington. She was buried in Duncan Cemetery, Georgetown, Arkansas. Johnnie Theron, who was born April 12, 1919, died September 2, 1993. He married Helen Francis King on Febru-ary 15, 1941.

"Aaron and Mary Pennington lived in Wesley, Arkansas, from 1921 to 1926."

Then, following Trudy's story about the trip to see Earl and Jewel, she just had to say something about the trip itself and Marti Hyder's part in it:

I Remember Marti
by Trudy Tobias

"Marti Hyder and I will never forget this day, February 2, 1996. For sometime we had been making plans to take a trip to Dinuba to visit two relatives that neither one of us had ever seen, Jewel Hall and her father, Earl.

"I knew how desperate Marti was to meet these people because despite the fog, having to leave her son, David, with his young friend, Michael, and her husband, Ray, to fend for themselves all day, she was determined to go. In addition, she had never been to Dinuba and had no address for Earl Hall and his daughter. Normally, a thing like this would have been unthinkable. A trip like this on such a day would have been *outside her realm*, for she is not one to brave the elements and launch out into unfamiliar realms.

"I was, to put it mildly, proud of her to reach out and go beyond her own fears."

A Visit to Japton and Drakes Creek, Arkansas
by Wesley E. Hall

In the spring of 1972, when I was teaching at Southwest Missouri State University, in Springfield, my oldest brother, Ezra, and my oldest sister, Gradie, and I made a trip to the old Hall homestead in Arkansas. The following is what I entered in my journal of that trip, which I entitled *Trip to Drakes' Creek*:

"May 10, 1972: Last Saturday my brother Ezra Marion and my sister Gradie swooped in upon me from Duncan, Oklahoma, and Fresno, California, wanting me to drive them down into Arkansas. Indeed, they wanted to go back to Madison County, where they were born. I was more than a little excited by the prospect, for I had heard much about this wild and woolly place in Madison County. I refer, of course, to Japton and Drakes Creek. It was the Drake's Creek Baptist Church where Grandfather Hall had preached, according to legend and hearsay; and in the church cemetery and nearby in the Old Ledbetter Cemetery many of our relatives had been buried.

"We got off to an early start, driving south from Spring-field through Branson and the Shepherd of the Hills country and crossing the Missouri state line into Arkansas around breakfast time. After Fayetteville, where the university is locat-ed, it became a bit hairy; but I had a good map and with God's help we ended up, at Ezra and Gradie's birthplace.

"I had grown up hearing my parents talk about a place in Arkansas called *Fedville*. After hearing my brother pronounce this word, I realized this fabled place was none other than the town where I had worked on my doctorate!

"We spent the day deep in the woods of southern Madison County, where Ezra and Gradie had been born and where they had lived until they were three and five, respectively. It was a beautiful, hot, sultry day; and I remember that the vegetation was the greenest green I had ever seen. Our plan was to look for cemeteries and talk to as many old friends of the family as we could. We weren't disappointed.

"It did not take us long to find people who remembered our grandfather, for he was something of a local character. Over and over we heard people refer to him as *the best shot in the county*, *the smoothest talker in six states*, and *Reverend Hall*. Everybody, it seemed, had stories to tell about him and Old Blue, his hound (*the best durned hound that ever lived*), and his horse (*the fastest mare in the county*). My grandfather was carrying a lot of superlatives around with him!

"In one version of *The Panter Story*, he was riding along mindin' his bidness when he heard a woman screaming for help down close to a creek. He rode fast, discovered that a black panther had leaped out of a tree onto her horse's back and was about to eat her. Of course, he *nailed* the cat with his first shot. And, ever since, the creek has been called *Panter Crik*. I couldn't wait to find an Arkansas state road map to see if such a creek existed. It did, and not far from Japton.

Another version of this story (We heard them both that day) goes like this: "Uncle Will was ridin' along 'mindin' his own bidness' when a black panter leaped out of a tree right on top of him. He was crossin' a crik at the time and passin' beneath a large tree on which the panter had been crouchin'. Wal, you know whut? Uncle Will must've heerd or 'spected sumpin fer he looked up and seen thet panter hurlin' through the air.

Know whut he did? He brought his rifle up and farred right pintblank in that panter's mouth!"

"This second storyteller, who had been just a boy when Uncle Will had moved away, went on to say that the panther had been terrorizing the neighborhood for months and had, on one occasion, come close to killin' a young girl. Anyway, in recognition of the occasion of the shooting, the creek got the name *Panter Crik.*

"We had no trouble finding cemeteries where our kin had been buried. At the Drake's Creek Baptist Church, where Grandpa had preached, we found a well-kept graveyard; and in a cow pasture a few miles away we found another, the Old Ledbetter Cemetery. In this one was a large impressive granite tombstone, the most outstanding stone in the cemetery. It belonged to Green Berry Hall, an uncle of mine.

"This particular Green Berry, had been born in 1854, according to the 1860 Bullock County, Georgia, census records. But on the granite tombstone the date of birth was August 12, 1842! I reasoned that it was not likely that he had deliberately made himself twelve years older, and I had to believe the information chiseled in stone, which surely proved that he was the third child of my grandparents, right after William Newton and Tarry.

"Also in the Ledbetter Cemetery we found the grave of one 'Tyre Hall. The birthday chiseled on the stone was 1838, leaving no doubt that this was indeed our Uncle Tarry. According to the Madison County census records for 1840, Tarry was born in 1838 near Charleston, South Carolina; but Green Berry Jr., his younger brother, according to the1850 census records, was born in Bullock County in August, 1842. [This would establish the time of the move of the Halls from South Carolina to Georgia at about 1840.]

"It was a most satisfying journey for the three of us that day back 1972. I, for one, learned a great deal about my family and I know that it gave Ezra and Gradie a lot of pleasure to see their old birthplace one last time.

I also became addicted to nosing around cemeteries and dabbling in genealogy as a result of that trip!"

Lee and Charity Rogers
by Wesley E. Hall

On an earlier occasion, in the late 1960's, I had visited the Drakes Creek, Japton area with a fellow genealogist, Daniel Littlefield, our excuse to visit my aunt and uncle, Charity and Lee Rogers. (Dan taught me a number of things about genealogy and constructing a family tree, two of which were removing names from old faded headstones with onionskin paper and a soft-leaded pencil and giving everybody in the family a number to keep things straight):

Lee and Charity were living in a little dilapidated house just down the road from Japton; and it was Charity who was deathly sick at this time. Uncle Lee offered us each a glass of water first thing, but Dan took one look at the one offered him and turned away. I accepted the dirty glass but pretended to be too interested in talking to my uncle to drink; and when he wasn't looking, I poured it just outside the kitchen door. It was obvious that Uncle Lee had not washed a dish or a glass in a week, and it occurred to me that both he and Aunt Charity probably had tuberculosis.

We had found my aunt and uncle by inquiring at the general store in Japton; and after we found them, visited awhile, and left, I felt a sickness in my stomach at the sight of them and their poor surroundings.

From there we visited the cemetery at Drakes Creek Baptist Church, not far from Japton, and the old Ledbetter Cemetery, on beyond that. In the latter, I found the tombstone of Uncle Green B. (who was born eleven years after William Newton), according to the inscription on the tombstone.

My Early Childhood
by Jim Gragg

Hindsight says I should have taken notes when family was talking. Here's a quick overview of my early childhood: I was born near Claremore Oklahoma (the County seat); I wore a clean white dress every day, before and after learning to walk; I walked miles to school and Church over snow covered hills (or so I was told); I would have had oodles of siblings (mom lost several before birth), but I had plenty of cousins to create family chaos; wild animals tried to get into our house (through the chimney as the story goes); we left Oklahoma for California when I was five; stopped in New Mexico for work in the fields (had ran out of money); arrived in Phoenix on Christmas Eve, 1939, during the infamous one hundred year flood; was raised on the desert (dogs and guns); always had family outings (picnics and fishing parties); and did my share of cotton, potatoes, onions and the like (went from home to the field, to school, back to the field and back home, every school day, Every Saturday and most Holidays were also dawn to dusk field work. Sunday was God's day. I was never ambitious but worked harder than most, did well in school, did even better in the Navy (22+ years), and later with the Arizona State Government (another 22+ years).

SKELETONS IN THE HALL CLOSET

Every branch of the Hall family has a treasure chest of mysteries and hand-me-downs that some of the family would just soon remain out of sight. I have ever been diligent to collect these skeletons whenever and wherever I could; and let me confess that I have been able to match most of what I have heard (and read) with equally true believe-it-or-nots from my own branch. Therefore, be it known that this chapter is not a pointing of the finger at one particular branch.

One of my favorite skeletons came to me in the snail mail one day from a collector like myself, Trudy Tobias. She was the granddaughter of one my uncles and the wife of a grandson of another; and you can believe what she said.

The Summer of 1933
by Trudy Tobias

One day during the summer of 1933 Patricia Sisemore went out with a girlfriend and a male cousin and stayed until it was very late that night. When they came in, she discovered that her dad, Logan, had been waiting up for her and was very upset. The next day while she was mopping the floors, he angrily told her either to marry Orville Rainey, who happened to be there at the time, or she would not 'see the light of day till she was eighteen'. She was only fifteen at the time. Later that day, she asked Orville, who was nineteen, how soon could they get married. Orville replied, 'This Saturday.'

That was how she came to marry Orville Rainey.

While he worked out in the fields, she played with the grandkids of the couple Orville was working for. She played jacks with them a lot, but she always got breakfast for her new husband.

Pat was convinced that Logan Sisemore wanted to get rid of his daughters fast. His boys would take care of him. She didn't love Orville and she told him so. They were both virgins when they got married, and she confessed to me they didn't know where to put it. They tried the belly button at first.

Pat's sister, Lucille, had married at the age of fourteen; and her husband was Orville's brother, Willie Rainey, who died in 1991 or 1992. But she had loved him more than Pat did Orville.

Eventually, Pat left Orville. Her family had told her she needed to get out more. Raising two boys and working out in the field was all that she knew. She agreed to go out with her sister, Lucille, once, and then another time, and by then she really liked it. She felt she wanted more freedom and maybe seeing other men. She couldn't do this to Orville and remain married; so a divorce followed.

At last, she found true love. He was a serviceman, and she truly loved him. In a short time, however, she came to realize that the love was one-sided. This man, whose name was Hayes, was stationed far away; and there came a time when he thought she had been unfaithful to him. So he step-ped out on her.

That was it, as far as she was concerned. After that point, she began to go out with other men and had serious relationships with them, only to hurt them intentionally, be-cause of the anger and pain she had endured in the relationship with her true love, Hayes.

And she knew it was wrong.

"If I could have found the right man, Pat said, that I really loved, I would have been a great wife.

She did marry a second time, this time to Jerry Hatcher. He turned out to be a Jekell and Hyde. When he drank, his forehead would become scaly.

The marriage lasted only about a year, because he physically abused her and she ended up with a broken bone in her back.

Later, she began to date other men, just to get back at Hatcher, because she was still hurting emotionally.

Greel Hall's Hitch at Leavenworth
by Wesley Hall

At least two of William Newton Hall's sons learned how to make moonshine whisky, which in Arkansas before the turn of the century was not against the law. My father, Greeley Tee-man Hall, started out a very devout Baptist but in the 1930's in Oklahoma learned how to make *after-breakfast toddies* for his father-in-law, Henry Allan Karr and ended up in Leavenworth Federal Prison, in Kansas. No one had ever seen him take a drink of alcoholic beverages until that time, and his first brush with the Law came in 1933 when his neighbor John Ginn turned him in and led the Seminole County, Oklahoma, sheriff to his still. His sentence was a year-and-a-day in the state penitentiary, at McAlester. After he returned, in the presence of anyone who would listen, he swore he would never make another drop of *white lightning* again. And he didn't. However, one morning in 1935, when the Dust Bowl and the Great Depression were at their worst, two long black automobiles swooped in and out spilled a dozen federal Intern-al Revenue agents. John Ginn had turned Papa in again and sworn that he was making whisky, but this time they couldn't find a still. The only *evidence* they found were a small wooden nail keg and a piece of brass tubing. These and Ginn's word were enough to get Papa a five-year sentence in the big house.

[Trudy told me a number of stories about the branches of the family that she knew so well, some of which I could not share with you. I know they were true stories, but in the end I decided not to include them in this book. The people that her stories were about are now dead, but it was their living relatives that I was thinking about. Originally, the title I had in mind for this family history was *Skeletons in the Hall Closet*; and had I carried through with my plan to include Trudy's stories and mine about our branches of the family, it wouldhave been an accurate one. But I decided to leave that for someone else. My wish is to put out the first serious Hall Family History, a beginning which will be followed by much more complete studies of where we came from and how far we have gone.]

Trudy died unexpectedly in 1999.

Trudy Tobias

One day in 1998 Trudy appeared out of cyberspace. I knew at once that she was an addict like me of things Hall and genealogy in general. She confessed to me that she was the granddaughter of one of William Newton Hall's sons and the wife of a grandson of another! Talk about marrying kissin' cousins! She had a lot of information about the Hall family and was willing to share it. And she did, about fifty pounds of Family Group Records, pictures, legends, and personal confessions. Ironically, when I sifted through the whole mess I learned that there wasn't a blessed thing about her! And to this day I have less information about her branch of the family than I do about almost any other.

How Papa Lost a Million Dollars
by Wesley Hall

Greel Hall, my old man, thought he could do no wrong. God Himself was only slightly more perfect than he was. He knew more than anybody else did, including lawyers, ordained preachers, bankers, and judges. The following is a very true story:

In the spring of 1927 two lawyers from Holdenville, Oklahoma, came to see Papa about trading a farm in Texas for our farm. It was a much larger place than ours, and it ran parallel with the King Ranch. It would not cost us a dime to move, and if we didn't like what we found there, we had one year to call the deal off and we would be moved back, lock, stock, and barrel, at no expense to us. Papa signed the papers and we went to the Rio Grande Valley of Texas. To make a long story short, we did not like the deal and came back (Going and coming we and all of our belongings, including the livestock and farm machinery, rode the train, free of charge). Time passed and one day the Lynch Brothers Drilling Company showed up and drilled a well on one corner of our farm. It came in good, not a gusher but good. We were about to be rich, no doubt about it. When the check came (It turned out to be the only one that would be coming), it was made out in the amount of one hundred and fifty dollars! A one-time payment for damages to the surface of the land.

After the explosion and a great deal of shouting and threatening, on Papa's part, we were shown the small print on the contract Papa had signed back in 1927. He had, without knowing it, signed away alternating five-acre strips of mineral rights to our farm. Of course, the Lynch Brothers had chosen to put down a well on a strip for which we did not have the mineral rights. Later, they brought in another well, which was at least as good as the first.

The Legendary William Newton Hall
by Delia Sisemore

[Most of the skeletons in the Hall closet were put there by none other than William Newton Hall himself. No male or female in the family has come close to raising as many eyebrows and as much hell as he did. The following is a brief summary of his escapades, as related to me by William Newton's daughter, Cordelia Mae Sisemore.]

William Newton Hall owned slaves and a great deal of land prior to the Civil War. And he was married and had a son named *Sid*. I was his favorite so he told me things he didn't tell anybody else. Nobody knew where he disappeared to for long periods of time but me. Of course, that was before my time, but it was after the family moved to Arkansas he would suddenly disappear and not be seen for weeks. He told me it was because he was looking for his long lost Sid. I never did know for sure that he married my mother, who was a lot younger than him.

During the war he tried to join the Blue Bellies but they wouldn't have him. On at least two occasions he tried to cross the lines and was almost killed. So he took up with a family in Atlanta, put on a dress and a bonnet and set out the war dis-guised like a woman. In that family, which was named Woods, was a young girl name Susan. After the war he took her to Arkansaw as his wife. She was my mother, but I never knew whether they was married or not.

Will the Real Susie Woods Stand Up?
by Wesley Hall

In at least one branch of the Hall family there are a number of skeptics that do not believe that *Susan Elizabeth Woods* was the name of William Newton Hall's wife. This despite the fact that a copy of the marriage license has circulated through this branch of the tree. They believe that the real mother of his children was Suzie Owens, half-Cherokee. And as proof they cite two documents, Ulysses S. Grant Hall's birth certificate and his application for a Social Security number. On both his mother's name is Susie Owens.

In a letter to Trudy Tobias dated March 6, 1995, Lucy Dawson, the wife of Guy Dawson and the daughter of Grant and Sylvania Hall, referred to William Hall's wife as *Susan Owen Hall.*

It is true that the single surviving picture of William Newton and his wife would seem to confirm that she was part Indian. And it does seem a bit curious that most of the children (The author has not seen *all* of them) of the redhaired William Newton look as if they have Indian blood in them. One member of the family reported that she had seen William N. Hall's name on the Cherokee Rolls.

Finally, there are other members of the family who believe that William N.'s wife's name was *Susan Elizabeth Jones* (His daughter Cordelia was heard on several occasions to say that her mother's maiden name was *Jones*). And at least one family member reports that he grew up believing that William Newton's wife was Susan Elizabeth Sizemore!

SHARECROPPERS AND GYPSIES

William Newton Hall had six sons; and according to one of his daughters he raised them by a very strict code, one that may have seemed a little out of place in that frontier area of eastern Arkansas where he and his two brothers, Tyre and Green B. settled. He insisted that they learn how to read, in order to be able to understand the *Bible*, and behave at all times like Southern gentlemen. His two daughters could come and go as they pleased, but they had to toe the mark or answer to him.

He taught them farming and blacksmithing and carpentry, which, he figured, would stand them in good stead no matter where they might wander in the years ahead. Grant and Greel became excellent blacksmiths, Arch excelled as a carpenter, and the other three became expert makers of wicker furniture.

The boys took turns trying to sell and barter the furniture that they turned out, going from neighborhood to neighborhood in the farm wagon. It was on one of these trips that Greel met and fell in love with a beautiful redhead in Wesley. She was Mallie Rue Karr, one of four very eligible daughters of Henry Allan Karr, whose family had migrated to Arkansas about the same time the Halls had made the trip. And, coincidentally, their former home had been in Cherokee County, Georgia, about thirty miles north of Atlanta and contiguous with Dawson County, whence the Halls had come.

Mallie Rue Carr Greeley Teeman Hall
(1882-1971)   (1877-1965)
[Photo taken in 1900]

On Mallie's eighteenth birthday (Greel had turned twenty-three more than three months before), without asking permission or even the blessing of their parents, the two set out by horseback for the Indian Territory. On November 17, 1900, two days later, they were married on the banks of Barron Fork Creek, in what was later to become Cherokee County, Oklahoma. A few miles south of them was Tahlequah, the capitol of the Cherokee Nation.

At any rate, in the spring of 1907 Greel and Mallie took up the new life of sharecroppers. They settled near Barron Fork Creek, where Ruth was born on January 4, 1908. Greel's younger brother Grant and his wife, Vane, had settled in the Cookson Hills of Oklahoma, near Sallisaw, where

Willie had been born way back on October 3, 1901; but by this time they had returned to Madison County, Arkansas.

They were still in Madison County in October, 1901, when Willie was born; but in the spring of 1903 their third child, Albert, was born near Sallisaw, in Oklahoma (Indian Territory). Shortly after that they returned to Madison County, Arkansas, where their other three children were born.

These were very hard times for my family, if we can judge by the moves they made down across Oklahoma. If they ever complained, it was not passed down to me, the last of the family. Ruth was born in 1908 in Cherokee County, Clara Mabel in 1910 in Kiowa County, Clifford in 1912 in Pottawatomie County, Delsie Dale in 1914 near Asher in Pottawatomie County, Luther in 1917 in Seminole (while my family was visiting at the home of my mother's brother, Hubert T. Carr). This was just prior to our move to the Horseshoe Bend, south of Konawa, in the spring of 1917, where Greeley Teeman paid down on a small farm. Vernon was born on the farm in 1920, Zack in 1923, I in 1925.

Green T., the youngest brother, who was thirteen when my parents got married and twenty (and still unmarried) when they moved to Oklahoma, finally caught up with us in Kiowa County, where Ernest Clifford was born on May 12, 1911. Their next child, Pearl, was born in Little Rock, Arkansas; but by May 7, 1916, when their third child, Marge, was born they were living near us again, this time in Seminole county.

About this time my father decided to change his name. He and Green Tee, both reluctant to go by their first names, were using their initials; and quite frequently Greel's important (sic) mail would go to Green, and visa versa. So Papa changed his name to Horace Greel, and from that momentous day on he was known as "H. G. Hall."

None of the Hall boys, as far as I know, had to go overseas during WWI. Greel had to register for the draft, and for a time the family braced itself for his call-up. It never happened. The Roaring Twenties came and went, Wall Street crashed, and the Great Depression took over the country. And although the River Bend, as it was being called, was not inside the

Dust Bowl, the rains stopped and the crops all dried up, forcing most of the sharecroppers in the Bend to go West. Our best friends, the Grants and the Riggses, packed up and went down Route 66. We hung on, living completely off the land. Clifford disappeared for long periods of time, riding the rails in the West.

The old River Bend was as good a place as any to live during the depression of the 'Thirties. I might have said *suffer*, but nobody that I knew did much suffering, especially from the lack of food. While the soup lines in Chicago and New York got bigger and bigger (according to drifters who dropped by the farm), the people of Bend went right on eating fried potatoes and beans and other simple, good foods. Like cornbread and sorghum molasses for breakfast and blinky milk, without the cereals!

The soil in the Bend was a sandy loam, and anything that grows on a vine loved it. Citrons grew wild in the lower Bend, but who is going to mess with a *cittern* when right over the hill is somebody's big watermelon patch?

Which reminds me of how much Papa disliked watermelon thieves.

I was about eight or nine and Papa had pretty well given up on farming because of the drought, everything, that is, but watermelons and sorghum cane (both of which required more water than cotton or corn and had always been his *money* crops). Anyway, he spent his days from right after breakfast till dusky dark on the east end of our front porch keeping an eye on his watermelon patch.

Beside him on the tongue-in-groove porch were his spit can, his old tattered Bible, and his double-barreled shotgun. And three or four *pot-licker* hounds.

This was in the time of Uncle Trigger and the Seventh Day Adventists down in the Thomas Pecan Grove, right before Grandpa Karr showed up and taught him how to make whiskey from sorghum cane juice. He would sit there mumbling and grumbling about what Job did and what God did to Job, and occasionally you would hear Uncle Trigger's name or maybe

Gene Thomas's name mentioned. Sometimes his voice would rise to the high heavens, and I knew that was no time to be within fly swat distance of him.

On a hot July afternoon when everybody was sprawled out on the front porch listening to Papa go on about the pitiful state of the world (He had taken to reading the first page of the Kansas City *Star*), here came two of the Thomas boys. They came over the First Hill from the direction of the mailbox and cut down through the center of the watermelon patch. But they didn't stop once or even bend over toward one of the melons, and it was a good thing. Papa had spotted them right off, and the second they stepped foot on the sacred ground he was on his feet with the shotgun.

Of course, if they had grabbed up melons and run with them, Papa's buckshot would not have reached them; but then he would more than likely have hunted them down, and they probably knew that.

As it was, they came right on across the creek to the house. It turned out to be Hershel and Paul Wayne, boys about Vernon's and Luther's ages.

"Hiddy, Mister Hall!" one of them called out from some distance away. "Yall shore got some watermelon patch over there!"

They came on and sat down on the east edge of the porch in the shade, while Papa studied them. The rest of us just grinned and nodded at them. The dogs hadn't even bothered to bark.

"Them melons is my money crop," said Papa finally, with emphasis. "Yore daddy put out any this year?"

"Oh, yeah," nodded Paul Wayne. "But yore's is twice as big as ourn."

Papa relaxed back into his chair, looking pleased (or maybe vindicated, because of all the water he had hauled from the well at the Sorghum Mill to keep those vines alive. In fact, all of us, including my sisters, had worked like slaves to keep that First Hill from drying up and blowing away.

"Well, I'll tell you boys, that stretch of ground back of the creek there is real good watermelon soil. I figger to make seventy-five, eighty dollars on that crop." He thought a minute, his heavy black eyebrows working. Then he said, "Aint nobody gettin' his hands on eny of them biggest uns."

Vernon, who never did have much sense where Papa was concerned, said, "I reckon it would be all right if I went over and picked out two or three little ones, since we've got company."

Papa almost swallowed his dip of snuff at this blasphemy. He whirled around and shouted, "I reckon i'twouldn't! I'll do all the pickin', if eny pickin's to be done! You worthless boys keep away from my melons! None of you know how to pick out a ripe one!"

Nothing was said for a long time after that blast. Papa swatted a few flies, getting a great deal of satisfaction out of each kill. I eased around and climbed up between Hershel and Wayne, and for a time our bare feet dangled together. One of them punched me in the ribs and the other pinched me on a leg, and I had a dickens of a time smothering my snickers. Eventually, Mama brought out a pitcher of lukewarm water and some snuff glasses.

Two days later the shinola hit the fan.

It was right after daylight, even before Papa had had his first cup of coffee; and I think I was the only other member of the family awake and out of bed. Suddenly, something heavy hit the front porch with a bang, rattling screendoors and windows; and before I had time to investigate, Papa's hysterical scream echoed throughout the house:

"Somebody's done busted six of my best melons!"

The family gathered on the porch to look at the mess Papa had caused. He had carried the remains of a ravaged giant dark-green melon all the way from the First Hill and thrown it right in front of the screendoor to the kitchen!

"What they didn't bust they plugged!" he added, his face beet red.

"What are you goin' to do, Greel?" asked Mama meekly.

"I'm going to teach them Thomas boys a lesson they'll never forget as long as they live!" he bellowed. "They won't get away with this!"

It looked like an open-and-shut case against Hershel and Wayne Thomas. Just two days before this these boys had boldly walked across his patch and then had the gall to sit on his front porch and comment on how much better they were than their own pappy's.

Mama tried to argue that they were both good boys and would not do a thing like that. It had to've been drifters.

But what she and the rest of us had to say had no effect on Papa. He was going to "fix them two boys" so that they would never steal another melon as long as they lived.

I had been carrying a deep, dark secret for a full day and a half. It was so deep and dark I wasn't sure I should even tell Mama. There never had been anything I couldn't tell her, after I had made her swear not to pass it on or do anything about it; but this time somebody's life was at stake. I had thought that if I didn't let it out, just keep my mouth shut and go on about my business, the worst that could happen would be that Hershel and Wayne's father would beat the tar out of them. I didn't know what Papa had in mind for them, but more than likely he would fume and spew for a few days and then go tell Mister Thomas.

My deep dark secret was something I had seen the very next morning after the Thomas boys had dropped by. At the time I was working with my cornstalk livestock in the sandbed beneath the hicker nut tree, and Papa was snoozing on the east end of the front porch. It was still early enough that the July heat hadn't penetrated the deep shade of my playground, and I don't know what it was that caused me to stand up and peep over the edge of the Bermuda Grass Hill. It was like a voice told me to.

The instant I focused upon the watermelon patch I knew the picture was all wrong! Somebody, definitely not Papa, was right out in the middle busting melons! At first I wasn't sure who it was because his back was to me and he was stooping over, but whoever it was was wearing striped overalls just like Vernon's!

I almost yelled at Papa when I saw the first melon hit the ground! But it was like I was paralyzed in the vocal chords! I watched as the bent figure stood up with the heart of a melon in both hands, and that's when I saw the bright red hair! It sure enough was Vernon!

When it came to nerve, old Vern had few peers. He had already had more whippings with the razor strop than all the older boys put together, and it was a known fact that he was not afraid of Papa or any other grownup. He had terrorized Zack and me since the three of us were babies, and the older he got the more dangerous his practical jokes and dirty tricks had become. And not for a second had he ever given a thought to the consequences of his acts.

Now, he was busting melon after melon, taking maybe two or three big bites, and then tossing the rest away! Some melons evidently failed to live up to his expectations; so he didn't even bother to stoop and remove the hearts. And on his way toward the Red Oak Grove, where the Sorghum Mill used to be and where he would be out of sight of Papa, he took out his knife and removed plugs from a number of melons that he was curious about. Not once did he bother to thump one before he either busted it or plugged it.

So I kept quiet, my secret a knot of pain in the pit of my stomach.

If I let it out that Vernon had done this awful thing, Papa would probably kill him. The least he would do would be to disown him, send him out upon Route Sixty-six, where he would become a drifter like Tolley Grant and Sigel Riggs.

Later, I regretted that I had kept all this in because Vernon came very close to killing both Zackie and me on more than one occasion.

Papa no longer dozed on the east end of the front porch. He sat wide-eyed and stared hard toward the First Hill, with his shotgun across his knees; and he didn't bother with the spit can any longer. I was hunkered down at the end of the porch with my Junior G-Man Seebackoscope, just out of his sight, when I first became aware that he was no longer using the can.

Despite all anybody could do or say, Mama's worrying that he was up to something that he orten to be and Vernon's wild ideas about what he would do to get even with anyone that would do that to his melons, Papa would not let it out what he planned to do to Hershel and Wayne. All he would say was, "I reckon they won't git away with hit."

As it turned out, Papa's first move was to set possum traps next to some of his very biggest melons and camouflage them with vines. (This I learned well after the fact.) About daylight the next morning when he did an on-site inspection, he found to his amazement all the traps sprung and more of his prize melons squashed.

That day he sat on the porch all day with the 25-35 deer gun cocked and ready, even though now he knew the thieves were working at night. I saw the busted melons from the house, and at that distance it seemed like red was beginning to be the dominant color on the First Hill.

Vernon, I noticed, now had an angry red welt on two sides of his right foot; but he was staying out of Papa's sight. With that kind of evidence to back me up, I should have turned him in. Although I didn't know it at the time, I was never again to have the goods on him like this. And in the years to come I came to realize that he was a genius at covering his tracks and making the grownups think he was innocent of the life-threatening things that plagued Zack and me.

Despite my already considerable expertise in the field of sleuthing, I once again had to learn secondhand what Papa was up to next. As it turned out, it was a drastic last-ditch, dirty, lowdown trick that came close to making a believer out of the melon thief. And it put Papa out of the watermelon business completely.

During the dark of night while the rest of the family was sound asleep, including me, Papa crutin-oiled all of the remaining ripe melons in his patch (the ones that had not already been plugged, that is). Crutin Oil, a chemical mixture that isn't even found in the dictionaries today, was a violent purgative that some Benders were said to have used on cats, using an extraneous method that took immediate effect.

It was around midnight of the same night Papa doctored his melons that the thief busted his first one and began to wolf down the heart. According to Papa, it couldn't have been an hour after he had plugged and poured a generous amount of that deadly Crutin Oil into the last melon and quit the patch that he heard the first agonized scream. This was followed by other, throatier, even more agonized carryings-on. It was enough to make Johnny Weismueller turn pale in shame and take up another line of work than yelling at apes on a movie set. The blood-curdling sounds echoed and re-echoed throughout the hills of the lower Bend, from Nigger Creek to Tommy Ragland's.

And that was the last any of us heard out of Vernon for at least a week.

It is amazing what insights time brings. Remember the old saying "Hindsight's always twice as good as foresight"? During the time I was growing up I had it all wrong about Papa, because nobody bothered to explain things to me and because (I'm convinced) nobody ever really put two and two together, about why he turned out the way he did.

You see, I was the last of eleven children, and a lot of water had gone under the bridge before I appeared on the scene. And my family did not waste much time filling me in on what I had missed, especially about the distant past and things that were better off left unsaid. There was no talk by the grownups about where we came from, what Grandpa Hall and Grandpa Karr had done back when they were young. If there were any skeletons in my folk's closets, I never knew anything about them as a child growing up in the Bend.

There were skeletons, I was to discover after I was grown up and out on my own. My Aunt Deely, my father's youngest sister and Grandfather Hall's "favorite," told me enough to fill half a dozen volumes of family history; and what I didn't learn from her I put together from scraps of gossip and family legend and a word or two here and there from other members of the family.

Papa was one of six sons of Susan Elizabeth Woods and William Newton Hall, who had been a Georgia planter before the Civil War; and, after a lifetime of misjudging him, I am convinced that he was a gifted son of a very gifted and daring father.

"Uncle Will," as the people around Japton and Drakes Creek, Arkansas, called Grandpa (this according to Aunt Deely), switched from planting cotton and tobacco (with an overseer and slaves doing all the work) and the life of a gentleman in Bullock County, Georgia, to preaching the gospel at the Drakes Creek Baptist Church, blacksmithing, making wicker furniture, and farming with a mule.

From him Papa learned the Bible, blacksmithing, carpentry, and farming; and once in the Bend farming his own land, he built his blacksmith shop, the only one in the Bend, a sorghum mill, again the only one south of Nigger Creek, and began to fill in at Pilgrim's Rest on Sundays when no ordained preacher showed up.

Most of these things I knew about Horace Greel Hall when I was a kid. I even knew, this from Delsie and Mabel, that he had once swapped our farm for one down in Texas; and when it didn't work out he had returned to the Bend and picked up where he had left off.

We had the biggest apple orchard in our part of the Bend, the only one that I knew of; and around our house were many signs of Papa's hard work and industry. In addition to the several varieties of apples, he had put in a plumb orchard, two very productive Bing cherry trees, two pear trees, and several crab apple trees. By himself he had built a large cement cellar with bins for sweet potatoes, Irish potatoes, apples, pears, peanuts. And above this he had built a smokehouse, again the only one in the Bend.

But mostly what I knew about Papa was that I did not like him. It never occurred to me to give him credit for all the things we had; and even if I had, I would still not have liked him or trusted him. Because he was not only a slave-driver, which he had always been if I could judge from what my older brothers and sisters had said over and over, but by the time I was old enough to take stock of things he was cruel and indifferent, and potentially brutal.

The two ends of my family had very different stories to tell about Papa. Ezra and Ollie and Grady, already married and on their own when I was born, would brook no criticism of him. He was a "very good man," a true

Christian, the first school board president at Pilgrim's Rest, a thoughtful and sensitive father. The younger children told a very different story. Most of them had been around when the big change began; and by the time Zackie, Vernon, and I were the only boys left, he was none of the things he had once been.

When I was a year-and-a-half old, hardly old enough to know, much less remember, what was what, two men in suits and ties showed up at our house in a shiny black touring car and propositioned Papa to trade our farm for one in the Rio Grande Valley. This I learned from Delsie one day several years later when she found me in a backroom of the house moping about something Papa had done or said to me.

The farm was much larger than the one in the Bend and had much richer soil. All it needed was a lot of hard work and it would make Papa a rich man. He could go look at it and if he didn't like what he saw, he could turn the proposition down with no hard feelings. And, if he ended up trading and later changed his mind, for any reason, he could return to the Bend and the all it would cost him would be a little time. The company the two men represented would foot the bill for the trip to check out the farm and the move by train of his family, livestock, and machinery.

Delsie was only twelve at the time of the move. To my question, "Did Papa wonder *why* this company wanted our farm?" she said she had no idea. Apparently, the owners of the farm in Texas had decided to look for a place in Oklahoma; but as far as she knew Papa hadn't even asked why they had settled on his.

Anyway, the big move took place in the early spring of 1927. Everything, all of the furniture and farm machinery, as well as the mules and the cows and two full grown hogs, were either hauled or herded across the South Canadian River to the train depot in Ada.

Details of the move and the stay in Texas were always very skimpy because Delsie couldn't remember and Mama would not say very much about any of it. She had liked no part of it and never gave it her blessing and in the process almost lost one of her children because of it. Papa would say nothing at all about it, and the older kids that went along (Clifford, Delsie, Mabel, Luther) got out of it only a few Mexican words, how wonderful the Mexican family just down the road was that made great hot tamales and would do anything to get all of the shucks from our corn.

But all of them at one time or another told me the story of *the big cat* that almost got me while I was playing in the frontyard.

Our farm paralleled the King Ranch for a mile or so, which was encircled by a high fence. On our side was farmland, on the other side jungle. Out of the jungle one day came this large animal that looked like a black panther. Somehow, it got through the fence and headed straight for me. Mama screamed at the top of her voice and at the last possible moment, just as the animal leaped, Papa appeared in the door with a rifle and with one shot killed it.

Almost the only other thing I was ever to learn about this *Texas Swop* was that Zackie became deathly sick on the water there. That was the reason passed down for our returning to the Bend. The water *had something in it*, and that's all it took. Mama panicked and, after a great deal of consternation and perturbation, Papa gave in and notified the Holdenville lawyers that the deal was off. Once again everything was loaded into boxcars, and the Halls returned to the Bend.

End of story? Oh, no. It was more like the beginning.

When the two lawyers from Holdenville showed up wanting to trade a farm in Texas for our little piece of ground, Papa had no idea they represented an oil company. Up to this point not a single well had been drilled in the Bend; and despite the fact that my Uncle John, on the Karr side of the family, had hit it rich over in Seminole, it would seem that the thought never occurred to Papa or any of my family that our little farm might have something of value beneath it.

Uncle John, according to rumors and hearsays, had twenty-seven acres smack in the middle of what came to be known as the "Seminole Oil Field." It was worthless land, wouldn't grow cockleburrs; and Papa was always a bit condescending when the subject of Uncle John's little farm came up. That is, until word came that he was suddenly a millionaire. Just before he sold out and went to Houston to live high on the hog, he told Mama that he had collected a million dollars on every acre of his sorry little plot of land.

Anyway, the swop was off and the family went on back to the Bend. It had been a great experience, one that they would never forget; and both Mama and Papa were anxious to put the whole thing behind them. But, as it turned out, Papa had failed to "read the fine print" in the proposition he had signed with the Holdenville lawyers! What he thought he had signed was a simple agreement that if "for any reason" at the end of one year he did not want to make the exchange, he could have his Oklahoma farm back. Period.

Well, not exactly.

The decade of the Roaring Twenties had ended with a whimper for us, but for most of the country, especially the big cities, it had ended disastrously. In November, 1929, the biggest banks in the country closed their doors, and that brought on what the newspapers were calling the *Great Depression*. Then, in the early 'Thirties, a drought so severe and so widespread hit the middle of the country that much of western Oklahoma, the Panhandle of Texas, and southern Kansas became known as the Dust Bowl.

And although technically the Bend was on the rim of the Bowl, rain was so scarce most of the time families were barely able to grow enough food for their tables. Grasshoppers and locusts, after devastating Kansas, swarmed across our little farm in greater numbers than anyone had ever seen, eating everything in their path. Our main creek west of the house dried up and the ground became so hard-baked in the Willow Bottom the crawdads were unable to dig holes to escape me.

I was impervious to the blistering heat of summertime, not even bothering to wear a straw hat most of the time; food had always been a low priority with me when I could be outside playing; so, as far as I was concerned, the Dust Bowl years were about the same as any other years, only perhaps a bit warmer. I continued to build forts and hideouts in the Willow Bottom on our place, the Red Clay Ditches on Jack Hensley's land, and the Sand Canyons down close to the South Canadian River. (Which had become a barren stretch of flat red sand.)

We managed to grow in the bottoms just about everything we needed, and so nobody ever went hungry; but I remember one particular morning out at the cow lot I cornered Zack and demanded to know why we had to eat cornbread for breakfast. He came back with something about the mill in town refusing to trade their flour for our shelled corn anymore, that times were hard.

This was news to me. "Why can't we just buy some flour?"

"With what?" asked Zack. "We don't have any money."

We were out at the cow lot getting milk for Papa's butter. He would not eat day-old butter and our watercooler just wouldn't keep it fresh overnight. Therefore, every morning somebody had to crawl out of bed early enough to milk old Two-Teat, who just gave about a half-gallon of milk at best, so that somebody else would have time to churn it before breakfast. On this particular morning Zackie was doing the milking, so I would have to do the churning.

"You know, Dock, it don't make no sense to me at all."

"What, hard times?"

"No. I mean what's the use of goin' to this trouble when all we've got to go with the butter is cornbread and sorghum molasses."

"We're goin' to the trouble because Papa wants fresh butter. It don't make no difference what he does with it. Besides, cornbread, fresh butter, and sorghum is more'n a lot of people have," he said, always the serious one.

"If our cane had made it the way it usually does," I said, standing close by so I could grab the bucket and run to the churn with it, "we could've made a fortune this year, I bet." I was remembering that people from as far away as Ada and Wewoka had come to our house during the summer asking about our sorghum molasses.

"No," he said with finality, "we wouldn't have made a thing."

"How about all them people that come askin'?"

"They came to git somethin' for nothin'. None of them had any money. Don't you pay any attention to anything? Papa gave our syrup to them people, saving back just enough to get us through the winter."

It was the early part of 1933 that the first oil well was drilled in the Bend.

One morning early (I was on my way to Punky Ginn's, having skipped out on breakfast) I heard a distant roaring over in the direction J. D. Cypert's house and East Fairview. I had just topped the last hill before the section line road, which is where Punky lived, and the noise was a lot louder. And, it was definitely heading in my direction.

It sounded to me like an army of big trucks invading the Bend. I mulled that over for a time and then sat down in the shade of some willows with Old Ring and waited. I had never heard so much noise at any one time, and the thought occurred to me that finally the Law in Konawa had talked the Army into taking us over. I was torn between waiting to see the spectacle and running to warn Papa.

I waited and it turned out to be two pickup trucks and a big flatbed truck loaded down with lumber and concrete blocks and barrels of creosote and wheelbarrows and a lot of stuff I had never seen before! And while Old Ring and I watched, that day and each day from then on, they proceeded to bring in a mountain of stuff; and right where John Ginn's leased land ended and Gene Thomas's farm began, there on the west side of the section line road where nothing but trees had ever been before, the Lynch Brothers Drilling Company built a large storage building and the prettiest little house I had ever seen.

And about a week after that first caravan showed up, here came the biggest thing I had ever seen on wheels. It was an oil well drilling rig!

By this time, Old Ring and I were having trouble seeing above the heads and around the shoulders of other Benders who had heard the great news. In fact, everybody in the Bend would eventually show up and, standing at a polite distance, pass judgment on the trees being sawed down, the height of the wooden oil rig, the noise and stink of the machinery (the likes of which nobody had ever seen before).

It was the most exciting thing I had ever seen, by far.

In the winter of 1935, late in November, Papa received word from the Lynch Brothers Oil Drilling Company that a well was going to be drilled on our land!

All semblance of seriousness and hard work around our place ended immediately, because we were going to be rich from this oil well. (To be perfectly honest, there hadn't been much to do all year, what with the Dust Bowl and grasshoppers and money so scarce Papa hadn't even been able to buy seed corn to plant.) Nobody had any doubt about whether the well would come in or not, despite the cautious talk around the breakfast table. Our Karr relatives in Seminole had become so rich two years before they couldn't live in Oklahoma any longer, and everybody knew Uncle John's briar patch was just about the sorriest piece of ground in the country. One well in the Bend should be worth all twenty-seven of the ones the oil people had drilled on his.

"Even if it comes in a dry hole, we'll git damages won't we?" asked Clifford one morning. "I'll bet that'll amount to quite a bit of money."

"One hundred and fifty dollars," said Papa, slurping his coffee and frowning tragically. Then he surprised everybody by adding, "But I reckon there's probably a little oil down there. Maybe enough so we can give this weed patch back to the Indins."

The drilling had started on November 30, and all month long it had continued, right through Christmas, with us expecting any day to be so rich we would have to move to Texas just to be able to brag about all the money we had in the bank.

We could hear the big rotary drill working away clean up to the house, and every time it went CHUG-CHUG at the bottom of its turn Papa's spirits would rise again and he would get a thoughtful look on his face. I guess he was thinking about all the things he was going to buy with the piles of money we would get. Sometimes I would look at him and there would be a pleased, almost gleeful look on his old kisser, like somebody had just told him a joke you can't talk about in front of women and children.

On Christmas Eve, Zackie and me went looking for a tree down in the Willow Bottom, where the drill rig was, even though there wasn't no good cedars there. It didn't take much urging for me to get him as far as the dam, because he was curious about all the goings-on, same as me. But when I tugged on his sleeve and told him I wanted to ask Mike a question he balked.

"Who's Mike?" he asked, sounding suspicious, like he thought I was leading him into a trap.

"He's the guy in the blue shirt. Come on, it won't take but a minute."

"You better stay away from that thing," he warned, not budging an inch. Then he demanded, "Do you know all the men that work for the oil company?"

"Just the driller, Ed, and the tool-pusher, Mike, and the roustabout over there taking a smoke break. That's Pete."

"Well, that sounds like all of them."

Old Ring followed right at my heels as I worked my way over the dam to Mike, who was always in a good mood. I could tell by Ring's behavior he was not on good terms with this crew, but evidently he thought as long as he stuck close to me he would be all right.

"Hey, Red!" yelled Mike. "Got your stockin' on the mantel?"

"Sure, how about you?"

Mike laughed like I had told a joke and repeated what I had said to Ed. Then he stuck his hand out and pointed toward my chest, "Better back up a little, I might git some black gold on you."

I swear he said 'black gold'. Ed came over and stood beside me and wanted to know if Santa Claus was going to visit me. I told him Santa Claus had not found the Bend yet, as far as I knew. Besides, if he did show up, the dogs would bark at him and Papa would probably shoot him with buckshot. It was now Ed's turn to laugh like a hyena and repeat to Mike what I had just said.

"How far down are you?" I asked.

"Twelve-ninety or so, I reckon," replied Ed, grinning. "You anxious for us to bring in a gusher? Tell your dad it should be anytime now."

Zackie was waving and working his mouth, pretending to yell at me. I thanked Ed and dashed back across the rough ground to the dam, trying to leave Old Ring at the mercy of the Lynch Brothers. But he caught and passed me and looked back over his shoulder with his tongue lolled out, like he had showed me a thing or two.

We found a decent cedar on the hill behind our barn and sawed the bottom straight so it would sit on crossed one-bys. Mabel had a thing or two to say to us for taking so long and couldn't wait to get us back out of the house on another errand. It was snowing by this time and pretty soon we would be leaving for the Christmas program at Pilgrim's Rest School. Both of us, as well as everybody else in school, was in the play about Joseph and Mary and the baby in the manger. We did this same play with hardly any variations every year, but our teacher saw to it we didn't get the same parts. This year I was supposed to be the Wise Man with Frankincense.

Anyway, the well came in on New Year's Eve, at twenty-five hundred and thirty-one feet; and although it was not a gusher, it came in good and so Papa said a special prayer of benediction at the breakfast table the next day and ended by saying as how he was planning to buy a new truck and drive it down Route Sixty-six to California. I glanced at Mama right after the *amen* and knew at once by her pursed lips she wasn't the least bit pleased with the way that prayer had ended.

"Why do you want to go there?" she asked, querulously.

"To find out what all the fallderol's about," he came back. "Almost ever'body we know has gone down Sixty-six, looking for a pot of gold. Well, we'll just go down it, too, and see if any of them found it."

When the check came from the Lynch Brothers in May of that year, it was in the amount of one hundred and fifty dollars; and the typed letter on company stationery said quite bluntly that this was the sum of the damages for easement rights to the drilling site. Papa read the letter a number of times, getting madder and madder. I was rushed out of his presence for my own protection, and later I learned that Papa had just about busted a gasket over the pitiful amount he was being paid for what appeared to be a very productive oil well.

Suddenly, I was not privy to anything that was going on. Papa made a trip to Wewoka, I knew, for the purpose of meeting with the shyster lawyers, as he never failed to call them; but it wasn't until much later that I learned the rest of the story: The lawyers, just a bit amused, had spelled it out for him. When he made the swop for the farm in Texas, he had given up a five-acre strip of mineral rights on our Oklahoma farm. Yes, it was in the agreement, in small print, but it was quite legal. Too bad Lynch Brothers had decided to sink a well on that five-acre strip. Perhaps they would dig other wells and one or more might be on us.

This blow to Papa's pride, not to mention his ambitions and aspirations, changed his life completely. That he had gone from the good father and serious citizen of my brother Ezra's time to the mean and bitter old man of mine I knew very well, but I had never understood why.

Papa had believed himself incapable of making a mistake. His father had come down from the planter class in Georgia to dirt farmer and ordained Baptist minister in raw, new Oklahoma; but God had had a hand in that. Through no fault of his own had William Newton Hall been reduced to such a lowly state; and his legacy to his sons was a pride and self-assurance that would allow for no mistakes.

Who can say what another man would have done under the circumstances? Papa did not change overnight from the devout Christian he had always been. He had never been a talkative and outgoing man, even with his family; and so the change that was taking place inside him was not apparent to outsiders and his small redhaired son, who was in a world of his own creation most of the time. But, of course, Mallie knew, and felt a coldness inside her body she had never felt before.

The blow dealt Papa by the lawyers brought him to his knees, but it is possible he might have gotten to his feet again had it been the only one of such magnitude. There were several over the years, delivered not by lawyers but by Fate, or whatever it is that enjoys hitting a man when he is down. Each of these I saw not as end results but as causes. Papa, to me, was who he was because he had become a selfish and egotistical old man.

It was at about this time that my maternal grandfather, Henry Allan Karr, taught my father how to make whisky so that he could have a *toddy* before breakfast. A neighbor, John Ginn, urged on by his Christian wife, turned him in. He spent a "year and a day" in McAlester State Prison. Back at home, his honor tarnished and his pride destroyed, my father took up a position on the front porch to tell anyone who would come along just how unjust the world was. In 1936 the Law returned to our house, this time led by the Feds, and took him away. The charge, making and selling moonshine liquor. No still was found because there was no still, but on the word of our closest neighbor, Mr. John Ginn, he was found guilty and sent to Leavenworth Prison for five years.

In the summer of 1938 he was back home on probation, all vestiges of respect and pride gone. He was about as low as a human being could get. On December 22 he loaded what was left of his family into his old truck and took us to Buckeye, Arizona, to live in the "Red Camp" (formerly the residence of sheep) and pick cotton for the Miller Cattle Company. The next spring we continued on to the San Joaquin Valley of California.

We had become Okies.

THE HALLS OF DISCINCTION

[Almost all people named *Hall* are, by nature and inclination, potentially outstanding. Down through history there have been a great number of them who made names for themselves. Of course, there were a few black sheep in the flock; and these, sorry to say, have received far more attention than they deserved. The following is a mere sampling of Halls who have attracted national and international attention (and at least one who attracted no attention at all).]

Anthony Hall (1968, Boston-)

Michael Anthony Thomas Charles Hall (more often just Anthony Michael Hall) first won accolades in *National Lampoon's Vacation* (1983), but is more often remembered as the *geek* who pursued Molly Ringwald in *Sixteen Candles* (1984). Hall appeared in several other teen films, including *The Breakfast Club* and *Weird Science* (both appeared in 1985).

Arsenio Hall (1955-)

Actor, comedian, and television host. Host and eponym of *The Arsenio Hall Show* (1989-1994); starred in television series *Martial Law* (1998-). [Tyree Hall (1838) married a girl named *Arcenia,* and the name Arsenio shows up in a number of early Hall families from Georgia.]

Asaph Hall (1829-1907)

U.S. astronomer, born in Goshen, Connecticut; Harvard University professor; discovered two moons of planet Mars, determined the period of rotation of Saturn.

Basil Hall (1788ñ1844)

British naval officer and traveler. In the service from 1802 to 1823, he commanded vessels on scientific assignments and voyages of exploration. He wrote of them in his *Account of a Voyage of Discovery to the West Coast of Corea and the Great Loo-Choo* (1818); in *Extracts from a Journal Written on the Coasts of Chile, Peru, and Mexico* (2 vol., 1823, reprinted 1968); and in *Fragments of Voyages and Travels* (1831ñ33). These were written in three series, each series amounting to three volumes. After leaving the navy he traveled in the United States, and his *Travels in North America* (3 vol., 1829) were a valuable early description of America.

Charles Francis Hall (1821-71)

U.S. explorer, born in Rochester, N.H.; searched for Franklin party 1860-69; died on North Pole expedition.

Charles Martin Hall (1863-1914)

Inventor of electric aluminium smelting.

Chester Moor Hall (1703-71)

British lawyer, mathematician, and inventor; born in Leigh, Essex; first person to make an achromatic refracting telescope.

Edward Hall (1498-1547, London)

English historian whose chronicle was one of the chief sources of William Shakespeare's history plays.

Edwin Herbert Hall (1855-1938)

Discoverer of the *Hall Effect* (1879): an electric current applied perpendicularly to a magnetic field generates an electric field that is perpendicular to both the current and the magnetic field.

Elizabeth Hall (1608-1670)

Mrs. Elizabeth Hall Nash Bernard. Lady Bernard was the daughter of Susanna Shakespeare and John Hall; granddaughter of William Shakespeare and Ann Hathaway (the last surviving direct descendant of Shakespeare).

Fawn Hall (1959-)

Secretary to Oliver North during the Iran-Contra affair.

Granville Stanley Hall (1844-1924)

U.S. psychologist, educator, and editor; born near Ashfield, Massachusetts; president and professor of psychology at Clark University, Worcester, 1888-1920. Founder of the *American Journal of Psychology*. His most important work is *Adolescence* (2 vol., 1904). Published his autobiography in 1923.

Gus Hall (1910-)

Began as Arro Kusta Hallberg. U. S. Communist politician; secretary-general of U. S. Communist Party 1959-; Communist presidential candidate 1972, 1976, 1980, 1984.

James Hall (1793-1868)

American author and editor who also served as a soldier, attorney, judge, and civil servant during his diverse career. He was born in Philadelphia, Pennsylvania, and served a soldier in the War of 1812 (1812-1815). He was court-martialed in 1817 for insubordination, but his punishment was canceled by President James Monroe. He studied law at Pittsburgh until 1820, when he traveled down the Ohio River in a keelboat to Shawneetown, Illinios. He lived in Illinois for twelve years, becoming a prosecuting attorney, a district judge, a newspaper editor, an author of prose and verse, and the state treasurer. From 1830 to 1836, he founded and edited the *Illinois Monthly Magazine*, subsequently called the *Western Monthly Magazine*, the first literary periodical west of Chicago, Illinois. His many novels include *Letters from the West* (1828), *Legends of the West* (1832), *The Soldier's Bride and Other Tales* (1833), *Tales of the Border* (1835), and, with Thomas L. McKenney, *The History of the Indian Tribes of North America* (3 volumes, 1836-1844). After 1833 Hall lived in Cincinnati, Ohio, working as a banker.

James Hall (1811-1898)

American geologist and paleontologist. Born in Hingham, Massachusetts, graduated from Rensselaer School (later Rensselaer Polytechnic Institute), in 1832. An authority on stratigraphy and invertebrate paleontology, he joined the New York state geological survey in 1836 and in 1839 he became the state geologist for New York.

James Norman Hall (1887-1951)

U.S. writer of distinction. He was born in Colfax, Iowa, but lived many years in Tahiti. He wrote the *Doctor Dogbody's Leg* tales, *My Island Home*, his autobiography, and, with C. B. Nordhoff, he wrote *Mutiny on the Bounty*, *Pitcairn's Island*, *The Hurricane*, and *The Dark River*.

John H. Hall

Inventor of the breech-loading rifle (1833).

John Hall (1575-1635)

English physician and Puritan; husband of Susanna Shakespeare (m. 1607); son-in-law of William Shakespeare; father of Elizabeth Hall (1575-1635).

Sir John Hall (1824-1907)

New Zealand (English-born) politician; prime minister of New Zealand 1879-1882.

Joseph Hall (1574-1656)

Born July 1, 1574, in Ashby-de-la-Zouch, Leicestershire, England, and died September 8, 1656, at Higham, Norfolk. English bishop, moral philosopher, and satirist; remarkable for his literary versatility and innovations. He was the first English satirist to successfully model Latin satire (*A Harvest of Blows*, 1597-1602). As a moral philosopher he achieved a European reputation for his Christianization of Stoicism. Educated under Puritan influences at the Ashby School and the University of Cambridge (from 1589), he was elected to the university lectureship in rhetoric. He became rector of Hawstead, Suffolk, in 1601 and concentrated chiefly on writing books to make money "to buy books." He wrote, among other things, *Mundus Alter et Idem* (*The World Different and the Same*), ca. 1605, an original and entertaining Latin satire that influenced Jonathan Swift's *Gulliver's Travels*.

Joyce Clyde Hall (1891-1982)

Businessman in Nebraska and Kansas, creator of the Hallmark Company, which he ran with his brother Rollie.

Kevin Peter Hall (1955-1991)

Actor; starring in the television series *Misfits of Science*, 1985-1986 (in the role of Dr. Elvin Lincoln); *227*, 1989-1990 (in the role of Warren Merriwether), *Harry and the Hendersons*, 1990-1991 (in the roll of Harry). He starred in the following movies: *Predator*,1987 (as the Predator), *Harry and the Hendersons*,1987 (as Harry), *Predator 2*, 1990 (as the Predator).

Leonard Wood Hall (1900-1979)

U. S. Republican politician; chairman of Republican National Committee 1953-1957.

Lloyd Augustus Hall (1894-1971)

His research led to improved curing salts, which led to improved meat preservation. He also discovered a method for sterilizing spices, which had applications in other fields. His methods are today used to sterilize medicine, medical supplies, and cosmetics. In addition, he patented a method that dramatically cut the amount of time necessary to cure meats. Instead of a six-day to fifteen-day period, meats can now be cured in hours. His research resulted in more than one hundred patents in the United States, Great Britain, and Canada. Recognition for his work came when, as the first African-American to be so honored, he was elected to the National Board of Directors of the American Institute of Chemists. After his retirement in 1959, he spent six months in Indonesia as a consultant for the FAO, (the Food and Agriculture Organization of the United Nations).

Lyman Hall (1724-90)

The famous one, a physician and an American Revolutionary War leader, born in Wallingford, Conn.; signer of Declaration of Independence; first governor of Georgia (1783-85). A county in Georgia was named after him.

Lyman Hall (1859-1905)

Not so famous, but, nevertheless, a U. S. educator and mathematician, as well as a president of Georgia Institute of Technology (1896-1905).

Marshall Hall (1790-1857)

English physician and physiologist, M. D. from the University of Edinburgh (1812). He practiced medicine in Nottingham and in London. He opposed bloodletting and devised a method of artificial respiration named for him. As a result of his experiments with animals he read a paper before the Royal Society (1833) advancing the theory of reflex action; despite some opposition to the theory it was later universally accepted. His works also include *The Diagnosis of Diseases* (1817) and *Memoirs on the Nervous System* (1837).

Monty Hall (1924?-)

Began as Monty Halparin. Canadian-born television game show host; immigrated to U. S. 1955; host of game show *Let's Make a Deal* (1964-1986); honorary mayor of Hollywood (1973-1979).

Nathan Kelsey Hall (1810-1874)

Born in Ondanga, NY, served as Postmaster general under Millard Fillmore, and latr as a federal judge.

Prince Hall (1735?-1807)

Barbadian-born Freemason; founded first black Masonic Lodge in the U. S. (1775); eponym of Prince Hall system of lodges.

Robert N. Hall (1919-)

Born in New Haven, Connecticut. Invented the high-voltage, high-power semiconductor pin rectifier. This invention boosted efficiency and reduced wasted power and destructive heat build-up in large-scale power transmission (1994).

Robert Hall (ca, 1948-1996)

New Zealand Mountaineer/guide who perished on May 14, 1996, on Mount Everest, along with seven others, in the greatest Everest disaster in history.

Samuel Hall (1781-1863)

From Nottinghamshire, England. Engineer and inventor of the steam condenser for boilers.

Samuel Read Hall (1795ñ1877)

American educator and clergyman, born in Croydon, New Hampshire. After teaching in Rumford, Maine, and Fitchburg, Massachusetts, he founded a training school for teachers (1823) in Concord, Vermont, one of the first in the United States. He also helped to organize the American Institute of Instruction (1830), the oldest educational association in the United States. He became principal of the teachers seminary at Phillips Academy (1830-1837), of Holmes Plymouth Academy (1837-1840), and of Craftsbury Academy (1840-1846), to which he added a teachers training department. From 1846 to 1875 he served as pastor in Brownington and in Granby, Vermont. He wrote numerous textbooks, and his famous *Lectures on School-Keeping* (1829) were republished by A. D. Wright and G. E. Gardner in 1929, with a biography of him and a bibliography of his works.

Sam Hall

Then there is the famous chimney sweep, Sam Hall, *aka* Jack Hall, who was hanged in 1701. He inspired a song with dozens of different lyric versions, including one sung by Carl Sandburg which begins:
James W. Clements posted this limerick on a genealogical web site:
> O my name, it is Sam Hall, it is Sam Hall;
> My name, it is Sam Hall, it is Sam Hall,
> And I hate you one and all,
> Yes I hate you one and all.
> God damn your eyes!

Wesley Elmo Hall, B. A., M. A., Ph. D

The eleventh child of an Oklahoma dirt farmer, attended Bugscuffle School in the River Bend of Seminole County, learned to read upside down and backwards (because there was only one book in the home), learned mathematics playing dominoes, became a vagabond on Route Sixty-six at the age of fourteen, never had an address until he joined the Navy. In his youth he traveled and wrote his books, and in his dotage he published them. He became a missionary English teacher, an author of sorts, a follower of no one.

[There are, of course, many other outstanding Halls, some of whom I could find no dates that would attach to their names: The Sir John Hall who was the first Director of the Bank of America, the Geoffrey Hall who was an Admiral in the American Navy, the Harold Hall who was a Judge; the Kenneth Hall who was a General in the American Army; the Peter Hall who was a Professor of Geography; the Sir Noel Hall who was a Principal at Brasenose College; the William Hall who was a Nuclear Physicist, and many, many more. Let us not overlook the David Hall who was a partner of Dr. Benjamin Franklin in their printing establishment, or that the wife of Sir William Shakespeare and even Shakespeare himself was the father of a daughter named Susan Hall.]

THE FIRST GENERATION

John Hall (b. 1769)

The name *John*, scribbled inside a tiny box on the ancient census paper caught my eye (I was looking at a microfiche screen); and for a minute it was all I could do to keep the tears back. In less than a week after I had discovered that *Hiram Hall* and *Charity* were the parents of my grandfather, here was the name of my great-great-grandfather! It appeared to be tangible evidence. Maybe not absolutely conclusive, but solid evidence. And in the next small rectangular box, where my grandfather's mother's name was supposed to be, was *Mary*! And, God be my witness, their place of birth and the year each was born were also there! All the many hours of research in dim and dusty libraries had paid off!

The family tree had just grown a whole new set of roots!

John Hall, from near Charleston, South Carolina, was born in 1769. There it was, on an official federal census for the county of Carroll in the state of Georgia for the year of our lord 1840! That meant the branch of the Hall family to which I belonged had been in this country before it was a country, while it was still just a scattering of colonies! Furthermore, it meant that my ancestor was living near Charleston before it was *Charleston*! Well, a little before. In 1770 the rapidly-growing seaport town of Charlestown would decide to christen it *Charleston*.

Mary, according to the faded, difficult-to-read census, had been born in 1770, in the same area.

Since the federal census did not begin until 1790 (and then only as a bare bones listing of heads of households), I knew there was little likelihood I would find my farthest-back relatives (and be able to positively identify them). John and Mary were fine names, respectable names, but they were so common it would be most difficult singling them out from all the other such combinations.

But I went to work and found a John Hall who had married a Mary Ann Dodd on April 10, 1774. Girls marry young in the South, but there was no way my farthest-back relative would give up his freedom at the age of 5! In the 1790 census for York County, South Carolina, this John was listed as "free white male under age 16." In the 1800 census for York County a John Hall was listed, but York County is a long way from the Charleston area. In 1820 there was a John B. Hall listed, and in 1840 there were two John Halls on record. Sometime during the following decade these Johns must have died or moved out of the county because there was no further census record for him in York County.

At least now we could say with some certainty that our first American Hall was in the Charleston area in the last half of the Eighteenth Century. And although guessing and speculation are frowned upon by some family historians, it will be permitted on this occasion. John's and Mary's parents almost certainly arrived (together perhaps) in this country by ship around 1750. Immigration from England, Ireland, and Scotland was at an all-time high during this period.

John and Mary raised a family in the Charleston area, and we are now convinced that our Hiram Hall was one of their children. It is altogether possible, while we're surmising, that another of their children, several years younger than Hiram, was named Green Berry. In the next chapter, we will look at this individual a bit closer and attempt to make a case for him as a member of our family. Regrettably, we have been unable to find tangible proof that Hiram and Mary were his parents.

After countless hours of poring over ships' passenger lists, I concluded that while it is interesting to speculate about all the John Halls and William Halls that came to this country in the early 1800's, nothing much is likely to come of such an exercise.

THE SECOND GENERATION

The children of John and Mary Hall:

Hiram Hall (1795-ca.1870)

Hiram Hall, who was born near Charleston, South Carolina, in 1795, left home as a young man and made his way across the states of South Carolina and Georgia to Carroll County, on Georgia's extreme western border. Exactly when he made this trip is not known, but he was in Carroll County well before 1820, when he married a local girl named Charity, who was eighteen years old. It is possible that Hiram was accompanied by a sister, Precilla; but it is almost certain that his parents remained behind. All we know about Charity is that she was born in 1802 in Carroll County, Georgia, and, over a period of twenty-five years, had ten children.

Arminda (Armindy) (1823, Carroll County, Georgia)
John Hall (1824, Carroll County, Georgia)
Nancy Hall (1829, Carroll County, Georgia)
William Newton Hall (1831, Carroll County, Georgia)
Emeline Hall (1836, Carroll County, Georgia)
Tyre [Tyree] Hall (1838, Carroll County, Georgia)
Green B. (1842, Carroll County, Georgia)
Elander (Ailey) Hall (1843, Carroll County, Georgia)

Claracy [Charity] Hall (1847, Carroll County, Georgia)
Parthena Hall (1848, Carroll County, Georgia)

Precilla Hall (ca. 1794-)

Precilla showed up in the 1820 census for Hall County, Georgia, not far from Carroll. She was listed as head of household, without husband but with a son, age ten to fifteen years old. From other sources I learned that she had married a man named Wyatt Williams, and the son's name was Wyatt N. Williams, born in 1814. (It is not clear where this child was born because in three separate censuses his place of birth was different. In one it was Tennessee, in another it was Georgia, and in the third it was South Carolina!) However, it is known that Wyatt N. became a judge in Carroll County and was widely known. Precila showed up in the 1830 census of Carroll County as the wife of Nathan Gann.

Green Berry (1823-)

Green Berry Hall, born near Charleston, South Carolina, moved to Georgia around 1840, settling first in Dawson County. Like his older brother, he married a girl named Charity, who was also from the Charleston area. Their first child was born in Dawson County, Georgia, in 1843. This gives us some idea of when he and Charity made the trip from South Carolina.

Anxious to put down roots and failing to find what he wanted in Dawson County, Green Berry probably made only one crop there before moving his family to Bulloch County, in the southeastern corner of the state. They were settled in by the time John Wesley was born in 1844, and, following him in quick succession, came James (1846), Mary Anne (1848) Charity (1849), and, finally, the twins, Froni R. and Isom R. (1853), all born in Bulloch County. [Because of Charity's age at the last two came along, it has been conjectured that they may have been the children of colored servants in the house.]

Nancy Hall (1843, Dawson County, Georgia)

John Wesley Hall (1844, Bullock County, Georgia)

James Hall (1846, Bullock County, Georgia)

Mary Anne Hall (1848, Bullock County, Georgia)

Charity Hall (1849, Bullock County, Georgia)

Froni R. Hall (1852, Bullock County, Georgia)

Isom R. Hall (1852, Bullock County, Georgia)

[It might be noted here that William Newton, Tyre (Tyree), and Green B. Hall (the Younger) were for a time thought to be members of the Green Berry and Charity Hall family of Bulloch County. It is a sad fact of life that some family researchers (and even an occasional professional genealogist) take it upon themselves to add or eliminate information from official census rolls, or pass as authentic their own prefabricated census rolls. Sometimes this happens when a frustrated sleuth tries a bit too hard to find slots for familiar-looking names. In the case of these three Halls, I had what I thought were official census records that placed them with Green Berry and Charity. Then one day I was offhandly informed by a Hall searcher that William N. Hall, Tyree, and Green B. were the sons of Hiram and Charity Hall, of Carroll County. Another searcher corroborated this with copies of *bonafide* census rolls for this county in Georgia that I had never heard of (at that time). Another researcher sent me the same census information, but this time the county was *Haralson*. Still another searcher suggested that undoubtedly some energetic genealogist, on discovering that the two families looked so much alike, had taken the liberty of adding those names to the Bulloch County family. While this fire was raging, I ran upon an amazing thing on the Interrnet. It was a public warning from the Director of something called *America's First Families* (cf. *GenForum*), a man named Harold Oliver. It began with a question: "Have you run across any typed manuscripts on the Hall family?

The reason I am asking is that Gustave Anjou (c1863-1942), the genealogy forger, is credited as creating false *Hall* lines." He went on to say that
this Gustave Anjou had deliberately planted whole pages of errors, had
indeed received money to do it.]

THE THIRD GENERATION

The children of Hiram and Charity Hall:

Arminda Hall (1823-1915)

Armindy, the first child of Hiram and Charity Hall, was born in Carroll County, Georgia, on March 17, 1823, and died in Walker County, Alabama, in 1915. She married Thomas S. Herron on November 25, 1847. Thomas was born December 29, 1812, and died July 19, 1899. They left Georgia in 1857 with five children and moved to Walker County, Alabama. Only three of the children survived the trip, and they located in the area of Carbon Hill or Eldridge. Armindy and Thomas are buried in the Pisgaugh Cemetery of Carbon Hill, Alabama.

James Herron (1848, Carroll County, Georgia)
Hiram Herron (1850, Carroll County, Georgia)
Charity Herron (1852, Carroll County, Georgia)
D. F. Herron (1854, Carroll County, Georgia)
Jane Herron (1857, Haralson* County, Georgia)
Pierce Herron (1860, Walker County, Alabama)
Green Herron (1862,, Walker County, Alabama)
Missouria Herron (1864, Walker County, Alabama)

[In 1856 Haralson County was created from the northern third of Carroll County.]

Murry John Hall (1824-1898)

John Hall was the first son of Hiram and Charity Hall. He was born October 1, 1824, in Carroll County, Georgia, and died in Childress (Childress County), Texas, on August 3, 1898. He married Nancy Hamilton, the daughter of John Lewis Hamilton and Margret Ann Reid, on January 20, 1848, at Nancy's home two miles northeast of Bremen, Carroll County, Georgia. Nancy was born April 3, 1828, in Gwinnett, Georgia, and died in Childress, Texas, on March 6, 1914. In 1851 they moved with one or more of John's brothers (and families) to Searcy County, Arkansas. There Madison Monroe was born. By 1854 they were living in Frederickstown, Madison County, Missouri, where Richard LaFayette and the rest of the children were born. Eventually, sometime after the Civil War, they moved to Springtown, Texas, where they put down roots.

Delilah Emiline Hall (1848, Carroll County, Georgia)
Robert Jefferson Hall (1850, Carroll County, Georgia)
Madison Monroe Hall (1852, Searcy County, Arkansas)
Richard Lafayette Hall (1854, Madison County, Missouri)
Janette Ardelia Hall (1856, Madison County, Missouri)
Mary Ann (Lee) Hall (Madison County, Missouri)
Nancy Lanore Hall (1859, Madison County, Missouri)
Margret Charity Hall (1861, Madison County, Missouri)
Mary (Maty) Ann Hall (1866, Madison County, Missouri)

The Hall Family 1911 or 1912

Nancy Hall (1829-1883)

Nancy was born in Carroll County, Georgia, in 1829. She married Jefferson Dean, of South Carolina, and they moved to Haralson County, Georgia. In 1883 she died in Buchannon, Haralson Co., of smallpox. They had six children:

Susan Dean (Haralson County, Georgia)
Loucinda Dean (Haralson County, Georgia)
Charity M. Dean (Haralson County, Georgia)
Martha Joe Dean (Haralson County, Georgia)
Vianna Dean (Haralson County, Georgia)
Jefferson Savannah Dean (Haralson County, Georgia)

William Newton Hall (1831-1923)

William Newton Hall, Hiram and Charity's fourth child, was born in Carroll County, Georgia, in August, 1831, and died in Seminole County, Oklahoma, in 1923. He is buried in Egypt Cemetery, near Ada,

Oklahoma (Pontotoc County), in an unmarked grave. It is possible that he married a woman named Darcas when he was a young man; but if he did we have no record of this marriage. Darcas was born in 1836 in Dawson County, Georgia, and was on the census rolls as the wife of a William Hall (born in Florida in 1830. [There was also a Green B Hall (b. 1823) living in the county at this time, possibly his uncle.] In the 1860 Dawson County census record, Darcas and William had four daughters:

Sarah Hall (1851, Dawson Co., Georgia)

Susan Hall (1853, Dawson Co., Georgia)

Mary Hall (1856, Dawson Co., Georgia)

Margaret Hall (1859, Dawson Co., Georgia)

[According to one of William Newton's daughters, Cordelia, after he left Georgia and moved to Arkansas, he made more than one trip back to Georgia searching for a son named Sid. It is possible, of course, that Darcas bore William a son after the 1860 census was taken; however, no evidence of such a son has been found. Following the Civil War she and the daughters seems to have disappeared.]

In 1868 William Newton Hall married Susan Woods in Haralson County, not far from Dawson County. This would seem to suggest that if, in fact, he had been married to Darcas, he must have had some knowledge of her whereabouts at this time. It is possible that she did not survive the war; and if so William Newton would more than likely have known about it.

Again according to William Newton's daughter Cordelia, he had become acquainted with Susan while he was hiding out in her family's residence in Atlanta, a deserter from the Confederate cavalry. It has been substantiated that William Newton remained in the Georgia Cavalry until the spring of 1865 (The war ended April 15), was indeed the Company Commander of Company E, Second Battalion, Fifth Regiment, of the Georgia Cavalry.

Susan Elizabeth Woods was born in Atlanta, Fulton County, Georgia, in 1851, making her twenty years younger than William Newton. According to Carl Watson Hall (b. 1940, son of Carl Bud Hall) Susan's full name was Susan Mahalia Wood, her father's name was Jeremiah Wood, and her grandparents were Jeremiah Wood and Mary A.Dehart. This has not been substantiated. It has been established that she died in Seminole County, Oklahoma, in 1918. She and Will had eight children:

Archie Brooklyn Hall (1871, Waldron, Scott County, Arkansas)

Dock Walter Hall (1873, Waldron, Scott County, Arkansas)

Greeley Teeman Hall (1877, Drakes Creek, Madison County, Arkansas)

Ulysses S. Grant Hall (1880, Drakes Creek, Madison County, Arkansas)

Sidney William Hall (1882, Drakes Creek, Madison County, Arkansas)

Cordelia Mae Hall (1884, Huntsville, Madison County, Arkansas)

Charity Hall (1885, Drakes Creek, Madison County, Arkansas)

Green T. (Tyree) Hall (1887, Drakes Creek, Madison County, Arkansas)

Emeline Hall (1836-1911)

Emeline Hall, the fifth child of Hiram and Charity Hall, was born in Carroll County, Georgia, in 1836, and died there in 1911. She married Graves Eaves, who died in 1912. They were buried in the Piney Woods Cemetery, in Haralson County. Hiram Hall, who apparently died sometime during the Civil War, left a will in Haralson County; but, unfortunately, the old Will Book A, in which the details would be listed, is missing. Only the index is still there. It lists Graves Eaves as administrator of Hiram Hall's estate with the year 1884 after his name. According to the 1880 Haralson County, Georgia, census Emeline and Graves had four children, all born in Haralson County, Georgia:

Ava E. (Elander Ally) Eaves (1858, Haralson County, Georgia)

Gracy L. Eaves (1868, Haralson County, Georgia)

James Grant Eaves (1871, Haralson County, Georgia)

Amanda C. Eaves (1873, Haralson County, Georgia)

Tyre (Tyree) Hall (1838-)

Tyree was born near in Carroll County, Georgia, the sixth child of Hiram and Charity Hall. He was called *Tarry* and was very likable. He married a woman named Arcina N. Merett in Dawson County on January 20, 1859. She was born in Georgia in 1838 (Occasionally, her name was written *Arcenia* or *Arcena*, and, once, on the Dawson County marriage list, it was *Arseeney Merett*). During the Civil War Tarry was a private in Company G., 40th Georgia Infantry Regiment (called the *Haralson Defenders*). He was drafted on April 10, 1862, but sometime later deserted and was captured on October 24, 1864, near Dallas, Georgia. He was released on May 12, 1865, and the following remarks were written on his release papers: "Claims to have been loyal. Was conscripted into Confederate Army. Deserted to avail himself of amnesty proclamation."

In 1880, Tarry and Arcenia had nine children:

David Hall (1860, Dawson County, Georgia)
Lenora Hall (1862, Dawson County, Georgia)
Charity E. Hall (1867, Dawson County, Georgia)
Mary A. Hall (1870, Dawson County, Georgia)
James W. Hall (1871, Dawson County, Georgia)
Lucy A. Hall (1872, Dawson County, Georgia)
Margaret Hall (1875, Madison County, Arkansas)
Arcina Hall (1878, Madison County, Arkansas)
George W. Hall (1879, Madison County, Arkansas)

[When Tarry was fifty-eight, he married Annie Cox, who was twenty-five at the time. She was born in May, 1875, in Alabama; her father was born in Georgia, and her mother was born in Alabama. Theodore S. Cox, her brother, was staying with them in 1900. Theodore was born in Alabama in June, 1870.]

Green Berry Hall (1842-1930)

Green B. was the seventh child of Hiram and Charity Hall, of South Carolina, and probably a nephew of the Bulloch County Green Berry Hall. He was born in Carroll County, Georgia. According to his tombstone in the Ledbetter Cemetery near Japton, Arkansas, he was born August 12, 1842, and died January 5, 1930, in Madison County, Arkansas.

During the *War Between the States* he was a private, like his brother Tyree, in Company G, 40th Georgia Infantry Regiment, made up entirely of Carroll (and Haralson) County men. He was captured at Vicksburg, Mississippi, on July 4, 1863, but released two days later (July 6), with no explanation given on his release papers. He was reported absent without leave from November 23 to December 31, 1863, after which there was no further record.

He married Sarah Elender Bradley April 15, 1866. She was born January 12, 1850, in Carroll County, Georgia, and died July 23, 1911, in Madison County, Arkansas.

Although he is buried beside his first wife in Ledbetter Cemetery, Madison County, Arkansas, Green B. married twice again after Sarah died. His second wife was Virginia Anderson, twenty-five years younger, whom he married the year following Sarah's death, on November 26, 1912. She was born in 1869, and the wedding took place in Madison County, Arkansas. In 1928, just two years before he died, he married Nancy Leievenia Magnolia (Nola) Burell.

In the Haralson *County*, Georgia, census for the year 1860, Green B. and Sarah, twenty-five and twenty years old, respectively, had two children: William, three years old, and Mary, one. In the 1880 Madison County, Arkansas, census records, in addition to William and Mary, they had Liza A. [Elizabeth], seven, and Jessica, two. On this record, William and Mary were born in Dawson County, Georgia, and Liza and Jessica were born in Madison County, Arkansas.

On the Madison County, Arkansas, census roll for 1900, Green B. and Sarah had the following children: Angus, sixteen, Rena, thirteen, Green M., eleven, Hyram, eight, and Olga, five.

About 1872 Green B. (the Younger) and Sarah E. Hall, moved from Dawson or Haralson County, Georgia, to Madison County, Arkansas, and, eventually, had at least eight children [Note the gap in years between Jessica and Rena]:

William Hall (1867, Haralson County, Georgia)
Mary E. Hall (1869, Haralson County, Georgia)
Elizabeth A. Hall (1873, Madison County, Arkansas)
Jessica Hall (1878, Madison County, Arkansas)
Rena Hall (1887, Madison County, Arkansas)
Green M. Hall (1888, Madison County, Arkansas)
Hyram Hall (1892, Madison County, Arkansas)
Olga Hall (1895, Madison County, Arkansas)

Elander (Ailey) Hall (1843-)

Ailey was the eighth child of Hiram and Charity Hall. She was born in Carroll County, Georgia, in 1842. According to the census roll for 1860, she had a child named Delia Sandford, who was nine months old. According to another census record, Ailey was born in 1836, married to William Sandford, who was born in 1842 in Georgia, and had Delilah and two other children:

Delilia Sandford (1848, Carroll County, Georgia)
Frances Sandford (1851, Carroll County, Georgia)
Rebecca Sandford (1859, Haralson County, Georgia)

Charity Hall (1847-)

Claracy, as Charity was called, was the ninth child of the Hiram and Charity family. She was born in Carroll County, Georgia, in 1847.

Parthena Hall (1848-)

Parthena, the ninth and last child of Hiram and Charity, was born in Carroll County, Georgia, in 1848. She married James Thompson on March 3, 1870; G. B. Brown on November 3, 1874; and William R. Day on November 23, 1889. Her last marriage took place in Anderson County, Texas. She had a daughter, Electious, in 1866, possibly by James Thompson, and a son, John, almost definitely by Thompson. In the 1880 Harralson County, Georgia, census, Charity (Hiram's wife?) listed a grandson named John Thompson.

The children of Green Berry (b. 1823) and Charity (b. 1815) Hall:

Nancy Hall (1843-)

Nancy was the first child of Green Berry (1823-), and Charity (1815-) Hall. She was born in 1843 in Dawson County, Georgia.

John Wesley Hall (1844-)

John Wesley was born in Bulloch County, Georgia.

James Hall (1846-)

James was born in Bulloch County, Georgia.

Mary Anne Hall (1848-)

Mary was born in Bulloch County, Georgia.

Charity Hall (1849-)

Charity was born in Bulloch County, Georgia.

Froni R. Hall (1852-)

Froni was born in Bulloch County, Georgia.

Isom R. Hall (1852-)

Isom R. was Froni's twin, who apparently died while an infant.

THE FOURTH GENERATION

The children of Armindy (Hall) and Thomas S. Herron:

James Herron (1848-1935)

James was the first child of Armindy Hall and Thomas S. Herron. He was born November 4, 1848, in Carroll County, Georgia, and died October 21, 1935, in Eldridge, Walker County, Alabama. He married Catharine Rosetta Webster, on December 4, 1897, in Fayette (Fayette County), Alabama.

Hiram Herron (1850-1909)

Hiram was born July 25, 1850, in Carroll County, Georgia, and died September 18, 1909, in Walker County, Alabama. On December 26, 1872, he married Martha Francis Guttery, whose parents were Isham Guttery and Rebecca Pike. Martha was born February 18, 1850, in Townley, Walker County, Alabama, and died January 15, 1927, in Walker County, Alabama.

Elijah Isham Herron (1873-1875, Walker County, Alabama)
Newman Herron (1876-1893, Walker County, Alabama)
James Thomas Herron (1879-1966, Walker County, Alabama)
Arminda Elvira Herron (1881, Walker County, Alabama)
Cora Ann Herron (1883-1960, Walker County, Alabama)
Julia Frances Herron (1886-1965, Walker County, Alabama)
Savannah Silvany Herron (1888, Walker County, Alabama)
Lunceford Osro Herron (1891-1977, Walker County, Alabama)

Charity Herron (1852-1857)

Charity was born May 17, 1852, in Carroll County, Georgia, and died in Haralson County, Georgia, on July 25, 1857.

D. F. Herron (1854-1857)

D. F. was born July 8, 1854, in Carroll County, Georgia, and died in Haralson County, Georgia, on August 8, 1857.

Jane Herron (1857-?)

Jane was born February 4, 1857, in Haralson County, Georgia. She married George W. Whitehead on September 26, 1878, in Walker County, Alabama.

Pierce Herron (1860-1902)

Pierce was born January 4, 1860, in Walker County, Alabama, and died September 15, 1902. He married Laura Abraham on December 24, 1890, in Lonoke County, Arkansas.

[The date and place of Pierce's birth establishes the approximate time of the trip that Arminda and Thomas Herron made from Georgia: between the spring of 1857 and the winter of 1859-1860.]

Green Herron (1862-1925)

Green was born July 23, 1862, in Walker County, Alabama, and died January 5, 1925. It is very likely that he was named after Green Berry, the uncle born twenty years earlier. He married Rhoda A. Miller on June 4, 1881, in Walker County, Alabama. Rhoda was born in 1862.

Missouria Herron (1864-1945)

Missouria, the last child of Armindy and Thomas Herron, was born April 13, 1864, in Walker County, Alabama, and died October 16, 1945. She married J. L. (Jim) Ingle on September 11, 1887, in Walker County, Alabama. Jim was born in 1864, also.

The children of Murry John Hall and Nancy (Hamilton):

Delilah Emiline Hall (1848-)

Delilah was the daughter John Hall and Nancy Hamilton and the granddaughter of John (1769-) and Mary (1770-) Hall. She was born in Carroll County, Georgia.

Robert Jefferson Hall (1850-1944)

Robert Jefferson was the son of John and Nancy (Hamilton) Hall and the grandson of Hiram and Charity Hall. He was born on March 25, 1850, in Carroll County, Georgia, and died June 15, 1944, in Broken Arrow (Tulsa County), Oklahoma. On January 24, 1875, he married Sara Jane Brewer on in Oak Grove, Oregon County, Missouri. She was born October 2, 1856, in Factor's Fork, Wayne County, Tennessee, and died June 1, 1940, in Oak Grove, Oregon County, Missouri. Her parents were Josiah Brewer and Susan C. Risner.

Robert spent most of his life in Missouri, but he lived the last twelve years near Broken Arrow, Tulsa County, Missouri. He died in a convalescent home there. He and Sara Jane had nine children.

Wellington C. Hall (1879-1964, Oregon County, Missouri)

Thomas Cleveland Hall (1884-1965, Oregon County, Missouri)

Darien C. Hall (1887-1922, Oregon County, Missouri)

Marien Hall (1887-1889, Oregon County, Missouri)

Cara E. Hall (1892-1893, Oregon County, Missouri)

Voyd Hall (1894-1968, Oregon County, Missouri)

Earnest Thurman Hall (Oregon County, Missouri)

Larry Wise Hall (Oregon County, Missouri)

Mary Anice Hall (1899, Oregon County, Missouri)

Madison Monroe Hall (1852-1928)

Madison was the third child of John Hall and Nancy Hamilton. He was born August 20, 1852, in Searcy County, Arkansas, and died May 8, 1928, in Gainesville, Cook County, Texas. He moved to a farm six miles northeast of Gainesville about 1902, and he was still living there when he died. He was buried in Fairview Cemetery. He married Annette Elefel Tilgal Frey on March 1, 1875, in Montague County, Texas. She was born March 27, 1854, in Greenville, Muhlenberg County, Kentucky, and died November 26, 1925, in Gainesville, Cook County, Texas. She is buried in Fairview Cemetery, Gainesville, Texas. They had nine children.

Ida Lenora Hall (1876, Gainesville, Cook County, Texas)
Violet May Hall (1879, Gainesville, Cook County, Texas)
Harriet Lillian Hall (1881-1902, Gainesville, Cook County, Texas)
Josephine Pearl Hall (1883-1926, Gainesville, Cook County, Texas)
Ernest Edward Hall (1886, Gainesville, Cook County, Texas)
Raynard Lafayette Hall (1888, Gainesville, Cook County, Texas)
Ethel Hall (1890, Gainesville, Cook County, Texas)
Anita Gertrude Hall (1895, Gainesville, Cook County, Texas) (twin)
Rosamond Del Hall (1895, Gainesville, Cook County, Texas) (twin)

Richard Lafayette Hall (1854-?)

Richard, the fourth child of John and Nancy Hall, was born December 9, 1854, in Madison County, Missouri.

Janette Ardelia Hall (1856-?)

Janette was born February 11, 1856, in Frederickstown, Madison County, Missouri, and died there in early childhood.

Nancy Lanore Hall (1859-1923)

Nancy was born October 20, 1859. She married (?) on October 13, 1885, in Parker County, Texas. She died in Childress, Texas, in 1923.

Margret Charity Hall (1861-1936)

Margret was born November 23, 1861, and died in Memphis, Texas, on August 23, 1936. She was married in Missouri and had two children there. Her other children, five in all, were born in Texas. (Names and birthdays unavailable)

Mary Ann Lee Hall (1866-?)

Maty, as she was called, was the last child of John and Nancy Hall. She was born February 9, 1866, in Frederickstown, Madison County, Missouri, and died there in early childhood.

The children of Nancy (Hall) and Jefferson Dean:

Susan Dean (?)

Loucinda Dean (?)

Charity M. Dean (?)

Martha Joe Dean (?)

Vianna Dean (?)

Jefferson Savannah Dean (?)

The children of William Newton Hall and Susan Elizabeth (Woods):

Archie Brooklyn Hall
Nancy Caroline McDougal
abt. 1952

Archibald Brooklyn Hall (1871-1955)

Archie was born April 25, 1871, in Waldron, Scott County, Arkansas, and died May 31, 1955, in Nowata, Nowata County, Oklahoma. The cause of death was *cirrhosis* of the liver. He is buried in Memorial Park Cemetery, Nowata. On July 7, 1892, he married Nancy Caroline McDougal, who was born May 3, 1876, five miles from Huntsville, Madison County, Arkansas. Nancy died May 26, 1955, in Nowata (Nowata County), Oklahoma, and was buried in the Nowata Cemetery.

The cause of her death was *myocarditis*, a heart condition. Her father was James Jefferson McDougal, who was born in 1850 in Tennessee. Her mother was Elizabeth Elsey.

For most of Archie's life he lived on his farm at Alluwe, Nowata County, Oklahoma, where he raised cotton, tobacco, corn, and broom corn. On this farm he had horses, cows, pigs, chickens, and turkeys. For a period of three years, sometime around 1940, it rained nonstop, flooding the entire country. During the last year of the flood Archie tried to free some horses tangled in a wire fence and fell, breaking his hip. From this point on he gave up farming, and for the rest of his life he walked with a crutch. He sold the farm and moved to Nowata, where he chewed tobacco and sold bootleg whisky from the home. He stored all of his money in coffee cans.

Nancy Caroline, who was called *Clancy* and whose Indian name was *Sukie*, gets high marks from her children, especially Jessie Mae, who said, "Nancy Caroline was a wonderful lady. She encouraged me with my education by helping with my homework. I knew my ABC's and could read before I started school. I went from first grade into second my first year, and I give her credit. When she was candleing eggs or churning butter, we were working on spelling or math. Grandmother Nancy sold eggs, butter, and milk to the markets. She always kept her money. She played the pump organ, and she dipped snuff and always wore her hair in a bun and kept a scarf tied around her head. And she always had her arms covered with long sleeves and wore long skirts."

Nancy and Archie had eight children. And although the list is far from complete, we know that they had at least nine grandchildren, twenty-seven great-grandchildren, eleven great-great-grandchildren, and one great-great-great-grandchild.

About living on the farm in Alluwe, Jessie Mae said this: "Grandpa's farm was located in Alluwe, Nowata County, along the Verdigris River. He raised cotton, corn, tobacco and broom corn. My grandmother, Nancy Clementine McDougal Hall was half Cherokee Indian. They were married on July 7, 1892, in Stigler; and my parents [Jesse Newton Hall (1899-1994) and Dora Bell Lawson (1904-1947)] married in Stigler, OK, June 27, 1919."

Minnie Aloony (Aluna) Hall (1894-1910)
Annie Dona Hall (1896-1956)
Jesse Newton Hall (1899-1995)
Carl (Bud) Tyre Hall (1901-1965)
Pearl Ellen Hall (1903-1985)
Birtha Elizabeth Hall (1905-2000)
Aaron Granville Hall (1907-1964)
Cecil Hall (1912-1912)

Dock Walter Hall (1873-1951)

Dock was the second child of William Newton Hall and Susan Elizabeth Woods. He was born December 22, 1873, in Waldron, Scott County, Arkansas. (Some sources give *Waldron* as his middle name.) He died May 8, 1951, in Dinuba, Tulare County, California. He married Kate K. Elsey, who was born February 4, 1883, near Japton, Madison County, Arkansas, and died January 16, 1977, in Dinuba, California. She is buried in the Smith Mountain Cemetery in London, Tulare County, California.

About 1910, Dock and Kate Elsey moved to a farming area near Huntsville, Arkansas, where they had their first three children. After the third child, Cecile, they moved to another farming region near Konawa, Oklahoma, where Jewell, a girl, was born on September 19, 1915. Their last two children, Dovie and Oma, were born in that area. In March of 1936 they made the bit move out west, to Dinuba, California. [Cf. *Stories and Legends*, below.]

Arthur Hall (1902-1995, Huntsville, Arkansas)
Earl Hall (1903-1999, Huntsville, Arkansas)
Cecile Hall (1908-1957, Huntsville, Arkansas)

Jewel Hall (1915, Konawa, Seminole County, Oklahoma)
Dovie Hall (1918, Konawa, Seminole County, Oklahoma)
Oma Hall (1922, Konawa, Seminole County, Oklahoma)

The Greely Teeman-Mallie Carr Family in 1924 (all but the last, Wesley Elmo, who would be born the following year) Top: Ezra M., Gradie, Ruth, Ollie; 2nd: Mabel, Greel, Delsie, Mallie, Clifford; front: Vernon, Zack, Luther.

The Greeley Teeman Hall Family
[Photo taken in 1926]

Greeley Teeman Hall (1877-1965)

Greel was the third son of William Newton Hall and Susan Elizabeth Woods. He was born near Japton, Madison County, Arkansas, on August 24, 1877, and died in Kern County, California, on March 6, 1965. His death was caused by internal bleeding from a broken hip. He is buried in Memorial Gardens, Fresno, California. On November 17, 1900, he married Mallie Rue Carr (sometimes *Karr*) in Welling, Indian Territory. They eloped on horseback from their homes in Madison County, Arkansas. Mallie was born November 15, 1882, in Wesley, Madison County, Arkansas, and died July 12, 1971, in Fresno, California. When she eloped with Greel, she was eighteen, redheaded, and very pretty; and Greel, at age twenty-two, was not an unattractive man. Mallie's father was Henry Allan Carr, who was born December 6, 1852, in Cherokee County, Georgia, and died in 1940 in Shawnee, Oklahoma, where he is buried. Her mother was Alice Howard.

They sharecropped down across Oklahoma to the River Bend, of Seminole County, and there they bought a 165-acre farm. Once settled, Greel decided to change his name to *Horace Greel*, which, he thought, would put a stop to his brother Green T. getting his mail. Since their initials were the same and both were reluctant to use their given names in business matters, it seemed logical to Greel to change his.

    Ezra Marion Hall (1902-1986, Madison County, Arkansas)
    Grady Hall (1904-1990, Madison County, Arkansas)
    Ollie Ida Hall (1906-1934, Madison County, Arkansas)
    Ruth Hall (1908-1976, Cherokee County, Oklahoma)
    Clara Mabel Hall (1910-1964, Kiowa County, Oklahoma)
    Clifford Cleborn Hall (1912-1974, Pottawatomie County, Oklahoma)
    Delsie Dale Hall (1914-1998, Pottawatomie County, Oklahoma)
    Luther Leonard Hall (1917-1972, Seminole, Seminole County, Oklahoma)
    Vernon Hall (1920-1974, Seminole County, Oklahoma)
    Zack Oberon Hall (1923-1969, Seminole County, Oklahoma)
    Wesley Elmo Hall (1925, Seminole County, Oklahoma)

Ulysses S. Grant Hall (1880-1964)

Grant was the fourth son of William Newton Hall and Susan Elizabeth Woods. He was born March 31, 1880, near Japton and Drakes Creek, Madison County, Arkansas, and died July 9, 1964 (at 7:15 a. m.), in Tipton, Tulare County, California. He was eighty-four. He died of *carcinomatosis* of the head and face (*arteriosclerotic* C-V), (facial cancer). He was living at 273 Newman Road with his daughter, Ella Crisler, at this time, and she had him buried in the Tipton, Pixley County, Cemetery.

On October 12, 1899, he married Sylvania (Vane) Pennington, whose parents were Aaron Pennington and Mary Sisemore. Vane was born February 25, 1880, in Uker, Clay County, Kentucky, and died March 11, 1936, in Buckeye, Maricopa County, Arizona.

Grant and Vane remained in Madison County, Arkansas, until they first two children were born, Viola Helen in 1900 and Willie in 1901.

This was where Albert was born. Shortly after that they moved back to Madison County, where their other three children were born. In 1936 the family moved to California. On the way Vane became very ill with cancer and pneumonia and died March 11, 1936, in a motel in Buckeye, Arizona. She was buried in Phoenix. Grant settled in Tipton, California, and lived there from 1952 until his death in 1964.

Viola Helen Hall (1900-1982, Madison County, Arkansas)
Willie Hall (1901-1906, Madison County, Arkansas)
Albert Hall (1903-1916, Cookson Hills, Indian Territory)
Maggie Lee Hall (1905-1935, Madison County, Arkansas)
Mary Elizabeth Hall (1906-1989, Madison County, Arkansas)
James Arnold Hall (1908-1993, Madison County, Arkansas)
Ella Zona Hall (1910-1990, Madison County, Arkansas)
Goldie Mae Hall (1913-1916, Madison County, Arkansas)
Lucy Florence Hall (1915-, Madison County, Arkansas)
Iva Alice Hall (1916-1921, Madison County, Arkansas)
Johnnie Theron Hall (1919-1993, Madison County, Arkansas)

[Lucy, at last report, was living in Arizona. One of Grant's grandsons, Raymond Jesse Hyder, son of Mary Elizabeth Hall, of Tipton, California, married a woman named Marti (family name not available), who has worked on the Hall family tree. Ella Zona's son Clyde Theron Crisler, another grandson of Grant and Vane, married Trudy, who was a granddaughter of Green T. Hall, and a family researcher.]

Sidney William Hall (1882-1972)

Sidney was the fifth (consecutive) son of William Newton Hall and Susan Elizabeth Woods; and, very possibly, he was named for the *lost Sid* Aunt Delia talked about.

Sid was born December 30, 1882, in Japton (Madison County), Arkansas, and died in 1972 in Cecil, Franklin County, Arkansas. He was buried in Broken Arrow, Oklahoma. On August 30, 1902, he married Cordelia Eubanks, who was born in 1887 in Kingston, Madison County, Arkansas. Sid was nineteen and Cordelia was fifteen. They had four children. Their three sons settled in and around Tahlequah, Oklahoma; and their daughter, Nadine, married a medical doctor named McKissick, and they moved to Tulsa. She died in 1999. Clint was in a nursing home in 1987. Orville has four children, all of whom live in the Tahlequah, Oklahoma, area.

Melvin (Red) Hall (?-)
Clint Hall (?-)
Nadine Hall (?-)
Orville Hall (?-1940)

Cordelia Mae Hal (1884-1992)

Cordelia (Delia, affectionately known as *Aunt Deely*) was the first daughter of William Newton Hall by Susan Elizabeth Woods. She was born in Huntsville, Madison County, Arkansas, on March 15, 1884 (In later life she decided that she had been born on March 15, 1890). She died in a Watsonville, California, hospital on December 12, 1982. At the time of her death she was living at Moss Landing, Monterey County, California. She is buried in Cherokee Memorial Gardens, Lodi, California.

On July 10, 1906, she married Logan Sisemore and they had seven children. Logan was born near Japton and Ball Creek, Madison County, Arkansas, on June 10, 1887, and died on December 14, 1973, in Lodi, San Joaquin County, California. He is buried beside Delia in Cherokee Memorial Gardens.

Logan's father was John Sisemore, Sr., and his mother was Sarah E. Neal, who was born March 15, 1884, and died December 12, 1982. He had two sisters, Abbie Scott and Rhoda Rogers.

In 1978, after Logan died, Delia moved to Santa Clara for a short time and then settled at Moss Landing.

Logan and Delia made the trip to California in 1935 and lived for a time in Madera, San Jose, and Mountain View before moving to Lodi in 1958. At last count they had nine grandchildren, twenty-five great-grand-children, and one great-great-grandchild.

Coleman Sisemore (1909-1991)

Theodore Sisemore (1911-1981)

Jack Sisemore (1914-1989)

Lucille Sisemore (1915-1977)

Buena Patricia Sisemore (1917-)

Thelma (Tommie) Sisemore (1922-1990)

Carl Sisemore (1926-1996)

Charity Hall (1885-1964)

Charity was born April 10, 1885, in Japton, Madison County, Arkansas, and died there in January, 1964. She married Lee Rogers, who was born April 25, 1886, and died one month before she did (December, 1963) in the same place. I paid them a visit just before they died. (Cf. *A Visit to Charity and Lee* in *Stories and Legends*.)

The following is the entry I made in my journal after a brief visit to see Aunt Charity and Uncle Lee in the late 1960's. I was on a *graveyard search* at the time, accompanied by a good friend who was a practicing genealogist, Daniel Littlefield:

Lee and Charity had two children:
Grace Rogers (?-)
Searls Rogers (1906-)

[Grace married a man named Thomas and was at last report living at 8051 E. 8th Street, Buena Park, CA 90621. Her telephone number was 714-523-3847. Searls, who was born August 11, 1906, in Japton (Madison County), Arkansas, died in Arkansas.]

Green T. (Tyree) Hall (1887-1967)

Uncle Green T. was my father's kid brother, and he brought his family to our house quite often when I was a child. He and Aunt Nanny had been just twenty and nineteen, respectively, when my parents made the move from Madison County, Arkansas, to the new state of Oklahoma; but by the time we were settled in the River Bend of Seminole County, Oklahoma, they caught up with us. And like my parents they share-cropped down across Oklahoma until they reached the Bend.

I remember hearing stories about the two families moving, separately, from one farm to another in wagons during the early 1900's. They took everything they owned with them including mules and milk cows.

Green T. was born on November 22, 1887, near Japton, Madison County, Arkansas, and died August 11, 1967, in Lodi, California. He was buried in Woodbridge, California. He married Nancy (Nanny) Eversole, who was born July 4, 1888, in Athens Valley, Kentucky. She died December 20, 1945, in Fayetteville, Arkansas, and is buried in Cherokee Memorial in Lodi, California. Nanny's father was John Eversole and her mother was Sarah F.

Ernest Clifford Hall (1911-)

Olen Hall (?-)

Pearl Zenia Hall (1914-1981)

Arizona (Marge) Lee Hall (1916-)

Delphi (Pat) Hall (1919-)

Irene Hall (1923-)

Imogene (Bonnie) Hall (1928-)

Robert Hall (adopted by the Kirks in1931-)

The children of Emeline Hall and Graves Eaves:

Ava Elander Eaves (1858-)

Ava was the granddaughter of Hiram and Charity Hall. In the Haralson County, Georgia, census for 1880, her name was listed as Ava E. In the 1860 and 1870 census rolls for that county she was listed as Elander Ally. She married C.A. Maner in December, 1882.

Gracy L. Eaves (1868-)

Gracy was born ten years after her sister Ally. Indeed, the entire Civil War took place between their births.

James G. Eaves (1871-)

James was born in Haralson County, Georgia.
Amanda C. Eaves (1873-).

Amanda was born in Haralson County, Georgia.

The children of Tyree Hall and Arcenia Meritt Hall:

David Hall (1860, Haralson County, Georgia)

Lenora Hall (1862, Haralson County, Georgia)

Charity E. Hall (1867, Haralson County, Georgia)

Mary A. Hall (1870, Haralson County, Georgia)

James W. Hall (1871, Haralson County, Georgia)

Lucy A. Hall (1872, Haralson County, Georgia)

Margaret Hall (1875, Madison County, Arkansas)

Arcina Hall (1878, Madison County, Arkansas)

George W. Hall (1879, Madison County, Arkansas)

[The dates and places of the births of Lucy and Margaret establish rather accurately the date of Tyree and Arcenia's move from Haralson County, Georgia, to Madison County, Arkansas.]

The children of Green Berry Hall (b. 1842) and Sarah Elender Bradley:

William Hall (1867, Haralson County, Georgia)

Mary E. Hall (1869, Haralson County, Georgia)

Elizabeth A. Hall (1873, Madison County, Arkansas)

Jessica Hall (1878, Madison County, Arkansas)

Rena Hall (1887, Madison County, Arkansas)

Green M. Hall (1888, Madison County, Arkansas)

Green was born October 18, 1888, in Madison County, Arkansas, and died there on April 17, 1985. On August 30, 1911, he married Grace E. Patrick, who was born September 17, 1893. She was the daughter of Merida and Maggie Parsley Patrick, who were buried in the Ledbetter

Cemetery near Drakes Creek and Japton, Madison County, Arkansas. In the 1920 census for Madison County, Arkansas, three children were listed:
Zelda Hall (1913-)
Irene Hall (1916-)
Ray Hall (1919-)

Hyram Hall (1892, Madison County, Arkansas)

Olga Hall (1895, Madison County, Arkansas)

[The dates and places of the births of Mary and Elizabeth establish rather accurately the move that Green B. and Sarah made from Haralson County, Georgia, to Madison County, Arkansas.]

THE FIFTH GENERATION

The children of Hiram Herron and Martha Guttery:

Elijah Isham Herron (1873-1875)

Elijah was born December 6, 1873, and died March 10, 1875, in Walker County, Alabama. He was the grandson of Arminda (Hall) and Thomas Herron and the great-grandson of Hiram and Charity Hall, of Harralson County, Georgia.

Newman Herron (1876-1893)

Newman was born May 16, 1876, and died November 21, 1893, in Carbon Hill, Walker County, Alabama.

James Thomas Herron (1879-1966)

James was born May 21, 1879, in Walker County, Alabama, and died in July, 1966, in Carbon Hill, Walker County, Alabama. He married Mintie Ardonia Cheatham on September 10, 1899, in Saragossa, Walker County, Alabama. She was born in July, 1880, in Walker County, Alabama, and died in June, 1951, in Walker County, Alabama.

Mamie Ethel (1900, Walker County, Alabama)
Walter James Herron (1902, Walker County, Alabama)
Clarence Herron (1904, Walker County, Alabama)
Flossie Herron (1906, Walker County, Alabama)
Edgar Herron (1908, Walker County, Alabama)

Donnie Mae Herron (1910, Walker County, Alabama)
Grady Herron (1912, Walker County, Alabama)
Esther Louise Herron (1915, Walker County, Alabama)
Earl Herron (1918, Walker County, Alabama)
Earnest Herron (1920, Walker County, Alabama)

Arminda Elvira Herron (1881-)

Arminda was born August 5, 1881, in Walker County, Alabama.

Cora Ann Herron (1883-1960)

Cora was born November 28, 1883, in Walker County, Alabama, and died April 27, 1960.

Julia Frances Herron (1886-1965)

Julia was born April 4, 1886, in Walker County, Alabama, and died August 28, 1965, in Walker County, Alabama.

Savannah Silvany Herron (1888-?)

Savannah was born August 25, 1888, in Walker County, Alabama. She married B. R. Ferguson.

Lunceford Osro Herron (1891-1977)

Lunceford was born November 27, 1891, in Walker County, Alabama, and died December 25, 1977, in Walker County, Alabama.

The children of Robert Jefferson Hall and Sara Jane Brewer:

Wellington Columbus Hall (1879-1964)

Wellington was born July 27, 1879, in Wellngton, Sumner County, Kansas, and died in 1964 in Oregon County, Missouri. He married Laura A. Sitton, who was born in 1883 and died in 1963. He was the first child of Robert Jefferson Hall and Sara Jane Brewer. His grandparents were John and Nancy (Hamilton) Hall. Both Wellington and Laura are buried in Garfield Cemetery, Oregon County, Missouri.

Thomas Cleveland Hall (1884-1965)

Thomas Cleveland was born December 9, 1884, in Garfield, Oregon County, Missouri, and died October 13, 1965, in Novato, Marin County,, California. On May 23, 1906, he married Margie Rena Roberts, who was born October 20, 1889, in Billmore, Oregon County, Misssouri. She died October 26, 1961, in Monticello, San Juan County, Utah. Her parents were Evan D. Roberts and Martha Jane Thomasson. Thomas and Margie had seven children.

Wayne Ambrose Hall (1907, Oregon County, Missouri)
Carlos Mentril Hall (1909, Oregon County, Missouri)
Therman Clement Hall (1914, Oregon County, Missouri)
Thomas Richard Hall (1916, Oregon County, Missouri)
Lloyd Evan Hall (1920, Oregon County, Missouri)
Mary Lenore Hall (1923, Oregon County, Missouri)
Victor Leon Hall (1928, Oregon County, Missouri)

Darien C. Hall (1887-1922)

Darien was born March 1, 1887, in Garfield, Oregon County, Missouri, and died January 22, 1922, in Oregon County, Missouri. He is buried there in Garfield Cemetery. He married a girl named Jessie (surname not available), who was born October 7, 1889, and died May 2, 1964. She is buried in Garfield Cemetery, Oregon County, Missouri. According to one source, Darien was also married at one time to Lillie Taylor.]

Marien Hall (1887-1889)

Marien, Darien's twin, died December 12, 1889, and is buried in Garfield Cemetery, Oregon County, Missouri.

Earnest Thurman Hall (1891-)

Earnest was born March 9, 1891, in Garfield, Oregon County, Missouri, and died November 14, 1982, in Cortez, Montezuma County, Colorado. On September 16, 1916, he married Roma Pritchard, who was born in 1900 and died in 1971.

Cara Ethel Hall (1892-1893)

Cara was born December 18, 1892, and died exactly one year later. She is buried in Garfield Cemetery, Oregon County, Missouri.

Voyd C. Hall (1894-1968)

Voyd was born July 9, 1894, in Garfield, Oregon County, Missouri, and died December 9, 1968. He is buried in New Salem Cemetery, Oregon County, Missouri. He married Mary P. Meyers, who was born September 24, 1895, and died October 28, 1970. She is buried in New Salem Cemetery, Oregon County, Missouri.

Larry Wise Hall (1898-)

Larry was born March 1, 1898, in Garfield, Oregon County, Missouri. He married Helen Jenkins on September 10, 1924.

Mary Anise Hall (1899-)

Mary Anise was born March 2, 1899, in Garfield, Oregon County, Missouri. She married Paris Cotton, who was born in March, 1872, and died of cancer on or about May 7, 1928, when his will was filed (It was signed by Voyd C. Hall and witnessed by A. P. Payne and Abner S. Rhodes on May 8, 1925). They had seven children:

Opal D. Cotton (?-)
Sarah F. Cotton (?-)
Nelma G. Cotton (?-)
Leamon R. Cotton (?-)
Rosco B. Cotton (?-)
Patrick Earl Cotton (?-)
Thelma Louise Cotton (?-)

The children of Madison Monroe and Annetta Elefel (Tilgal) Hall:

Ida Lenora Hall (1876-)

Ida was born September 27, 1876, in Alton, Oregon County, Missouri. She married Henry Mortimer Algood in 1895.

Violet May Hall (1879-)

Violet May Hall was born April 26, 1879, in Weatherford, Parker County, Texas. She married Iris Holmes Edmondson on May 6, 1912.

Harriet Lillian Hall (1881-)

Harriet was born November 6, 1881, in Forestburg, Montague County, Texas. She married Joseph H. Bryan on September 21, 1902.

Josephine Pearl Hall (1883-1926)

Josephine was born September 28, 1883, in Forestburg, Montague County, Texas, and died November 6, 1926. She married Herman Smith Holland on February 19, 1910.

Ernest Edward Hall (1886-)

Ernest was born March 24, 1886, in Forestburg, Montague County, Texas. He married Hiawatha Tillman in 1910.

Raynand Lafayette Hall (1888-)

Raynand was born September 23, 1888, in Forestburg, Montague County, Texas. He married Carrie Tillman on February 12, 1912.

Ethel Hall (1890-)

Ethel was born November 16, 1890, in Stoneburg, Montague County, Texas. She married Claude Robert Turner on July 8, 1918.

Anita Gertrude Hall (1895-)

Anita was born August 6, 1895, in Forestburg, Montague County, Texas. She married Roy Bolivar Robinson.

Rosamond Del Hall (1895-)

Rosamond was born August 6, 1895, in Forestburg, Montague County, Texas. On December 20, 1919, she married Chester Josiah Robb.

The children of Archie Brooklyn Hall and Nancy Caroline McDougal:

Minnie Aluna Hall (1894-1910)

Minnie was born December 14, 1894, in Japton, Madison County, Arkansas, and died in 1910.

Annie Dona Hall (1896-1956)

Annie Dona was born August 29, 1896, in Japton, Madison County, Arkansas; and died June 11, 1956, of *acute circulatory failure, secondary anemia*, and *Hodkin's Disease*, in Big Cabin, Oklahoma. She was buried in Memorial Park, Nowata. According to her death certificate, her mother's name was Nancy Ledbetter. She married Jeremiah William Swafford on April 28, 1924. and they had one child before they divorced.

Christopher David Swafford (1920-1983)

Annie's second husband was O. L. Irons, of Big Cabin, Oklahoma. He was born in1896. They had one child.

Jack Irons (?-)

Jesse Newton Hall (1899-1995)

Jesse was the son of Archie Brooklyn and Nancy (McDougal) Hall. He was born April 1, 1899, in Van Buren, Arkansas, and he died in Nowata, Oklahoma, on June 18, 1995. On June 27, 1919, he married Dora Bell

Lawson in Stigler, Oklahoma, and they had nine children before divorcing.

On July 22, 1950, Jesse married Finise E. Etter.

Dora Belle was born October 12, 1904, in Briartown, Oklahoma, and died in Yuma, Arizona, on November 23, 1947. She was buried in Steel Camp Cemetery, Oglesby, Oklahoma. Dora's parents were Charles Kendrick Lawson (b.1868) and Martha Jane Hudson. Her mother died when she was two and she was raised by her father and Martha Holt. She also married (2) Frank Gougler (on November. 23, 1947, in Yuma, Arizona), (3) Clifford Zinn, (4) Edward A. Pogue, and (5) Glenn Manier.

She worked at whatever she could, in order to make money to keep the family going. She was the bread winner in the family. Jesse did not work until after he and Dora Belle divorced and he re-married. Dora Belle had a saying during those days: "We might be poor and not have much but we will be clean. It takes only a bar of soap." The house was cleaned thoroughly every Saturday.

Jesse served in the U. S. Army during World War I. He and Dora Belle and the children lived in Alluwe and Nowata, Oklahoma, from 1922 until his death. He played the fiddle for dances in and around Porum, Oklahoma. He worked for the WPA during the Great Depression; and once, when he was using a sledge hammer he missed his mark and hit his leg. This would continue to bother him throughout his life. After he and Dora Belle divorced, he went to work for Nowata County as a truck driver for the Sanitation Department. He had TB during WWI and was admitted to the Indian Hospital in Nowata.

Elizabeth Imogene Horn (1920, Chelsea, Oklahoma)
Oliver Newton Hall (1921, Chelsea, Oklahoma)
Lois Hall (1925, Chelsea, Oklahoma)
Roy Lee Hall (1925, Chelsea, Oklahoma)
Jessie Mae Hall (1930, Chelsea, Oklahoma)
Helen Bernice Hall (1932, Chelsea, Oklahoma)
Dorothy Lee Hall (1934, Nowata, Oklahoma)

Shirley Ann Hall (1938, Alluwe, Oklahoma
Judy Hall (1941, Nowata, Oklahoma)
Jerry David Hall (1943, Nowata, Oklahoma)
James Alvin Hall (1943, Nowata, Oklahoma)

King Tyree (Carl Bud) Hall (1901-1965)

Bud Hall, a son of Archie and Nancy Hall, began life as King Tyre Hall; but when he got old enough he legally changed his name to Carl Tyre Hall, and that is the way it will go down in the history books. He was born April 27, 1901, in Japton, Madison County, Arkansas, and died October 13, 1965, in Trona, San Bernardino County, California. He was buried in Trona Cemetery. He married Caroline (Carrie) Melissa Taylor on May 10, 1921, in Stigler, Haskell County, Oklahoma.

Carrie was born November 25, 1902, in Waldron, Scott County, Arkansas, and died June 29, 1982, in Stigler. She was buried in Coleman Cemetery, Porum, Oklahoma. Her father was Milton Zachariah Taylor, and her mother was Catherine Ann Hale. One source claims that Bud was married even before Carrie and spent some time in the Army in Ft. Chaffee, Arkansas. His family lives in Porum, Oklahoma. Two daughters, Sadie (Hall) Rock and Iva Lorene (Hall) Blackwood live not far away.

Gladys Marie Hall (1922-1986)
Iva Loreen Hall (1924-)
Sadie Lee Hall (1926-)
James Oliver Hall (1928-)
Tyre Roland Hall (1929-)

His second wife was Nora May Howell, whom he married on May 2, 1934. She was born May 31, 1913, in Vinita, Craig County, Oklahoma. Her father was Curl Wasston Howell, and her mother was Asenah Bell Davis. Nora married again, to Harry Charles Rae. Carl and Nora were living in Chelsea when they had the following children:

Virginia Ruth Hall (1937, Chelsea, Oklahoma)
Carl Watson Hall (1940, Chelsea, Oklahoma)
Kenneth Franklin Hall (1943, Chelsea, Oklahoma)
Richard Douglas Hall (1945, Chelsea, Oklahoma)

Pearl Ellen Hall (1902-1985)

Pearl was born September 15, 1903, in Mulberry, Madison County, Arkansas, and died in Peoria, Maricopa County, Arizona, July 13, 1985. She married James Olin Gragg on September 29, 1920. Olen was born May 16, 1900, and died in September, 1972. His brother, Levi, married a woman named Nette, whose last name may have been Barns. Pearl and James Gragg had one son, who lives in Peoria, Arizona.

James Benjamin Gragg (1934-)

Birtha Elizabeth Hall (1905-1999)

Birtha was the sixth child of Arch and Nancy Hall and a granddaughter of William Newton Hall and Susan Elizabeth Woods. She was born April 7, 1905, in Japton Madison County, Arkansas, and died July 9, 2000, in Glendale, Arizona. She is buried at Resthaven Park Cemetery in Glendale. She married Steven Benjamin Edmond Gragg on September 29, 1920. He was born February 19, 1897, and died Oct 9, 1982. He is also buried at Resthaven. According to his grandson, Nelson Lee Gragg Jr., Ed's mother, Bettie Gragg, married William Henry Harrison Jones while he was still a child. She had been living with her parents, William and Hannah Adkins, in White Oak Township, Franklin County, Arkansas.

Archie Gragg (?-)
Mable Gragg (1922-)
Elizabeth (Lizzie) Gragg (1924-)
Flossie Gragg (1927-)
Frant Gragg (1930-)

Paul Gragg (1936-1986)
Betty Gragg (1938-ca. 1998)
Nelson Lee Gragg Sr. (1940-)
Hank Gragg (1944-)
Eddie Gragg (?-)

Aaron (Tank) Granville Hall (1907-1964)

Tank was a son of Arch and Nancy Hall. He was born May 2, 1907, in Japton, Madison County, Arkansas, and died June 8, 1964. He married Vera Pauline Aukaby (Huckaby?) on November 17, 1937.

Cecil Hall (1912-1912)

Cecil was the last child of Arch and Nancy Hall. He was born May 1, 1912, in Japton, Madison County, Arkansas, and died there a week later (May 8).

The children of Dock Walter and Kate (Elsey) Hall:

Arthur H. Hall (1902-1995)

Arthur was the first child of Dock Walter Hall and Kate K. Elsey. He was born in Huntsville, Arkansas, on March 29, 1902, and died March 15, 1995, in Exeter, California. He married Vernie V. Tyler, who was the daughter of Wes Tyler, of Konawa, Oklahoma. Vernie's sister, Emozett (Tyler) Phillips, the wife of (Vivien) Bill Phillips, of the River Bend south of Konawa, Oklahoma, said to me in a recent letter that she and Vernie were born in a *dugout* in John Vance's bottom in the Bend. Vernie gave her birthdate as December 31, 1925. Arthur and Vernie lived in Exeter, California, for many years. Vernie had Alzheimer's Disease and, according to Velta Lee (Hall) Domyan, their niece, after Arthur shot himself the children had to put Vernie in a rest home in Visalia, California, where she died May 5, 1995. Both are buried in the Exeter District Cemetery.

According to Trudy Tobias in 1996, Arthur and Vernie had five children, "all still living, married, with children and grandchildren."

LaVonna Hall (?-)

Johnnie Clifton (J. C.) Hall (?-)

LeRoy Hall (?-)

Earl Hall (1903-1999)

Earl was the son of Dock Walter Hall and Kate K. Elsey. He was born in Huntsville, Madison County, Arkansas, on December 19, 1903, and died in Cutler, California, November 4, 1999, having lived ninety-five years, ten months, and fifteen days. He married Stella Mae Scoggins, of Konawa, Seminole County, Oklahoma, on July 12, 1926, in Konawa. Stella was the daughter of Hiram Finley (Finn) Scoggins and Nancy Elizabeth Skelton. She died in Cutler, Tulare County, California, on March 7, 1993, after having complained of chest pains.

According to Velta, their third child, who was repeating what her mother had told her, as soon as the marriage ceremony was over Earl disappeared and was gone three days. Stella stayed with Gradie (Hall) and Arthur Lee Goff during that time; and when Stella's father heard about Earl's disappearance, he got out his shotgun and went looking for him.

On two later occasions he did the same thing, once when Bob, the fourth child, was born, and again when Oteka, the sixth and last child, was born! So in December, 1942, Earl took his family to the Cutler/Orose area near Tulare, California, stopping briefly in Oklahoma City to see Stella's younger sister, Thelma, and her husband, Otis Lewis. Velta said that her aunt and uncle begged Earl to "at least wait until it quit raining" but it was to no avail. They made that trip in a 1939 Dodge, which averaged "ever bit of 35 miles per hour." It took them about seven days to reach the San Joaquin Valley.

Stella and Earl had six children:

Durward Jack Hall (1927, Seminole County, Oklahoma)

Val Gene Hall (1928, Seminole County, Oklahoma)

Velta Lee Hall (1930, Seminole County, Oklahoma)

Bobby Ray (Bob) Hall (1932, Seminole County, Oklahoma)

Barbara Louise Hall (1935, Seminole County, Oklahoma)

Joyce Oteka Hall (1938, Seminole County, Oklahoma)

Cecile Hall (1908-1957)

Cecile was a daughter of Dock and Kate. She was born February 27, 1908, in Huntsville, Arkansas, and died of cancer May 17, 1957. She married Bill Lanphear and had two sons and two daughters. After Bill died, she married Kenny Campbell, who is now also deceased. Both husbands are buried in Smith Mountain Cemetery. One of Cecile's sons, Doyle, has married for the second time. They have children but no information is available on this family. Cecile's other son, Leon, died while still a baby. One daughter, Suevella, died of cancer in 1978 and is buried in Greene County Memorial Gardens, Paragould, Arkansas. The other daughter, Drucella, was still living in 1998 and was married and had children and grandchildren (names and dates unavailable).

Doyle Lanphear (?-)

Leon Lanphear (?-)

Suevella Lanphear (?-1978)

Drucella Lanphear (?-)

Jewel Hall (1915-)

Jewell Hall is a daughter of Dock and Kate. She was born September 19, 1915, in Konawa, Seminole County, Oklahoma. She married Connie

Lee (Bud) Beard, who was born August 17, 1909, and died February 15, 1957, in Dinuba, California. He is buried in the Smith Mountain Cemetery, near Sultana, California. Jewell lives in Dinuba, California.

Billy Ray Beard (1939-)

Oma Hall (1922-)

Omie, the youngest daughter of Dock and Kate, married Johnny Beard (now deceased) and they had twin daughters, Judy and Janet (who have disowned their mother, are both married, and now live in Visalia, California). Omie and Jewell married brothers. Their sister is the mother of Mary Louise (Valgene Hall's wife). That makes them Louise's aunts as well as the aunts of Stella and Earl's children: Jack, Valgene, Velta, Bob, Barb, and Oteka.

Judy Beard (?-)

Janet Beard (?-)

By a later husband, C. L. Payne, Oma had a daughter whom she named Brenda, who is married and lives in Reedley, California. According to Trudy Tobias, she had another daughter by Payne, named Linda. Omie now lives in Dinuba, California.

Brenda Payne (?-)

Linda Payne (?-)

The children of Greeley Teeman (Horace Greel) Hall and Mallie Rue Carr:

Ezra Marion Hall (1902-1986)

Ezra was the firstborn of Mallie and Greel Hall's big family. He was born near Japton and Drakes Creek, in Madison County, Arkansas, on September 29, 1902, and died of cancer on July 25, 1986, in Duncan, Stevens County, Oklahoma, where he is buried. His wife of over fifty years was Florence Viola Scoggins, who was born in Konawa, Seminole County,

Oklahoma, on April 25, 1905, and died in Duncan, Stevens County, Oklahoma, October 9, 1997.

For most of his life Ezra worked as a pumper for the Champlain Oil Company, moving his family from one little town to another, places like Konawa and Sasakawa and Noble, in Oklahoma, and Dalhart, in the panhandle of Texas. Finally, they settled in Duncan, Oklahoma, and put down roots.

Ezra and Florence had two children, Alton and Dot. The former had a difficult time settling down; but after a brief marriage he returned to the home of his parents and was there until his death. He was likable and easy to get along with; but like most of the Hall boys, he had a high temper. Dot, very likable and deserving, had a hysterectomy while still very young and from that time on had severe neurological problems.

Alton Lee Hall (1928, Seminole County, Oklahoma)

Dorotha Faye Hall (1931, Seminole County, Oklahoma)

Gradie Hall (1904-1990)

Gradie was the first daughter of Mallie and Greel Hall. She was born near Japton, in Madison County, Arkansas, on May 10, 1904, and died in Fresno, California, on October 23, 1990. She married Arthur Lee Goff, who was born in Konawa, Oklahoma, in 1907, and died in Fresno, California, in 1981.

From the time she was a young girl Gradie was making something pretty to sell, from artificial flowers to coffeetable curios to wedding arrangements. Her home was always a warm and safe place for her wayward brothers to land, and she loved nothing better than cooking for all who showed up there. Late in life she employed her daughters and granddaughters and even her own mother at times in her various business ventures, and took them and her flower arrangements to Anaheim, California, once a year to a big artificial flower show.

It was Gradie who kept the big Greel and Mallie Hall family together, planned re-unions for them, forced them stay in touch. At the time of her death she was writing to and talking on the telephone to cousins, aunts, uncles, on both sides of the family, on a regular basis.

She and Arthur had three daughters.

Inas Faye Goff (1926, Konawa, Seminole County, Oklahoma)
Maudie June Goff (1929, Konawa, Seminole County, Oklahoma)
Annie Jo Goff (1930, Konawa, Seminole County, Oklahoma)

Ollie Ida Hall (1906-1934)

Ollie was born near Japton, in Madison County, Arkansas, on November 13, 1906, and died from complications of childbirth on February 5, 1934, in Seminole County, Oklahoma. She was buried in the Konawa Cemetery. She married Lou Albin Smith, of Konawa, who was born July 16, 1898, and died in Konawa, Seminole County, Oklahoma, in 1989.

Ollie died when I was eight years, and what I remember about her is how sweet she was when I would stop by her house on my way to Pilgrim's Rest (Bugscuffle) School. I was a month younger than her daughter Flora Evelyn, and so I would stop by and the two of us would walk the remaining half-mile through sand and stickers and red clay ditches to Miss Lola's chart class. Everybody said that she was another Mallie, a wonderful mother and wife, someone who never raised her voice in anger, who made life better for all who came near her. When she died at twenty-eight, she left behind five small children to face the world without a mother. Lou did the best he could, but Ollie was not somebody who could be replaced. He took the four older ones to his parents' house in Konawa (Mr. and Mrs. Pat Smith) and the baby was raised by Hubert and Delphia (Smith) Grady, his sister and brother-in-law.

Flora Evaline Smith (1925, Konawa, Seminole County, Oklahoma)
Merle Eston (Bud) Smith (1927, Konawa, Seminole County, Oklahoma)

Lou Albin (L. A.) Smith (1929, Konawa, Seminole County, Oklahoma)
Mallie Avo Smith (1931, Konawa, Seminole County, Oklahoma)
Roy Joe Smith (1934, Konawa, Seminole County, Oklahoma)

Ruth Hall (1908-1976)

Ruth was born in Cherokee County, Oklahoma, January 4, 1908, and died in Henryetta, Oklahoma, on September 8, 1976, where she is buried. She married Joseph Benjamin Potter, who was born September 18, 1907, in Sasakwa, Oklahoma, and died in Konawa, Seminole County, Oklahoma, Wednesday, November 27, 1996, at 6 p.m. He was buried beside Ruth. Ben was the son of J. B. Potter, who was born March 23, 1870, and died in March, 1949, and Ora (Dennis) Potter, who was born August 18, 1872, and died June 30, 1941.

Ruthie was the poet(ess) of our family. She loved nothing better than to sit around making up verses, and the older she got the more she did this kind of thing and sent the results to her relatives.

Clara Dale Potter (1935, Seminole County, Oklahoma)
David Mitchel Potter (1937, Konawa, Seminole County, Oklahoma)
Beulah Jean Potter (1940, Konawa, Seminole County, Oklahoma)

Clara Mabel Hall (1910-1964)

Mabel, who spelled her name *Mable*, was born in Kiowa County on February 21, 1910, and died in August, 1964, in Phoenix, Arizona. She married James F. Holderby, of Tulsa, Oklahoma, a private in the U. S. Army, who died soon after the marriage. Times were hard in those days, and so the small widow's pension she received made her the richest human being in the River Bend country, where we lived. After the family sold the farm and went on the road, she married Melvin Merrill, of Phoenix, Arizona, giving up her pension. Melvin had the personality of an aging cabbage, with a secretive, mean streak to boot; and as soon as no other Halls were around he became abusive to my sister.

All during my boyhood she was a dominating force in our home. When she left home that one time, it was only long enough to secure that little check from the government; and then she was back, a permanent fixture until I was finally old enough to join the Navy and leave home myself. In fact, she was far more visible to me than any other adult throughout my childhood. My mother did not approve of her martinet ways, but Mabel managed to get around her. Unless it was snowing, hailing, sleeting, or storming, she would not allow me to enter the house during daylight hours.

Clifford Cleborn Hall (1912-1974)

Cliff, the first redhead in the family, was mostly heard about and seldom seen when I was a boy. He was born near Asher, in Pottawatomie County, Oklahoma, on June 3, 1912, and died December 29, 1974, in Fresno, California. He was found by the Fresno police unconscious in an alley in that city, and it was my sister Gradie's opinion that he had been murdered. But the Fresno police decided that he had died from exposure and malnutrition. Only a short while before his death he had checked into a clinic because of skin cancer.

Cliff was the only brother I had who *rode the rails* (became a hobo). During the Great Depression he panhandled across the western part of this country, and about once a year he would come home to rest up and get some nourishment. Almost always he would bring with him some ragged derelict, like himself a stray from some defunct Oklahoma farm.

His first adventure into matrimony was with Imogene White, of Asher, Oklahoma. Imogene had a much younger brother named Garland, who stayed with us for a time and became the kid brother I had wanted for so long. Cliff and Imogene were not married long, but during that time they had a daughter.

Frances Carol Hall (?-)

Later, Cliff married a girl from Maud, Oklahoma, a town not far from
Bowlegs, just a few miles from Asher, where he was born ("To reach Maud
you have to go through Bowlegs"). Her name was Georgia Marie Sage,
and she was born September 28, 1916, in Checotah, McIntosh County,
Oklahoma, and died October 30, 1976, in Riverbank, Stanislaus County,
California. Her parents were Charles Edward Sage and Louisa Emily
Roberts. They had three daughters before divorcing. Georgia later married
George Collins, of Riverbank, California.

Shirley Ann Hall (1937, Maud, Seminole County, Oklahoma)

Mary Jo Hall (1939, Maud, Seminole County, Oklahoma

Nancy June Hall (1943, Modesto, Stanislaus County, California)

Cliff was naturally gifted as a mechanic. He proved that on Route 66
when we made that trip time and again in an old rattletrap truck. At one
time he was the head mechanic of a first class garage in Fresno, California;
but, eventually, inevitably, he became an itinerant stoop laborer, compet-
ing with the wetbacks and Okies in the San Joaquin Valley of California.
He would show up at one of my sisters' places in Fresno every two or three
years, laugh and carry on a bit about his wanderings, and then disappear.
Once he disappeared for a long time; and when he finally surfaced, we
learned that he had found a job on a very large sheep ranch in Nevada that
was owned by a family of Basques. These people could not speak English
(nor did they wish to speak English), and Clifford could not speak
Basque; but somehow he had become the foreman of the ranch.

Delsie Dale Hall (1914-1998)

Delsie was born near Asher, Pottawatomie County, Oklahoma, on
August 30, 1914, and died in Fresno, California, on January 13, 1998.
She married William Clifford (Lucy) Bernard, of Shady Point and Red
Oak, Oklahoma. Lucy was born January 29, 1915, and died March 2,
1988, in Fresno, California.

Delsie was pretty and the best-tempered member of my family, and she loved nothing better than a party out on the Bermuda Grass Hill at our farm in the River Bend. It was she who care of me when I was a baby. After she married the good-natured Lucy (smooth, easy-going, full of stories and lies and Tom foolery) and they settled down in a grape vineyard in Fresno County, California, it was their house that became the place to go for fun times, lots of good food, and serious domino games. Lucy was the straw boss of John Ingle's vast holdings in the Valley, and for a time I was his shadow. Our hangouts were Kazarians' big general store in Rolinda and a little grocery store located at an intersection of two avenues in the vineyard country west of Fresno, not far from where Lucy and Delsie lived.

Lucy got his nickname back when he was a kid, undoubtedly because he became a bit too attached to some girl by that name. When he showed up in California, he applied for a driver's license and when it finally came, his name was spelled *Bernard*. According to Myrna, his oldest daughter, he was "just too lazy to have it changed."

During Delsie's advanced years she was plagued by Alzheimers Disease. Fortunately, she had two daughters, Myrna and Joyce, who saw to her needs on a daily basis, taking turns. She and Lucy had three daughters:

Myrna Jo Bernard (1939, Fresno County, California)
Sylvia Ann Bernard (1940, Fresno County, California)
Joyce Dean Bernard (1942, Fresno County, California)

Luther Leonard Hall (1917-1972)

Luther, who was *Luke* to his kinfolks and friends, was born in Seminole, Oklahoma, while my family was visiting our Uncle Hubert T. Carr and his family in Seminole, Oklahoma. The event took place on February 1, 1917, just months before Greel Hall was to invest in one hundred and sixty-five acres of sand burrs and bull nettles in the River Bend south of Seminole. He died of cancer near Drumright, Oklahoma, on September 15, 1972, and was buried in Mt. Vernon Cemetery, seven miles south of Stillwater, Oklahoma.

Luke was a steady, serious, hard worker; but he loved to drink home-brew and white lightning and play dominoes. In a land rich with good domino players, he was considered one of the best ever to walk through the sagging front doors of Garner's Pool Hall and Slim's Domino Parlor, in Konawa, Oklahoma.

When I returned to Konawa after WW2, Luke was pumping oil for the Champlain Oil Company, the same company Ezra worked for (In fact, the two of them were living within a stone's throw of each other in company houses) out southeast of town. One day he came along when I was on the highway trying to hitch a ride to Ada, fifteen miles away in Pontotoc County. Bill Archer was with me and when I saw my brother's old red pickup truck slowing down, I said, "Look who the dogs have dragged up." Luke picked us up and headed out of town into the thickets and briar patches toward Asher and Maud. When I finally got up enough courage to ask him where he was taking us, he said, "I want to introduce you to someone." That someone turned out to be a bootlegger who specialized in homebrew, a wanted man who lived a very cautious life. We spent the night there, and the next morning Bill confessed that he could not remember anything past the second bottle of brew.

For a long time Luke was married to Christine Clark, of Seminole County, Oklahoma, a cousin of Jack Thomas, perhaps the second-best fist-fighter in the entire Bend. My money was on Luke. Christine, how-ever, did a good job of keeping them apart. She was as close as a sister to me; and when she died in 1997, I knew I had lost a dear, dear friend. She and Luke had one child while they were living there near Konawa, Oklahoma.

Luther Ray (*Luke*) Hall (1940, Seminole County, Oklahoma)

Christine finally divorced old Luke because of his drinking and staying out late; but even though she married again, she continued to worry about him and look after him from time to time. He proceeded to marry again, also, this time to a lady named Alice (last name not available), of Odessa, Texas.

Vernon Hall (1920-1974)

Vernon was the second redhead in the family. Our mother had had flaming red hair as a child and young woman, as did both of our grandfathers. Even so, out of nine children, he was only the second. He was the first Hall to born in the River Bend. It happened on January 4, 1920, and he died in Fresno, California, on December 11, 1974, where he is buried. From an early age it was quite clear to everyone, especially to his two younger brothers, who came along a year and a half apart behind him, that Vernon was worthless, lazy, ornery, and dangerous. He was the only person I ever knew that enjoyed seeing someone else in pain. He wrecked and looted other people's personal belongings without a sign of conscience. And when he went away to the CCC in the mid-'Thirties, I rejoiced and sang *alleluias.*

By the time Vernon was old enough to join the Oklahoma National Guard, he was putting on some weight and had begun to look as mean and dangerous as he really was. The Guard finally mobilized in early 1942 and became part of the U. S. Army's 45th Infantry Division. Right off the bat this outfit went to Louisiana and *bivouacked,* getting ready for a trip overseas. Vernon had found a home. Japan had answered all his prayers by bombing Pearl Harbor, and everyone breathed a sigh of relief when the U. S. Army took him to war. The first thing any of us knew he was in North Africa with General Patton fighting Rommel and the Germans. His outfit went on to Sicily, hit Anzio Beach, crossed Italy and Belgium and entered Germany ahead of the Russians. Vernon was captured twice by the Germans, once in Belgium and again in Germany; and he escaped both times. He went from cook's assistant to military policeman to hardened infantry combat soldier. He was commissioned by General Patton himself on the field and given the temporary rank of Captain. After the war he stayed on in Germany as a *Constabulary Policeman* in West Berlin. He married the daughter of the Postmaster General of that city and they had a daughter. But when he showed up at home he was alone. The truth of the matter was he had been dabbling with the black market, and the U. S. Army had given him a choice: He could resign and never show his face again in the Army (and charges would not be brought against him), or he could face a court martial that would surely strip him of his rank and privileges.

Like Clifford before him and Zackie after him, Vernon became an itinerant ne'er-do-well in the San Joaquin Valley of California. He was, alternately, a cook in a variety of greasy spoons, the head chef of one of Fresno's (California) restaurants, a stoop laborer fighting and drinking his way up and down the valley, a bum that lived off his mother's meager little welfare commodities, and a sheepherder in Nevada working for his older brother. He was a real test of Mallie's love and forbearance.

Vernon was not given a middle name, but that was something the Army could not tolerate. Suddenly, he was *Vernon Tom Hall*, shortened for clerical purposes, to *Vernon T. Hall*.

When the war was over, he made it home before I did; and he returned to a hero's welcome in Konawa, the nearest town to the River Bend. The American Legion Post put a banner across main street (Muskogee Avenue) that read: *WELCOME HOME VERNON HALL!* And the first night he was home the Post and the VFW, which was new in town, threw a big dance in his honor at the American Legion Hut. Drinks were on the hut. What amazed me, when I showed up in town a month or so later, was how the American Legion (and the town, for that matter) knew about my brother's wartime exploits and the precise time he would get home. Did the guy have a press agent?

Zack Oberon Hall (1923-1969)

Dock, as my next older brother was called, came along on March 7, 1923, the second child to be born in the Bend. He died in Oroville,

California, on November 17, 1969, and is buried in the Butte County Cemetery, California, near Oroville. Those attending the funeral were Grady (Hall) Goff, Earl and Stella Hall, Bill Lanphear and his second wife, Thelma. Stella told her daughter Velta that it was the saddest funeral she had ever attended. Grady wrote a eulogy titled *In Memory of My Brother Zackie* (cf. the chapter titled *Memorials*).

For most of my childhood it was Zackie and me against Vernon and the world. His nickname in those days was *Dock*, and as far as I was concerned it fitted him to a T. I thought he was capable of anything. Our favorite thing to do in the wintertime was telling stories about the Black Natives of the South Seas. We built a tiny sheet-iron shanty down the hill a bit on the west side of the smokehouse, installed a makeshift stove in it (a discarded five-gallon bucket placed upside down on the floor), and hunkered around it to keep warm. Vernon was always a threat during such times, but when both of us faced him off the odds were about even. And he did not like those odds. He loved play practical jokes on us, jokes that were capable of killing us.

Zack was quiet-natured, pensive if you will, and, quite often, just a bit negative. The grownups called it *brooding*. It was I who thought up silly things to do, most of which he vetoed. What he wanted to do at any one time I never had the slightest notion; so I followed him around and waited. Being a part of whatever he thought up was all I asked. He trained a Jersey bull calf to pull a sled (and do anything else he demanded), and it was on this conveyance that we traveled all over the Bend. He called the bull *Billy*.

Following in the footsteps of Luke and Ezra, Zack got a job with an oil company and became a pumper. The Lynch Brothers Drilling Company built a small shotgun house on the hillside above where they had put down a well on our farm, and Zack moved into it. He was living there, quite contented with life I think, when the War in the Pacific began and I went off to California with our parents. While I was in California, I heard that he had married a Konawa girl named Edith Coonrod; and later, when

I was in the Pacific, I heard about the arrival of his two children, Karen and Jim. It was all so unbelievable, that Zackie was married and fathering children of his own, and I was so far away, in a world that looked very much like the one we had told stories about when we were kids.

Karen Hall (?-)

Jim Hall (?-)

Zack and Edith got a divorce about the time the war ended; and he went to California, leaving the children with Edith and joining the Navy. This I could not believe when the news reached me. When the country really needed him, he had preferred to pump gasoline. After all the fun stopped, there he was in the Pacific sending pictures of himself in dress blues and dungarees.

Edith married again and raised the kids; and, after his hitch in the Navy, Zack (lost boy that he was, always) married a woman named Kay, last name unknown, and moved to Burbank, California. He worked for a big aircraft company there in Burbank and in his spare time he invented a labor-saving device that the company adopted for its assembly line. The company saved a great deal of money because of this invention, and because of this he was given an immediate raise in pay, promised a promotion, and assured that he had a job for life. However, the joy had gone out of it for him. He had expected much more, and the longer he thought about it the less he liked it; and, so, one day he up and quit, leaving Kay and his little daughter as well as the job. As they used to say in Oklahoma, he had hit the owlhoot trail.

Sydney Lee Hall (1953-)

Sydney, lost to the family for many years, is doing quite well in Lufkin, Texas. She married Ken McKay, an engineer for Lockeed Martin, and they have two almost-grown daughters, Regina and Kristel.

Zack's last years were spent doing much the same thing Cliff and Vern were doing, stoop labor in the San Joaquin Valley, occasionally surfacing at Mama's or Gradie's for food and a place to sleep. Once in the mid-'Fifties when I was teaching English at Northeastern State College,

Tahlequah, Oklahoma, he paid me a visit. It was great to have him in my house, but almost immediately I saw that one of us had changed a lot. Things were not the same between us. He had embarrassed me a number of times over the years by calling me at the college and asking for emergency money; and now he was embarrassing me in my home by drinking too much and talking too loud both inside and outside the house. It was sad day for both of us when I took him to the edge of town and watched him thumb a ride for California. It was the last time I ever saw him.

Wesley Elmo Hall (1925-)

I was born September 18, 1925, in the River Bend of Seminole County, Oklahoma. Everywhere else in the country it was the middle of the Roaring Twenties, but in the Bend it was the Victorian Age. Money was a scarce as hens' teeth. I had red hair, like Vernon and Clifford, but there the similarities ended. Indeed, I had very little in common with any of my siblings. There were ten of them, most of whom were out on their own when I was born, either married and raising children or looking for work out west, or just gone to be away from our father.

From early childhood I liked to read and write and put words down on paper. We had almost no books in our house. The *King James Version of the Bible* was always present, but even that I was not allowed to pick up and read. Mabel, the only one in the family that ever had any money for frivolities, liked to read a Western magazine called *Ranch Romances*; but, of course, no one was permitted to touch one of those jewels. On rare occasions someone would come up with a quarter for a *Wild West Weekly*, and that would be shared by all who could read. I devoured every scrap of paper and book Zackie brought home from school, learned the alphabet without even being aware that I was doing so, and, by four, when I started to school, was reading the *Uncle Remus* stories in the first grade reader. I, who one day would be a college English teacher, learned proper Engish from Br'er Rabbit and Br'er Fox!

Unlike my brothers and sisters, I loved to collect things, write things down and sign my name to them, play detective and take every-body's fingerprint, tell stories about exotic lands, dream. My fantasy worlds were so real to me it caused talk, even outside the family. In a blade of grass I could sometimes see eternity, and a June bug rolling a ball of cow manure was enough to transfix me for an hour.

I was a poor excuse for a farm boy and Papa told me so on a number of occasions. He did not approve of *higher education*; that is, anything beyond the third grade, which is as far as he got. His argument was that he could read the *Bible* as well as anyone, and any schooling beyond that was not necessary for farming.

Every child must have a role model, but for me there was no one at all; so without giving it a thought I made Papa my *reverse* role model. If he liked something, that was reason enough for me to dislike it. When he had an opinion about something, I never failed to play the devil's advocate. When he looked at something and shook his head disapprovingly, I knew it had to be a winner.

In other words, I took the road he avoided. And it made all the difference. If it hadn't been for Papa I might have ended up a failed farmer.

On August 17, 1948, after Bugscuffle, four high schools, WW2, a hitch in the U. S. Navy (and during a hitch in the post-war U. S. Coast Guard), I married Bonita Pursiville in Ada, Pontotoc County, Oklahoma. We had four children:

Leslie Jeanne Hall (1952-)
Robert Christopher Hall (1959-)
Holly Denise Hall (1960-)
John Jeffrey Hall (1962-1982)

In February, 1982, my youngest was killed in a one-car accident on Highway 60, east of the little town of Fordland, Missouri. He was just twenty and home on leave from the U. S. Navy, and he left behind a wife and two babies, and a great emptiness in my heart.

On December 19, 1988, I married Sharon Jeanette Wright, who was born July 16, 1953, in Memphis, Tennessee. Her father was Bud Wright, who was born in Covington, Tennessee; and her mother is Sadie Walker, who, after Bud died, married Chuck Berry, an RVer retired from Boeing in Seattle, Washington.

The children of Ulysses S. Grant and Sylvania (Pennington) Hall:
Viola Helen Hall (1900-1936)

Helen was the first child of Grant and Vane Hall. She was born August 7, 1900, in Madison County, Arkansas, and died on March 11, 1936. On June 16, 1917, she married Ralph Cunningham Cannon. They had a boy and named him Ralph Cannon, Jr. In 1964 they were living in Tipton, California.

Ralph Cunningham Cannon, Jr. (ca. 1918-)

Willie Hall (1901-1906)

Willie was born October 3, 1901, in Madison County, Arkansas, and died December 6, 1906, in Sallisaw, Oklahoma. He was buried in Duncan Cemetery, Georgetown, Arkansas.

Albert Hall (1903-1916)

Albert, the son of Grant and Vane Hall, was born May 26, 1903, in Sallisaw, Oklahoma, and died April 19, 1916, in Sallisaw, Oklahoma. He was buried in Mt Comfort Cemetery, on B. A. Rudolph's place.

Maggie Lee Hall (1905-1935)

Maggie was born February 14, 1905, in Madison County, Arkansas, and died February 27, 1935, in Blaine Bottoms (Star County), Oklahoma. She is buried in Madison County, Arkansas. She married Floyd Harris and they had five children. One, Charles Harris, just a baby when she died, was raised by Mary E. Hyder. Lowell and Fay were raised by Ella Zona (Hall) and Clyde Crisler. Two died when they were still infants.

Lowell Harris (?-)
Fay (Clifton) Harris (?-)
Charles Harris (?-)

Mary Elizabeth Hall (1906-1989)

Mary Elizabeth was born September 19, 1906, in Madison County, Arkansas, and died October 6, 1989, in Tulare County, California. She was buried in the Tipton Cemetery. She married Toy Hyder and they had two boys, Ray and Jerry. They made the trip to California with Grant and Vane, but in 1938 they returned to Spiro, Oklahoma. They were married forty years before Toy died. Mary then married Everett Cole, and this marriage lasted until Everett's death twenty years later. Mary was living in Tipton, California, in 1964.

Jessie Raymond Hyder (?-)
Jerry Albert Hyder (?-)

James Arnold Hall (1908-1993)

Jim was born June 8, 1908, in Madison County, Arkansas, and died January 14, 1993, in Spiro (LeFlore County), Oklahoma. On September 10, 1932, he married Bessie Crumm, who was born September 17, 1915, in Spiro, Oklahoma. Her father was Elmer Crumm and her mother was Edyth (Clara) Norris. They had three children.

Kenneth Murl Hall (1934-)
Cecil Ferrell Hall (1943-)
Wanda Hall (1940-)

Ella Zona Hall (1910-1990)

Ella was born May 9, 1910, in Japton, Arkansas, and died May 10, 1990, in Tulare County, California. She was buried in Woodville Cemetery. She married Clyde Theron Crisler, and in 1964, when Ella's father died, they were living at 273 Newman Road, in Tipton, California.
Clyde Theron Crisler, Jr. (?-)

Goldie May Hall (1913-1916)

Goldie was born December 10, 1913, in Fayetteville (Washington County), Arkansas, and died April 20, 1916, of measles in Sallisaw, Oklahoma. She was buried in Mt. Comfort Cemetery on B. A. Rudolph's place.

Lucy Florence Hall (1915-)

Lucy was born March 6, 1915, in Fayetteville, Arkansas. Her first husband was John Davis, whom she married on September 14 (year not available). The second was Guy Dawson, who was born August 25, 1916, in Eastland, Texas. In 1964. Lucy and Guy were living in El Mirage, Arizona. They were still living together in March, 1995, when Lucy was eighty. By Guy she had four children.
Sylvia Dawson (1940-)
Alma Dawson (1941-)
Janet Dawson (1943-)
Phyllis Dawson (1952-)

Iva Alice Hall (1916-1921)

Iva was born May 2, 1916, in Fayetteville (Washington County), Arkansas, and died of measles August 15, 1921, in Wesley, Arkansas, at her grandparents' place (Aaron and Mary Pennington). She is buried in Duncan Cemetery, Georgetown, Arkansas.

John Theron Hall (1919-1993)

Johnny (John T.), the last child of Vane and Grant Hall, was born April 12, 1919, in Wheeler (Washington County), Arkansas, and died September 2, 1993, in Visalia, California. He was buried in the Tipton Cemetery. On February 15, 1941, he married Helen Francis King. His second wife's name was Dorothy Brandt. In 1964, when his father died, he was living in Sunnyvale, California. (One record shows his address at the time of his father's death as that of the home: 273 Newman Road, Tipton, California.)

The children of Sidney William and Cordelia (Eubanks) Hall:

Melvin Hall (?-)

Melvin (Red) was the first child of Sidney William and Cordelia (Eubanks) Hall and a grandson of William Newton and Susan Elizabeth (Woods) Hall. He has a son living in Tahlequah, Oklahoma.

Clint Hall (?-)

Clint was in a nursing home in 1987.

Nadine Hall (?-1999)

Nadine is Sidney William Hall's only daughter, as far as I know. She married a physician named McKissick and was living in Tulsa, Oklahoma, at the time her death in December, 1999.

Orville Hall (?-1940)

According to rumor and hearsay, Orville's four children are living in the Tahlequah, Oklahoma, area. The only reliable information is that he died in 1940.

The children of Cordelia Mae (Hall) and Logan Sisemore:

Coleman Sisemore (1909-1991)

Coleman, the first son of Delia Hall and Logan Sisemore, was born April 23, 1909, in Japton, Ball Creek township (Madison County), Arkansas, and died June 2, 1991, in Moss Landing, Monterey County, California. He married Argie Ewing November 12, 1927, in California. His second wife's name was Hill (first name unavailable), and his third wife was Flora Mae Miller.

Theodore Sisemore (1911-1981)

Ted was born February 3, 1911, in Japton (Madison County), Arkansas, and died October 8, 1981, in Kerman, Fresno County, California. He married Pearl Miller on October 18, 1930, in Chickasha, Grady County, Oklahoma. Ted and Pearl had two children.

Leon Sisemore (?-)
Lawrence Sisemore (?-)

Jack Sisemore (1913-1989)

Jack was born in Japton, Ball Creek, Madison County, Arkansas, on January 31, 1913, and died May 17, 1989, in Milpitas (Santa Clara County), California. He married Helen (last name unavailable) on September 10 (year not available). His second wife was Eula Guyton, and by her he had a daughter.

Francis Sisemore (?-)

Lucille Sisemore (1915-1977)

Lucy was born in Japton, Ball Creek (Madison County), Arkansas, on November 18, 1915. and died December 28, 1977, in Sacramento, California. Her first husband was Willie Kendrick Rainey, whom she married in 1932 in Pocassett, Grady County, Oklahoma. They had two children. Lucy's second husband was Tom Bratten.

Robert K. Rainey (?-)

Betty Jean Rainey (?-)

Buena Patricia Sisemore (1917-)

Pat was born in Japton, Ball Creek, Madison County, Arkansas, on January 12, 1918. She married Orville Lee Rainey on May 6, 1932, in Chickasaw, Grady County, Oklahoma. Orville was born in 1914 in Oklahoma, and died on June 17, 1995, in Oildale, Kern County, California. Pat divorced Orville in 1938 and later married Jerry Hatcher. They were living in Shasta, California, in 1982. Pat and Orville had two children.

Tommy Aubrey Rainey (1938-)

Jackie Ray Rainey (1934-)

Thelma Sisemore (1922-1990)

Tommie was born in Japton, Ball Creek, Madison County, Arkansas, on January 13, 1919, and died October 22, 1990, in Roseville, Placer County, California. Her first husband was Richard Hines, by whom she had one child. The name of the second husband was Rhoads. They were living in Nevada in 1982.
Beverly Hines (?-)

Carl Keith Sisemore (1926-1996)

Carl was born July 29, 1926, in Osage, Osage County, Oklahoma, and died March 25, 1996, in El Paso, El Paso County, Texas. He spent twenty years in the U. S. Army, serving in the Pacific during World War 2, in Korea in the 1950's, and Vietnam in the 1960's. He married a woman named Vickey (last name unavailable).

The children of Charity (Hall) and Lee Rogers:

Grace Rogers (1903-?)

Grace was the only daughter of Charity Hall and Lee Rogers. She was born in 1903 near Japton (Madison County), Arkansas. She married a man named Thomas and they had three children. At last report Grace was living at 8051 E. 8th Street, Buena Park, California 90621.
Thomas(?) Thomas (1936-)
Ginger Sue Thomas (1940-)
Dewey Thomas (1944-)

Searls Rogers (1906-?)

Searls was born on August 11, 1906, near Japton, Madison County, Arkansas. He married but his wife's name is unavailable. According to one source, he died in Arkansas. There were six children by this marriage:

Kenneth Rogers (?-)
Twila Rogers (?-)
Wayne Rogers (?-)
Brenda Rogers (?-)
Rick Rogers (?-)
Vickie Rogers (?-)

The children of Green T. and Nanny (Eversole) Hall:

Ernest Clifford Hall (1911-)

Ernest, the first son of Green T. Hall and Nanny Eversole, was born May 12, 1911, probably in Kiowa County, Oklahoma. In December, 1945, when his mother died, he was living in Fresno, California.

Pearl Zenia Hall (1914-1981)

Pearl was born March 28, 1914, in Little Rock, Arkansas, and died April 2, 1981, in Lodi, California. She is buried in the same cemetery as her mother. She married four times. Her husbands' names were Belser, Morrison, Leroy Earl Tobias, and Sukut (Sakut?). By Leroy Earl she had a daughter. In December, 1945, when her mother died, she was Mrs. Pearl Morrison, of Richmond, California.

Trudy Ellen Hall (?-1999)

Arizona Marge Hall (1916-1945)

Marge was born May 7, 1916, probably in Seminole County, Oklahoma. She married twice. Her husbands' names were Fletcher and Lee. In December, 1945, when her mother died, she was going by the name Mrs. Arizona Lee, of Vallejo, California.

Delphia Hall (1919-1975)

Pat was born August 21, 1919, in Mulberry, Arkansas, and died December 5, 1975, in Vancouver, Washington. She married three times. Her husbands' names were Hays, Avegio, and Kenneth Kodabaugh. The latter she married in Reno, Nevada. In December, 1945, when her mother died, she was Mrs. Delphia Hayes, of Richmond, California.

Irene Hall (1923-)

Irene was born November 29, 1923, in England, Arkansas, and died May 5, 1992, in Woodville, California. She married Brooks Bryant and a man named Geidt. When her mother died in December, 1945, she was Mrs. Irene Giedt, of Lodi, California.

Pauline Hall (1923-?)

Pauline was Irene's twin and died when she was in elementary school.

Imogene Hall (1928-)

Bonnie was born in 1928 in Seminole, Oklahoma. She married Russell Burrow. In a newspaper story about the death of her mother, in 1945, she was referred to as Mrs. *Energene* Burrow, of Acampo.

Robert Hall (1931-)

Bob was born November 21, 1931, in Spiro, Oklahoma, and died January 2, 1994, in Galt, California, of a heart attack. At age nineteen, after having carried the guilt (for seven years) of failing to prevent his father from bludgeoning his mother to death, he asked a man and a woman that he cared a lot about to adopt him. They were the Kirks, Orvilla and Walter, from Ohio. He confessed to his sister Bonnie that he wanted to get away from everything about Green T. Hall. In December, 1945, when his mother died, he was living in Acampo. He married Ella Coffee and they had four daughters. He is buried in Cherokee Memorial in Lodi.

THE SIXTH GENERATION

The children of James Thomas and Mintie Ardonia (Cheatham) Herron:

Mamie Ethel Herron (1900-1972)

Mamie was born September 30, 1900, in Ripley, Alabama, and died April 20, 1972, in Walker County, Alabama. She was the granddaughter of Hiram and Martha Herron and the great-granddaughter of Arminda (Hall) and Thomas Herron.

Walter James Herron (1902-1970)

Walter was born September 10, 1902, in Ripley, Alabama, and died July 13, 1970, in Merrillville, Indiana. He married Ceatrice Jenkins on January 11, 1927. She was born November 23, 1910, in Townley, Walker County, Alabama, and died July 25, 1996, in Crane Hill, Alabama. Her mother's name was Rosa.

Walter James Herron, Jr. (1929-)
Jerry Edward Herron (?-)
Larry Ray Herron (?-)
Norma Jean Herron (?-)
Douglas Wayne Herron (?-)
Glenda Gail Herron (?-)

Clarence Herron (1904-1986)

Clarence was born June 4, 1904, in Carbon Hill, Walker County, Alabama, and died April 20, 1986, in Huntsville, Alabama.

J. W. Herron (?-)
Opal Jean Herron (?-)
Billy Ray Herron (?-)
Bobby Joe Herron (?-)
Carl Dean Herron (?-)
Raymond D. Herron (?-)
Violet Mae Herron (?-)
Harvey Lee Herron (?-)
Mary Lou Herron (?-)
Jerry Don Herron (?-)
George Edward Herron (?-)

Flossie Herron (1906-1996)

Flossie was born February 12, 1906, in Carbon Hill, Walker County, Alabama, and died December 7, 1996.

Edgar Herron (1908-)

Edgar was born February 1, 1908, in Ripley, Alabama.

Donnie Mae Herron (1910-1995)

Donnie Mae was born august 4, 1910, in Ripley, Alabama, and died November 6, 1995, in Las Vegas, Nevada.

Grady Herron (1912-)

Grady was born December 14, 1912, in Ripley, Alabama.

Esther Louise Herron (1915-)

Esther was born January 31, 1915, in Carbon Hill, Walker County Alabama.

Earl Herron (1918-1977)

Earl was born January 7, 1918, in Ripley, Alabama, and died January 26, 1977, in Birmingham, Alabama.

Earnest Herron (1920-1971)

Earnest was born August 17, 1920, in Ripley, Alabama, and died April 17, 1971, in Walker County, Alabama.

The children of Thomas Cleveland and Margie Rena (Roberts) Hall:

Wayne Ambrose Hall (1907-1929)

Wayne was born March 26, 1907, in Billmore, Oregon County, Missouri, and died March 19, 1929, in El Centro, El Centro County, California. He was the first child of Thomas Cleveland Hall and Margie Rena Roberts and a grandson of Robert Jefferson Hall and Sara Jane Brewer.

Carlos Mentril Hall (1909-1964)

Carlos was born September 29, 1909, in Billmore, Oregon County, Missouri, and died August 20, 1965, in Monticello, San Juan Co., Utah. He married Winnifred Lorena Rogers on October 11, 1935. She was born October 11, 1917, in Spur, Dickens County, Texas. They had eight children:

Virginia June Hall (1936-1945)
Theodore Carlos Hall (1937-1962)
Roger Evan Hall (1939-)
Janette Arlene Hall (1941-)
Marjorie Evelyn Hall (1943-)
Barbara Joy Hall (1945-)
Winnifred Eileen Hall (1946-)
Marilyn Kaye Hall (1949-)

Therman Clement Hall (1914-2001)

Therman was born April 3, 1914, in Billmore, Oregon County, Missouri, and died October 29, 2001. He married Mary Virginia Rogers, who was born August 2, 1915, in Crosbyton, Crosby County, Texas. They had three children:

Allie Jane Hall (?-)
Richard Wayne Hall (?-)
Robert Lynn Hall (?-)

Thomas Richard Hall (1916-1920)

Thomas was born January 1, 1916, in Billmore, Oregon County, Missouri, and died May 4, 1920, in El Centro, El Centro County, California.

Lloyd Evan Hall (1920-1994)

Lloyd was born November 17, 1920, in El Centro, El Centro County, California, and died November 24, 1994, in Denver, Colorado. He married (1) Frieda Irene Wiederman and (2) Elizabeth Davis.

Mary Lenore Hall (?-)

Mary was born March 10, 1923, in Dove Creek, Dolores County, Colorado. She married Marion Lee Neely, who was born June 17, 1921, and died April 17, 1991. She is buried in Cahone, Dolores County, Colorado.

Victor Leon Hall (1928-)

Victor was born on October 16, 1928, in Dove Creek, Delores County, Colorado. On October 18, 1952, he married Phyllis Maurine Rice, who was born June 10, 1934, in Quinter, Gove County, Kansas. The wedding took place in Altura, Arapahoe County, Colorado. They had four children. Phyllis has been very helpful with the Hall Tree. She and Vic live Cahone, Colorado.

Steven Blane Hall (1954-)
Vickie Lynn Hall (1956-)
Timothy Wayne Hall (1959-)
Derek Duane Hall (1968-)

The children of Annie Dona (Hall) and J. W. Swafford:

Christopher David Swafford (1920-1983)

Christopher Swafford was the son of Annie Dona Hall and Jeremiah William Swafford and the grandson of Archie Brooklyn and Nancy Caroline (McDougal) Hall. He was born in Porum, Oklahoma, January 31, 1920, and died December 19, 1983, in Nowata, Oklahoma, He is buried in the Nowata Relocated Cemetery. He married Edna Marie Pettit, who was born in Pumpkin Center, Oklahoma. on March 24, 1918. They had three daughters.

Billie Ann Swafford (1953-)
Shirley Flo Swafford (1955-)
Judy Aline Swafford (1957-)

The children of Jesse Newton and Dora Belle (Lawson) Hall:

Elizabeth Imogene Hall (1920-)

Imogene was born January 26, 1920, in Chelsea, Rogers County, Oklahoma. She has married three times. They were Bill Reed, by whom she had a daughter, Charlie Williams, by whom she had two daughters, and Fayt Horne. She lives in Afton, Oklahoma, near her daughters. She enjoys reading and spending time with her grandchildren.

Kapatha Darlene Reed
Martha Joyce Wiliams (1944-)
Linda Bell Williams (1950-)

Oliver Newton Hall (1921-)

Newt was born December 22, 1921, in Chelsea, Rogers County, Oklahoma. He married Erma Lucille Cochran, who was born November

30, 1927, in Oklahoma, and died January 20, 1992. She is buried in the Chapel of Memories, Norwalk, California.

Newt served in the U. S. Army during WWII and saw action in Germany. He took his boot training at Ft. Campbell, Kentucky, where he contacted *spinal menningitis* and almost died. In Germany he developed a fungus on his feet, from wet shoes and socks. Shortly after that he found a dead German soldier and confiscated his boots. When he returned to the United States, he made his home in Globe, Arizona, where he worked in the copper mines. Later, he became a truck driver and drove eighteen-wheelers all over the country.

Lucille was half Cherokee Indian and loved by everybody. At Christmas she made picture cards of Oliver and herself and sent them to the family. She was hospitalized with tuberculosis for a number of years.

Carol Ann Kelly (1943-) (a stepdaughter)
Marion Jeanette Hall (1947-)
Saudonna Lea Hall (1951-)
Wendell Ralph Hall (1954-)

Lois Hall (1925-1931)

Lois was born in Chelsea, Rogers County, Oklahoma.

Roy Lee Hall (1925-)

Roy was born November 23, 1925, in Chelsea, Rogers County, Oklahoma. He served in the U. S. Army from 1956 to 1958. He married Sue Zinn and the had three children.

Patty Hall (?-)
April Hall (?-)
Peggy Hall (?-)

[The dates of Roy's and Lois's births have not been substantiated.]

Jessie Mae Hall (1930-)

Jessie Mae Hall, who prefers to be called *Jackie*, was born February 2, 1930, in Chelsea, Rogers County, Oklahoma. She finished high school and went to business college, training to be a medical secretary. She has always enjoyed working in the yard and growing flowers; and when her children were at home, she enjoyed making a lot of their clothes and some of her own. She was a volunteer in the local hospital for five years, and for a time she was a home room mother at school and a cub scout mother. There was always a need for cookies, it seemed. Going fishing was something the kids enjoyed doing, and it Jackie found out that it was a good way to get the yard weeded (The deal was that if they would dig up worms, she would take them fishing.) She married Kenneth Eugene Hollinsworth in California in 1948 and divorced him in Las Vegas in 1962. He was born March 25, 1926, in Delaware County, Oklahoma, and died November 2, 1999, in Hanford, California, and he was cremated. His wife, Martha, kept his ashes. The Holinsworth families gathered at the home of Dan Holinsworth and a tree was planted in the yard in remembrance of his passing. A head stone has been placed in the family lot in Nowata, Oklahoma. Ken served in the 101st Airborn in 1946 and 1947. He entered the service in Salt Lake City on February 2, 1946, went through basic training at Fort Lewis, Washington, and went to Japan to participate in the Occupation Japan Victory. He received the Good Conduct Medal and was released on October 5, 1947. His rank was PFC. His parents were Charles Jack Holinsworth (1887-1963) and Josephine Turner (1894-1963). They had four children. Her second husband was Lyndon Murray Hillis, whom she married on November 27, 1964, in California, and divorced December 5, 1975, in California. He was born on February 2, 1932, in Banning, California. She met Clair Eugene Heckathorn in California in 1980 and they were married in 1983. Gene Heckathorn a retired U. S. Navy captain, and the marriage took place on April 16, 1983, at the Naval Yard Chapel, Washington, D. C. Gene was born September 18, 1936, at RD 2, New Wilmington, Pennsylvania.

Michael Eugene Holinsworth (1949-1997)
Danny Ray Holinsworth (1950-)
Valerie Ann Holinsworth (1952-)
Rodney Lee Holinsworth (1956-)

Helen Bernice Hall (1932-)

Helen Bernice was born July 4, 1932, in Chelsea, Rogers County, Oklahoma. Through the years she has remained a homemaker. Her son Donald had AIDS and she took care of him in the home until his death on January 15, 1994. Her husband, Bill Orchid, now has *Alzhimers* and *Parkinson's Disease*, and she takes care of him. Her first husband was Ralph Dixon Ames, whom she married in 1945. He died in 1957 at Fort Eustis, Virginia. Her present husband's name is and William A. Orchid, and they have had one child.

Lola Mae Ames (1947-)
Vickie Melinda Ames (1949-)
Donald Eugene Ames (1952-1994)
Dora June Orchid (1955-)

Dorothy Lee Hall (1934-)

Dorothy Lee was born December 1, 1934, in Nowata, Nowata County, Oklahoma. Her first husband was Darrel Dixon. Her present husband, Bob Ross Hollinsworth, is the brother of Kenneth Eugene Holinsworth, who was married to Jessie Mae for a time. Bob Ross was born July 3, 1930. They had five children.

Allen Holinsworth (1952-1975)
Bobby Holinsworth (1955-)
Frank Holinsworth (1956-)
Debra Holinsworth (1958-)
Dewey Holinsworth (1959-)

Shirley Ann Hall (1938-)

Shirley was born March 28, 1938, in Alluwe, Nowata County, Oklahoma. She was, for a time, a baker for a grocery market, and she was also the cake decorator. She enjoys going to church and reading her Bible. She has been married three times: Clifford Zinn, who was born in Delaware, Oklahoma, and by whom she had one child; Edward A. Pogue, by whom she had four children; and Glenn Manier. When she was married to Edward Pogue, they visited prisons in the Los Angeles area and sang for the inmates. She accompanied with the accordion. During this time they also traveled about doing the same for people in homeless shelters and retirement homes. Shirley's son Robby, by Edward Pogue, was allegedly murdered by his wife and boyfriend for his insurance money. According to one source, they cut him into small pieces and buried his parts in different places. His head and his hands were never found. They were caught, tried, and are now serving prison sentences.

Linda Kay Zinn (1955-)
Laurie Kay Pogue (1963-)
Marjorie Marcelle Pogue (1965-)
Robert Edward Pogue (1961-1990)
Felecia Irene Pogue (1969-)

Judy Ilene Hall (1941-)

Judy Ilene Hall was born August 26, 1941, in Alluwe, Nowata County, Oklahoma. One source claims that she was married to a man named Boyd, but this has not been substantiated.

Jerry David Hall (1943-)

Jerry was born April 15, 1943, in Nowata, Nowata County, Oklahoma. He is now living in Artesia, California.

James Alvin Hall (1943-)

Jim was born in Nowata, Nowata County, Oklahoma, on August 20, 1943. He has married twice, the first time to Charlote Pagent, who was born in Indiana, and by whom he had three children:
James Alvin Hall, Jr. (1964-)
Guy Dean Hall (1965-)
Frank George Hall (1966-)

His second wife was Ella Moyer, and they also had three children:

Jamie Ann Moyer (1975-)
Brenda Louise Moyer (1976-)
John David Hall (1978-)

[The dates of Jerry's and James's births have not been substantiated.]

The children of Carl (Bud) Tyree and Carrie Melissa (Taylor) Hall:

Gladys Marie Hall (1922-1986)

Gladys was the granddaughter of Archie Brooklyn Hall and Nancy Caroline McDougal. She born March 18, 1922, in Porum, Muskogee County, Oklahoma, and died March 18, 1986, in Checotah, Muskogee County, Oklahoma. She married Vinnis Bervine Phillips on October 19, 1938, in Stigler, Haskell County, Oklahoma. He was born July 2, 1917, in Little Rock, Arkansas, and died March 29, 1969, in Pixley, California. His parents were Floyd Calvin Phillips (1895-1986) and Della Olean Cude (1896-1986). They had ten children:
Nancy Olene Phillips (?-)
Frankie Lee Phillips (?-)

Shirley Delores Phillips (?-)
Peggy Joyce Phillips (?-)
Richard Dwayne Phillips (?-)
Vinnis Leon Phillips, Jr. (?-)
Dianna Gail Phillips (?-)
Debra Marie Phillips (?-)
Kenneth Lee Phillips (?-)
Candy Phillips (?-)

Iva Lorene Hall (1926-)

Iva was born September 22, 1926, in Chelsea, Rogers County, Oklahoma. She married Charles Edward Smith on February 29, 1952, in Van Buren (Crawford County), Arkansas. Charles died in World War Two (June 6, 1944). They had one child.

Charles Henry Smith (?-)

Iva's second husband was Earl Milton Blackwood, whom she married on July 25, 1946. They had five children. She lives in Porum, Oklahoma.

Sadie Lee Hall (1926-)

Sadie was born September 22, 1926, in Chelsea, Rogers County, Oklahoma. She married Calvin (Cal) Ray Rock on February 29, 1952, in Van Buren, Arkansas. Her second husband was Elmer Shamblin, Jr., whom she married on November 13, 1961. With Cal Rock she had five children. She is living in Porum, Oklahoma.

Ervin Lee Rock (?-)
Calvin Ray Rock, Jr. (?-)
Janis Kaye Rock (?-)
Robbie Dale Rock (?-)
Janie Faye Rock (?-)

James Oliver Hall (1928-)

James was born February 19, 1928, in Muskogee, Muskogee County, Oklahoma. He married Leola Ezell (Leula Naomi Ezelle) on September 30, 1947. Leola was born May 8, 1930, in Boynton, Muskogee County, Oklahoma. Her father is LeRoy Ezell and her mother is Ola Ethel (Shomake). They had five children.
Judy Gail Hall (1949-)
James Larry Hall (1974-)
Kathy Ann Hall (1951-)
Mark Stephen Hall (1953-)
David Lee Hall (1959-)

Tyree Roland Hall (1929-)

Tyree Roland was born August 15, 1929, in Chelsea, Rogers County, Oklahoma. He married Ruby Benton September 22, 1950, in Eufaula, McIntosh County, Oklahoma, and they have six children.
Anna Mae Hall (?-)
Debra Sue Hall (?-)
Lillian Lou Hall (?-)
Bessie Jean Hall (?-)
Maye Belle Hall (?-)
Jackie Lee Hall (?-)

The children of Carl (Bud) Tyree and Nora Mae (Howell) Hall:

Virginia Ruth Hall (1937-?)

Virginia Ruth was born January 18, 1937, in Alluwe, Nowata County, Oklahoma. She married the following five men: Herbert Nieto

(December 19, 1954), Howard Norman Ronning (July, 1958), Lloyd Kay Klaus (November, 1970), John Ohl, and Gene Henderson. She had four children by Herbert Nieto (names unavailable).

Carl Watson Hall (1940-)

Carl was born Carl Wasston Hall but at the age of awareness changed that legally to Carl Watson Hall. He was born March 31, 1940, in Alluwe, Nowata County, Oklahoma. On July 8, 1967, he married Linda Marie Tolboe, better known as *Mae*.

Kenneth Franklin Hall (1943-)

Kenneth was born January 10, 1943, in Chelsea, Rogers County, Oklahoma. He married Erlene Endfinger on June 1, 1969.

Richard Douglas Hall (1945-)

Richard was born March 30, 1945, in Chelsea, Rogers County, Oklahoma. He married Kathleen Meyer on December 21, 1968, and Valerie Grace Hewitt on November 1, 1980.

The children of Pearl Ellen (Hall) and James Olin Gragg:

James Benjamin Gragg (1934-)

James was born September 7, 1934, in Claremore, Oklahoma. He married Opal M. Whinery, who was born July 10, 1937, and they had four children. His second wife's name is Andrea J. Carrillo. She was born May 2, 1944.

Lois Marie Gragg (1957-)

Annette Lynn Gragg (1959-)
Diana Dee Gragg (1962-)
Donald Ray Gragg (1964-)

The children of Birtha Elizabeth (Hall) and Ed Gragg:

Archie Gragg (?-)

Archie died at birth. His grandparents were Archie Brooklyn Hall and Nancy Caroline McDougal.

Mable Gragg (1922-)

Mable was born November 19, 1922. She married Billy Hales and they had twelve children. She died in Brownfield, Texas, where they had lived since the 1960's.
Utah Hales (?-)
Carl Hales (?-)
Clifford Hales (?-)
Buck Hales (?-)
Marty Hales (?-)
Tex Hales (?-)
Lena Hales (?-)
Cherry Hales (?-)
June Hales (?-)
Nita Hales (?-)
Brazil Hales (?-)
Tim Hales (?-)

Elizabeth Gragg (1924-)

Lizzie was born January 29, 1924. She married Edsel Gray and they live in Arizona. They had two children:
Curtis Gragg (?-)
Rickey Gragg (?-)
Other children of Lizzie's (father's name not available):
Johnny Gragg (?-)
Minnie Gragg (?-)
Mike Gragg (?-)
Doris Jean Gragg (?-)
Eugene Gragg (?-)
Martha Gragg (?-)
Calvin Gragg (?-)
Lulu Gragg (?-)
Mitchell Paul Gragg (?-)

Flossie Gragg (1927-)

Flossie married a man named Edward Duncan and they live in Arizona. They have one son.
Tommy Gragg (?-)

Frant Gragg (1930-)

Frant was born April 1, 1930. He married Thelma Tatharow (an Apache). They have seven children and live in Anadarko, Oklahoma.
Joseph Frant Gragg (?-)
Rachel Gragg (?-)
Neva Gragg (?-)
Kelly Gragg (?-)
Tracy Gragg (?-)

Josh Gragg (?-)
Jeremy Gragg (?-)

Paul Gragg (1936-1986)

Paul was born June 20, 1936. He married Aleen Felther and they had five children. He was killed in an auto accident between Surprise and Wickenburg, Arizona, sometime in 1986. He is buried in Resthaven Cemetery, Glendale, Arizona.

Brenda Gragg (?-)
Paula Gragg (?-)
Sandi (Sandy) Gragg (?-)
Tammi (Tammy) Gragg (?-)
Donita (Donia) Gragg (?-)

Betty Gragg (1938-ca. 1998)

Betty was born October 14, 1938. She married Billy Bob Williams and they had four children. Her second husband's name was K. C. Broder. She died about 1998 in Phoenix, Arizona, and is buried in Resthaven Cemetery, Glendale, Arizona.

Debbie Williams (?-)
Linda Williams (?-)
Steve Williams (?-)
Sonny Williams (?-)

Nelson Lee Gragg Sr. (1940-)

Nelson Lee Gragg, Sr., was born May 13, 1940, in a tent near Dirty Creek, in Muskogee, Oklahoma. He was married and had a child (Tylene) before he married Marion Bacon, who was born November 29, 1941, in

Caroway, Arkansas. They were divorced about 1966, after being married six or seven years. They had four children:

Nelson Lee Gragg, Jr. (1960-)

Brian Lynn Gragg (1961-)

Andrea Marion Gragg (1963-)

Rose Michelle Gragg (?-)

Hank Gragg (1944-)

Eddie Hank was born July 11, 1944, in Whittman, Arizona. He married Billie Crotcher, a full-blood Apache, and they had four children. They live at 22243 Lone Mountain Road, Whittman, Arizona 85361.

Richard Shane Gragg (?-)

Thomas Gragg (?-)

Eddie Gragg (?-)

Polly Gragg (?-)

The children of Earl and Stella (Scoggins) Hall:

Durward Jack Hall (1927-)

Jack is the grandson of Dock Walter Hall and Kate Elsey. He was born April 13, 1927, in Konawa, Seminole County, Oklahoma. He married Sarah Gladys Slentz on February 24, 1954, in Bay St. Louis, Hancock County, Mississippi; and they now live in Oklahoma City. Sarah was born September 27, 1931, in Green Forest, Carroll County, Arkansas, and died May 5, 1981, in Oklahoma City, Oklahoma. She was the daughter of Herbert Lavon Slentz and Alicie M. Holder. She and Jack had two children.

Larry Wayne Hall (1955-)

Tracy Kay Hall (1957-)

Val Gene Hall (1928-)

Val Gene Hall is the son of Earl Hall and Stella (Scoggins) and the grandson of Dock and Kate Hall. He was born Sept. 23, 1928, near Konawa, Seminole County, Oklahoma. He married Louise Elms in October, 1949, in Las Vegas, Clark County, Nevada. Louise was born December 25, 1930, in Seminole County, Oklahoma. She is the daughter of Leo C. Elms and Willie Beard. They now live in Madera, California, and have two children.

Phyllis Jean Hall (1950-)
Ronald Hall (1951-)

Velta Lee Hall (1930-)

Velta Lee was born October 5, 1930, near Shawnee, Pottawatomie County, Oklahoma. She married Andrew J. (Mike) Domyan on December 6, 1956, near Konawa, Seminole County, Oklahoma. Mike was born July 12, 1925, in Pennsylvania. He is the son of Jacob Domyan and Anna Gonka. Velta and Mike now live in Oceanside, California. They have one child.

Nathan Domyan (1958-)

Bobby Ray Hall (1932-)

Bob was born November 24, 1932, near Konawa, Seminole County, Oklahoma. He married Anita Marquez on September 10, 1955, in Las Vegas, Clark County, Nevada. Anita is the daughter of Arthur Marquez and Inez Chavez. Bob and Anita live in Fresno, California, and have four children.

Robert James Hall (1956-)
Debra Ann Hall (1957-)

Dianna Lynn Hall (1958-)
Denise Hall (1962-)

Barbara Louise Hall (1935-)

Barbara was born July 13, 1935, near Konawa, Seminole County, Oklahoma. She married William Charley Helton on November 30, 1959, in Beaufort, Beaufort County, South Carolina. William was born in Corbin, Whitley County, Kentucky, on November 21, 1932. He is the son of William Virgil Helton and Annette Watts. Their present address is Clovis, California, and they have one child.

William Charles Helton (1960-)

Joyce Oteka Hall (1938-)

Oteka was born December 21, 1938, near Konawa, Seminole County, Oklahoma. She married Edward S. Browne on November 17, 1960, in Sacramento, Sacramento County, California. Edward is the son of William Renedcos Browne and Candelaria Santa Maria. Their present address is Sacramento, California, and they have two children.

Rochelle Candine Browne (1961-)
Lindsay Edward Hall Browne (1963-)

The children of Cecile (Hall) and William Lanphear:

Doyle Lanphear (?-)

Doyle is the grandson of Dock Walter and Kate (Elsey) Hall and the grandson of William Newton and Susan Elizabeth (Woods) Hall. He has married a second time and has children, but no information is available on this family. According to Velta (Hall) Domyan, his aunt, his first wife, Joy, died mysteriously in February of 1962.

Leon Lanphear (?-?)

Leon died when he was a baby.

Suevella Lanphear (?-1978)

Suevilla died of cancer in 1978 and is buried in Greene County Memorial Gardens, Paragould, Arkansas.

Drucella Lanphear (?-)

Drucella is married and has children and grandchildren but no information about this family is available.

The children of Jewel (Hall) and Connie Lee (Bud) Beard:

Billy Ray Beard (?-)

Billy Ray Beard was born April 17, (year unavailable), in Kerman, Fresno County, California. He is the grandson of Dock Walter and Kate (Elsey) Hall. He married Cathy Stucky, who died of cancer in the early 1990's in Visalia, California. Dr. Drake, a physician in Kerman, California, delivered Billy Ray. Connie died in the Tulare County Hospital. Bill does body and fender work in Dinuba. His son Keith works with him. Gregory works at the Fresno Airport.

Gregory Beard (1961-)
Keith Beard (1963-)

The children of Dovie (Hall) and Lou Peak:

Darrell Dean Peak (?-)

Dean is the grandson of Dock Walter and Kate (Elsey) Hall. He married and has two sons, one of whom committed suicide.

The children of Ezra Marion and Florence (Scoggins) Hall:

Alton Lee Hall (1928-1989)

Alton was born in Seminole County, Oklahoma, on March 10, 1928, and died in Oklahoma City, Oklahoma County, Oklahoma, on October 11, 1989. He was the grandson of Mallie Rue (Carr) and Greeley Teeman (Horace Greel) Hall. He married Jeanetta Ramsey, of Konawa, Seminole County, Oklahoma, on March 17, 1948. She was born December 2, 1932, in Oklahoma City, Oklahoma, and was the daughter of Bill and Ruth Ramsey. They had one child.
Ginger Kaye Hall (1949-)

Dorotha Faye Hall (1931-2000)

Dot was a very likable and deserving but while she was quite young things began to go wrong for her. She was born near Konawa, Seminole County, Oklahoma, on January 28, 1931, and died November 11, 2000, in Duncan, Oklahoma. She married Marlin Joe (Mack) Schornick, of Konawa, Oklahoma, on November 2, 1948. Mack was born in Konawa, Oklahoma, on January 18, 1927, and died in an accident in Duncan, Oklahoma, August 7, 1980. His father was Lester Schornick and his mother's last name was Snyder. They had two children.
Terrye Lee Schornick (1951-)
Mickey Joe Schornick (1957-)

The children of Gradie (Hall) and Arthur Lee Goff:

Inas Faye Goff (1926-)

Faye was the first child of Gradie (Hall) and Arthur Lee Goff and the second grandchild of Greel and Mallie Hall. She was born in Konawa, Seminole County, Oklahoma, on October 31, 1926. She married Steve Kandarian, who was born May 19, 1918, in Fresno, California, where he died on December 9, 2001, at the age of eighty-three. He had Parkington's Disease, but the actual cause of his death was a hip injury.

Katherine Louise Kandarian (1944-)

Patricia Ann Kandarian (1946-)

Maudie June Goff (1929-)

June was born in Konawa, Seminole County, Oklahoma, on January 22, 1929. She married Joseph Lamanuzzi, Jr., of Fresno, California, who was born on January 31, 1930. They had two children.

Joseph Arthur Lamanuzzi (1953-)

Linda Faye Lamanuzzi (1955-)

Annie Jo Goff (1930-1995)

Annie Jo was the daughter of Gradie (Hall) and Arthur Lee Goff and a granddaughter of Greel and Mallie Hall. She was born in Konawa, Seminole County Oklahoma, on November 15, 1930, and died in Fresno, California, on April 5, 1995. She married Angelo Papagni, of Fresno, California, who was born October 1, 1928, and died February 28, 1981. They had three children.

Sandra Elizabeth Papagni (1953-)

Judith Anne Papagni (1956-)

Carlo Nicholas Papagni (1960-)

The children of Ollie Ida (Hall) and Lou Smith:

Flora Evaline Smith (1925-)

Flora was the first child of Ollie Ida (Hall) and Lou Smith and the first grandchild of Greel and Mallie Hall. She was born in Haskell, Oklahoma, on August 20, 1925, almost exactly one month before yours truly was born (I was an uncle before I was born). She married John Nuckells, of Fresno, California, in June, 1950. He died that October and she later married James Lee Putler, who was born March 28, 1930, in Sugar Pine, California. Jim is the son of Elma Irene Judkins and Francis Owen Putler. They had two children.

Nancy Kay Putler (1961-)
David Allen Putler (1961-1961)

Muriel Eston Smith (1927-2000)

Bud was born in Raymondville, Texas, on March 29, 1927, and died in Blanchard, Oklahoma on April 29, 2000. Greel Hall had swapped our farm for one down in the Rio Grande Valley, and Lou and Ollie had made the trip, too. That explains why Buddy was born in Texas. He married Florene, last name unavailable, of Fresno, California. She was born on Christmas Day (year unavailable). After a long-time residence in Fresno, they moved to Blanchard, Oklahoma.

Lou Albin (L. A.) Smith (1929-)

L. A. was born in Seminole County, Oklahoma, on May 3, 1929. He has been an artist, a taxidermist, and a gourmet barbecue cook (specializing in a barbecue sauce he created himself and marketed under the name *Smoky Smith's Famous BQ Sauce*). He married Lucille Cleveland, who was born April 1, 1929, in Ada, Oklahoma, and died in Oklahoma City, Oklahoma, in April, 2000. They had three children.

Gary Smith (1949-)

Bridget Evelyn Smith (1953-)

Gregory Paul Smith (1959-)

Mallie Avo Smith (1931-)

Avo was born in Seminole County, Oklahoma, in 1931. She excelled in high school and became the Superintendent Jack Davis's secretary after she graduated. She married Frank Rincon, who was born in Fresno, California, on June 13, 1925; and for many years they had a grocery store in Clovis, California, where they still live. They have raised four children.

Mark Anthony Rincon (1951-)

Debra Ann Rincon (1953-)

Robert Harlan Rincon (1954-)

Kelley Maria Rincon (1957-)

Roy Joe Smith (1934-1996)

Joe was the third son of Ollie (Hall) and Lou Smith and the grandson of Greel and Mallie Hall. He was born in Seminole County on January 29, 1934 (His mother died in childbirth). He married a woman named Alma (last name unavailable), became an electrical engineer, raised three children, and died April 29, 1996, at the age of sixty-two in Houston, Texas. He was raised by Hubert and Delphia Grady, his father's sister and brother-in-law.

Michael Smith (?-)

Donna Smith (?-)

Douglas Smith (?-)

The children of Ruth (Hall) and Ben Potter:

Clara Dale Potter (1935-)

Clara was the first child of Ruth (Hall) and Ben Potter and the grand-daughter of Greel and Mallie Hall. She was born in Konawa, Seminole County, Oklahoma, on September 13, 1935. She married Carl Swann, of Oklahoma City, and, after three children, they divorced. Clara has made her home in Oklahoma City, where she is secretary of her church.

Steve Nolan Swann (1956-)
Gary Alan Swann (1957-)
Sandra Gail Swann (1963-)

David Mitchel Potter (1937-)

Mitchel was born in Seminole County, Oklahoma, May 31, 1937. He married Martha Ann Hinson, and they adopted a boy, who was reclaimed by the natural birth mother; then they had two boys of their own and later divorced. On March 27, 1987, Mitchel married Charolotte DeGraffenreid Mixon, who was born August 27, 1936.

Joel Austin Potter (1970-)
Timothy Mark Potter (1971-)

Beulah Jean Potter (1940-)

Jean was born in Okmulgee, Oklahoma, on November 12, 1940. She is a granddaughter of Greel and Mallie Hall. She married Jack Finley, of Grand Island, Nebraska. Jack preaches and manages a church in Hemet, California. They have two children.

Darcy Marlane Finley (1964-)
Nia Clarice Finley (1966-)

The children of Clifford Cleborn Hall and Imogene White:

Frances Carol Hall (?-)

Frances Carol, the daughter of Imogene (White) and Clifford Hall and the granddaughter of Greel and Mallie Hall, was born in Asher, Pottawatomie County, Oklahoma, sometime in the mid-Thirties.

The children of Clifford Cleborn Hall and Georgia Marie Sage:

Shirley Ann Hall (1937-1989)

Shirley was the first child of Clifford Hall and Georgia Marie (Sage) and a granddaughter of Greel and Mallie Hall. She was born in Maud, Seminole County, Oklahoma, on September 26, 1937, and died February 16, 1989, in Oakdale, Stanislaus County, California. She is buried in Knight's Ferry, California. On July 3, 1953, she married William Dean Terrill, who was born June 25, 1935, in Modesto, Stanislaus County, California, and died May 27, 1993, in Manteca, San Joaquin County, California. His parents were Robert Alfred Terrill and Mary Viola Jeffries. Shirley and Bill had five children before they divorced. Shirley later married (1) Harvey Taylor and (2) Henry Barnett. Bill married Helen Jarvis.
David Philip Terrill (1955-)
Kathleen Marie Terrill (1958-)
Merry Susan Terrill (1960-)
Cara Lee Terrill (1962-)
Mark Allen Terrill (1964-)

Mary Jo Hall (1939-1993)

Mary Jo was born in Maud, Seminole County, Oklahoma, on December 27, 1939, and died February 26, 1993, in Modesto, Stanislaus

County, California. She married John Richard Sheppard, who was born on January 21, 1937, in Fresno, California. They had one son and divorced. Later, she married Bob Musgraves, an accountant in Modesto, California.

John Richard Sheppard, Jr. (1957-)

Nancy June Hall (1943-)

Nancy was born in Modesto, Stanislaus County, California, in June of 1943. She married Jesse Kilborn Holmes, who was born June 3, 1940, in California. They had three children.

Jesse Kilborn Holmes, Jr. (1965-)
Michelle Holmes (?-)
Kimberly Holmes (?-)

The children of Delsie Dale Hall and William Clifford (Lucy) Bernard:

Myrna Jo Bernard (1939-)

Myrna is the oldest daughter of Delsie (Hall) and Clifford (Lucy) Bernard and a granddaughter of Greel and Mallie Hall. She was born in Kerman, Fresno County, California, on October 18, 1939. She married Anthony Louie Ceccarelli, born April 22, 1934, in Ecorse, Michigan, and died February 17, 2000, in Fresno, California. Recently, Myrna has begun research on a Bernard family tree. They had four children.

Adam Rocco Ceccarelli (1961, Fresno, California)
Matthew Christopher Ceccarelli (1962, Fresno, California)
Michael John Ceccareli (1967-1988, Fresno, California) (twin)
Anna Rue Ceccarelli (1967, Fresno, California) (twin)

Sylvia Ann Bernard (1940-)

Sylvia was born in Kerman, California, on October 4, 1940. She married (1) Neil Allen Williams, who was born January 11, 1940, in Fresno, California; (2) Randal Mello; (3) Jerry Cole; and (4) Ted (Theo) Stathakis. By her first husband she had three children, whom Jerry Cole adopted. By her last husband she had one child.

Richard Allen Williams (1957-) [Cole by adoption]
Cheryl Ann Williams (1958-) [Cole by adoption]
Jack Wesley Williams (1959-1974) [Cole by adoption]
Randy Allen Mello, Jr. (1977-)

Joyce Dean Bernard (1942-)

Joyce was born in Kerman, Fresno County, California, on February 4, 1942. She married Steve Manning Birdman, of Los Angeles, California, and they had one child, a daughter, before they divorced. Her second husband was David Crockett Robinson, of Waeldor, Texas, and they had one child, a daughter.

Margo Janeen Birdman (1962-)
April Dawn Robinson (1963-)

The children of Luther Leonard Hall and Christine Clark:

Luther Ray Hall (1940-)

Luke is the only child of Luther Hall and Christine (Clark) and a grandson of Greel and Mallie Hall. He was born in 1940 in Seminole County, Oklahoma. He married Norma Jean Maddie, who was born in 1941, and they had two boys and divorced in 1958. Connie re-married, a man named Smith. Sometime in the 1970's both boys legally changed their names to Smith.

Luther Ray (Hall) Smith, Jr. (1957-)

Richard Allen (Hall) Smith (1958-)

On May 23, 1965, Luke married Connie Beth Rorabaugh, who was born June 15, 1947, and they had three children before they divorced in May, 1982.

Angela Rae Hall (1966-)

Darrin Dewayne Hall (1967-2001)

Debra Dawn Hall (1971-)

On July 23, 1984, Luke married Debra Sue Lancaster; and they live in Milfay, Oklahoma. Debbie has been a great help with both the Hall and the Carr family trees.

The children of Zack Hall and Edith Coonrod:

Karen Jo Hall (?-)

Karen is the daughter of Zack Hall and Edith Coonrod and the grand-daughter of Greel and Mallie Hall. She was born in Seminole County, Oklahoma. She married R. C. Lawyer, and for a time they owned a grocery store in or near Ada, Oklahoma. In the 'Seventies her address was R. R. #3, Konawa, Oklahoma 74849. They had two children.

Terri Jo Lawyer (?-)

Michael (Butch) Dewayne Lawyer (?-)

Jim Hall (?-1996)

Jim was the son of Zack and Edith Hall. He was born in Seminole County, Oklahoma, and died on November 2, 1996, in Prague,

Oklahoma, where he was a deputy sheriff for years. He is buried in the Dora Cemetery in Konawa, Oklahoma. He married Gale, last name unavailable, whom he divorced in October, 1969. On September 2, 1970, he married Trecias Jo, last name unavailable, and they had one child, whom they named Trecias. Shortly before the birth of their daughter, Jim wrote the following letter to his Aunt Gradie Goff (my sister) in Fresno, California:

Dear Aunt Grady,

I got your letter and pictures. I will treasure them. At leas I know what my family looks like. Thank you very much. You better count yourself lucky I don't write very many letters. I don't set still too long at a time. Always too busy to write. Karen has two kids. They are sweet but spoiled. The last part is my fault. I love them very much. The girl is the oldest. her name is Terri Jo. The boy's name is Mikeal (Butch) Dewayne. We were looking at some of my baby pictures. Butch and I look like twins. Well, I am going to tell you a few things about me. I hope it don't bore you.

I went to school at Asher, first to the third. We moved back to Konawa during the summer between 3rd and 4th grades. When I was in the 7th I knocked my right hip out of socket and had surgery. They put 3 pins in to hold it in place. I was bedfast for 8 months in a cast. I walked on crutches for a year afterwards. In about 8 or 9 months my left hip went out of socket. Same story on it. I went to school on a stretcher. all my friends were wonderful, caring for me from one class to another. This is one thing I will always be grateful for. Well, I was back walking by the middle of the 9th grade. Everything went great the rest of school. I won a few awards in F. F. A. I was State Star Farmer in 1964, class president my senior year. I graduated with a B average in 1964. I worked at different jobs for the next year.

In 1965 I got a new Chevrolet. On June 11, 1966, I got married. her name was Gale. We got a new house and new furniture, color TV, then had bad luck hit again. I hurt my right knee. I couldn't work for a year and a half. Well, I finally got back on my feet, got the house and all paid for. We got another new car and Gale finished beauty school and opened a shop. This was where the real trouble started. She decided she was boss because was making more money than me. Well, I finally took all I could take. We were divorced in October of 1969.

She took everything but my 1963 Ford pickup. House and all. Well, there I was back single again. One thing good about it, we didn't have any kids. I got me another house and got new furniture and met the most wonderful person in the world. her name is Trecias Jo. Yes, we got married on September 2, 1970. Just a little while before you were here. I am the most happiest man around here. She has long blond hair, the real color, too. And real sweet, too.

Well, we live and learn. You had better thank you're something special. This is the longest letter I ever wrote! Tell everybody that I love them, especially Grandma Hall. Tell her I weill send her a picture of the wife and I when we have some made.

Love, Jim

The children of Zack Hall and Katherine (last name unavailable):

Sydney Lee Hall (1953-)

Sydney, the daughter of Zack Hall and Kay, and the granddaughter of Greel and Mallie Hall, was born in Burbank, California, on September 20, 1953. After her parents divorced, Sydney was passed about from place to place. For a time she stayed with my sister Mable and Melvin Merrill. Then she disappeared and the rumor was that she had been taken in by her mother's folk in Texas. Today, she lives in Lufkin, Texas, is married to Ken McKay, an engineer for Lockeed Martin there in Lufkin n, and has two daughters. She has worked in a daycare center for six of the seven years they have lived in Lufkin. Regina, nineteen, is a student at Angelina Junior College in Lufkin, and Kristel, seventeen, is a senior in high school.

Regina McKay (December 17,1983-)

Kristel McKay (October 7, 1984-)

The children of Wesley Elmo Hall and Bonita Pursiville:

Leslie Jeanne Hall (1952-)

Leslie was born in Valley View Hospital, Ada, Oklahoma, on February 4, 1952, while her parents were living in Pawnee, Oklahoma. (Her father was a high school English teacher there.) She is the granddaughter Greel and Mallie Hall, and her maternal grandparents were Nolan Franklin Pursiville and Mary Etier, of Ada, Oklahoma Les married a young musician named John Gott, of Springfield, Missouri, on September 25, 1970. They divorced on July 25, 1972, and later Leslie married her college photography teacher, Alan Harry Brown, of Cedar Rapids, Iowa, who was born on November 17, 1942. They bought a house on Normal Street, one block from Southwest Missouri State University, Springfield, where Alan was teaching. Les completed her bachelor's degree in art there and then a master's in psychology, before becoming an art therapist in Springfield. They had two children, moved into a lovely two-story antique on Cherry Street, and built a reputation for themselves in photographic art, showing their work internationally. The children grew up in Springfield, but eventually both moved to California.

Matthew Alan Brown (1975-)
Lauren Elizabeth Brown (1977-)

Robert Christopher Hall (1959-)

Chris was born in Tahlequah, Oklahoma, on April 2, 1959, where his father was teaching English in the local state college. He served in the U. S. Army Infantry as a tour guide at the DMZ in Korea, then returned to the States and was stationed at Ft. Leonard Wood, in Missouri, where he met and married Valorie Chase, an Army brat born in Tennessee. After he was discharged, they settled in Springfield, Missouri, for a time and had two boys. In 1993 they were divorced. Chris is now head of Planning and Zoning in Franklin County, Missouri, and Valorie and the boys are living in eastern Tennessee next door to her parents. Chase, it is rumored, has exemplary writing talent, unlike his paternal grandfather.

Chase Wesley Hall (1989-)

Tyler Cody Hall (1992-)

Holly Denise Hall (1960-)

Holly was born in Tahlequah, Oklahoma, on October 31, 1960. She served in the U. S. Air Force as an Air Traffic Controller in the Azores Islands, then, back in the States, she became a medical assistant. She married Doug Melton, of Oldfield, Missouri, who was also in the Air Force. They divorced and she later married Steve Katona, of New Jersey. They divorced and she later married Sean FitzPatrick, and they have three sons, all named after saints. In 2001 both Holly and Sean, who had completed masters' degrees in psychology in St. Louis, Missouri, enlisted in the U. S. Air Force as medical therapists. Both went through Commissioned Officer Training (COT) in Alabama and came out captains. Their first assignment turned out to be Scott AFB, Illinois, near St. Louis.

Nicholas Michael FitzPatrick (1995-)

Brendan Miles FitzPatrick (1997-)

Patrick Stephen FitzPatrick (1999-)

John Jeffrey Hall (1962-1982)

Jeff was born in Tahlequah, Oklahoma, on May 7, 1962, the last child of Wesley and Bonita Hall. His parents took him to Modesto, California, where his father taught English at the local junior college and his mother taught elementary school. After two years they took him to Springfield, Missouri, where his father taught English at Southwest Missouri State

University and his mother taught remedial reading at Logan Elementary School. In 1972, when he was ten, his parents built a new home in the hills of Christian County, twenty miles from Springfield. There he came into his own. He loved the hills, woods, and streams of that part of the country; and he made many friends among the locals (who were rather clannish). When he graduated from Chadwick High School, in 1981, he joined the Navy, just as his father had at the same age. He married his childhood sweetheart, Ronda Marie Grimes. On February 12, 1982, while he was on leave of absence from his ship in Charleston, South Carolina, he was killed in an automobile accident near Fordland, Missouri. He was buried in the Old Boston Cemetery, just down the road from his home. It overlooks Swan Creek at a point where the fishing was always good. He and Ronda had two children.

David Jeffrey Grimes (1980-)

Latisha Marie Hall (1981-)

The children of Viola Helen (Hall) and Ralph Cunningham Cannon, Sr.:

Ralph Cunningham Cannon, Jr. (ca. 1918-)

Ralph is the grandson of Ulysses Grant and Sylvania (Pennington) Hall and the great-grandson of William Newton and Susan Elizabeth (Woods) Hall.

The children of Maggie Lee (Hall) and Floyd Harris:

Lowell Harris(?-)

Lowell was raised by Ella (Hall) Crisler. He is the grandson of Ulysses Grant and Vane Hall and the great-grandson of William Newton and Susan Elizabeth (Woods) Hall.

Fay Clifton Harris (?-)

Fay was also raised by Ella (Hall) Crisler.

Charles Harris (?-)

Charles' mother died when he was a baby, and he was raised by Mary E. Hyder.

The children of Mary Elizabeth (Hall) and Ray Hyder:

Raymond Jessie Hyder (1924-)

Ray is the grandson of Ulysses Grant and Vane Hall and the great-grandson of William Newton and Susan Elizabeth Hall. He was born May 8, 1924. By his first wife, name unavailable, he had two children.
Michael Ray Hyder (1950-)
Pamela Elaine Hyder (1953-)
In 1982 Ray married Marti, who was born in 1940, when she was forty-two and he was fifty-eight; and Marti raised the two children by his first wife (Michael Ray was born September 15, 1950, and Pamela Elaine was born May 26, 1953). Then on September 7, 1982, they had a boy of their own, David. Marti collaborated with Trudy Tobias in research on the family tree until Trudy's death in 1999. She and Ray and David live in Tipton, California, where they have a video repair shop on their property and, as Marti puts it, they make enough extra money to finance what the young one thinks he must have.
David Hyder (1982-)

Jerry Hyder (?-)

Jerry is the son of Mary Elizabeth (Hall) and Toy Hyder, of Spiro, Oklahoma. He is the grandson of Grant and Vane Hall. Presently, he lives in Tipton, California.

The children of James Arnold Hall and Bessie Crumm:

Kenneth Murl Hall (1934-)

Kenneth is the son of James (Jim) Arnold Hall and Bessie Crumm and the grandson of Grant and Vane Hall. He was born January 11, 1934, in Spiro, Oklahoma; and he married Rena Irene Walker, who was born August 15, 1937, in Spiro, Oklahoma. Her father was Alvin Walker and her mother was Dollie Scarberry.
Kathy Irene Hall (1955-)
Ricky Murl Hall (1957-)

Cecil Ferrell Hall (1942-)

Cecil is the son of James Arnold Hall and Bessie (Crumm) and the grandson of Grant and Sylvania Hall. He was born September 29, 1942, and he married Patricia Bolt on April 12 (year unavailable), in Spiro, Oklahoma. Cecil dropped in on me when I was living at Lake of the Ozarks, in Missouri, to discuss the Hall family tree. He travels a lot and has a business called C & H Sales and Service, Inc., located in Wagoner, Oklahoma; and he enjoys talking about the family and searching for the burial places of the old folks. He and Walter Sisemore, of Tahlequah, Oklahoma, have contributed many headstones to unmarked graves. Cecil and Patricia have one daughter, and they live in Wagoner, Oklahoma.
Rebecca Jane Hall (?-)

Wanda Hall (1940-)

Wanda was born April 11, 1940, in Red Hill, Cacher Bottoms, Spiro, LeFlore County, Oklahoma. She married William Dale Smith (b. February 11, 1938) in Stigler, Oklahoma. William Dale was born in Spiro and died there. His father is William Jefferson Smith, and his mother is Rhoda Bell French. Wanda and Dale were married on May 21, 1958, in Stigler; and they have three children.

Larry Dale Smith (1960-1983)
Tawnya Danita Smith (1961-)
Tammy Denise Smith (1962-1963)

The children of Ella Zona (Hall) Clyde Theron Crisler:

Clyde Theron Crisler, Jr. (?-)

Clyde is the son of Ella Zona Hall and Clyde Theron Crisler, and the grandson of Grant and Vane Hall. He married Trudy Tobias, the granddaughter of Green T. Hall and his second cousin.

The children of Lucy Florence (Hall) and Guy Dawson:

Sylvia awson (1940-)

Sylvia is a granddaughter of Grant and Vane Hall. She was born April 17, 1940, in Buckeye, Arizona. She married twice, to Dean Parker on January 1, 1937, in Arkansas, and to Sisto Benevidez on August 25, 1950, in New Mexico.

Alma Dawsn (1941-)

Alma was born June 16, 1941, in Buckeye, Arizona. She married twice, Alois Schmidt on April 19, 1935, and Loy Fulbright (date unavailable).

Janet Dawson (1943-)

Janet was born July 14, 1943, in Buckeye, Arizona. She married twice, Darrell Belcher on July 19, 1939, in Oklahoma, and David Weekley (date and place unavailable).

Phyllis Dawson (1952-)

Phyllis was born June 15, 1952, in Lancaster, California. She married twice, to Donnie Price on January 1, 1945, in Cement, Oklahoma, and Leon Ellison on May 3, 1950, in Iowa.

The children of Ted and Pearl (Miller) Sisemore:

Leon Sisemore (?-)

Leon is the grandson of Delia (Hall) and Logan Sisemore and the great-grandson of William Newton and Susan Elizabeth (Woods) Hall.

Lawrence Sisemore (?-)

Lawrence is another son of Ted Sisemore and Pearl (Miller) and a grandson of Delia (Hall) and Logan Sisemore.

The children of Jack Sisemore and Eula Gutten:

Francis Sisemore (?-)

Francis is the granddaughter of Delia (Hall) and Logan Sisemore and the great-granddaughter of William Newton and Susan Elizabeth (Woods) Hall.

The children of Lucille Sisemore and Willie Rainey:

Robert K. Rainey (?-)

Robert is the granddaughter of Delia (Hall) and Logan Sisemore and the great-grandson of William Newton and Susan Elizabeth (Woods) Hall. He married a woman named Marion (family name unavailable), and they had three children.
Robert K. Rainey, Jr. (?-)
Evelyn Rainey (?-)
Karen Rainey (?-)

Betty Jean Rainey (?-)

Betty Jean is the daughter of Lucille (Lucy) (Sisemore) and Willie Rainey and the granddaughter of (Delia) Hall and Logan Sisemore.

The children of Pat Buena Sisemore and Orville Rainey:

Tommy Aubrey Rainey (1938-)

Tommy Aubrey is the grandson of (Delia) Hall and Logan Sisemore. He married twice. By his first wife (name not available) he had three children. The name of his present wife is Wanda (surname unavailable).

Thomas Rainey ((1956-1982)
Jack Rainey (?-)
William Rainey (?-)

Jackie Ray Riney (1934-)

Jackie married a woman named Helen (last name unavailable) and they had four children:
Mitzi Rainey (?-)
 Brenda Rainey (?-)
Esta Rainey (?-)
Christine Rainey (?-)

The children of Thelma Sisemore and Richard Hines:

Beverly Hines (?-)

Beverly is the daughter of Thelma (Sisemore) and Richard Hines and the granddaughter of (Delia) Hall and Logan Sisemore.

The children of Grace (Rogers) and (?) Thomas:

Thomas (?) Thomas (1936-)

Thomas [if that is his name] was the first son of Grace (Rogers) and a man named Thomas (first name not available) and the grandson of Charity (Hall) and Lee Rogers. He was born in Japton (Madison County), Arkansas, on May 23, 1936.

Ginger Sue Thomas (1940-)

Ginger was born April 17, 1940, in Madison County, near Japton, Arkansas.

Dewey Thomas (1944-)

Dewey was born in Fullerton, California, on April 26, 1944.

The children of Searls Rogers (wife's name unavailable):

Kenneth Rogers (?-)

Kenneth was born near Japton, Madison County, Arkansas.

Twila Rogers (?-)

Twila was also born near Japton, in Madison County, Arkansas.

Wayne Rogers (?-)

Wayne was also born in Madison County, Arkansas. Could this be the Wayne Rogers of M*A*S*H fame?

Brenda Rogers (?-)

Brenda was born in Madison County, Arkansas.

Rick Rogers (?-)

Rick was born in Madison County, Arkansas.

Vickie Rogers (?-)

Vickie was born in Madison County, Arkansas.

THE SEVENTH GENERATION

The children of Walter James Herron and Ceatrice Jenkins:

Walter James Herron, Jr. (1929-)

Walter James, Jr., was born July 19, 1929, in Flat Creek, Alabama. He was the grandson of James Thomas Herron and Mintie Cheatham, the grandson of Hiram Hall and Martha Guttery, and the great-grandson of Arminda Hall and Thomas Herron. He married Norma Faye Heaton on January 14, 1950, in Ensley, Alabama. She was born August 22, 1929, in Sequim, Washington. Her parents were William Heaton and Alice Sutherby.

Dennis James Herron (1951-)
William Allen Herron (1953-)

The children of Clarence Herron and Meatrice Odom:

J. W. Herron (?-)

Opal Jean Herron (?-)

Billy Ray Herron (?-)

Bobby Joe Herron (?-)

Carl Dean Herron (?-)

Raymond D. Herron (?-)

Violet Mae Herron (?-)

Harvey Lee Herron (?-)

Mary Lou Herron (?-)

Jerry Don Herron (?-)

George Edward Herron (?-)

The children of Carlos Mentril Hall and Winnifred Lorena Rogers:

Virginia June Hall (1936-1945)

Virginia June. the daughter of Carlos Mentril Hall and Winnifred Lorena Rogers and the granddaughter of Thomas Cleveland Hall and Margie Rena Roberts, was born October 11, 1917, in Spur, Dickens County, Texas, and died July 11, 1945, in Durango, La Plata County, Colorado.

Theodore Carlos Hall (1937-1962)

Theodore was born April 7, 1937, in Dove Creek, Dolores County, Colorado, and died November 13, 1962, in Monticello, San Juan County, Utah. He married Beverly Daniels, and they had two children:
Wendy Lee Hall (1960-)
Thea Joy Hall (1961-)

Roger Evan Hall (1939-)

Roger was born December 12, 1939, in Dove Creek, Dolores County, Colorado; and in 1962 he married Sharon Lynn Holland. They had two children:
Jeffrey Evan Hall, Jr. (1967-)
David Theodore Hall (1970-)

Janette Arlene Hall (1941-)

Janette was born Decembeer 12, 1941, in San Francisco, California. She married John Knuckles April 6, 1963, and they had two children:
Valorie June Knuckles (1964-)

John Roger Knuckles 1968-)

Marjorie Evelyn Hall (1943-)

Marjorie was born June 14, 1943, in San Francisco, California. She married Floyd Johnson, who was born in Grants, New Mexico, in 1961, and they had two children:
William Troy Johnson (?)
Raymond Kent Johnson (?)

Barbara Joy Hall (1945-)

Barbara was born February 20, 1945, in Albuquerque, Bernalillo County, New Mexico. On September 21, 1963, she married Charles Bradley Pearson, who was born May 4, 1964, in Mancos, Montezuma County, Colorado. His parents were R. L. Pearson and Ruth Stephenson. They had five children:

Pamela Ann Pearson (1964-)
Lorena Ruth Pearson (1966-)
Charles Bradley Pearson, Jr. (1969-)
Rena Lyn Pearson (1970-)
Tricia Danette Pearson (1971-)

Winnifred Eileen Hall (1946-)

Winnifred was born November 17, 1946, in Moab, Grand County, Utah; and she married Danny Anderson, who was born June 10 (?). They had two children:
Danny Carlos Anderson (1967-)
Steven Terry Anderson (1969-)

Marilyn Kaye Hall (1949-)

Marilyn was born June 7, 1949, in Monticello, San Juan County, Utah. She married Dennis Hendric and they had two children:
Austen Reed Hendric (1979-)
Arin Hendric (1981-)

The children of Therman Clement Hall and Mary Virginia Rogers:

Allie Jane Hall (?)

Richard Wayne Hall (?)

Robert Lynn Hall (?)

The children of Victor Leon Hall and Phyllis Maurine Rice:

Steven Blane Hall (1954-)

Steven was born May 21, 1954, in Denver, Denver County, Colorado. He married Connie Corrine Taylor on September 12, 1975.

Vickie Lynn Hall (1956-)

Vickie was born April 18, 1956, in Denver, Arapahoe County, Colorado. She married Robert Eugene Cooke on November 20, 1976.

Timothy Wayne Hall (1959-)

Timothy was born January 6, 1959, in Albuquerque, Bernallio County, New
Mexico. He married (1) Lori Ann Turner, (2) Janet Gardner, and (3) Delilah (De-De) Shelley. The last wedding took place on August 16, 1997.

Derek Duane Hall (1968-)

Derek was born February 14, 1968, in Moab, Grand County, Utah. On May 16, 1993, he married Kim Denise Weiler of Inglewood, Los Angeles County, California. She was born March 1, 1970.

The children of Christopher David Swafford and Edna Marie Pettit:

Billie Ann Swafford (1953-)

Billie was born June 17, 1953, in Nowata, Oklahoma. She married a man named Minugh. She now lives in Springdale, Arkansas, and works on the family tree. She is the granddaughter of Annie Dona (Hall) and J. W.

Swafford, and the great-granddaughter of Archie Brooklyn Hall and Nancy Caroline McDougal.

Shirley Flo Swafford (1955-)

Shirley was born April 8, 1955, in Nowata, Oklahoma, where she lives today.

Judy Aline Swafford (1957-)

Judy was born March 2, 1957, in Nowata, Oklahoma, and she lives in Birmingham, Alabama.

The children of Oliver Newton Hall and Lucille Cochran:

Carol Ann Kelly (1943-)

Carol was born March 8, 1943. She was Lucille's daughter by a previous marriage.

Marion Jeanette Hall (1947-)

Marion was born November 17, 1947, in Globe, Arizona. She is the granddaughter of Jessie Newton and Dora Belle (Lawton) Hall, and the great-granddaughter of Archie Brooklyn Hall and Nancy Caroline McDougal.

Saudonna Lea Hall (1951-)

Saudonna was born February 3, 1951, in La Mesa, California. She has had two husbands: Michael Gene Dodgin and James Dean Donato.

Wendell Ralph Hall (1954-)

Wendell was born November 22, 1954.

The children of Jessie Mae Hall and Kenneth E. Holinsworth:

Michael Eugene Holinsworth (1949-1997)

Mike was the grandson of Jessie Newton Hall and Dora Belle Lawson, and the great-grandson of Archie Brooklyn Hall and Nancy Caroline McDougal. He was born in Twin Falls, Idaho, on January 29, 1949, and died of *chronic myeloenous leukemia* on January 9, 1997. He married four times, and his wives' names were Cindy Springer, Sandy Robards, Margret Morton, and Lauara Leann Stewart. According to his mother he is in construction, a trade he learned from father. He built a lot of the Pizza Huts and chilli restaurants across the southwest. He was also a rodeo rider. In fact, he was the Number Six overall Cowboy in California for a few years.

Danny Ray Holinsworth (1950-)

Danny was born in San Diego, California, on September 28, 1950. He is an electrician and lives in California. According to his mother he is a Ventilator Quad, whatever that is. He married Judith Kennedy and has a son. John Holinsworth (?-)

Valerie Ann Holinsworth (1952-)

Valerie was born in Lancaster, California, on June 10, 1952. She has been employed with Motorola for twenty-eight years and is in management, which she enjoys a great deal. She married (1) Mark Fenton Jones and, at another time, (2) Richard S. Priola. One of the marriages took place in Reno, Nevada, in 1973; and one of the divorces took place in San Jose, California, in 1975. She lives in Phoenix, Arizona, and has one daughter.

Michelle Hollinsworth (?-)

Rodney Lee Holinsworth (1956-1978)

Rodney was born July 4, 1956, in Pomona, California, and died June 2, 1978, in Iona, California. He was married to a Mexican girl named Irma (surname unavailable), and he was killed by a Mexican gang for marrying her. He had been warned not to marry her, and after one week of marriage he was killed.

The children of Gladys Marie (Hall) and Vinnis Bervine:

Nancy Olene Phillips (?-)

Nancy and her brothers and sisters are the grandchildren of Carl (Bud) Tyre Hall, and the great-grandchildren of Archie Brooklyn Hall and Nancy Caroline McDougal.

Frankie Lee Phillips (?-)

Shirley Delores Phillips (?-)

Peggy Joyce Phillips (?-)

Richard Dwayne Phillips (?-)

Vinnis Leon Phillips, Jr. (?-)

Dianna Gail Phillips (?-)

Debra Marie Phillips (?-)

Kenneth Lee Phillips (?-)

Candy Phillips (?-)

The children of Iva Loreen Hall and Charles Edward Smith, Sr.:

Charles Henry Smith, Jr. (?-)

Charles is grandson of Carl (Bud) Hall and Carrie Taylor, and the great-grandson of Archie Brooklyn Hall and Nancy Caroline McDougal.

The children of Sadie Lee (Hall) and Calvin Rock, Sr.:

Ervin Lee Rock (?-)

Ervin and is brothers and sisters are the grandchildren of Carl (Bud) Hall and Carrie Taylor and the great-grandchildren of Archie Brooklyn Hall and Nancy Caroline McDougal.

Calvin Ray Rock, Jr. (?-)

Janis Kaye Rock (?-)

Robbie Dale Rock (?-)

Janie Faye Rock (?-)

The children of James Oliver Hall and Leola Ezell:
Judy Gail Hall (1949-)

Judy Gail Hall and her sister and brothers are the grandchildren of Carl (Bud) Hall and the great-grandchildren of Archie Brooklyn Hall. She was born March 13, 1949, in Porum, Muskogee County, Oklahoma. She married Michael Merrill Lloyd on August 30, 1974, in Salt Lake City. Michael was born October 16, 1951. He is the son of John Clifton Lloyd and Ramona Woolley, of Salt Lake City. Judy and Michael have four children.

Gwendolyn Lloyd (1975-)
Carrie Anne Lloyd (1977-)
Rachel Leona Lloyd (1979-)
Brett Lloyd (?-)

James Larry Hall (1951-)

James Larry was born March 28, 1951, in Fallbrook, San Diego County, California. He married Paula Jean Parfumorse on April 4, 1972, in Escondido, San Diego County, California. Paula was born June 20, 1954, and died in July, 1989, in Boston, Massachusetts. She is buried in Richmond, Sagadahoc County, Maine. They had a daughter, Melanie Ann Hall, then divorced in 1973 and James Larry later married Janet Louise Andrew (January 30, 1976) in Tulsa, Oklahoma. Paula married Danny Livesay after she and Larry split up. In 1989, Livesay adopted Melanie Ann Hall.

Melanie Ann Hall (?-)

Kathy Ann Hall (1952-)

Kathy Ann was born August 2, 1952, in Fallbrook, San Diego County, California. She married (1) Johnnie Lee Duke on May 2, 1970, in Porum, Muskogee County, Oklahoma; (2) Michael McCormick on March 19, 1973; (3) David Bruce Wright, of Broken Arrow, Oklahoma, on October 3, 1975. David Bruce brought to the family from another marriage two children: Steven Bruce Wright, who was born August 16, 1966, in L. A., California, and William Floyd Wright, who was born July 11, 1967, in Los Angeles, California. [This last according to Kenneth R. Lawrence.] Kathy and Bruce had two children of their own, born in the 'Seventies.

Steven Bruce Wright (1966-)
William Floyd Wright (1967-)
Angela Michelle Wright (1973-)
Robert Daryl Wright (1976-)

Mark Stephen Hall (1953-)

Mark was born October 5, 1953, in Fallbrook, San Diego County, California. He married Robin Hirschi on December 30, 1980, in Idaho Falls, Idaho. Robin was born June 27, 1954, in Rexburg, Idaho. They have two children.

Marcus Oliver Hall (1985-)
Greta June Hall (1992-)

David Lee Hall (1959-)

David was born October 18, 1959, in Escondido, San Diego County, California. He married Paula Kay Eakin on July 25, 1980, in Broken Arrow, Tulsa County, Oklahoma. They have two children.

Corey Douglas Hall (?-)
Amber Brooke Hall (?-)

The children of Tyre Roland Hall and Ruby Benton:

Anna Mae Hall (?-)

Anna Mae and her sisters and brother are the grandchildren of Carl (Bud) Hall and Carrie Taylor, and the great-grandchildren of Archie Brooklyn Hall and Nancy Caroline McDougal.

Debra Sue Hall (?-)

Lillian Lou Hall (?-)

Bessie Jean Hall (?-)

Maye Belle Hall (?-)

Jackie Lee Hall (?-)

The children of James Benjamin and Opal M. (Whinery) Gragg:

Lois Marie Gragg (1957-)

Lois and her sisters and brother are the grandchildren of Pearl Ellen (Hall) and James Olin Gragg, and the great-grandchildren of Archie Brooklyn Hall. She was born November 5, 1957.

Annette Lynn Gragg (1959-)

Annette was born May 16, 1959.

Diana Dee Gragg (1962-)\
Diana was born April 12, 1962.

Donald Ray Gragg 1964-)

Donald was born March 10, 1964.

The children of Mabel Gragg and Billy Hales:

Utah Hales (?-)

Utah Hales is the grandson of Birtha (Hall) and Ed Gragg and the great-grandson of Archie Brooklyn and Nancy Caroline (McDougal). He married Sandy (surname not available) and they had one child:
Billy Hales Jr. (?-)

The children of Nelson Lee Gragg, Sr. (1940-), and Marion Bacon:

Nelson Lee Gragg, Jr. (1960-)

Nelson Lee, Jr., and his brother and sisters are the grandchildren of Birtha (Hall) and Ed Gragg and the great-grandchildren of Archie Brooklyn and Nancy Caroline (McDougal) Hall. He was born January 24, 1960, in Phoenix, Arizona. On December 20, 1980, he married Wendi Leigh Noland in Mt. Angel, Oregon. She was born August 16, 1961. Nelson grew up with his father on a farm near El Mirage (the area where Birtha (Hall) and Ed Gragg moved to in the 1940's). They now live in Emmitt, Idaho, where Nelson Jr. has a small construction company. They have five children:
Gideon Gragg (1982-)
Seth Gragg (1983-)

Amanda Gragg (1987-)
Jesse Paul Gragg (1988-)
Caleb Gragg (1991-)

Brian Lynn Gragg (1961-)

Brian was born February 4, 1961, in Phoenix, Arizona. He married Cindy Grantham and they have three children and live in Buckeye, Arizona.

Aaron Gragg (?-)
Evan Gragg (?-)
Cathrine Gragg (?-)

Andrea Marion Gragg (1963-)

Andrea was born January 26, 1963, in Phoenix, Arizona. She married a man named Schocher (first name not available) and they have three children and live in Salem, Oregon.

Tyler Gragg (?-)
Tiffany Gragg (?-)
Brodie Gragg (?-)

Rose Michelle Gragg (?-)

The children of Durward Jack Hall and Sarah Gladys Slentz:

Larry Wayne Hall (1955-)

Larry and his sister Tracy are the grandchildren of Earl and Stella Hall and the great-grandchildren of Dock Walter Hall and Kate Elsey. He was born August 27, 1955, and on August 27, 1974, he married Christie

Mason in Edmond, Oklahoma County, Oklahoma. Christie was born December 9, 1956, in Blackwell, Kay County, Oklahoma. They had three children.

Justin Wayne Hall (1975-)
Bryan David Hall (1979-)
Matthew Reid Hall (1981-)

Tracy Kay Hall (1957-)

Tracy was born March 12, 1957. She married Chuck Hoenshell, and they have two children.

Kari Dawn Hoenshell (1980-)
Eric Ryan Hoenshell (1983-)

The children of Val Gene Hall and Louise Elms:

Phyllis Jean Hall (1950-)

Phyllis was born May 30, 1950, in Dinuba, Tulare County, California. She and her brother Ronald are the grandchildren of Earl and Stella Hall and the great-grandchildren of Dock Walter and Kate (Elsey) Hall. She married Milton Kenneth Hendrickson on August 21, 1971, in Madera, California. They had one child, who died in April, 1996.

Robert Earl Hendrickson (1978-1996)

Ronald Hall (1951-)

Ronald was born August 23, 1951. He married Dahlia Josephina Ortiz, who was born May 4, 1954. They had one child. They divorced in late

1990, and he married Elizabeth Melindez Espinoza, born June 26, 1956. There were no children by this marriage.

Aaron Lee Hall (1982-)

The children of Velta Lee Hall and Mike Domyan:

Nathan Domyan (1958-)

Nathan was born October 21, 1958. He is the grandson of Earl and Stella Hall and the great-grandson of Dock Walter and Kate (Elsey) Hall.

The children of Bob Hall and Anita Marquez:

Robert James Hall (1956-1956)

Robert was born April 6, 1956, in California, and died June 24, 1956, in California.

Debra Ann Hall (1957-)

Debbie was born April 27, 1957. She and her sisters are the grandchildren of Earl and Stella Hall and the great-grandchildren of Dock Walter Hall and Kate Elsey. She married David Robert Nelson, who was born October 15, 1954. They had two children and divorced in 1985. Her second husband, Robert Eugene Stafford, whom she married in 1991, was born December 28, 1948. There were no children by the second marriage.

Lee David Nelson (1980-)

Donny Ray Nelson (1982-)

Dianna Lynn Hall (1958-)

Dianna was born June 27, 1958. She married Jay Dee Liles, who was born February 2, 1957). They had two children.
Jason Dee Liles (1978-)
Amy Christine Liles (1981-)

Denise Marie Hall (1962-)

Denise was born August 27, 1962. She married Donald Michael Smith in 1984. He was born August 10, 1956. They had three children:
Nicole Marie Smith (1985-)
Kathrine Ray Smith (1987-)
Daniel Miles Smith (1988-)

The children of Barbara Louise Hall and William Charles Helton:

William Charles Helton (1960-)

William is the grandson of Earl and Stella Hall, and the great-grandson of Dock Walter and Kate (Elsey) Hall. He was born August 26, 1960.

The children of Joyce Oteka (Hall) and Edward S. Browne:

Rochelle Candine Browne (1961-)

Rochelle Candine is the granddaughter of Earl and Stella Hall, and the great-granddaughter of Dock Walter and Kate (Elsey) Hall. She was born

June 15, 1961. She had a son on December 31, 1963. (Father's name unavailable)
Lindsay Edward Hall Browne (1963-)

The children of Alton Lee Hall and Jeanetta Ramsey:

Ginger Kaye Hall (1949-)

Ginger Kaye is the granddaughter of Ezra and Florence Hall, and the great-granddaughter of Greel and Mallie Hall. She was born in Oklahoma City, Oklahoma, on June 24, 1949. She married David Landers, who was born in Houston, Harris County, Texas, on April 21, 1945. They had a daughter. Ginger divorced Landers and later married Gary Ramsey, who was born June 4, 1947, in Lindsay, Garvin County, Oklahoma. By him she has had two children. They now live in the former home of Florence and Ezra Hall at 711 E. Main, Duncan, Oklahoma 73533.
Lavina Ruth Landers (1963-)
Marcella Diane Ramsey (?-)
Tina Lynn Ramsey (1970-)

The children of Dorotha Faye Hall and Mack Schornick:

Terrye Lee Schornick (1951-)

Terrye is the granddaughter of Ezra and Florence Hall, and the great-granddaughter of Greel and Mallie Hall. She was born in Duncan, Stephens County, Oklahoma, on September 25, 1951. She married Neil Hugentober. They are now divorced and Terrye lives in Indiana, working in Home Health Care.

Mickey Joe Schornick (1957-)

Mickey was born in Duncan, Oklahoma, on January 9, 1957. He married Cynthia (Cindy) Sue Coder on April 16, 1985, in Wichita Falls, Wichita County, Texas. Cindy was born September 11, 1959, in Comanche, Stephens County, Oklahoma. She is the daughter of Richard Lee Coder and Joan Cunningham. Mickey and Cindy now live in Duncan, Oklahoma. They have two children.

Sarah Schornick (?-)
Katelyn JoAnn Schornick (1988-)

The children of Faye Goff and Steve Kandarian:

Katherine Louise Kandarian (1944-)

Kathy is granddaughter of Gradie (Hall) and Arthur Lee Goff, and the great-granddaughter of Mallie and Greel Hall. She was born November 6, 1944, in Fresno, California. She married Steve Diebert, of Fresno, California. They have two daughters.

Stephanie Leann Diebert (1971-)
Melissa Ann Diebert (1975-)

Patricia Ann Kandarian (1946-)

Patricia was born August 28, 1946, in Fresno, California. She married Richard Lehman. They divorced.

The children of June Goff and Joe Lamanuzzi:

Joseph Arthur Lamanuzzi (1953-)

Joey was born on the Travis Air Force Base, in California, on December 12, 1953. He and his sister, Linda, are the grandchildren of Gradie Hall and Arthur Lee Goff and the great-grandchildren of Mallie and Greel Hall.

Linda Faye Lamanuzzi (1955-)

Linda was born in Fresno, California, on December 7, 1955. She married John Rice in 1989 and divorced him in 1996. She goes by the name *Miss Linda Lamanuzzi.*

The children of Annie Jo Goff and Angelo Papagni:

Sandra Elizabeth Papagni (1953-)

Sandy was born in Fresno, California, on May 27, 1953. She married James Ray on October 9, 1972, and they had two children. James died in May, 1988. She and her sister, Judy, and brother, Carlo, are the grandchildren of Gradie (Hall) and Arthur Lee Goff and the great-grandchildren of Mallie and Greel Hall.
Kristina Ray (1973-)
James Ray, Jr. (1975-)

Judith Ann Papagni (1956-)

Judy was born in Fresno, California, on July 12, 1956. She married John Biggs, who died in 1976. Judy later married Danny Akins, and they have a daughter named Jodi Angela Papagni. She was born May 16, 1991.
Jodi Angela Papagni (1991-)

Carlo Nicholas Papagni (?-)

Nick was born February 12, 1960, in Fresno, California. He married Teri Laplaca in 1991, and they have a daughter, Gianna Maria Papagni, who was born January 4, 1992.

The children of Flora Smith and Jim Putler:

Nancy Kay Putler (1961-)

Nancy was born January 11, 1961, in Yuba City, California. She is the granddaughter of Ollie (Hall) and Lou Smith, and the great-granddaughtrer of Greel and Mallie Hall. She married James Robert Kemp II, who was born in Delvan, Wisconsin, on August 23, 1963. They had two children and then were divorced August 2, 1996.
James Robert Kemp III (1991-)
Patrick Owen Kemp (1993-)

David Allen Putler (1961-1961)

This infant son of Flora (Smith) and Jim Putler died in childbirth.

The children of L. A. Smith and Lucille Cleveland:

Gary Lynn Smith (1949-)

Gary was born in Ada, Oklahoma, on May 20, 1949. He and his brother and sister are the grandchildren of Lou and Ollie (Hall) Smith and the great-grandchildren of Mallie Carr and Greel Hall. He married

Cinderella (Cindy) Meismer, who was born April 11, 1948, and they have two children.

Ries Nathaniel Smith (1978-)
Katy Nina Smith (1979-)

Bridget Evelyn Smith (1953-)

Bridget was born in Oklahoma City, Oklahoma, on September 12, 1953. By Michael Thomas O'Leary she had a daughter, Heather, who recently (2000) married a man named John, in Oklahoma City. By Charles Patrick Antis, whom she married (ca. 1973) she had another daughter, Heather, who has a son (Patrick, b. August 13, 1998). Bridget lives in Portland, Oregon, and turns out the Oregon *Historical Gazette* newsletter and does websites for the deserving.

Heather Marie Smith O'Leary (1971-)
Crystal Katherine Freedom Antis (1975-)

Gregory Paul Smith (1959-)

Greg was born on October 19, 1959, in Oklahoma, City, Oklahoma. On July 18, 1987, he married Pebbles A. McDonald, who was born August 1, 1965, in Oklahoma City, where they are living. They have five children.

Jessica Lynn Smith (1987-)
Geoffrey Paul Smith (1990-)
Megan Elizabeth Smith (1994-)
Catherine Michelle Smith (1996-)
Patricia Lucille Smith (1999-)

The children of Avo Smith and Frank Rincon:

Mark Anthony Rincon (1951-)

Mark was born in Fresno, California, on October 18, 1951. He and his sisters and brother are the grandchildren of Lou and Ollie (Hall) Smith and the great-grandchildren of Mallie Rue Carr and Greel Hall. He married Sherry Rene Hoffman, who was born November 12, 1953. They have two sons.

Trenton Mark Rincon (1977-)
Troy Anthony Rincon (1979-)

Debra Ann Rincon (1953-)

Debi was born in Fresno, California, on March 9, 1953. She married David Scott Beach, who was born May 8, 1953. They have two sons.

Jonathan David Beach (1992-)
Justan Scott Beach (1994-)

Robert Harlan Rincon (1954-)

Harlan was born in Fresno, California, June 9, 1954. He married a woman named Ada Karen Lohne, who was born May 9, 1955. They live in Madera, California, and have two children.

Melissa Anne Rincon (1976-)
Robert Neal Rincon (1978-)

Kelly Maria Rincon (1957-)

Kelly was born in Fresno, California, on February 14, 1957. She married Steven Farrell Brizendine on April 30, 1954. They live in Lodi, California, and have two daughters.

Erica Allison Brizendine (1980-)
Jillian Morgan Brizendine (1983-)

The children of Roy Joe and Alma Smith:

Michael Smith (?-)

Michael and his sisters are the grandchildren of Ollie (Hall) and Lou Smith, and the great-grandchildren of Greel and Mallie Hall.

Donna Smith (?-)

Donna was born in Oklahoma City, Oklahoma. She is married, but the name of the husband is not available. They have two boys and a girl (names unavailable).

Douglas Smith (?-)

Douglas was born in Oklahoma City and he is married, but the name of the wife is unavailable. They had two children, but the names of their children are unavailable.

The children of Clara Potter and Carl Swann:

Steve Nolan Swann (1956-)

Steve was born in Texas on January 4, 1956. He and his brother, Gary, and his sister (Sandra) are the grandchildren of Ruth (Hall) and Ben Potter, and the great-grandchildren of Greel and Mallie Hall. He married Jan Durelle Greenwood, and they live in Catoosa, near Tulsa. At last report, Steve was a State Farm agent and was coaching basketball on the side. Jan was filling in as one of his secretaries. They have two children.

Kristyn Durelle Swann (1981-)

Jessica Leanne Swann (1984-)

Gary Alan Swann (1957-)

Gary was born in Texas on November 1, 1957. He married Becky, last name unavailable. They divorced. Gary works at the Oklahoma City courthouse downtown, three blocks from the federal building that was bombed by terrorists. He has two daughters.
Erika Swann (?-)
Melissa Rae Swann (1982-)

Sandra Gail Swann (1963-)

Sandra was born in Stockton, California, on April 12, 1963. She married Mike Bellamy, who was born in Ft. Worth, Texas, Tarrant County, on May 3, 1956. They live in Arnold, California, but get their mail in Murphy's, California. She was, at last report, a student at the University of the Pacific, working on a master's degree in physical therapy. They have two children.
Erica Nicole Bellamy (1983-)
Brandon Michael Bellamy (1985-)

The children of Mitchel Potter and Martha Ann Hinson:

Joel Austin Potter (1970-)

Joel was born in Stockton, California, on July 8, 1970. He and his brother are the grandchildren of Ruth (Hall) and Ben Potter and the great-grandchildren of Mallie Rue (Carr) and Greeley Teeman (Horace Greel) Hall. He now lives in Denver.

Timothy Mark Potter (1971-)

Mark was born in Idaho on November 30, 1971. He also lives in Denver.

The children of Jean Potter and Jack Finley:

Darcy Marlane Finley (1964-)

Darcy was born in California, on December 16, 1964. She and her sister are the grandchildren of Ruth (Hall) and Ben Potter and the great-grandchildren of Mallie and Greel Hall. She married Danial Jefferson Langston, and they live in Salmon, Idaho. Danny lived in a foster home as a child and didn't have a family. Years later, after he and Darcy were married and had children, his foster parents adopted him and the entire family, giving them their name. She and Danny have three children.
Danita Jasmine Langston (1987-)
David Mitchel Langston (?)
Dillon James Langston (?)

Nia Clarice Finley (1966-)

Nia was born February 4, 1966, in California. She married Phillip (P. J.) Langston, Jr., (Danny Langston's foster brother) on December 24 (year unavailable). They live in Salmon, Idaho, and they have four children.
Renae Charise Langston (?-)
Chistow (Keestow) Langston (?-)
Bowdrie Langston (?-)
Jude Alonzo Langston (1998-)

The children of Shirley (Hall) and William Terrill:

David Philip Terrill (1955-)

Dave and his sisters and brother are the grandchildren of Clifford Hall and Georgia Sage, and the great-grandchildren of Mallie and Greel Hall. He was born in Escalon, San Joaquin County, California, on October 17, 1955. He graduated from California State University, Fresno, in 1978 with a B. S. degree in journalism, and for years he was the Publicity Director of the Fresno District Fair. He married Karen Sue Bonds on October 28, 1984, at Lake Tahoe, Douglas County, Nevada. She was born January 2, 1951, in Oklahoma City, Oklahoma. Her parents are Clifford LeRoy Bonds and Dollie Mae Reed. Formerly, Karen was married to Ron Freitas.

Karen and Dave live in Gold River, California, in the outskirts of Sacramento. Dave designs and maintains web sites for businesses, associations, and non-profit organizations. Karen, at last report, worked for the forestry service as a spokesperson.

Kathleen Marie Terrill (1958-)

Kathleen was born in Escalon, San Joaquin County, California, on August 29, 1958. She married Arnold Ulloa on June 16, 1979, in Riverbank, Stanislaus County, California, and they live in Riverbank, California. The last word was that Kathleen was a loan officer in a Modesto bank, and Arnold was a barber there. They have three children.

Jacquelyn Renee Ulloa (1982-)
Audrey Lynn Ulloa (1985-)
Olivia Ulloa (1988-)

Merry Susan Terrill (1960-)

Merry was born in Escalon, California, on March 4, 1960. She married Francis (Frank) Rock on September 4, 1982, in Modesto, Stanislaus County, California, and they live in Modesto, California.

Cara Lee Terrill (1962-)

Cara was born in Escalon, San Joaquin County, California, on May 25, 1962, graduated from Modesto Junior College, married Les Burns, and they had two children before divorcing. She married Perry Vierra on December 23, 1992, at Lake Tahoe, Douglas County, Nevada. The last news from her was that she was a single parent living with her son Kyle and daughter Elise in Waterford, California, and working for a cellular service provider.

Kyle Burns (1983-)

Elise Burns (1987-)

Mark Allen Terrill (1964-)

Mark was born in Modesto, Stanislaus County, California, on January 11, 1964. He married Gerilyn Silva and they live in Gustine, California. Geri was born October 8, 1964. In the early 'Ninties Mark was working in the security field (home and auto), and Geri was working for the family support division of Stanislaus County as a temp.

The children of Mary Jo Hall and John Richard Sheppard, Sr.:

John Richard Sheppard, Jr. (1957-)

John Richard was born in Merced, Merced County, California, on July 17, 1957. He is the grandson of Clifford and Georgia (Sage) Hall, and the great-grandson of Mallie and Greel Hall. On June 1, 1985, he married Theresa Kathleen Parker in Oakdale, Stanislaus County, California.

The children of Nancy Hall and Jesse Kilborn Holmes, Sr.:

Jesse Kilborn Holmes, Jr. (1965-)

Jesse was born in Modesto, Stanislaus County, California, on June 18, 1965. He and his sisters are the grandchildren of Bill and Shirley Terrill and the great-grandchildren of Mallie and Greel Hall.

Michelle Holmes (?-)

Michelle was born in Modesto, California.

Kimberly Holmes (?-)

Kimberly was also born in Modesto, California.

The children of Myrna Barnard and Anthony Ceccarelli:

Adam Rocco Ceccarelli (1961-)

Adam was born in Fresno, California, on September 1, 1961. He and his brother and sister are the grandchildren of Delsie Dale (Hall) and William (Lucy) Bernard, and the great-grandchildren of Greel and Mallie

Hall. In 1997 he married Mary Louise Dewitt, who was born September 3, 1963. They divorced in 1998.

Matthew Christopher Ceccarelli (1962-)

Matthew was born in Fresno, California, on December 20, 1962. By Pam Fitzpatric, a friend, he had one child in 1984. He married Lisa Barkley, who was born June 29, 1964, in Sanger, California., and they had one child.

Shannon Fitzpatric Ceccarelli (1984-)
Alissa Ceccarelli (1986-)

Michael John Ceccarelli (1967-1988)

Michael, the first of twins, was born in Fresno, California, on March 13, 1967. He died on June 16, 1988. By Lee Ann Turner he had a child.

(?) Ceccarelli (1988-)

Anna Rue Ceccarelli (1967-)

Anna was also born on March 13, 1967, in Fresno, California, where she lives.

The children of Sylvia Bernard and Neil Allen Williams:

Richard Allen Williams (1957-)

Richard was born February 17, 1957, in Fresno, California. He is the grandson of Delsie Dale (Hall) and Clifford (Lucy) Bernard, and the great-grandson of Greel and Mallie Hall. He and his sister, Cheryle, and his brother, Jack Wesley, were adopted by Jerry Cole, their mother's second husband.

Cheryle Ann Williams (1958-)

Cheryl was born July 12, 1958, in Fresno, California. She married Tom Patterson and they had two children. By her second husband, Randal Mello, she had one child.
Amber Patterson (1984-)
Thomas Patterson, Jr. (1986-)

Jack Wesley Williams (1959-1974)

Jack was born May 21, 1959, in Fresno, California; and on July 27, 1974, he was killed while riding his bicycle in front of his home.

The children of Joyce Dean Bernard and Steve Birdman:

Margo Janeen Birdman (1962-)

Janeen and her sister, April, are the daughters of Joyce Bernard and Steve Birdman, the granddaughters of Delsie Dale (Hall) and William Clifford Bernard, and the great-granddaughters of Greel and Mallie Hall. She was born in Fresno, California, on September 13, 1962. She married (1) Steven Boone and (2) Rick Randolph.
Amanda Summer Boone (1980-)
Ashley Dawn Boone (1988-)(?-)
Madison Ariel Boone (1999-)
Jessica Randolph (?-)

The children of Joyce Dean Bernard and David Crockett Robinson:

April Dawn Robinson (1963-)

April was born in Fresno, California, on April 1, 1963. She is the granddaughter of Delsie Dale (Hall) and William Clifford Bernard, and the great-granddaughter of Greel and Mallie Hall. Dave was born in Waeldor, Texas.

The children of Luther Ray and Rebecca (Smith) Hall:

Luther Ray Hall, Jr. (1957-)

Luther Ray, Jr. (Luke Junior) was born in Oklahoma in 1957. He is the grandson of Luther Leonard Hall and Christine Clark, and the great-grandson of Greel and Mallie Hall. When he was about eighteen he chose to legally change his name to Smith. He married Rebecca Smith and they had two girls.
Rosalie Jean Smith (1977-)
Amanda Yvonne Smith (1980-)

Richard Allen (Hall) Smith (1958-)

Richard Allen (Hall) Smith also chose to change his name legally to Smith.

The children of Luther Ray (Luke) Hall and Connie Beth Rorabaugh:

Angela Rae Hall (1966-)

Angie was born on May 23, 1966, married Jose Refuigeo Ramirez Corona Aquilar, who was born July 14, 1968. They have two sons:
John Ross Hall (1991-)
Michael Dewayne Hall (1993-)

Darrin Dewayne Hall (1967-)

Darrin, was born in Perry, Oklahoma, on May 25, 1967, and died in Drumright, Oklahoma, on January 27, 2001 (Cf. *Obituaries*). He graduated from Drumright High School, and at the time his death he was employed as a lineman for ProfLine Cable Company of Tulsa. He married Mary Elizabeth Harmon, of Bristow, Oklahoma, who was born October 4, 1968 and they had two children:
Zachary Thomas Hall (1991-)
Matthew Lucas Hall (1997-)

Debra Dawn Hall (1971-)

Debra Dawn was born July 28, 1971. She married Johnny Dewayne Bell (b. July 26, 1968) about 1990, and they had a daughter before divorcing. Debbie next married Mark Kevin Hockett, who was born July 16, 1962, and they have a baby that was born November 28, 2001.
Lyndsey Renee Bell (1991-)
Darrin James Hockett (2001-)

The children of Karen Hall and R. C. Lawyer:

Terri Jo Lawyer (?-)

Terri Jo is the daughter of Karen (Hall) and R. C. Lawyer and the granddaughter of Zackary Oberon Hall and Edith Coonrod. She was last reported living in or near Ada, Oklahoma.

Michael (Butch) Dewayne Lawyer (?-)

Butch is the son of Karen (Hall) and R. C. Lawyer, who some years ago owned a grocery store near Ada, Oklahoma.

The children of Jim Hall and Trecias Jo (surname not available):

Trecias Hall (?-)

Trecias is the granddaughter of Zack Hall and Edith Coonrod.

The children of Zackary Oberon Hall and Katherine (surname unavailable):

Sydney Lee Hall (1953-)

Sydney, the granddaughter of Mallie Rue (Carr) and Greeley Teeman (Horace Greel) Hall, was born in Burbank, California, on September 20, 1953. Today, she lives in Lufkin, Texas, is married to Ken McKay, an engineer at Lockeed Martin there in Lufkin, and has two daughters. Sydney has worked in a day care center for six of the seven years they have lived in Lufkin. Regina, nineteen, is a student at Angelina Junior College in Lufkin, and Kristel, seventeen, is a senior in high school.
Regina Mckay (1983-)
Kristel Mckay (1984-)

The children of Leslie Jeanne Hall and Alan Harry Brown:

Matthew Alan Brown (1975-)

Matt is the first grandson of the compiler of this family history. His maternal grandmother was Bonita Pursiville. He and his sister, Lauren, are the great-grandchildren of Mallie and Greel Hall. He was born in Springfield, Missouri, on May 3, 1975. After a year in college, Matt took a computer software job in California, where he is presently working steadily up the microchip corporate ladder. Recently, he has moved to the Hollywood area.

Lauren Elizabeth Brown (1977-)

Lauren, the first granddaughter of the compiler of this family history, was born in Springfield, Missouri, on March 23, 1977. She graduated from Southwest Missouri State University, Springfield, in the spring of 2000 and is presently pursuing an acting career in Hollywood, California.

The children of Robert Christopher Hall and Valorie Chase:

Chase Wesley Hall (1989-)

Chase was born in Springfield, Missouri, at 11:56 a.m. on Thursday, March 16, 1989. He is the grandson of Wesley Hall and Bonita Pursiville, the great-grandson of Mallie and Greel Hall, and the great-great-grandson of William Newton and Susan Elizabeth (Woods) Hall. At an early age he and his younger brother were taken to eastern Tennessee by his mother. He has done well in school and has attracted statewide attention with his writing! [This on good authority from his father.]

Tyler Cody Hall (1992-)

Tyler, the second son of Chris Hall and Valorie Chase, was born in Springfield, Missouri, September 16, 1992. While Chase may be the writer in the family, Tyler is the talker.

The children of Holly Denise Hall and Sean FitzPatrick:

Nicholas Michael FitzPatrick (1995-)

Nicholas is the son of Holly (Hall) and Sean FitzPatrick, the grandson of Wesley Hall and Bonita Pursiville, and the great-grandson of Greel and Mallie Hall. He was born in Bolivar, Missouri, on Sunday, November 18, 1995. As this goes to press he and his two brothers are residing with his parents and two younger brothers at Scott Air Force base in Illinois.

Brendan Miles FitzPatrick (1997-)

Brendan was born in Bolivar, Missouri, on Sunday, April 20, 1997. At birth he weighed seven pounds and six ounces, and he was (for a very brief time) twenty-one and one-half inches long.

Patrick Stephen FitzPatrick (1999-)

Patrick was born May 4, 1999, in Miami, Florida. Specifically, in the St. Tropez Apartments in a section of Miami known as Miami Lakes.

The children John Jeffrey Hall and Ronda Grimes:

David Jeffrey Hall (1980-)

David is the son of Jeff Hall and Ronda (Grimes) Muilenburg, the grandson of Wesley Hall and Bonita Pursiville, and the great-grandson of Greel and Mallie Hall. He was born in Chadwick, Missouri, on July 11, 1980. His father died in an automobile accident in 1982, and his mother has since become Mrs. Jim Muilenburg, of Nixa, Missouri. David married Christy Heard, who was born Aug. 9, 1981, in Chadwick, Missouri, where they now live; and on August 19, 2001, around 3 p. m., Christy gave birth to an eight-pound, six-ounce daughter, the delight of their life.
   Courtney Lea Grimes (2001-)

Latisha Marie Hall (1981-)

Tish was born in Chadwick, Missouri, on July 18, 1981, and is now living in an apartment in Nixa, Missouri, and working for Walgreen Drugs as a druggist's assistant. She has recently graduated from Nixa High School.

The children of Kenneth Murl Hall and Rena Irene Walker:

Kathy Irene Hall (1955-)

Kathy is the granddaughter of James Arnold and Bessie (Crumm) Hall and the great-granddaughter of Grant and Vane (Pennington) Hall. She married a man named Burney (first name unavailable) and had two boys.
   Allen Joseph Burney (1976-)
   Aaron Joshua Burney (1979-)

The children of Wanda Hall and William Dale Smith:

Larry Dale Smith (1960-1983)

Larry and his sister Tawnya are the grandchildren of James Arnold Hall and Bessie Crumm and the great-grandchildren of Grant Hall and Sylvania Pennington. (His other sister, Tammy, is deceased.)
Jeremy Don Smith (1978-)
Misty Dawn Smith (1980-)

Tawnya Danita Smith (1961-)

Tawnya has three children by two men, one of whom is James David Daugherty and the other a man named Kelley (first name not available).
James David Daugherty II (1980-)
Andrea Nicole Kelley (1984-)
Bridgett Leann Kelley (1986-)

Tammy Denise Smith (1962-1963)

The children of Raymond Jessie Hyder and (?):

Michael Ray Hyder (1950-)

Mike, the first son of Ray (Jessie) Hyder (mother's name unavailable), and his sister, Pamela, are the grandchildren of Mary Elizabeth (Hall) and Toy Hyder, and the great-grandchildren of Grant and Vane Hall. He was born September 15, 1950, in Tipton, California, and raised by Marti, his father's second wife.

Pamela Elaine Hyder (1953-)

Elaine was born May 26, 1953, in Tipton, California. Marti, her father's second wife, Marti, also raised her.

The children of Raymond Jesse Hyder and Marti (surname unavailable):

David Hyder (1982-)

David is the grandson of Mary Elizabeth (Hall) and Toy Hyder, and the great-grandson of Grant Hall and Sylvania Pennington. He was born September 7, 1982, in Tipton, California.

The children of Robert K. Rainey, Sr., and Marion (surname not available):
Robert K. Rainey, Jr. (?-)

Robert and his sisters, Evelyn and Karen, are the grandchildren of Lucille (Sisemore) and Willie Kendrick Rainey and the great-grandchildren of Delia (Hall) and Logan Sisemore.

Evelyn Rainey (?-)

Karen Rainey (?-)

The children of Tommy Aubrey Rainey and (name of wife unavailable):

Thomas Rainey (1956-1982)

Thomas and his two brothers are the grandchildren of Pat Buena (Sisemore) and Orville Rainey, and the great-grandchildren of Delia (Hall) and Logan Sisemore.

Jack Rainey (?-)

William Rainey (?-)

The children of Jack Ray Rainey and Helen (surname unavailable):

Mitzi Rainey (?-)

Mitzi and her sisters are the grandchildren of Pat Buena (Sisemore) and Orville Rainey, and the great-grandchildren of Delia (Hall) and Logan Sisemore. She has married three times, has a daughter by the third husband (whose name is not available), and they live in Texas.

Sage Rainey (?) (1995-)

Brenda Rainey (?-)

Esta Rainey (?-)

Christine Rainey (?-)

Christine married John (last name unavailable), and they have two boys and a girl and live in Big Bear, California. (names unavailable)

THE EIGHTH GENERATION

The children of Walter James Herron, Jr., and Norma Faye Heaton:

Dennis James Herron (1951-)

Dennis was born January 29, 1951, in Fairfield, Alabama. He and his brother, William, are the grandsons of Walter James and Mintie (Cheatham) Herron, Sr., the great-grandsons of James Thomas Herron and Mintie Cheatham, the great-great-grandsons of Hiram and Martha (Guttery) Herron, and the ggg-grandsons of Arminda Hall and Thomas Herron.

William Allen Herron (1953-)

William was born August 23, 1953, in Gary, Indiana.

The children of Theodore Carlos Hall and Beverly Daniels:

Wendy Lee Hall (1960-)

Wendy was born December 2, 1960, in Monticello, San Juan County, Utah. She and her sister, Joy, are the granddaughters of Carlos Mentril and Winnifred Lorena (Rogers) Hall, and the great-granddaughters of Thomas Cleveland and Margie Rena (Roberts) Hall.

Thea Joy Hall (1961-)

Joy was born October 4, 1961, in Monticello, San Juan County, Utah.

The children of Roger Evan Hall and Sharon Lynn Holland:

Jeffrey Evan Hall (1967-)

Jeffrey was born August 20, 1967, in Moab, Grand County, Utah. He and his brother, David, are the grandchildren of Carlos Mentril and Winnifred Lorena (Rogers) Hall, and the great-grandchildren of Thomas Cleveland and Margie Rena (Roberts) Hall. He

David Theodore Hall (1970-)

David was born in February, 1970.

The children of Janette Arlene Hall)and John Knuckles:

Valorie June Knuckles (1964-)

Valorie was born in July, 1964. She and her brother, John, are the grand children of Carlos Mentril and Winnifred (Rogers) Hall, and the great-grandchildren of Thomas Cleveland and Margie Rena (Roberts) Hall,

John Roger Knuckles (1968-)

Roger was born December 23, 1968.

The children of Marjorie Evelyn Hall and Floyd Johnson:

William Troy Johnson (?)

Troy and his brother, Raymond, are the grandchildren of Carlos Mentril and Winnifred (Rogers) Hall and the great-grandchildren of Thomas Cleveland and Margie Rena (Roberts) Hall.

Raymond Kent Johnson (?)

The children of Barbara Joy Hall and Charles Bradley Pearson:

Pamela Ann Pearson (1964-)

Pam was born May 4, 1964, in Monticello, San Juan County, Utah. She and her sisters and brother are the grandchildren of Carlos Mentril and Winnifred Lorena (Rogers) Hall, and the great-grandchildren of Thomas Cleveland and Margie Rena (Roberts) Hall. On October 8, 1988, she married Jeffrey Royce Hanson at Red House Ranch, Carlin, Elko County, Nevada. They have two children:
Emily Louise Hanson (1991-)
Jared Ryan Hanson (1993-)

Lorena Ruth Pearson (1966-)

Lorena was born October 12, 1966, in Moab, Grand County, Utah. On January 8, 1983, she married Michael Royce Allred in Monticello, San Juan County, Utah. They have two children:
Tana Elaine Allred (1983-)
Kena May Allred (1993-)

Charles Bradley Pearson (1969-)

Charles was born February 18, 1969, in Moab, Grand County, Utah. On May 7,
1990, he married Judy Lynn Housekeeper in Wellington, Carbon County, Utah. They have two children:
Charles Garrett Pearson (1991-)
Paige Kay Pearson (1994-)

Rena Lynn Pearson (1970-)

Rena was born March 25, 1970, in Monticello, San Juan County, Utah. On December 3, 1988, she married Glenn Shane Prestwich, in Monticello, San Juan County, Utah. They have one child:
Kamie Lyn Prestwich (1994-)

Tricia Danette Pearson (1971-)

Tricia was born June 10, 1971, in Monticello, San Juan County, Utah. On May 18, 1991, she married Richard Gregory Van Wagoner, in Cleveland, Emery County, Utah. They have four children.
Lacey Shay Van Wagoner (1992-)
Tia Chantel Van Wagoner (1993-)
Rondee Leah Van Wagoner (1997-)
Shalae Dacy Van Wagoner (2001-)

The children of Winnifred Eileen Hall and Danny Anderson:

Danny Carlos Anderson (1967-)

Danny was born February 2, 1967. He and his brother, Steven, are the grandsons of Carlos Mentril and Winnifred Lorena (Rogers) Hall, and their great-grandparents were Thomas Cleveland and Margie Rena (Roberts) Hall.

Steven Terry Anderson (1969-)

Steven was born February 14, 1969.

The children of Marilyn Kaye Hall and Dennis Hendric:

Austin Reed Hendric (1979-)

Austin was born in 1979. His and his brother Arin's grandparents were Carlos Mentril and Winnifred Lorena (Rogers) Hall, and their great-grandparents were Thomas Cleveland and Margie Rena (Roberts) Hall.

Arin Hendric (1981-)

Arin was born in 1981.

The children of Judy Gail Hall and Michael Merrill Lloyd:

Gwendolyn Lloyd (1975-)

Gwen was born August 1, 1975, in Salt Lake City, Utah. Her and her sisters' and brother's grandparents were James Oliver and Leola (Ezell) Hall, their great-grandparents were Carrie (Taylor) and Carl (Bud) Hall, and their gg-grandparents were Archie Brooklyn and Nancy Caroline (McDougal) Hall. She had a daughter in 1992 by a man named Lopez (first name unavailable).

Celina Renee (Lloyd) Lopez (1992-)

Carrie Anne Lloyd (1977-)

Carrie was born February 6, 1977, in Salt Lake City.

Rachel Leona Lloyd (1979-)

Rachel was born January 4, 1979, in Phoenix, Arizona.

Brett Lloyd (?-)

The children of James Larry Hall and Paula Jean Parfumorse:

Melanie Ann Hall (1973-)

Melanie was born in Escondido, San Diego County, California. After her mother died in 1989 in Boston, she was adopted by her stepfather, Danny Livesay. She is the granddaughter of James Oliver Hall, the great-granddaughter of Carl (Bud) Hall, and the gg-granddaughter of Archie Brooklyn and Nancy Carolyn (McDougal) Hall.

The children of Kathy Ann Hall and David Bruce Wright:

Steven Bruce Wright (1966-)

Steven and his brothers, William Floyd and Robert Daryl, and his sister, Angela Michelle, are the grandchildren of James Oliver Hall and Leola Ezelle, the great-grandchildren of Carl (Bud) Hall and Carrie Taylor, and the great-great-grandchildren of Archie Brooklyn Hall and Nancy Caroline McDougal.

William Floyd Wright (1967-)

Angela Michelle Wright (1973-)

Robert Daryl Wright (1976-)

Robert was born May 21, 1976, in Tulsa, Oklahoma.

The children of Mark Stephen Hall and Robin Hirschi Hall:

Marcus Oliver Hall (1985-)

Marcus and his sister, Greta June, are the grandchildren of James Oliver Hall and Leola Naomi Ezell, the great-grandchildren of Carl (Bud) Hall and Carrie Taylor, and the gg-grandson was Archie Brooklyn Hall and Nancy Caroline McDougal.

Greta June Hall (1992-)

The children of David Lee Hall and Paula Kay Eakin:

Corey Douglas Hall (?-)

Corey was born on May 15 (year unknown). She and her sister, Amber, are the grandchildren of James Oliver Hall and Leola Naomi Ezell, the great-grandchildren of Carl (Bud) Hall and Carrie Taylor, and the great-great-grandchildren of Archie Brooklyn and Nancy Caroline (McDougal) Hall.

Amber Brooke Hall (?-)

The children of Utah Hales and Sandy (surname unavailable):

Billy Hales, Jr. (?-)

Billy is the grandson of Mabel Gragg and Billy Hales, the great-grandson of Birtha Elizabeth Hall and Ed Gragg, and the great-great-grandson of Archie and Nancy Hall.

The children of Nelson Lee Gragg, Jr., and Windi Leigh Noland:

Gideon Gragg (1982-)

Gideon and his brothers and sister are the grandchildren Nelson Lee Gragg, Sr., and Marion Bacon, and the great-grandchildren of Birtha (Hall) and Ed Gragg.

Seth Gragg (1983-)

Amanda Gragg (1987-)

Jesse Paul Gragg (1988-)

Caleb Gragg (1991-)

The children of Brian Lynn Gragg and Cindy Grantham:

Aaron Gragg (?-)

Aaron is the grandson of Nelson Lee Gragg, Sr., and Marion Bacon and the great-grandson of Ed and Birtha (Hall) Gragg. He is married and has one child (name and date of birth unavailable).

The children of Larry Wayne Hall and Christie Mason:

Justin Wayne Hall (1975-)

Justin Wayne was born on March 18, 1975. He and his brothers, Bryan and Matthew, are the grandsons of Durward Jack Hall and Sarah Gladys Slentz and the great-grandsons of Earl and Stella Hall, and the gg-grand-sons of Dock Walter and Kate (Elsey) Hall.

Bryan David Hall (1979-)

Bryan was born May 22, 1979.

Matthew Reid Hall (1981-)

Matthew was born August 8, 1981.

The children of Tracy Kay Hall and Chuck Hoenshell:

Kari Dawn Hoenshell (1980-)

Kari was born August 2, 1980, in Oklahoma City, Oklahoma County, Oklahoma. She and her brother, Eric, are the grandchildren of Jack Hall and Sarah Slentz, the great-grandchildren of Earl Hall and Stella Scoggins, and the great-great-grandchildren of Dock Walter and Kate (Elsey) Hall.

Eric Ryan Hoenshell (1983-)

Eric was born February 17, 1983.

The children of Phyllis Jean Hall and Milton Kenneth Hendrickson:

Robert Earl Hendrickson (1978-)

Robert was born December 20, 1978. He is the grandson of Jack and Sarah Hall, great-grandson of Earl and Stella Hall, and the great-great-grandson of Dock Walter and Kate (Elsey) Hall.

The children of Ronald Hall and Dahlia Josephina Ortiz:

Aaron Lee Hall (1983-)

Aaron Lee was born November 10, 1983, in California. He is the grandson of Val Gene Hall and Louise Elms, the great-grandson of Earl and Stella Hall, and the great-great-grandson of Dock Walter Hall and Kate Elsey.

The children of Debra Ann Hall and David Nelson:

Lee David Nelson (1980-)

Lee was born July 8, 1980. He and his brother, Donny, are the grandsons of Bob Hall and Anita Marquez, the great-grandsons of Earl and Stella Hall, and the great-great-grandsons of Dock Walter Hall and Kate Elsey.

Donny Ray Nelson (1982-)

Donny was born February 11, 1982.

The children of Diana Lynn Hall and Jay Dee Liles:

Jason Dee Liles (1978-)

Jason was born December 16, 1978. He and his sister, Amy, are the grandchildren of Bob Hall and Anita Marquez, the great-grandchildren of Earl and Stella Hall, and the great-great-grandchildren of Dock Walter and Kate Hall.

Amy Christine Liles (1981-)

Amy was born August 15, 1981.

The children of Denise Marie Hall and Donald Michael Smith:

Nicole Marie Smith (1985-)

Nicole was born August 8, 1985. She and her sister, Kathrine, and her brother Daniel, are the grandchildren of Bob Hall and Anita Marquez, the great-grandchildren of Earl and Stella Hall, and the great-great-grandchildren of Dock Walter and Kate Hall.

Kathrine Ray Smith (1987-)

Kathrine was born February 19, 1987.

Daniel Miles Smith (1988-)

Daniel was born April 14, 1988.

The children of Ginger Kaye Hall and David Landers:

Lavina Ruth Landers (1963-)

Lavina was born in Ft. Stockton, Texas, on December 7, 1963. She is the granddaughter of Alton and Jeanetta Hall, the great-granddaughter of Florence and Ezra Hall, and the great-great-granddaughter of Mallie and Greel Hall. She married Ronald Cardona and they have three children. They have recently moved to Duncan, Oklahoma, and are living in the former home of Ezra and Florence Hall, her maternal great-grandparents.
Christopher Lee Cardona (1984-)
Andrew DeWayne Cardona (1987-)

Aaron Raymond Cardona (?-)

The children of Ginger Kaye Hall and Gary Ramsey:

Marcella Diane Ramsey (1968-)

Marcella and her sister, Tina, are the granddaughters of Alton and Jeanetta Hall, the great-granddaughters of Ezra and Florence Hall, and the great-great-granddaughters of Mallie and Greel Hall. She married Randall Jones, who was born in 1947, and they have two daughters.
Brandi Jo Jones (1989-)
Beth Marie Jones (1991-)

Tina Lynn Ramsey (1970-)

Tina has two children (father's name not available).
Justin Davis Ramsey (1988-)
Felisha Marie Diane Ramsey (1990-)

The children of Mickey Schornick and Cynthia Sue Coder::

Sarah Schornick (?-)

Sarah and her sister Katelyn, are the granddaughters of Dorotha Faye Hall and Mack Schornick. Her great-grandparents were Ezra and Florence Hall, of Duncan, Oklahoma; and her great-great-grandparents were Mallie and Greel Hall.

Katelyn JoAnn Schornick (1988-)

JoAnn was born on May 16, 1988, in Duncan, Stephens County, Oklahoma.

The children of Kathy Kandarian and Steven Diebert:

Stephanie Leann Diebert (1971-)

Stephanie was born in Fresno, California, on February 6, 1971. She and her sister Melissa, are the granddaughters of Faye and Steve Kandarian. Her maternal great-grandparents were Gradie (Hall) and Arthur Lee Goff, and her maternal gg-grandparents were Mallie Rue (Carr) and Greeley Teeman (Horace Greel) Hall. She graduated from the University of California at Davis; and, on November 9, 1996, she married Kenneth Jeffrey Price, of Beverly Hills. Ken was born October 2, 1968.

Melissa Ann Diebert (1975-)

Melissa was born in Fresno, California, on July 20, 1975. On July 20, 2001, she married Layne Bartley Lev, who was born August 14, 1973.

The children of Sandra Elizabeth Papagni and James Edward Ray, Jr.:

Kristina Ray (1973-)

Kristina was born in Fresno, California, on April 29, 1973. She and her brother James, are the grandchildren of Annie Jo Goff and Angelo Papagni. Their maternal great-grandparents were Gradie (Hall) and Arthur Goff, and their maternal great-great-grandparents were Mallie and Greel Hall.

James Edward Ray, Jr. (1975-)

James was born in Fresno, California, on September 30, 1975.

The children of Judith Ann Papagni and Danny Akins:

Jodi Angela Papagni (1991-)

Jodi was born May 16, 1991, in Fresno California. He is the grandson of Annie Jo Goff and Angelo Papagni and the great-grandson of Gradie (Hall) and Arthur Lee Goff.

The children of Carlo Papagni and Teri Laplaca:

Gianna Maria Papagni (1992-)

Maria was born in Fresno, California, on January 4, 1992. She is the granddaughter of Annie Jo(Goff and Angelo Papagni and the great-granddaughter of Gradie (Hall) and Arthur Lee Goff.

The children of Nancy Kay Putler and James Robert Kemp II:

James Robert Kemp III (1991-)

James was born on April 8, 1991, in Fremont, California. He and his brother, Patrick, are the grandsons of Flora Smith and James Putler, of Fremont, California. Their maternal great-grandparents were Ollie and Lou Smith, and their maternal great-great-grandparents were Mallie and Greel Hall.

Patrick Owen Kemp (1993-)

Patrick was born in Fremont, California, on October 2, 1993.

The children of Gary Lynn Smith and Cindy Meismer:

Reis Nathaniel Smith (1978-)

Reis was born April 23, 1978, in Oklahoma City. He and his sister Katy, are the grandchildren of L. A. and Lucille Smith, of Oklahoma City, Oklahoma, the great-grandchildren of Ollie and Lou Smith, and the great-great-grandchildren of Mallie and Greel Hall.

Katy Nina Smith (1979-)

Katy was born December 16, 1979, in Oklahoma City.

The children of Bridget Evelyn Smith and Michael Thomas O'Leary:

Heather Marie O'Leary (1971-)

Heather was born in Oklahoma City on January 1, 1971. She is the granddaughter of L. A. and Lucille Smith, of Oklahoma City (Her grandmother, Lucille, died in 2000). Her great-grandparents are Ollie and Lou Smith, and her great-great-grandparents are Mallie and Greel Hall. She recently married a man named John (last name unavailable), of Oklahoma City.

The children of Bridget Evelyn Smith and Charles Patrick Antis:

Crystal Katherine Freedom Antis (1975-)

Crystal was born in Wichita, Kansas, on January 1, 1975 (same day four years after her sister was born), where she is now living. She has a son (father's name not available). She is the granddaughter of L. A. and Lucille (Cleveland) Smith and the gg-granddaughter of Lou and Ollie (Hall) Smith.
Patrick Antis (1998-)

The children of Greg Smith and Pebbles A. McDonald:

Jessica Lynn Smith (1987-)

Jessica was born September 20, 1987, in Oklahoma City. She and her brother and sisters are the grandchildren of L. A. and Lucille Smith, the great-grandchildren of Ollie and Lou Smith, and the great-great-grandchildren of Mallie and Greel Hall.

Geoffrey Smith (1990-)

Geoffrey was born in Oklahoma City on March 20, 1990.

Megan Elizabeth Smith (1994-)

Megan was born in Oklahoma City on March 11, 1994.

Catherine Michelle Smith (1996-)

Catherine was born in Oklahoma City on June 4, 1996.

Patricia Lucille Smith (1999-)

Trisha is the fifth blessing of Pebbles and Gregory Smith, of Oklahoma City. She was born at 12:47 p.m. on May 27, 1999, in Oklahoma City.

The children of Mark Rincon and Sherry Hoffman:

Trenton Mark Rincon (1977-)

Trent was born March 10, 1977, in Fresno, California. He and his brother, Troy, are the grandsons of Avo Smith and Frank Rincon, the great-grandsons of Ollie and Lou Smith, and the great-great-grandsons of Mallie and Greel Hall.

Troy Anthony Rincon (1979-)

Troy was born February 9, 1979, in Fresno, California.

The children of Debra Angelina Rincon and David Scott Beach:

Jonathan David Beach (1992-)

Jonathan was born February 11, 1992, in Fresno, California. He and his brother Justan, are the grandsons of Avo Smith and Frank Rincon, of Cutler, California. Their maternal grandparents are Lou Smith and Ollie Hall, and his maternal great-grandparents were Mallie Rue Carr and Greeley Teeman (Horace Greel) Hall.

Justan Scott Beach (1994-)

Justan was born May 8, 1993, in Fresno, California.

The children of Robert Harlan Rincon and Ada Karen Lohne:

Melissa Anne Rincon (1976-)

Melissa was born October 23, 1976, in Fresno, California. She and her brother, Robert, are the grandchildren of Avo and Frank Rincon, of Fresno, California, and the great-grandchildren of Ollie and Lou Smith. She has attended Fresno City College, working part-time. Her ambition, as a young girl, was to become a fashion designer.

Robert Neal Rincon (1978-)

Robert was born April 6, 1978, in Fresno, California.

The children of Kelly Maria Rincon and Steven Farrell Brizendine:

Erica Allison Brizendine (1980-)

Erica was born was born December 12, 1980, in Fresno, California. She and her sister, Jillian, are the grandchildren of Avo (Smith) and Frank Rincon, of Cutler, California. Her maternal great-grandparents are Ollie and Lou Smith, and her maternal great-great-grandparents are Mallie and Greel Hall.

Jillian Morgan Brizeondine (1983-)

Jillian was born September 18, 1983, in Fresno, California.

The children of Steve Nolan Swann and Jan Durelle Greenwood:

Kristyn Durelle Swann (1981-)

Kristen was born in Oklahoma City, Oklahoma, on October 9, 1981. She and her sister, Jessica, are the granddaughters of Clara Potter and Carl Swann. Her maternal great-grandparents are Ruth (Hall) and Ben Potter, and her maternal great-great-grandparents are Mallie and Greel Hall.

Jessica Leanne Swann (1984-)

Jessica was born in Oklahoma City on September 24, 1984.

The children of Gary Alan Swann and Becky (surname unavailable):

Erika Swann (?-)

Erika and her sister, Melissa, are the granddaughters of Clara Potter and Carl Swann, the great-granddaughter of Ruth (Hall) and Ben Potter, and the great-great-granddaughter of Mallie and Greel Hall. She was born in Oklahoma City.

Melissa Rae Swann (1982-)

Melissa was born in Oklahoma City, Oklahoma, on December 3, 1982.

The children of Sandra Gail(Swann and Mike Bellamy:
Erica Nicole Bellamy (1983-)

Erica was born in Oklahoma City, Oklahoma, on February 9, 1983. She and her brother, Brandon, are the grandchildren of Clara Potter and Carl Swann, the great-granddaughter of Ruth (Hall) and Ben Potter, and the great-great-granddaughter of Mallie and Greel Hall.

Brandon Michael Bellamy (1985-)

Brandon was born in Oklahoma City, Oklahoma, on May 29, 1985.

The children of Darcy Marlane Finley and Danial Jefferson King:

Danita Jasmine King (1987-)

Danita was born March 11, 1987 in Salmon, Idaho. She and her brothers, David and Dillon, are the grandchildren of Jean Potter and Jack Finley, the great-granddaughter of Ruth and Ben Potter, and the great-great-granddaughter of Mallie and Greel Hall.

David Mitchel King (?-)

David was born in Salmon, Idaho, on November 8 (year unavailable).

Dillon James King (?-)

Dillon was born in Salmon, Idaho, in November (year not available).

The children of Nia Clarice Finley and Phillip Langston, Jr.:

Renae Charise Langston (?-)

Renae was born in Salmon, Idaho, on September 19 (year unavailable). She and her siblings are the grandchildren of Jean Potter and Jack Finley, the great-grandchildren of Ruth and Ben Potter, and the great-great-granddaughter of Mallie and Greel Hall.

Chistow Langston (?-)

Chistow (pronounced Kees-tow) was born January 7 (year unavailable)

Bowdrie Langston (?-)

Bowdrie was born in Salmon, Idaho, in August (year unavailable).

Jude Alonzo Langston (1998-)

Jude Alonzo was born April 15, 1998, in Salmon, Idaho, and weighed eight pounds and three ounces.

The children of Kathy Terrill and Arnold Ulloa:

Jacquelyn Renee Ulloa (1982-)

Jacquelyn was born on December 26, 1982, in Modesto, Stanislaus County, California. She and her sisters, Audrey and Olivia, are the grandchildren of Shirley Hall and Bill Terrill, the great-granddaughter of Clifford Hall and Georgia Sage, and the great-great-grandchildren of Mallie and Greel Hall.

Audrey Lynn Ulloa (1985-)

Audrey Lynn was born on April 29, 1985, in Modesto, Stanislaus County, California.

Olivia Ulloa (1988-)

Olivia was born on December 12, 1988, in Modesto, Stanislaus County, California.

The children of Cara Lee Terrill and Les Burns:

Kyle Burns (1983-)

Kyle was born April 29, 1983. He and his sister, Elise, are the grandchildren of Shirley Hall and Bill Terrill, the great-grandchildren of Clifford Hall and Georgia Sage, and the great-great-grandchildrenof Mallie and Greel Hall.

Elise Burns (1987-)

Elise was born August 12, 1987.

The children of Matthew Ceccarelli an Pam Fitzpatric:

Shannon Ceccarelli Fitzpatric (1984-)

Shannon was born on February 1, 1984, in Fresno, California.

The children of Matthew Ceccarelli and Lisa Barkley:

Alissi Ceccarelli (1987-)

Alissa was born December 16, 1986, in Fresno, California. She is the granddaughter of Myrna Bernard and Tony Ceccarelli, of Fresno, California. Her great-grandparents were Delsie Dale Hall and William Clifford Lucy Barnard, and her great-great-grandparents were Mallie and Greel Hall.

The children of Michael John Ceccarelli and Lee Ann Turner:

(?) Ceccarelli (1988-)

This daughter of Michael Ceccarelli's was born January 19, 1988.

The children of Cheryle Ann Williams Cole and Tom Patterson:

Amber Patterson (1984-)

Amber is born February 29, 1984, the granddaughter of Sylvia Ann Bernard and Neil Allen Williams. Her mother was adopted by Jerry Cole, her stepfather, when she was a child. Amber's grandparents were Sylvia Ann Bernard and Neil Allen Williams, and her great-grandparents were William Clifford Bernard and Delsie Dale Hall.

Thomas Patterson (1986-)

Thomas was born August 9, 1986.

The children of Cheryle Ann Williams Cole and Randel Mello:

Randel was born August 25, 1977. He is the grandson of Sylvia Ann Bernard and Neil Allen Williams.

The children of Margo Janeen Birdman and Steven Boone:

Amanda Summer Boone (1980-)

Amanda was born August 17, 1980, in Fresno, California. She and her sisters, Ashley and Ariel, are the granddaughters of Joyce Dean Bernard and Steve Manning Birdman and the great-granddaughters of Delsie and Lucy Bernard, of Fresno, California. Their great-great-grandparents were Mallie and Greel Hall.

Ashley Dawn Boone (1988-)

Ashley was born April 29, 1988, in Fresno, California.

Madison Ariel Boone (1999-)

Ariel was born February 28, 1999.

The children of Margo Janeen Birdman and Rick Randolph:

Jessica Randolph (?-)

The children of Luther Ray (Luke) Hall, Jr., and Rebecca Smith:

Amanda Yvonne Smith (Hall) (1980-)

Amanda is the granddaughter of Luther Ray Hall and Norma Jean Maddy, the great-granddaughter of Luther Leonard Hall and Christine Clark, and the great-great-granddaughter of Mallie and Greel Hall. She has one son (father's name unavailable).

Zackary Tyler Smith (1998-)

The children of Angela Rae Hall and Jose Refuigeo Ramarez Corona Aquilar:

John Ross Hall (1991-)

John Ross and his brother, Michael, are the grandsons of Luther Ray Hall and Connie Rorabaugh, the great-grandsons of Luther Hall and Christine Clark, and the great-great-grandsons of Mallie and Greel Hall.

Michael DeWayne Hall (1993-)

The children of David Grimes and Christy Heard:

Courtney Lea Grimes (2001-)

Courtney was born in St. John's Hospital, Springfield, Missouri, about 3 p. m., August 19, 2001. She is the first grandchild of Jeff Hall and Ronda (Grimes) Muilenburg, and the first great-grandchild of Wesley and Bonita (Pursiville) Hall. On her paternal side, she descends from Mallie Rue Carr and Greeley Teeman (Horace Greel) Hall and William Newton Hall and Susan Elizabeth Woods. Her parents currently live in Chadwick, Missouri.

THE NINTH GENERATION

The children of Pamela Ann Pearson and Jeffery Royce Hanson:

Emily Louise Hanson (1991-)

Emily was born July 11, 1991, in Elko, Elko County, Nevada. She and her brother descend from the John and Nancy (Hamilton) Hall branch of the family. They are the grandchildren of Barbara Joy (Hall) and Charles Bradley Pearson.

Jared Ryan Hanson (1993-)

Jared was born April 24, 1993, in Elko, Elko County, Nevada.

The children of Lorena Ruth Pearson and Michael Royce Allred:

Tana Elaine Allred (1983-)

Tana was born June 20, 1883, in Price, Carbon County, Utah. She and her sister Kena, are the grandchildren of Barbara Joy (Hall) and Charles Bradley Pearson. Their great-grandparents were John Hall (1824-1898) and Nancy Hamilton (1828-1914), and their gg-grandparents were Hiram and Charity Hall, of Haralson County, Georgia.

Kena May Allred (1993-)

Kena was born May 25, 1993, in Price, Carbon County, Utah.

The children of Charles Bradley Pearson and Judy Lynn Housekeeper:

Charles Garrett Pearson (1991-)

Charles was born April 13, 1991, in Price, Carbon County, Utah. He and his sister, Paige, are the grandchildren of Barbara Joy (Hall) and Charles Bradley Pearson. Their great-grandparents were John Hall and Nancy Hamilton.

Paige Kay Pearson (1994-)

Paige was born May 10, 1994, in Provo, Utah County, Utah.

The children of Rena Lyn Pearson and Glenn Shane Prestwich:

Kamie Lyn Prestwich 1994-)

Kamie was born June 10, 1994, in Provo, Utah County, Utah. She is the granddaughter of Barbara Joy (Hall) and Charles Bradley Pearson. Her great-grandparents were John Hall and Nancy Hamilton.

The children of Tricia Danette Pearson and Richard Gregory Van Wagoner:

Lacey Shay Van Wagoner (1992-)

Lacey was born February 2, 1992, in Price, Carbon County, Utah. She and her sisters are the granddaughters of Barbara Joy (Hall) and Charles Bradley Pearson. Their great-grandparents were John Hall and Nancy Hamilton.

Tia Chantel Van Wagoner 1993-)

Tia was born November 18, 1993, in Price, Carbon County, Utah.

Rondee Leah Van Wagoner (1997-)

Rondee was born August 22, 1997, in Price, Carbon County, Utah.

Shalae Dacy Van Wagoner (2001-)

Shalae was born August 30, 2001, in Price, Carbon County, Utah.

The children of Gwenolyn Lloyd and Lopez (first name unavailable):

Celina Renee Lopez (1992-)

Celina is the granddaughter of Judy Gail Hall and Michael M. Lloyd, the great-granddaughter of James Oliver Hall and Leola Naomi Ezelle, the great-great-granddaughter of Carl (Bud) Hall and Carrie Melissa Taylor, and the great-great-great-granddaughter of Archie Brooklyn Hall and Carolyn McDougal.

The children of Lavina Ruth Landers and Ronald Cardona:

Christopher Lee Cardona (1984-)

Christopher Lee and his brothers are the grandsons of Ginger Kaye Hall and David Landers, the great-grandsons of Alton and Jeanetta Hall, the great-great-grandsons of Ezra and Florence Hall, and the great-great-great-grandsons of Mallie and Greel Hall. His family is living in Duncan, Oklahoma.

Andrew Dewayne Cardona (1987-)

Andrew is a twin.

Aaron Raymond Cardona (1987-)

Aaron turned out to be Andrew's twin.

The children of Marcella Diane Ramsey and Randall Jones:

Brandi Jo Jones (1989-)

Brandi and her sister, Beth, are the granddaughters of Ginger Kaye Hall and Gary Ramsey, the great-granddaughters of Alton and Jeanetta Hall, the great-great-grand-daughters of Ezra and Florence Hall, and the great-great-great-grand-daughters of Mallie and Greel Hall.

Beth Marie Jones (1991-)

The children of Tina Lynn Ramsey (name of husband unavailable):

Justin Davis Ramsey (1988-)

Justin and his sister, Felisha, are the grandchildren of Ginger Kaye Hall and Gary Ramsey, the great-grandchildren of Alton and Jeanetta Hall, the great-great-grandchildren of Ezra and Florence Hall, and the great-great-great-grandchildren of Mallie and Greel Hall.

Felisha Marie Diane Ramsey (1990-)

The children of Amanda Yvonne Hall (name of father unavailable):

Zackary Taylor Smith (Hall) (1998-)

Zackary Taylor was born December 20, 1998. He is the grandson of Darrin Dewayne Hall and Mary Elizabeth Harmon Hall, the great-grandson of Luther Ray (Luke) Smith and Connie Rorabough, the great great-grandson of Luther Leonard Hall and Christine Clark, and the great-great-great-grandson of Mallie and Greel Hall.

THE FIRST FAMILIES

Arminda (Hall) and Thomas Herron

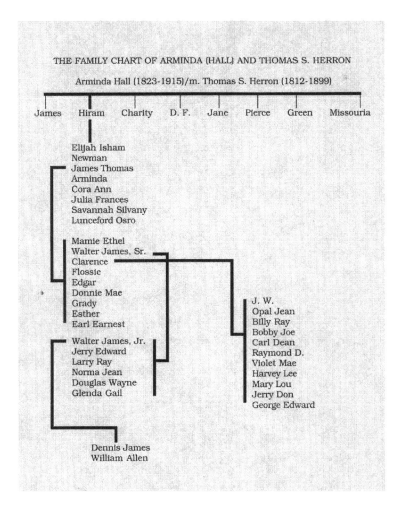

THE FAMILY CHART OF ARMINDA (HALL) AND THOMAS S. HERRON

Arminda Hall (1823-1915)/m. Thomas S. Herron (1812-1899)

James   Hiram   Charity   D. F.   Jane   Pierce   Green   Missouria

Elijah Isham
Newman
James Thomas
Arminda
Cora Ann
Julia Frances
Savannah Silvany
Lunceford Osro

Mamie Ethel
Walter James, Sr.
Clarence
Flossie
Edgar
Donnie Mae
Grady
Esther
Earl Earnest

Walter James, Jr.
Jerry Edward
Larry Ray
Norma Jean
Douglas Wayne
Glenda Gail

J. W.
Opal Jean
Billy Ray
Bobby Joe
Carl Dean
Raymond D.
Violet Mae
Harvey Lee
Mary Lou
Jerry Don
George Edward

Dennis James
William Allen

3.1 Arminda Hall (1823-1915) and Thomas S. Herron (1812-1899)

    4.1 James Herron (1848-1935)

    4.2 Hiram Herron (1850-1909) + Martha Guttery (?-?)

        5.1 Elijah Isham Herron (1873-1875)

        5.2 Newman Herron (1876-1893)

        5.3 James Thomas Herron (1879-1966) + Mintie Cheatham (?-)

            6.1 Mamie Ethel Herron (1900-1972)

            6.2 Walter James Herron Sr. (1902-1970) + Ceatrice Jenkins (?-)

                7.1 Walter James Herron, Jr. (1929-)

                    8.1 Dennis James Herron (1951-)

                    8.1 William Allen Herron (1953-)

                7.2 Jerry Edward Herron (?-)

                7.3 Larry Ray Herron (?-)

                7.4 Norma Jean Herron (?-)

                7.5 Douglas Wayne Herron (?-)

                7.6 Glenda Gail Herron (?-)

            6.3 Clarence Herron (1904-1986) + Meartice Odom (?-)

                7.1 J. W. Herron (?-)

                7.2 Opal Jean Herron (?-)

                7.3 Billy Ray Herron (?-)

                7.4 Bobby Joe Herron (?-)

                7.5 Carl Dean Herron (?-)

                7.6 Raymond D. Herron (?-)

                7.7 Violet Mae Herron (?-)

                7.8 Harvey Lee Herron (?-)

                7.9 Mary Lou Herron (?-)

                7.10 Jerry Don Herron (?-)

                7.11 George Edward Herron (?-)

            6.4 Flossie Herron (1906-1996)

            6.5 Edgar Herron (1908-?)

6.6 Donnie Mae Herron (1910-1995)

6.7 Grady Herron (1912-)

6.8 Esther Louise Herron (1915-)

6.9 Earl Herron (1918-1977)

6.10 Earnest Herron (1920-1971)

5.4 Arminda Elvira Herron (1881-?)

5.5 Cora Ann Herron (1883-1960)

5.6 Julia Frances Herron (1886-1965)

5.7 Savannah Silvany Herron (1888-?)

5.8 Lunceford Osro Herron (1891-1977)

4.3 Charity Herron (1852-1857)

4.4 D. F. Herron (1854-1857)

4.5 Jane Herron (1857)

4.6 Pierce Herron (1860-1902)

4.7 Green Herron (1862-1925)

4.8 Missouria Herron (1864-1945)

John Hall and Nancy Hamilton

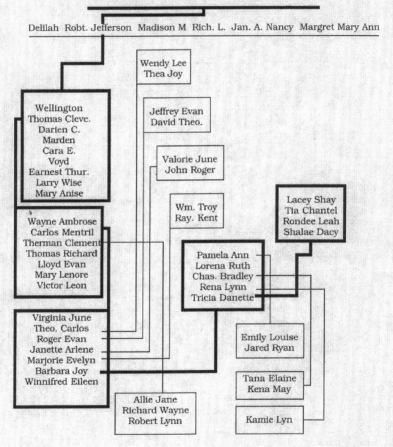

THE FAMILY CHART OF JOHN HALL AND NANCY HAMILTON

John Hall (1824-1898)/Nancy Hamilton (1828-1914)

Delilah Robt. Jefferson Madison M Rich. L. Jan. A. Nancy Margret Mary Ann

Wendy Lee
Thea Joy

Wellington
Thomas Cleve.
Darien C.
Marden
Cara E.
Voyd
Earnest Thur.
Larry Wise
Mary Anise

Jeffrey Evan
David Theo.

Valorie June
John Roger

Wm. Troy
Ray. Kent

Lacey Shay
Tia Chantel
Rondee Leah
Shalae Dacy

Wayne Ambrose
Carlos Mentril
Therman Clement
Thomas Richard
Lloyd Evan
Mary Lenore
Victor Leon

Pamela Ann
Lorena Ruth
Chas. Bradley
Rena Lynn
Tricia Danette

Virginia June
Theo. Carlos
Roger Evan
Janette Arlene
Marjorie Evelyn
Barbara Joy
Winnifred Eileen

Emily Louise
Jared Ryan

Tana Elaine
Kena May

Allie Jane
Richard Wayne
Robert Lynn

Kamie Lyn

3.2 John Hall (1824-1898) and Nancy Hamilton (1828-1914)

    4.1 Delilah Emeline Hall (1848)

    4.2 Robert Jefferson Hall (1850-1944) + Sara Jane Brewer (1856-1940)

        5.1 Wellington Columbus Hall (1879-1964)+Laura A. Sitton (1883-1963)

        5.2 Thomas Cleveland Hall (1884-1965)+Margie Rena Roberts (1889-1961)

            6.1 Wayne Ambrose Hall (1907-1929)

            6.2 Carlos Mentril Hall (1909-1965)+Winnifred Lorena Rogers (1917)

                7.1 Virginia June Hall (1936-1945)

                7.2 Theodore Carlos Hall (1937-1962)+Beverly Daniels (?-)

                    8.1 Wendy Lee Hall (1960-)

                    8.2 Thea Joy Hall (1961-)

                7.3 Roger Evan Hall (1939-) + Sharon Lynn Holland (?-)

                    8.1 Jeffrey Evan Hall (1967-)

                    8.2 David Theodore Hall (1970-)

                7.4 Janette Arlene Hall (1941-) + John Knuckles (?-)

                    8.1 Valorie June Knuckles (1964) (?-)

                    8.2 John Roger Knuckles (1968) (?-)

                7.5 Marjorie Evelyn Hall (1943) + Floyd Johnson (?-)

                    8.1 William Troy Johnson (?-)

                    8.2 Raymond Kent Johnson (?-)

                7.6 Barbara Joy Hall (1945-)+Charles Bradley Pearson (1940-)

                    8.1 Pamela Ann Pearson (1964-)+Jeffrey R. Hanson (1964-)

        9.1 Emily Louise Hanson (1991-)

        9.2 Jared Ryan Hanson (1993-)

  8.2 Lorena Ruth Pearson (1966-)+Michael Allred (1964-)

        9.1 Tana Elaine Allred (1983-)

        9.2 Kena May Allred (1993-)

  8.3 Chas. Bradley Pearson (1969-)+Judy Housekeeper (1970-)

        9.1 Charles Garrett Pearson (1991-)

        9.2 Paige Kay Pearson (1994-)

  8.4 Rena Lynn Pearson (1970-)+Glenn S. Prestwich (1966-)

        9.1 Kamie Lyn Prestwich (1994-)

  8.5 Tricia D. Pearson (1971-)+Richard Van Wagoner (1958-)

        9.1 Lacey Shay Van Wagoner (1992-)

        9.2 Tia Chantel Van Wagoner (1993-)

        9.3 Rondee Leah Van Wagoner (1997-)

        9.4 Shalae Dacy Van Wagoner (2001-)

7.7 Winnifred Eileen Hall (1946-) + Danny Anderson (?-)

  8.1 Danny Carlos Anderson (1967-)

  8.2 Steven Terry Anderson (1969-)

7.8 Marilyn Kaye Hall (1949-) + Dennis Hendric (?-)

  8.1 Austin Reed Hendric (1979-)

8.1 Arin Hendric (1981-)

6.3 Therman Clement Hall (1914-2001)+Mary V. Rogers (1915-)

    7.1 Allie Jane Hall (?-)

    7.2 Richard Wayne Hall (?-)

    7.3 Robert Lynn Hall (?-)

6.4 Thomas Richard Hall (1916-1920)

6.5 Lloyd Evan Hall (1920-1994)+Frieda Wiederman+Eliz. Davis

6.6 Mary Lenore Hall (1923-1991) + Marion Lee Neely (?-)

6.7 Victor Leon Hall (1928-) + Phyllis Maurine Rice (1952-)

    7.1 Steven Blane Hall (1954-) + Connie Corrine Taylor (?-)

    7.1 Vickie Lynn Hall (1956-) + Robert Eugene Cooke (?-)

    7.1 Timothy Wayne Hall (1959-)+Lori Turner+Gardner

    7.1 Derek Duane Hall (1968-) + Kim Denise Weiler (?-)

5.3 Darien C. Hall (1887-1922) + Jessie (1889-1964) + Lillie Taylor (?-)

5.4 Marien Hall (1887-1889) (Darien's twin)

5.5 Cara Ethel Hall (1892-1893)

5.6 Voyd Hall (1894-1968) + Mary P. Meyers (1895-1970)

5.7 Earnest Thurman Hall (1891-1982) + Roma Pritchard (1900-1971)

5.8 Larry Wise Hall (1898-) + Helen Jenkins (1924-)

5.9 Mary Anice Hall (1899-?) + Paris Cotton (1872-1928)

4.3 Madison Monroe Hall (1852-1928)

5.1 Ida Lenora Hall (1876-?)

5.2 Violet May Hall (1879-?)

5.3 Harriet Lillian Hall (1881-?)

5.4 Josephine Pearl Hall (1883-1926)

5.5 Ernest Edward Hall (1886-?)

5.6 Raynand Lafayette Hall (1888-?)

5.7 Ethel Hall (1890-?)

5.8 Anita Gertrude Hall (1895-?)

5.9 Rosamond Del Hall (1895-?)

4.4 Richard Lafayette Hall (1854-?)

4.5 Janette Ardelia Hall (1856-?)

4.6 Nancy Lanore Hall (1859-?)

4.7 Margret Charity Hall (1861-?)

4.8 Mary Ann Hall (1866-?)

Archie Brooklyn Hall and Nancy Caroline McDougal

THE FAMILY CHART OF ARCHIE BROOKLYN HALL

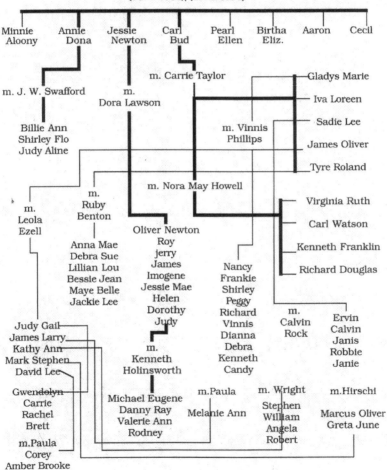

Archie B. Hall/m. Nancy Caroline McDougal
(1871-1955)/(1876-1955)

Minnie Aloony / Annie Dona / Jessie Newton / Carl Bud / Pearl Ellen / Birtha Eliz. / Aaron / Cecil

m. Carrie Taylor

m. J. W. Swafford

m. Dora Lawson

Gladys Marie
Iva Loreen
Sadie Lee
James Oliver
Tyre Roland

Billie Ann
Shirley Flo
Judy Aline

m. Vinnis Phillips

m. Nora May Howell

m. Leola Ezell

m. Ruby Benton

Anna Mae
Debra Sue
Lillian Lou
Bessie Jean
Maye Belle
Jackie Lee

Oliver Newton
Roy
jerry
James
Imogene
Jessie Mae
Helen
Dorothy
Judy

Virginia Ruth
Carl Watson
Kenneth Franklin
Richard Douglas

Nancy
Frankie
Shirley
Peggy
Richard
Vinnis
Dianna
Debra
Kenneth
Candy

m. Calvin Rock

Ervin
Calvin
Janis
Robbie
Janie

Judy Gail
James Larry
Kathy Ann
Mark Stephen
David Lee

m. Kenneth Holinsworth

Gwendolyn
Carrie
Rachel
Brett

m.Paula
Corey
Amber Brooke

Michael Eugene
Danny Ray
Valerie Ann
Rodney

Melanie Ann

m.Paula

m. Wright

Stephen
William
Angela
Robert

m.Hirschi

Marcus Oliver
Greta June

4.1 Archie Brooklyn (1871-1955) and Nancy Caroline (McDougal) (1876-1955):

    5.1 Minnie Aloony Hall (1894-1910)

    5.2 Annie Dona Hall (1896-1956)+Jeremiah William Swafford (?-?)

        6.1 Christopher David Swafford (1920-1983)

            7.1 Billie Ann Swafford (1953-)

            7.2 Shirley Flo Swafford (1955-)

            7.3 Judy Aline Swafford (1957-)

    5.3 Jesse Newton Hall (1899-?)

    5.4 Carl (Bud) Tyre Hall (1901-1965)+Carrie Taylor (?-?)

        6.1 Gladys Marie Hall (1922-1986) + Vinnis Bervine Phillips (?-?)

            7.1 Nancy Olene Phillips (?-)

            7.2 Frankie Lee Phillips (?-)

            7.3 Shirley Delores Phillips (?-)

            7.4 Peggy Joyce Phillips (?-)

            7.5 Richard Dwayne Phillips (?-)

            7.6 Vinnis Leon Phillips, Jr. (?-)

            7.7 Dianna Gail Phillips (?-)

            7.8 Debra Marie Phillips (?-)

            7.9 Kenneth Lee Phillips (?-)

            7.10 Candy Phillips (?-)

        6.2 Iva Loreen Hall (1926-)+Charles Edward Smith (?-?)

            7.1 Charles Henry

        6.3 Sadie Lee Hall (1926-)+Cal Rock (?-?)

            7.1 Ervin Lee Rock

            7.2 Calvin Ray Rock, Jr.

            7.3 Janis Kaye Rock

            7.4 Robbie Dale Rock

            7.5 Janie Faye Rock

        6.4 James Oliver Hall (1928-)+Leola Ezell (?-?)

            7.1 James Larry Hall (1974-)

            7.2 Kathy Ann Hall (1951-)

            7.3 Mark Stephen Hall (1953-)

7.4 David Lee Hall (1959-)

6.5 Judy Gail Hall (1949-)+Michael Merrill Lloyd (?-?)

7.1 Gwendolyn Lloyd (1975-)+(?) Lopez (?-)

8.1 Celina Renee Lopez (1992-)

7.2 Carrie Anne Lloyd (1977-)

7.3 Rachel Leona Lloyd (1979-)

7.4 Brett Lloyd (?-)

6.6 Tyre Roland Hall (1929-)+Ruby Benton (?-?)

7.1 Anna Mae Hall

7.2 Debra Sue Hall

7.3 Lillian Lou Hall

7.4 Bessie Jean Hall

7.5 Maye Belle Hall

7.6 Jackie Lee Hall

5.4 Carl (Bud) Tyre Hall (1901-1965)+Nora May Howell (?-?)

6.1 Virginia Ruth Hall (1937-1954)

6.2 Carl Watson Hall (1940-)

6.3 Kenneth Franklin Hall (1943-)

6.4 Richard Douglas Hall (1945-)

5.5 Pearl Ellen Hall (1903-1985)

5.6 Birtha Elizabeth Hall (1905-1999)

5.7 Aaron Granville Hall (1907-1964)

5.8 Cecil Hall (1912-1912)

Dock Walter Hall and Kate K. Elsey

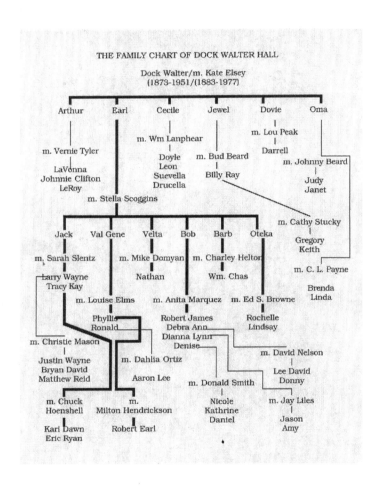

THE FAMILY CHART OF DOCK WALTER HALL

4.2 Dock Walter Hall (1873-1951) and Kate K. (Elsey) (1883-1977)

    5.1 Arthur H. Hall (1902-1995)+Vernie Tyler (1925-)

        6.1 LaVonna Hall (?-)

        6.2 Johnnie Clifton (J. C.) Hall (?-)

      6.3 LeRoy Hall (?-)

5.2 Earl Hall (1903-)

      6.1 Durward Jack Hall (1927-)

          7.1 Larry Wayne Hall (1955-)

              8.1 Justin Wayne Hall (1975-)

              8.2 Bryan David Hall (1979-)

              8.3 Matthew Reid Hall (1981-)

          7.2 Tracy Kay Hall (1957-)

              8.1 Kari Dawn Hoenshell (1980-)

              8.2 Eric Ryan Hoenshell (1983-)

      6.2 Val Gene Hall (1928-)

          7.1 Phyllis Jean Hall (1950-)

              8.1Robert Earl Hendrickson (1978-)

          7.2 Ronald Hall (1951-)

              8.1 Aaron Lee Hall (1983-)

      6.3 Velta Lee Hall (1930-)

          7.1 Nathan Domyan (1958-)

      6.4 Bobby Ray (Bob) Hall (1932-)

          7.1 Robert James Hall (1956-)

          7.2 Debra Ann (Hall) Stafford (1957-)

              8.1 Lee David Nelson (1980-)

              8.2 Donny Ray Nelson (1982-)

          7.3 Dianna Lynn (Hall) Liles (1958-)

              8.1 Jason Dee Liles (1978-)

              8.2 Amy Christine Liles (1981-)

          7.4 Denise Marie Hall (1962-)

              8.1 Nicole Marie Smith (1985-)

              8.2 Kathrine Ray Smith (1987-)

              8.3 Daniel Miles Smith (1988-)

      6.5 Barbara Louise Hall (1935-)

          7.1 William Charles Helton (1960-)

      6.6 Joyce Oteka Hall (1938-)

7.1 Rochelle Candine Browne (1961-)

7.2 Lindsay Edward Hall Browne (1963-)

5.3 Cecile Hall (1908-1957)

6.1 Doyle Lanphear (?-)

6.2 Leon Lanphear (?-)

6.3 Suevella Lanphear (?-1978)

6.4 Drucella Lanphear (?-)

5.4 Jewel Hall (1915-)

6.1 Billy Ray Beard (?-)

7.1 Gregory Beard (1961-)

7.2 Keith Beard (1963-)

5.5 Dovie Hall (?-)

6.1 Darrell Dean Peak (?-)

5.6 Oma Hall (1922-)

6.1 Judy Beard (?-)

6.2 Janet Beard (?-)

6.3 Brenda Payne (?-)

6.4 Linda Payne (?-)

Greeley Teeman Hall and Mallie Rue Carr

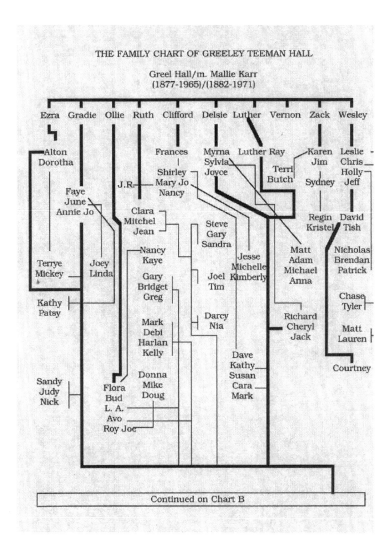

THE FAMILY CHART OF GREELEY TEEMAN HALL

Greel Hall/m. Mallie Karr
(1877-1965)/(1882-1971)

Ezra Gradie Ollie Ruth Clifford Delsie Luther Vernon Zack Wesley

Alton
Dorotha

Frances
Shirley
J.R. Mary Jo
Nancy

Myrna Luther Ray
Sylvia
Joyce

Karen Leslie
Jim Chris
Terri
Butch Holly
Sydney Jeff

Faye
June
Annie Jo

Clara
Mitchel
Jean

Steve
Gary
Sandra

Regin David
Kristel Tish

Nancy
Kaye

Jesse
Michelle
Kimberly

Matt
Adam
Michael
Anna

Nicholas
Brendan
Patrick

Terrye
Mickey

Joey
Linda

Joel
Tim

Gary
Bridget
Greg

Chase
Tyler

Kathy
Patsy

Mark
Debi
Harlan
Kelly

Darcy
Nia

Richard
Cheryl
Jack

Matt
Lauren

Dave
Kathy
Susan
Cara
Mark

Courtney

Sandy
Judy
Nick

Flora
Bud
L. A.
Avo
Roy Joe

Donna
Mike
Doug

Continued on Chart B

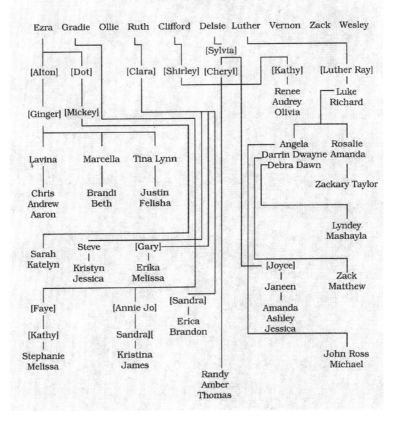

CHART B [continued from Chart A]

THE FAMILY CHART OF GREELEY TEEMAN HALL

Greel Hall/m. Mallie Karr
(1877-1965)/(1882-1971)

4.3 Greeley Teeman Hall(1877-1965) and Mallie Rue Carr (1882-1971)

    5.1 Ezra Marion Hall (1902-1986) + Florence Viola Scoggins (1905-1997)

        6.1 Alton Lee Hall (1928-1989) + Jeannetta Ramsey (1932-)

            7.1 Ginger Kaye Hall (1949-) +David Landers (1945-)

8.1 Lavina Ruth Landers (1963-) +Ronald Cardona (?-)

    9.1 Christopher Lee Cardona (1984-)

    9.1 Andrew DeWayne Cardona (1987-

    9.1 Aaron Raymond Cardona(1987-)

8.2 Marcella Diane Ramsey (?-) Randall Jones (1947-)

    9.1 Brandi Jo Jones (1989-)

    9.2 Beth Marie Jones (1991-)

8.3 Tina Lynn Ramsey (1970-) +(?)

    9.1 Justin Davis Ramsey (1988-)

    9.1 Felisha Marie Diane Ramsey (1990-)

6.2 Dorotha Faye Hall (1931-2001) + Mack Schornick (1948-1980)

    7.1 Terrye Lee Schornick (1951-) + Neil Hugentober (?-)

    7.2 Mickey Joe Schornick (1957-) + Cynthia Sue Coder (1959-)

        8.1 Sarah Schornick (?-)

        8.2 Katelyn JoAnn Schornick (1988-)

5.2 Grady Hall (1904-1990) + Arthur Lee Goff (1907-1981)

    6.1 Inas Faye Goff (1926-) + Steve Kandarian (1918-2001)

        7.1 Katherine Louise Kandarian (1944-) + Steve Diebert (?-)

            8.1 Stephanie Leann Diebert (1971-)+Kenneth J. Price (1968-)

            8.2 Melissa Ann Diebert (1975-) + Layne Bartley Lev (1973-)

        7.2 Patricia Ann Kandarian (1946-)

    6.2 Maudie June Goff (1929-) + Joseph Lamanuzzi, Jr. (1930-)

        7.1 Joseph (Joey) Arthur Lamanuzzi (1953-)

        7.2 Linda Faye Lamanuzzi (1955-)

    6.3 Annie Joe Goff (1930-1995)+Angelo Papagni (1928-1981)

        7.1 Sandra Elizabeth Papagni (1953-) + James Ray (?-1988)

            8.1 Kristina Ray (1973-)

8.2 James Ray (1975-)

7.2 Judith Anne Papagni (1956-) + John Biggs (?-1976)+Danny Akins

7.3 Carlo Nicholas Papagni (1960-)

5.3 Ollie Ida Hall (1906-1934) + Lou Albin Smith (1906-1934)

6.1 Flora Evaline Smith (1924-) + James Putler (1930-)

7.1 Nancy Kay Putler (1961-) + James Robert Kemp II (1963-)

8.1 James Robert Kemp III (1991-)

8.2 Patrick Owen Kemp (1993-)

7.2 David Allen Putler (1961-1961)

6.2 Merle Eston (Bud) Smith (1927-2001) + Florene (?)

6.3 Lou Albin (L. A.) Smith (1929-) & Lucille Cleveland (1929-2000)

7.1 Gary Lynn Smith (1949-) + Cindy Meismer (1948-)

8.1 Reis Nathaniel Smith (1978-)

8.2 Katy Nina Smith (1979-)

7.2 Bridget Evelyn Smith (1953-) + O'Leary + Antis

8.1 Heather O'Leary (1971-) + John (?)

8.2 Crystal Antis (1975-)

7.3 Gregory Paul Smith (1959-) + Pebbles A. McDonald (1965-)

8.1 Jessica Lynn Smith (1987-)

8.2 Geoffrey Paul Smith (1990-)

8.3 Megan Elizabeth Smith (1994-)

8.4 Catherine Michelle Smith (1996-)

8.5 Patricia Lucille Smith (1999-)

6.4 Mallie Avo Smith (1931-) + Frank Rincon ?

7.1 Mark Anthony Rincon (1951-)

8.1 Trent Rincon (1977-)

8.2 Troy Rincon (1979-)

7.2 Debra (Debi) Ann Rincon (1953-)

8.1 Jonathan Beach (1992-)

8.2 Justan Beach (1994-)

7.3 Robert Harlan Rincon (1954-)

8.1 Melissa Rincon (1976-)

8.2 Robert Neal Rincon (1978-)

7.4 Kelly Maria Rincon (1947-) + Brizendine

8.1 Erica Allison Brizendine (1980-)

8.2 Jillian Morgan Brizendine (1983-)

6.5 Roy Joe Smith (1934-1996) + Alma (?)

7.1 Donna Smith (?-)

7.2 Michael Smith (?)

7.3 Douglas Smith (?)

5.4 Ruth Hall (1908-1976) + Benjamin Potter (1907-1996)

6.1 Clara Dale Potter (1935-) + Carl Swann (?-)

7.1 Steven Nolan Swann (1956-) + Jan Durelle Greenwood (?-)

8.1 Kristyn Durelle Swann (1981-)

8.2 Jessica Leanne Swann (1984-)

7.2 Gary Alan Swann (1957-) + Becky (?-)

8.1 Melissa Rae Swann (1982-)

7.3 Sandra Gail Swann (1963-) + Mike Bellamy (?-)

8.1 Erica Nicole Bellamy (1983-)

8.2 Brandon Michael Bellamy (1984-)

6.2 David Mitchel Potter (1937-) + Martha Ann Hinson + Mixon

7.1 Joel Austin Potter (1970-)

7.2 Timothy Mark Potter (1971-)

6.3 Beulah Jean Potter (1940-) + Jack Finley (?-)

7.1 Darcy Marlane Finley (1964-) + D. J. Langston (?-)

8.1 Danita Jasmine Finley (1987-)

8.2 David Mitchel Finley (?)

8.3 Dillon James Finley (?)

7.2 Nia Clarice Finley (1966-) + P. J. Langston, Jr. (?-)

8.1 Renae Charise Langston (?-)

8.2 Chistow Langston (?-)

8.3 Bowdrie Langston (?-)

8.4 Jude Alonzo Langston (1998-)

5.5 Clara Mabel Hall (1910-1964) + James F. Holderby + Melvin Merrill

5.6 Clifford Cleborn Hall (1912-1974) + Imogene White (?-)

6.1 Frances Carol Hall (?-)

5.6 Clifford Cleborn Hall (1912-1974) +Georgia Marie Sage (1916-1976)

6.2 Shirley Ann Hall (1937-1989)+William Dean Terrill (1935-1993)

7.1 David Philip Terrill (1955-) + Karen Sue Bonds (1951-)

7.2 Kathleen Marie Terrill (1958-) + Arnold Ulloa (?-)

8.1 Jacquelyn Renee Ulloa (1982-)

8.2 Audrey Lynn Ulloa (1985-)

8.3 Olivia Ulloa (1988-)

7.1 Merry Susan Terrill (1960-) + Frank Rock (?-)

7.2 Cara Lee Terrill (1962-) + Les Burns + Perry Vierra (?-)

8.1 Kyle Vierra (1983-)

8.2 Elise Vierra (1987-)

7.3 Mark Allen Terrill (1964-)

6.3 Mary Jo Hall (1939-1992) + John R. Sheppard (?-) + Robert Musgraves

7.1 John Richard Sheppard, Jr. (1957-)

6.4 Nancy June Hall 1943-) + Jesse Kilborn Holmes, Sr. (1940-)

7.1 Jesse Kilborn Holmes, Jr. (1965-)

7.2 Michelle Holmes (?-)

7.3 Kimberly Holmes (?-)

5.7 Delsie Dale Hall (1914-1998) + William Clifford Bernard (1915-1988)

6.1 Myrna Jo Bernard (1939-) + Anthony Ceccarelli (1934-2001)

7.1 Adam Rocco Ceccarelli (1961-) + Mary Louise Dewitt (1963-)

7.2 Matthew Christopher Ceccarelli (1962-) + Lisa Barkley

8.1 Alissa Ceccarelli (1986-)

8.2 Shannon Ceccarelli Fitzpatric (1984-)

7.3 Michael John Ceccarelli (1967-1988) + Lee Ann Turner

    8.1 (?) Ceccarelli (1988-)

7.4 Anna Rue Ceccarelli (1967-) (a twin)

6.2 Sylvia Ann Bernard (1940-) + Neil AllenWilliams (1940-)

    7.1 Richard Allan Williams Cole (1957-) [Adopted by Cole]

    7.2 Cheryle Ann Williams Cole (1958-) + Tom Patterson (?-)

        8.1 Amber Patterson (1984-)

        8.1 Thomas Patterson (1986-)

    7.2 Cheryle Ann Williams Cole (1958-) + Randal Mello (?-)

    7.3 Jack Wesley Williams (1959-1974)

6.3 Joyce Dean Bernard (1942-) + Steve Manning Birdman (?-)

    7.1 Margo Janeen Birdman (1962-) + Steven Boone -)

        8.1 Amanda Summer Boone (1980-) + Marco Manfredo (?+)

        8.2 Ashley Dawn Boone (1988-)

        8.3 Madison Ariel Boone (1999-)

    7.2 April Dawn Robinson (1963-)

5.8 Luther Leonard Hall (1917-1972) + Christine Clark (?-1997)

6.1 Luther Ray Hall (1942-) + Norma Jean Maddie (?-)

    7.1 Luther Ray Jr. (1957-) + Rebecca Smith (?-)

        8.1 Rosalie Jean Smith (1977-)

        8.2 Amanda Yvonne Smith (1980-) + (?)

            9.1 Zackary Taylor (Hall) Smith (1998-)

    7.2 Richard Allen Hall (1958-)

    7.3 Angela Rae Hall (1966-) + Jose Aquilar (?-)

        8.1 John Ross Hall (1991-)

        8.2 Michael Dewayne Hall (1993-)

    7.4 Darrin Dewayne Hall (1967-) + Mary Elizabeth Harmon (?-)

        8.1 Zackary Thomas Hall (1991-)

        8.2 Matthew Luke Hall (1997-)

    7.5 Debra Dawn Hall (1972-) + Johnny Dewayne Bell (?-)

8.1 Lyndey Renee Bell (1991-)

5.9 Vernon Hall (1920-1974)

5.10 Zack Oberon Hall (1923-1969) + Edith Coonrod (?-)

    6.1 Karen Hall (?-)+ R. C. Lawyer (?-)

        7.1 Terri Jo Lawyer (?-)

        7.2 Michael (Butch) Dewayne Lawyer (?-)

    6.2 Jim Hall (?-1996) + Trecias Jo (?) (?-)

        7.1 Trecias (?-)

5.10 Zack Oberon Hall (1923-1969) + Katherine (?)

    6.3 Sydney Lee Hall (1943-) + Ken McKay (?-)

        7.1 Regina McKay (1983-)

        7.2 Kristel McKay (1984-)

5.11 Wesley Elmo Hall (1925-) + Bonita Pursiville (1929-1987)

    6.1 Leslie Jeanne Hall (1952-) + Alan Brown (1942-)

        7.1 Matthew Alan Brown (1975-)

        7.2 Lauren Elizabeth Brown (1977-)

    6.2 Robert Christopher Hall (1959-) + Valorie Chase (?-)

        7.1 Chase Wesley Hall (1989-)

        7.2 Tyler Cody Hall (1992-)

    6.3 Holly Denise Hall (1960-) + Sean FitzPatrick (?-)

        7.1 Nicholas Michael FitzPatrick (1994-)

        7.2 Brendan Miles FitzPatrick (1997-)

        7.3 Patrick Stephen FitzPatrick (1999-)

    6.4 John Jeffery Hall (1962-1982) + Ronda Grimes (?-)

        7.1 David Jeffrey Grimes (1980-) + Christy Heard (?-)

            8.1 Courtney Lea Grimes (2001-)

        7.2 Latisha Marie Hall (1981-)

Ulysses S. Grant Hall and Sylvania Pennington

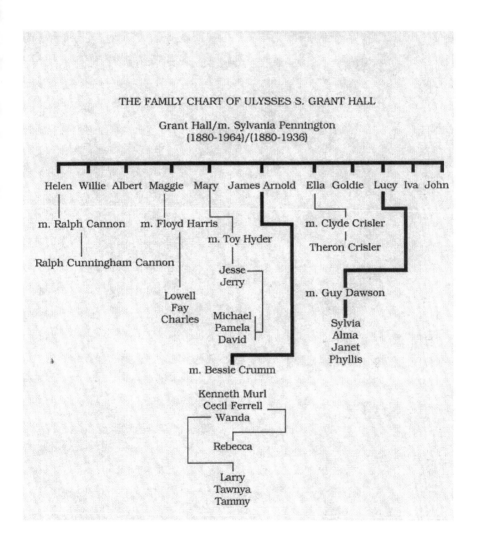

THE FAMILY CHART OF ULYSSES S. GRANT HALL

Grant Hall/m. Sylvania Pennington
(1880-1964)/(1880-1936)

Helen Willie Albert Maggie Mary James Arnold Ella Goldie Lucy Iva John

m. Ralph Cannon   m. Floyd Harris

m. Toy Hyder

Ralph Cunningham Cannon

m. Clyde Crisler

Theron Crisler

Jesse
Jerry

Lowell
Fay
Charles   Michael
           Pamela
           David

m. Guy Dawson

Sylvia
Alma
Janet
Phyllis

m. Bessie Crumm

Kenneth Murl
Cecil Ferrell
Wanda

Rebecca

Larry
Tawnya
Tammy

4.4 Ulysses S. Grant Hall (1880-1964) and Sylvania Pennington (1880-1936)
   5.1 Viola Helen Hall (1900-1982)+Ralph Cunninghame Cannon, Sr. (?-)

6.1 Ralph Cunningham Cannon, Jr. (ca. 1918-)

5.2 Willie Hall (1901-1906)

5.3 Albert Hall (1903-1916)

5.4 Maggie Lee Hall (1905-1935) + Floyd Harris (?-)

    6.1 Lowell Harris (?-)   •

    6.2 Fay (Clifton) Harris (?-)

    6.3 Charles Harris (?-)

5.5 Mary Elizabeth Hall (1906-1989) + Toy Elmo Hyder + Everett Cole

    6.1 Jessie Raymond Hyder (?-) + (?)

        7.1 Michael Ray Hyder (1950-)

        7.2 Pamela Elaine Hyder (1953-)

    6.2 Jessie Raymond Hyder (?-) + Marti (?)

        7.3 David Hyder (1982-)

    6.3 Jerry Hyder (?-)

5.6 James Arnold Hall (1908-1993) + Bessie Crumm (1915-)

    6.1 Kenneth Murl Hall (1934-) + Rena Irene Walker (1937-)

        7.1 Kathy Irene Hall (1955-) + (?_ Burney (?-)

            8.1 Allen Joseph Burney (1976-)

            8.1 Aaron Joshua Burney (1979-)

        7.2 Ricky Murl Hall (1957-) + La Donna Broughton (?-)

            8.1 Brandon Murl Hall (1985-)

    6.2 Cecil Ferrell Hall (1942-) + Patricia Bolt (?)

        7.1 Rebecca Jane Hall (?-)

    6.3 Wanda Hall (1940-) + William Dale Smith (1938-)

        7.1 Larry Dale Smith (1960-1983) + Tresa Ann Masterson (?-)

            8.1 Jeremy Don Smith (1978-)

            8.2 Misty Dawn Smith (1980-)

        7.2 Tawnya Danita Smith (1961-)+James D. Daugherty (?-)

            8.1 James David Daugherty II (1980-)

        7.2 Tawnya Danita Smith (1961-) + Theo Kelley III (?-)

            8.2 Andrea Nicole Kelley (1984-)

            8.3 Bridgett Leann Kelley (1986-)

7.3 Tammy Denise Smith (1962-1963)

5.7 Ella Zona Hall (1910-1990) +Clyde Theron Crisler (?-) + (?) Tobias

      6.1 Clyde Theron Crisler, Jr. (?-) + Trudy Ellen Smith (-1999)

5.8 Goldie Mae Hall (1913-1916)

5.9 Lucy Florence Hall (1915-)+Guy Dawson (1916-)

      6.1 Sylvia Dawson (1940-) + Dean Parker + Sisto Benevidez

      6.2 Alma Dawson (1941-) + Alois Schmidt + Loy Fulbright

      6.3 Janet Dawson (1943-) + Darrell Belcher + David Weekley

      6.4 Phyllis Dawson (1952-) + Donnie Price + Leon Ellison

5.10 Iva Alice Hall (1916—1921)

5.11 Johnnie Theron Hall (1919-1993)

Sidney William Hall and Cordelia Eubanks

4. 5 Sidney William Hall (1882-1972) + Cordelia Eubanks (1887-?)

    5.1 Melvin Hall (?-)

    5.2 Cling Hall (?-)

    5.3 Nadine Hall (?-) + (?) McKissck (?-)

    5.4 Orville Hall (?-1940)

Cordelia May Hall and Logan Sisemore

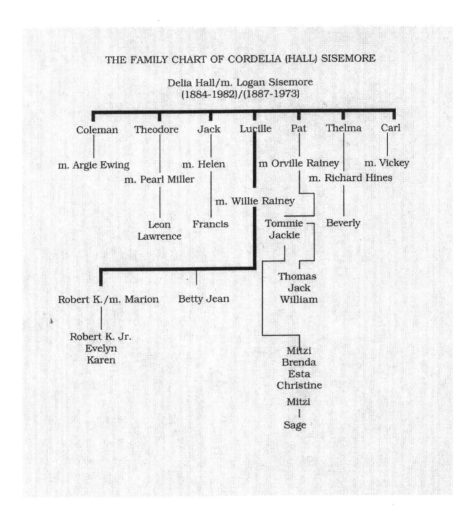

THE FAMILY CHART OF CORDELIA (HALL) SISEMORE

Delia Hall/m. Logan Sisemore
(1884-1982)/(1887-1973)

4.6 Cordelia Mae Hall (1884-1982) and Logan Sisemore (1887-1973)

    5.1 Coleman Sisemore (1909-?)

    5.2 Theodore Sisemore (1911-1981)

6.1 Leon Sisemore (?-)

6.2 Lawrence Sisemore (?-)

5.3 Jack Sisemore (1914-1989)

6.1 Francis Sisemore (?-)

5.4 Lucille Sisemore (1915-1977)

6.1 Robert K. Rainey, Sr. (?-)

7.1 Robert K. Rainey, Jr. (?-)

7.2 Evelyn Rainey (?-)

7.3 Karen Rainey (?-)

6.2 Betty Jean Rainey (?-)

5.5 Patricia (Buena) Sisemore (1917-)

6.1 Tommy Aubrey Rainey (1938-)

7.1 Thomas Rainey (1956-1982)

7.2 Jack Rainey (?-)

7.3 William Rainey (?-)

6.2 Jackie Ray Rainey (1934-)

7.1 Mitzi Rainey (?-)

8.1 Sage Rainey (1995-)

7.2 Brenda Rainey (?-)

7.3 Esta Rainey (?-)

7.4 Christine Rainey (?-)

5.6 Thelma (Tommie) Sisemore (1922-1990)

6.1 Beverly Hines (?-)

5.7 Carl Sisemore (1926-)

Charity Hall and Lee Rogers

4.7 Charity Hall (1885-1964) and Lee Rogers (1886-1963)

5.1 Grace Rogers (?-) + (?) Thomas

6.1 Thomas (?) Thomas (1936-)

6.2 Ginger Sue Thomas (1940-)

6.3 Dewey Thomas (1944-)

5.2 Searls Rogers (1906-) + (?)
>6.1 Kenneth Rogers (?)
>6.2 Twila Rogers (?)
>6.3 Wayne Rogers (?)
>6.4 Brenda Rogers (?)
>6.5 Rick Rogers (?)

Green Tyree Hall and Nanny Eversole

4.8 Green T. Hall (1887-1967) and Nancy Eversole (1888-1945)

5.1 Ernest Clifford Hall (1911-)

5.2 Pearl Zenia Hall (1914-1981)
>6.1 Trudy Ellen Hall (?-)

5.3 Arizona (Marge) Lee Hall (1916-)

5.4 Delphia Patricia (Pat) Hall (1919-)

5.5 Irene Hall (1923-)

5.6 Imogene (Bonnie) Hall (1928-)

5.7 Robert (Bob) Hall (1931-) + Ella Coffee (?-) (Adopted by Orvilla and Walter Kirk at age 19)

OBITUARIES

Archie Brooklyn Hall (1871-1955)

[Jesse Mae (Hall) Heckathorn, the daughter of Jesse Newton Hall and Dora Belle (Lawson) and the granddaughter of Archie Brooklyn Hall, sent me the following obituary, which was printed in the Nowata, Oklahoma, newspaper. The date of the funeral was May 31, 1955, just five days after his wife died.]

Headline: ARCHIE B. HALL DIES AT AGE OF 84 RITES SATURDAY

Archie B. Hall, 84, died at the home, 716 North Elm, at 4:30 p. m., Tuesday, shortly after funeral services were held for his wife, the late Nancy C. Hall. Mr. Hall was born in Walden [Waldron], Arkansas.

Survivors are three sons, Jess and H. E. (?) Hall, Nowata, and Carl T. Hall, Fromia, Calif.; three daughters, Mrs. J. O. Greggs [Gragg], Peoria, Ariz., Mrs. Ed Greggs [Gragg], Gila Bend, Ariz., and Mrs. Annie [Dona] Irons, Big Cabin, Okla.; four brothers, Sidney Hall, Adair, Greel Hall, Carmen [Kerman], Calif., and Greentree [Green Tyree] Hall and Grant Hall, both of Porterville, Calif.; two sisters, Mrs. Charity Rogers, Japton, Ark., and Mrs. Dellie Sizemore [Delia Sisemore], Mountain View, California; 33 grandchildren and 66 great grandchildren.

Funeral services will be conducted Saturday at 3 p. m. in the R. W. Benjamin chapel. Rev. A. A. Davis, pastor of the First Baptist Church, will be in charge.

Burial will be in Memorial Park. Four grandsons will serve as pall bearers.

Nancy Caroline McDougal Hall (1876-1955)

[This obituary was also printed in the Nowata, Oklahoma, newspaper on the day of Nancy's death, May 26, 1956. Nancy was buried beside Archie in Memorial Park, Nowata, Oklahoma.]

Headline: MRS. NANCY HALL DIES AT AGE OF 79 SERVICES PENDING

Mrs. Nancy C. Hall, 79, died at the home, 716 North Elm, at 8 a. m. today. She had been ill for the past eight months. The family has resided in the Nowata vicinity for twelve years.

Survivors are the husband, A. B. Hall, of the home, three sons, Jess and H. E. Hall, Nowata, and Carl T. Hall, Fromia, Calif., and three daughters, Mrs. J. O. Greggs, Peoria, Ariz., Mrs. Ed Greggs, Gila Bend, Ariz., and Mrs. Annie Irons, Big Cabin, Okla.

Funeral arrangements are pending with the R. kW. Benjamin Funeral Service.

Kate Hall (1883-1977)

DINUBAóFuneral services were held today [January 19, 1977] in the Dopkins Funeral Chapel for Kate Hall, 93, a thirty-year reident of Dinuba.

Mrs. Hall, a native of Arkansas, died Sunday in a Dinuba convalescent hopital.

Her husband, Dock W. Hall, died in 1951.

She is survived by two sons, Earl Hall, of Orosi, and Arthur Hall, of Exeter; three daughters: Jewel Beard, Dovie Braun, and Oma Payne, all of Dinuba; 19 grandchildren, 44 great-grandchildren, and seven great-great-grandchildren.

Burial was in the Smith Mountain Cemetery. The Rev. John Carr officiated at the services.

Ulysses S. Grant Hall (1880-1964)

July 9, 1964. Grant S. Hall

Grant S. Hall, 84, retired Arkansas farmer who has lived in Tipton since 1952, died today in a Tulare hospital following a lengthy illness.

He was born at Drakes Creek, Ark., and came to California in 1942. He was a member of the free Will Baptist Church in Mulberry, Ark.

Survivors include two sons, John T. Hall, Sunnyvale, and James Hall, Spire, Okla.: four daughters, Mrs. Ralph (Viola) Cannon, Mrs Toy (Mary) Hyder and Mrs. Clyde (Ella) Crisler, Tipton, and Mrs. Guy (Lucy) Dawson, El Mirage, Ariz.: three brothers, G. T. Hall, Lodi, and Grill and Sidney Hall; a sister, Mrs. Della Sizemore, Lodi, 21 grandchildren and 44 great-grandchildren.

Funeral services will be announced by the Goble Fuuneral Chapel.

Mallie Rue Carr Hall (1882-1971)

[Mallie was the daughter of Henry Allan Carr, the wife of Greel Hall, and the mother of eleven children: Ezra, Ollie, Gradie, Ruth, Clifford, Mabel, Delsie, Luther, Vernon, Zack, and Wesley Elmo.]

Mallie Rue Hall, 89, died in Fresno on July 12, 1971. Born in Arkansas, lived 34 years in Fresno. A homemaker and mother of Mrs. Grady Goff, Mrs. Ruth Potter, Mrs. Delsie Bernard, Clifford and Vernon Hall of Fresno, Ezra Hall of Beaver, Okla., Dr. Wesley Hall of Springfield, Mo., and Luther Hall of Odessa, Texas; sister of Mrs. Zora Hartness of Monett, Mo., Mrs. Myrtle Sherman of Sapulpa, Okla., and Mrs. Ethel Upperman of Phoenix, Ariz. Twenty-eight grandchildren, forty-seven great-grandchildren, and five great-great-grandchildren also survive. Funeral services held Tuesday afternoon, John N. Lisle Chapel. Interment in Fresno Memorial Gardens.

Cordelia Mae Hall Sisemore (1884-1982)

[Delia was the daughter of William Newton Hall and Susan Elizabeth Woods and the wife of Logan Sisemore]

Delia Mae Sisemore, 92, a former Lodi resident, died in a Watson-ville hospital late Sunday morning. Mrs. Sisemore was living at Moss Landing, Monterey County, at the time of her death. She was born and reared in Japtown [Japton], Ark. She married Logan Sisemore there in July, 1905.

The couple came to California in 1935 and lived in Madera, San Jose, and Mountain View before moving to Lodi in 1958. Mr. Sisemore died in 1973. In 1978, Mrs. Sisemore moved to Santa Clara for a brief time, and then Moss Landing.

Mrs. Sisemore is survived by: three sons Coleman Sisemore of Moss Landing, Jack Sisemore of Milpitas, and Carl Sisemore of Mexico; two daughters Patricia Hatcher of Shasta and Thelma Rhoads of Nevada; niece Grace Thomas of Buena Park; also many grandchildren.

Services will be conducted Tuesday at 2 p. m. in the Lodi Funeral Home Chapel with Scott Harrison of the Church of Christ officiating. Burial will follow in the Cherokee Memorial Park.

Nancy (Nanny) Eversole Hall (1888-1945)

[Nanny Eversole was the wife of Green T. Hall. She was referred to as *Annie E.* in newspaper accounts of her death. On her tombstone she is *Nanny E.* The following is a newspaper story about her death.]

Headline in the newspaper: MRS. A. HALL CRASH VICTIM

An automobille accident in Fayetteville, Arkansas, claimed the life of Mrs. Annie Hall of Acampo on Thursday, December 20th, as she was on her way with her husband, Green T. Hall, to visit relatives in Alma, Arkansas, over the Christmas holidays.

Mrs. Hall was 59 years of age. She is survived by her husband, her father, John Eversole of Alma, and leaves the following children: Mrs. Irene Geidt of Lodi, Mrs. Pearl Morrison of Richmond, Calif., Mrs. Delphia Hayes of Richmond, Mrs. Arizona Lee of Vallejo, Mrs. Energene Burrow of Acampo, Ernest Hall of Fresno and Robert Hall of Acampo.

She was the sister of Preston Eversole of Richmond, Raymond Eversole of Arkansas, Lyge Eversole of Fresno, Joe Eversole of Alma, Arkansas, Wes Eversole of Alma, Jim Eversole of Alma, and Mrs. Belle Eversole of Alma.

Dora Belle (Lawson) Gougler

[Dora Bell was married to Jessie Newton Hall for over twenty years and raised eleven children with him in Nowata County, Oklahoma.]

Dora Bell Gougler, 85, Nowata [Oklahoma] died early Tuesday morning, Nov. 28, 1989, in the Nowata Nursing Home.

Mrs. Dougler was born October 12, 1904, in Van Buren, Ark. the daughter of Charles and Martha Lawson. She was married to Frank Gougler Nov. 23, 1947 in Yuma, Arizona.

The couple resided in California for some time before they returned to the Nowata area in 1980.

Mrs. Gougler was a member of the Mormon Church.

Survivors include four sons: Oliver Hall, Norwalk, Calif.; Roy Hall, Vinita; Jerry Hall, Artesia, Calif.; and Jim Hall, Coffeeville, Kans.; six daughters: Imogene Horn, Afton; Jessie Hillis, Eugene, Oregon; Jessie Hillis, Eugene, Ore.; Helen Orchid, Lakewood, Calif.; Dorothy Holinsworth and Judy Boyd, both of Nowata; and Shirley Mainer,

Abbesford, Wisc.; two step-daughters: Sonja Moncade, Reno, Nevada; and Shirley Ginther, St. Joseph, Mo.; 56 grandchildren and 38 great-grandchildren.

Graveside funeral services for Mrs. Gougler will be held at 3 p. m. Thursday, Nov. 30 in the Steel Camp Cemetery, Oglesby, with the Rev. Arthur Stookey officiating.

Arrangements are by the Stumff-Nowata Funeral Home.

Delsie Dale Hall Bernard (1914-1998)

[Delsie was the wife of William Clifford (Lucy) Bernard and the mother of three daughters: Myrna, Sylvia, and Joyce.]

Delsie was born Delsie Dale Hall, the tenth [eighth] child of Horace G. Hall and Mallie Rue Carr, near Asher, Oklahoma, on August 30, 1914.

The family moved to California in the 'Thirties. They settled in Fresno, where Delsie met and married William Clifford (Lucy) Bernard on November 26, 1938.

Delsie and Lucy are survived by their three daughters, Myrna Ceccarelli and her husband Tony, their children, Anna, Matthew and his children Alissa Ceccarelli and Shannon Fitzpatric, and Adam and his wife, Mary; Sylvia Cole of Santa Barbara, her children, Richard Cole, Cherl Patterson and friend Jim French, their children, Randy Mello, Amber Patterson and Thomas Patterson; and Joyce Robinson, her children, April Robinson, Janeen Randolph, her husband Rick, their children, Amanda and Ashley Boone, Jessica Randolph; and many nieces and nephews. Her one surviving brother is Wesley E. Hall and wife Sharon of Highlandville, Missouri.

Delsie was a devoted mother and grandmother. She will be remembered by old friends for her hospitality and good cooking and for all the good times everyone had at Lucy and Delsie's home while her children were growing up.

Delsie never lost her sense of humor, good temper, and sweet smile.

Memorial Services will be held at Chapel of the Light, Friday, January 16, 1998, at 1 P. M.

Remembrances may be made to the Alzheimer's Disease Center of Central California, 1343 N. Wishon, Fresno, CA 93728.

Thomas L. Rainey (1956-1982)

[Thomas L. was the son of Tommy Aubrey Rainey, grandson of Pat (Buena) Sisemore and Orville Rainey, great-grandson of Delia (Hall) and Logan Sisemore]

Newspaper headline: SUNNYVALE MAN DIES IN CAR CRASH

Sunday, Dec. 5, 1982 [San Jose Mercury newspaper]

A 26-year-old man was killed Friday night [?] when his car went out of control and flipped over near Highway 101 in Mountain View, CA. The victim was identified Saturday by the Santa Clara County Coroner's Office as Thomas L. Rainey, a carpet-layer from Sunnyvale. The driver had turned onto Fairchild Drive near Leong Drive when his jeep rolled at least once, pinning his head between the vehicle's rollbar and the ground, according to a coroner's office investigator. He was pronounced dead at the scene.

Darrin Dewayne Hall (1967-2001)

[Darrin was the son of Luther Ray (Luke) Hall and Connie (Rorabough) Hall, the grandson of Luther Leonard and Christine (Clark) Hall.]

Funeral services for rural Drumright resident Darrin Dewayne Hall was held at 2 p. m., Saturday, January 27 (2001), at Olive Baptist Church.

Rev. George Brock, Sr. officiated and special music was provided by "The Lights of Christ." Interment followed on the family farm south of Drumright.

Serving as casket bearers were Richard Smith, Keith Miller, Keith Andrews, Brad Andrews, Alvin Andrews, and Dusty Roach. Honorary bearers were Zackary Hall, Matthew Hall, John Ross Hall, Michael Hall, and Lance Andrews.

Funeral arrangements were entrusted to Michael's Funeral Home of Drumright.

Darrin was born in Perry (Oklahoma) to Luther R. Hall and Connie (Rorabough) Hall on May 25, 1967. He died unexpectedly on Wednesday, Jan. 25, 2001 at the age of 33 years.

He had lived all of his life in this area and was a 1985 graduate of Drumright High School. He was currently employed as a lineman for ProLine Cable Company of Drumright.

Although his time with us was brief, he touched many lives. He'll be remembered as a loving father, son, brother, and friend and will be dearly missed by all who knew him.

His remaining family includes two sons and their mother, Zackary and Matthew Hall and Mary Harmon, all of Bristow; his mother, Connie Hall Bryant, of Drumright; his father and stepmother, Luke and Debbie Hall of Milfay; sisters Angie Hall and Debra Hall, of Drumright; stepsister Sue Scott, of Ada; half-brothers Richard Hall and Luther Hall, both of Kansas; stepbrother Keith Hall, of Drumright; two nephews, John Ross Hall and Michael Hall; a niece, Lindsey Bell; several aunts, uncles, other nieces and nephews and numerous friends, including his family of the heart, Dawna Flatt and Valerie Hatchett.

Dorotha Faye Hall Schornick (1931-2000)

[Dot was the beloved daughter of Florence Viola Scoggins and Ezra Marion Hall, of Duncan, Oklahoma.]

Dorotha Faye (Dot) Schornick, 69, died Saturday, Nov. 11, 2000, in the Wilkins Nursing Home. Service will be at 2 p. m. Monday at the Bailes-Polk Funeral Chapel, with the Rev. Winston Curtis officiating. Burial will be in the Duncan Cemetery following the service, under the direction of the Bailes-Polk Funeral Home.

Mrs. Schornick was born Jan. 27, 1931, to Ezra and Florence (Scoggins) Hall in Konawa [Oklahoma]. She attended the Konawa Schools. She married Marlin (Mac) Schornick in 1948 in Konawa. He preceded her in death in 1980.

Survivors include a son, Mickey Schornick of Duncan; a daughter,

Terrye Hugentober of Bloomfield, Ind.; and two granddaughters, Katelyn Joann and Sarah Ann Schornick, both of Duncan.

IN MEMORIAM

Mallie Rue Carr Hall
November 15, 1881-July 12, 1971
Tuesday, July 13, 1971 at 1 P. M.
Interment in Memorial Gardens, Fresno, California

Horace Greel Hall
[nÈe Greeley Teeman Hall]
[Son of William Newton Hall, husband of Mallie Rue Carr]
August 23, 18766March 6, 1965
Interment Memorial Gardens
Fresno, California

Kate Elsey Hall
February 4, 1883
January 16, 1977
Funeral service in Dopkins Chapel
Dinuba, California
The Rev. John Carr officiating
Tuesday, January 18, 1977, at 2 P. M.
Interment in Smith Mountain Cemetery

Dock Walter Hall
[Son of William Newton Hall, husband of Kate K. Elsey]
December 22, 1873
May 8, 1951
Funeral service at Dopkins Chapel

Dinuba, California
Thursday, May 10, 1951, at 2 p. m.
Interment Smith Mountain Cemetery

Ruth Hall Potter
[Daughter of Mallie Rue and Greel Hall, wife of Benjamin Potter]
Age 68
Born January 4, 1908
Tahlequah, Oklahoma
Died September 8, 1976
Henryetta, Oklahoma
Services 2:00 P. M. Friday, September 10, 1976
Chruch of Christ, Henryetta, Oklahoma
Interment Westlawn Cemetery, Henryetta, Oklahoma
Shurden Funeral Home

Delsie Dale Hall Bernard
[Daughter of Mallie Rue and Greel Hall, wife of William C. Bernard]
Born August 29, 1914, Asher, Oklahoma
Died January 13, 1998, Fresno, California
Funeral services Friday, January 18, 1998, at 1:00 P. M.
Chapel of the Light, Fresno, California

She always leaned to watch for us,
Anxious if we were late,
In winter by the window
In summer by the gate,

And though we mocked her tenderly,
Who had such foolish care,
The long way home would seem more safe
Because she waited there.

Her thoughts were all so full of us, She never
could forget!
And so I think that where she is
She must be watching yet,
Waiting till we come home to her, Anxious if we
are late, Watching from Heaven's window,
Leaning from Heaven's gate.

William Clifford Bernard
[Husband of Delsie Dale Hall]
Born January 29, 1915, Shady Point, Oklahoma
Died March 1, 1988, Fresno, California
Funeral services Friday, March 4, 1988,
Chapel of the Light, 11:00 A. M.
Fresno, California

Bonita Pursiville Hall

[Daughter of Mary and Nolan Franklin Pursiville, Sr., and the wife of
Wesley E. Hall]

Born August 18, 1929
Found eternal rest October 15, 1989
Services Saturday, October 21, 1989, 10 a. m.
Old Boston Cemetery, Oldfield, Missouri
The Rev. Kenneth McGill officiating
Adams Funeral Home, Ozark, Missouri
Zack Oberon Hall
In Memory of My Brother, Zackie
by Gradie (Hall) Goff
(November 17, 1969)

[When Zack, one of Greel and Mallie Hall's boys, died in Lodi, California, in 1969, his sister Gradie was the only member of the family present at the cemetery, and so moved was she at the pitiful scene she wrote the following.]

My brother Zack lies in Butte County cemetery.
In Butte County cemetery so very far awayómy darling brother Zackie lies today.
He was so handsome and so still as he lay in the casket at Scheer Memorial Chapel on Olive and Foot Hill.
It was so lonely and sad that his three children could not see their dad. He has a daughter Karen and a son Jim that never did really get to know him. But, his daughter Sydney, the youngest of them all, is proud to say her name is Sydney Hall. He also has a mother so sweet and so dear, who has loved him so much and shed many a tear.
He tried his very best to say, "I love my darling children anyway."
Dear brother, you had five brothers and five sisters, and there are only eight of us left to mourn for you.
Zack lost his dad March 9, 1965. He didn't get to see him because Dad was buried before Zack arrived.
We lost our dear sister Ollieóand Mable, too. It is so sad, dear God. We now turn to you, with your love and guidance from above. We know, dear God, we have your continuing love; and if we obey your command we will meet again in another land. I am sure it won't be sad and dreary like that spot in Butte County cemetery. But that is OK little brother. On Judgement Day we will all meet together in Heaven some way.
As we were going up Olive and Foot Hill down by a big library, we found this sad spot called the Butte County cemetery. I want you to know, my brothers and sisters who couldn't be there, it was a sad, lonely spot and so bare. There were only three graves as I could see, in that lonely Butte County cemetery. Our brother Zack could have had a military funeral if things had not gone wrong, and then maybe we could have at least had

one song. The song we requested was "On a Hill Far Away." That was the song they sang for Dad on that sad day.

Dear brothers and sisters, we know we have God's love and if we are lucky, we will all meet above. There is one thing we are sure of: God knows best, and if we trust him He will do the rest.

But dear brother, Zack, I am wondering why in this spot at Olive and Foot Hill I can still see your sweet face so still and dear. It just breaks my heart to leave you there. Now, my dear brother, I must go. But we will meet again, for the Bible tells us so.

CENSUS ROLLS & OTHER DOCUMENTS

Although the Hall family history is based primarily upon federal census records and the state and county records on file in Georgia, Arkansas, and Oklahoma, a great deal of effort has been expended elsewhere, such as the *Archives of the Church of Jesus Christ of Latter-Day Saints*, in Salt Lake City, Utah, and personal interviews with the oldest surviving members of the family. Since our family was in the American South prior to and during the Civil War, a great deal of valuable family information was undoubtedly lost; however, the 1840, 1860, and 1870 census records of Carroll, Haralson, Dawson, and Bullock counties did survive.

COUNTY CENSUS RECORDS

1840 CARROLL COUNTY, GEORGIA
   Hall, Hiram 813th District M704 Roll 38 21

1850 CARROLL COUNTY, GEORGIA

   1167 1 Cynthia Hale 51 f GA
   1167 2 Martha Hale 23 f GA

   1267 1 Hiram Hale 55 m SC (b. 1795)
   1267 2 Charity Hale 48 f GA (b. 1802)
   1267 3 Nancy Hale 21 f GA (b. 1829)
   1267 4 William Hale 19 m GA (b. 1831)
   1267 5 Eveline Hale 14 f GA (b. 1836)

1267 6 Tyra Hale 12 m GA (b. 1838)
1267 7 Ailey Hale 7 f GA (b. 1843)
1267 8 Parthena Hale 2 f GA (b. 1848)
1267 9 Green Hale 6 m GA (b. 1849)

[The year 1842 was chiseled on Green's tombstone, in Ledbetter Cemetery, Madison County, Arkansas. The surname in this census record is obviously misspelled.]

Thos. Herrin	30 M	Farmer	Ga.
Wife:	Arminda	25 F	"
Children:	Jas.	2 M	"
	Hiram	6/12 M	"

1134 1 John Hall 26 m GA (b. 1824)
1134 2 Nancy Hall 22 f GA (b. 1828)
1134 3 Delilah Hall 2 f GA (b. 1848)
1134 4 Robert Hall 6m m GA (b. 1850)

[These last two entries are Hiram and Charity's eldest daughter and son.]

1850 LUMPKIN COUNTY, GEORGIA

Greenbury Hall (27) (1823, S. C.) farmer 400
    Wife: Charity (34) (1816, S. C.)
    Children: Nancy (8) (1842, Ga.)
                John (6) (1844, Ga.)
                James (5) (1845, Ga.)
                Mary Ann (3) (1847, Ga.)
                Charity (2) (1848, Ga.)
[This is probably Hiram's younger brother.]

1860 HARALSON COUNTY, GEORGIA

[First census for this new county. Cf. Carroll County. Etna REEL NO: m653-126 PAGE NO: 373 and 374. Submitted by Wynell Simpson, Sept. 20, 2001.]

Hiram Hall (64 M FARMER 100 700 b. 1795, S. C.)
  Wife: Charity (58 F b. 1802, Ga.)
   Children: Elander (19 F WEAVER b. 1841, Ga.)
        Greer (17 M b. 1843, Ga.)
        Parthonia (12 F b. 1848, Ga.)
   Other: Martha Ayres (18) (1842, Ga.) WASHER
   Other: Henry Ayres (16) (1844, Ga.)
   Other: Clarance Ayres (13) (1847, Ga.)
   Other: Delilah (9/12) (1860, Ga.)

[Elender is married to William Sandford (b. 1842), who is not present for this census. Delilah is their daughter. Martha]

1860 DAWSON COUNTY, GEORGIA
Shoal Creek District - June 6

Green B. Hall (37) (1823, S. C.) farmer, 900, 300
  Wife: Charity (45) (1815, N. C.)
   Children: Nancy (17) (1843, Ga.)
        John Wesley (16) (1844, Ga.)
        James (14) (1846, Ga.)
        Mary Ann (12) (1848, Ga.)
        Charity (11) (1849, Ga.)
        Isom R. (8) (1852, Ga.)
        Green B. (6) (1854, Ga.)

[The similarities between this family and the Hiram and Charity Hall family are so striking the only conclusion that can be drawn is that they were closely related. For example, both have a son named Green B. Cf. the 1870 census.]

1860 DAWSON COUNTY, GEORGIA
Barretts District - July 10

William Hall (30) (b. 1830, FLA FARMER 30)
        Wife: Darcus (24), (1836, Ga.)
        Children: Sarah (9) (1851, Ga.)
                   Susan (7) (1853, Ga.)
                   Mary (4) (1856, Ga.)
                   Margaret (2) (1858, Ga.)

[Cordelia Hall, William Newton Hall's daughter, was convinced that her father had another family in Georgia. This would explain his disappearances for weeks at a time when the family was in Arkansas. She said he was returning to Georgia to search for his *long, lost Sid.* Darcas has been suggested as his first wife. This William Hall is thirty, he is from Florida, and there is no Sid. The first two discrepancies could be slips of the pen (of the census taker), and Sid could have been born after the 1860 census. Dawson County was where Green Berry Hall was living at this time. There is no record of this family after the Civil War. It is possible that Darcas and the children did not survive the terrible devastation of Sherman's *March to the Sea.*]

1870 HARALSON COUNTY, GEORGIA

Hall, Charity (68) (1802, Ga.) 700 200
        Daughter: Partheny Hall (23) (1847, Ga.)

Granddaughter: Electious Hall (2) (1868, Ga.) [Parthena's daughter]

Sandford, William (28) (1842, Ga.) farming 100
Wife: Elender (36) (1836, Ga.)
Children: Delilia Sandford (12) (1848, Ga.)
              Frances Sandford (9) (1851, Ga.)
              Rebecca Sandford (1) (1859, Ga.)

[Hiram, who would have been seventy-five, is absent from this 1870 census, suggesting that the Hall farm has been turned over to William Sandford, who has returned home from the war, Delilah is now twelve, and she has two sisters. These are Hiram and Charity's grandchildren. Tyre and Green B., who are now thirt and twenty-five, respectively, are probably sharecropping the farm with William.]

Tyree Hall (30) (1840, Ga.)
Wife: Arsenia (30) (1840, Ga.)
Children: Davis (10) (1860, Ga.)
              Lenorah (8) (1862, Ga.)
              Charity (5) (1865, Ga.)
              Mary (1) (1869, Ga.)

Green Hall (25) (1835, Ga.) farm laborer 150
Wife: Sarah Hall (20) (1840, Ga.)
Children: William (3) (1857, Ga.)
              Mary (1) (1859, Ga.)

1870 DAWSON COUNTY, GEORGIA

Hall, Green B. (48) M Farmer Ga.

Wife:	Charity (54) F Keeping House		Ga.
Children:	Mary Ann	21 F	Ga.
	Charity	19 F	Ga.
	Isom R.	17 M	Ga.
	Green B.	16 M	Ga.

1880 DAWSON COUNTY, GEORGIA
Shoal Creek Dist.

G. B. Hall (55) Self M M W Minister S.C.

Wife:	Charity (62)	wife F M W	N.C.
Children:	Mary A.	32 F	Ga.
	Charity	30 F	Ga.
	Green B.	25son M	Ga.
Other:	J. Summerout	11 (black)	Ga

[Green Berry Hall (the Elder) is now a minister of the gospel; but it is obvious from the names of his wife and children it is the same Green Berry.]

1880 MADISON COUNTY, ARKANSAS
Union Township

Green B. Hall (36) (1844, Ga.) father, S. C.; mother, Ga.

Wife:	Sarah E. Bradley (30) (1850, Ga.)
Children:	William (13) (1867, Ga.)
	Mary E. (11) (1869, Ga.)
	Liza A. (7) (1873, Ark.)
	Jessica (2) (1878, Ark.)

[From this it can be assumed that Green B. and Sarah made the trip from Haralson County, Georgia, to Madison County, Arkansas, between 1869 and 1873.]

1880 MADISON COUNTY, ARKANSAS
Richland Township

William N. Hall (49) (1831, Ga.) father S. C; mother Va.
    Wife: Susan E. (29) (185, Ga.) father, Ga; mother, Ga.
    Children: Acha B. (Archibald) (8) (1871, Ark.)
                   Doctor W. (6) (1874, Ark.)
                   Greeleserteemone (1) (1879, Ark.) [1877]
                   Ulsee Grant (2 mos.) (Mar. 1880, Ark.)

[It is obvious that William Newton and Susan Hall made the trip from Georgia to Arkansas before 1871, when Archie was born. We know from other records that they did not go directly to Madison County, however. It is very likely that the three brothers, including Tyre, arrived there about the same time.]

Tyre Hall (42) (1838, Ga.)
    Wife: Ascena (Arcenia) (42) (1838, Ga.)
    Children: David (20) (1860, Ga.)
                   Lenoria (18) (1862, Ga.)
                   Charity E. (13) (1867, Ga.)
                   Mary A. (10) (1870, Ga.)
                   James W. (9) (1871, Ga.)
                   Lucy A. (8) (1872, Ga.)
                   Maggie (5) (1875, Ark.)
                   Aurena (Arcenia) (2) (1878, Ark.)
                   George K. (1) (1879, Ark.)

[From this it is clear that Tyree and Arcenia did not leave Georgia until after Lucy was born in 1872. My conclusion is Green B. and Sarah and Tyree and Arcenia made the trip in the year 1873, and William and Susan, who were already in Waldron, Scott County, joined them in 1875. My father, Greeley Teeman, was born there in 1877.]

1880 BULLOCK COUNTY, GEORGIA
Census Place: Hagans, Bulloch, Georgia

William N. Hall (41) (1839, Ga. Father: Ga. Mother: Ga.)
    Wife: Martha (39) (1841, Ga.) father: Ga.; mother, Ga.)
    Children: Maggie Hall (14) (1866, Ga.)
              Ann E. Hall (12) (1868, Ga.)
              James R. Hall (7) (1873, Ga.)
              Mary D. Hall (5) (1875, Ga.)
              William Hall (3) (1877, Ga.)
              Samuel A. Hall (1) (1879, Ga.)
    Laborer: Joel Foster (36) (1844, Ga.)

[For a time I entertained the idea that this William N. was my grandfather.]

1880 HARRALSON COUNTY, GEORGIA

Charity Hall (83) (1797, Ga.) father, S. C.; mother, S. C.)
    Grandson: John Thompson (Ga.) [Parthena's son?]

1900 MADISON COUNTY, ARKANSAS
Union Township

William Hall (69) (April, 1831, Ga.)
  Wife: Susie E. (43) (July, 1857, Ga.) [1851]
  Children: Sidney W. (17) (April, 1883, Ark.) [1882]
                 Charity A. (15) (April, 1885, Ark.)
                 Green T. (12) (November, 1887, Ark.)
                 Cordelia (Delia) (9) (March, 1891, in Ark.) [1884]

[An excellent example of the carelessness of census takers]

1900 MADISON COUNTY, ARKANSAS

Green B. Hall (56) (Aug., 1843, Ga.) father, N. C.
  Wife: Sarah E. (50) (January, 1850, Ga.)
  Children: Angus (16) (Nov. 1883, Ark.)
                 Rena (13) (April, 1887, Ark.)
                 Green M. (11) (Oct. 1888, Ark.)
                 Hyram (8) (Feb. 1892, Ark.)
                 Olga (5), (April, 1895, Ark.)

Tyre Hall (58) (Dec. 1841, Ga.) father, N. C.
  Wife: Annie (25) (May, 1875, Ala.) father, Ga.; mother,
                 Ala.
  Other: Theodore S. Cox (29), brother-in-law, Ala.

1910 MADISON COUNTY, ARKANSAS
Dutch Creek Township, April 19-20

Tyre Hall (49) (1861, Ark.) father, Tnn., mother, Ark.
  Wife: Liza (47) (1863, Ark.) father, Tnn., mother, Ark.
  Children: Ida (18) (1892, Ark.)

1920 SEMINOLE COUNTY, OKLAHOMA
Konawa Township

Harris G. Hall (45) (1875, Ark.) father, Ga., mother, Ga. [Horace Greely]
      Wife: Mallis (39) (1881, Ark.) father, Ga,, mother, Ark.)
              [Mallie]
      Children: Ezra (17) (1903, Ark.)
              Gradie (15) (1905, Ark.)
              Ollie (14) (1906, Ark.)
              Ruthie (12) (1908, Ok.)
              Mable (9) (1911, Ok.)
              Clifford (7) (1913, Ok.)
              Delsie (5) (1915, Ok.)
              Luther (3) (1917, Ok.)
              Vernon (2 mos.) (1920, Ok.)

FROM THE ARCHIVES OF THE LATTER-DAY SAINTS
Salt Lake City, Utah

HARRALSON COUNTY, GEORGIA

Hiram Hall, born near Charleston, S. C., b. 1795 m.1822 in Georgia, father,1769; mother,1770)
      Wife: Charity, m. in 1822 (b. 1802, in Haralson Co., Ga).
      Children: Arminda Hall (b. 3-17-1823; m. Thos. S. Herron, Carrol Co., Ga. 11-25-47; d. 1915
              John Hall (b. 1824, Haralson Co., Ga.; m. Nancy Hamilton, b. 1824)
              Nancy Hall (b. 1829, Haralson County, Georgia)
              William N. Hall (b. 1831, Haralson Co., Ga.; m. Susan Wood 10-
17-1868 in Atlanta, Ga.)

Emeline Hall (1836, Haralson Co., Georgia)
Tyre Hall (b. 1838, Haralson Co., Ga.; m. Arseeney
Merett 1-20-
1859 in Haralson Co., Ga.; m. Annie Cox from Alabama)
Elander (Ailey) Hall (b. 1842, Haralson Co., Georgia)
Green B. Hall (b. 1844 or 1845, Haralson Co., Ga; m.
Sarah
Elvira Bradley on 4-15-1866 in Haralson Co.)
Clarency (Charity) Hall (b. 1847, Haralson Co., Ga)
[1860 census]
Parthena Hall (b. 1848, Haralson Co., Ga.; m. (1) James
Thompson 3-3-1870, Haralson Co.; (2) G. B. Brown 11-3
1874, Haralson Co.; (3) Wm. R. Day, of Anderson Co.,
Tex., on 11-23-1889)
Delila Hall (1859, Haralson Co., Ga)

Tyre Hall (1838, Haralson County, Ga.)
    Wife: (1) Arseeney Merett (Jan. 20, 1859, Haralson Co.,
                   Ga.;
                   (2) Annie Cox from Alabama)
    Children: Elander (Ailey) Hall (1842, Haralson Co., Ga.)

Green B. Hall (1845, Haralson Co., Ga.)
    Wife: Sarah Elvira Bradley (April 15, 1866, Haralson
                   Co., Ga.)
    Children: Claracy Hall (1847, Haralson Co., Ga.)
    Other: Parthena Hall (1848, Haralson Co., Ga.) m. (1)
                   James Thompson March 3, 1870, Haralson Co.,
                   Ga.; (2) G. B. Brown, Nov. 3, 1874, Haralson
                   Co., Ga.; (3) William R. Day of Anderson
                   County, TX, 11-23-1889.

[Parthena, of course, belonged to the Hiram and Charity family; but Green B. was her older brother. Haralson County did not exist until January 26, 1856, when it was created from Carroll and Polk counties.]

FROM THE NATIONAL ARCHIVES & RECORDS
Washington, D. C.

William Newton Hall (1841-ca. 1923) [1831-1923]
    Wife: Susan E. Woods (1851-ca. 1920) [1851-1918]
    Children: Archie Brooklyn (April 25, 1871, Waldron, Scott Co., Ark.)
                    Doctor Waldron (7) (1873, Ark.) [Dock Walter]
                    Charity (5) (1875, Ark.) [188]
                    Greele (1) (1877, Ark.) [Greely Teeman]
                    Ulsee Grant (3 mos.) (1880, Ark.) [Ulysses]
                    Sidney William
                    Delia

FAMILY ARCHIVES

Almost every branch of the Hall family has contributed something of historical interest and sentimental value to the Family Archives: pictures, letters, stories, legends, obituaries, copies of marriage licenses (and other similar documents), Family Group Records, maps, etc. These have been inventoried, classified, and stored in a safe place for the use of family members. For information regarding this write to me at 1463 Hwy 7 N, Holly Springs, MS 38635, or send me an email: <wehall@dixie-net.com>.

CERTIFICATES AND LICENSES

1. Birth Certifiicate - Grant Hall (born March 31, 1880) - State of Arkansas - Bureau of Vital Statistics - July 10, 1942 -Born in Drakes Creek, Japton Township, Madison Co., Arkansas. Father's name: William Hall; Mother's name: Susan Elizabeth Owens. Father's age: 40; Mother's age: 35. (2 copies)

2. Birth Certificate (delayed) - Greely Teeman Hall (April 7, 1942) Born August 24, 1877.

3. Birth Certificate (delayed) - Delsie Dale Hall (August 30, 1914). Place of residence: Asher, Oklahoma.

4. Marriage License - William N. Hall and Susan Wood -State of Georgia - Haralson County - October 17, 1868 - Justice of the Inferior Court, Haralson Co., John L. Phelps, M. G. (2 copies)

5. Marriage License - Greely Teeman (Horace Greel) Hall and Mallie Rue Karr - Welling, Indian Territory, November 17, 1900 (now Cherokee Co., Oklahoma) - Greely T., 22 years old; Mallie Karr, 18 years old.

6. Marriage License for Jesse Hall (21) of Porum, Muskogee Co., Okla., and Dora Lawson (16) of Briartown, Muskogee Co., Okla. Marriage place: Stigler, Oklahoma. Marriage date: June 27, 1919.

7. Application for Marriage License - for O. A. Peters (52) and Annie Hall (16). Signed by A. B. Hall on Dec. 12, 1912,

8. Application for Marriage License - for J. W. Swafford (38) and Annie Hall (26). Signed by A. B. Hall on April 28, 1924.

9. Request for Social Security Number - Grant Hall (June 3, 1937) - Born March 31, 1880, Madison Co., Arkansas) - U. S. Social Security Act (Application for Account Number) - Employed by W. P. A., LeFlore County, Oklahoma - Father's name: William Hall; Mother's name: Susy Owens.

10. Request for Social Security Number - Green Hall (December 5, 1938) (51 years old) - Born November 22, 1887, Japton, in Madison Co., Arkansas - Father's name: Wiliam N. Green; Mother's name: Susie Woods.

11. Death Certificate for Archie Brooklyn Hall. Born April 25, 1871; died May 31, 1955. Father's name: Wm. M. Hall [sic]; mother's name: unknown. Informant: Dave Swafford, Nowata, Oklahoma.

12. Death Certificate - Green T. Hall - Born November 22, 1888 - Died August 11, 1967 (He was 79)- Father's name: William M. Hall; Mother's name: Susan E. Woods, Tennessee.

13. Death Certificate - Jessie Newton Hall - Born April 1, 1891 - Died June 18, 1994. Buried: Nowata, Oklahoma. (2 copies)

14. Death Certificate for Nancy Clancy [sic] Hall. Born May 3, 1876; died May 26, 1955. Father's name: J. J. McDougal; mother's name: Elizabeth Elzido. Informant: A. B. Hall, Nowata, Oklahoma.

15. Death Certificate - Annie (Hall) Irons - Born Aug. 29, 1896 - Died May 9, 1956.

16. Dawes/Guion Miller Rolls - 1898-1914 (allotments of land in the Cherokee Nation). The following Halls are listed: Zula Lee, Annie, Jessie Mae, Newton, Walter, Wattie, William Newton. Pages 190-191.

17. "Some Madison County [Arkansas} Marriages"óExtracted by John B. Little, Box 63, Kingston, Arkansas 72742.

18. List of Marriage Licenses Issued 1856-1882 - Haralson County, Georgia (cf. p. 2) - William N. Hall and Susan Wood - October 17, 1868 - Tyre Hall and Arseeney Merett - January 20, 1859 - Green Hall and Sarah Elvira Bradley - April 15, 1866.

FAMILY GROUP RECORDS (FGR)

[Genealogy forms produced by the Church of Jesus Christ of Latter-day Saints and filled out by independent genealogists and family researchers.]

Judy G. Lloyd, 6115 W. Riveria Dr., Glendalee, AZ 85304 submitted the following Family Group Records:

1. Hiram Hall (1795-) and Charity (1802-)
2. Archie Brooklyn Hall (April 25, 1871-May 31, 1955) and Nancy Caroline McDougal (May 2, 1876-May 26, 1955)
3. Doctor Waldron Hall (Dec. 22, 1873-May 8, 1951)
4. Harris G. (Greele) Hall [sic] (August 23, 1875-March 6, 1965) and Mallis [sic] Carr (Nov. 15, 1881-July 12, 1971)

Trudy Tobias, P. O. Box 4129, Woodville, California, submitted the following FGR's:

5. Ulysses Grant Hall (March 31, 1880-July 9, 1964) and Sylvania Pennington (Feb. 25, 1880-March 11, 1936)
6. Sidney William Hall (Dec. 30, 1882-1972)
7. Logan Sisemore (June 10, 1882-Dec. 12, 1973) and Delia May (Cordelia) Hall (March 15, 1884-Dec. 1982)

8. Lee Rogers (April 25, 1886-Dec. 1963) and Charity Hall (April 10, 1885-Jan. 1964)

9. Green Tyre Hall (Nov. 22, 1887-Aug. 12, 1967) and Nancy (Nanny) Eversole (July 4, 1888-Dec. 20, 1945)

10. Guy Dawson (Aug. 25, 1916-) and Lucy Florence Hall (March 6, 1915) Letter written by Lucy March 6, 1995, to Trudy Tobias.

Mildred Guernsey, P. O. Box 105, Midway, Utah, submitted the following FGR's:

11. Thomas S. Herron (Dec. 12, 1812-July 19, 1899) and Arminda (Armindy) Hall (March 17, 1823-1915)

12. Earl Hall (Dec. 19, 1903-) and Stella Scoggins (Oct. 20, 1906-March 7, 1993)

Debra Shamblin, Rt. 1, Box 151, Webbers Falls, OK, submitted the following:

13. Carl Tyre Hall (April 27, 1901-Oct. 13, 1965) and Carrie Melissa Taylor (Nov. 25, 1903-June 29, 1982)

14. John Hall (Oct. 1, 1824-Aug. 3, 1898) and Nancy Hamilton (April 3, 1928-March 6, 1914)

15. Bud Hall (d. 1931) and Lissa Caroline (Carrie)Taylor (Nov. 22, 1902-June 29, 1982) (Cf. Carl Tyre Hall and Carl (Bud) Tyre Hall below.)

16. James Arnold Hall (June 8, 1908-Jan. 14, 1993) and Bessie Crumm (Crumb?) (b. Sept. 17, 1915)

17. Kenneth Murl Hall (Jan 11, 1934-) and Rena Irene Walker (Aug. 15, 1937-)

18. Ricky Joe Burney and Kathy Irene Hall (July 5, 1955-)

19. Ricky Murl Hall (July 18, 1957-) and La Donna Broughton

20. William Dale Smith (Nov. 2, 1938-) and Wanda Hall (April 11, 1940) (2 copies)

21. Larry Dale Smith (Feb. 8, 1960-June 2, 1983) and Tresa Ann Masterson)

22. James David Daugherty and Tawnya Danita Smith (Aug. 25, 1961)

23. Theo Kelley III and Tawnya Smith (Aug. 25, 1961)

24. C. L. Payne and Oma Hall (1922)

25. John Beard and Oma Hall (1922)

26. Arthur Hall and Vernie Tyler

27. Arthur G. [sic] Goff and Gradie Hall (1905)

28. Orville Rainey (1914-June 17, 1995) and Bunah (Patricia) Sisemore (Jan 12, 1918)

29. Jackie Ray Rainey (Aug. 8, 1934) and Helen (d. ca. 1934)

30. Thomas Aubrey Rainey (May 6, 1938)

31. James Braun and Dovie Hall (Nov. 25, 1918)

32. Peek and Dovie Hall (Nov. 25, 1918)

33. Connie Lee (Bud) Beard (d. ca. 1946) and Jewel Hall (sept. 19, 1915)

34. Billy Ray Beard (April 17) and Cathy Stucky (d. 1990)

35. Bill Landphear (? spelling) and Cecil (Cecilia) Hall

Ramona Lloyd, 2833 E. 4510 S., Salt Lake City, Utah 84117) submitted the following FGR's:

36. Michael Merrill Lloyd (Oct. 16, 1951) and Judy Gail Hall (March 13, 1949)

37. Calvin (Cal) Rock, Sr. and Sadie Lee Hall

38. Charles Smith (d. 1944) and Iva Lorene Hall

Kathy Ann Wright, 16116 Cindy Lane, Broken Arrow, OK 74014, submitted the following FGR's:

39. David Bruce Wright and Kathy Ann Hall (Aug. 2, 1952)

40. James Larry Hall (March 28 1951-) and Paula Jean Parfum/Livesay (June 20, 1954-July, 1989)

41. Vinnis Phillips and Gladys Marie Hall

42. Tyre Roland Hall (aug. 15, 1929-ca. 1931) and Ruby Benton

43. Mark Stephen Hall (Oct. 5, 1953-) and Robin Hirschi (June 27, 1954)

44. Carl Tyre Hall (April 27, 1901-Oct. 13, 1965) and Nora (May) Mae Howell (May 31, 1913-)

Carrie Hyslop, Rt. 2, Box 129, Porum, OK 74455, submitted the following FGR's:

45. Carl Tyre (Bud) Hall (April 27, 1901-Oct. 13, 1965) and Carrie Lisa Taylor (Nov. 25, 1902-June 29, 1982)

46. Ocie Dwight Hyslop (Sept. 22, 1899-May 9, 1976) and Lissa Caroline "Carrie" Taylor (Nov. 22, 1902-June 29, 1982)

Leola Hall, 311 N. 14th St., Broken Arrow, OK 74455, submitted the following FGR's:

47. James Oliver Hall (Feb. 19, 1928-) and Leola Ezell (May 8, 1930)

48. David Lee Hall (Oct. 18, 1959-) and Paula Kay Eakin

The following Family Group Records were submitted by Richard Gregory Van Wagoner, Cleveland, Emery County, Utah:

49. John Hall (1769-?) and Mary (1770-?) (2 copies)

50. Hiram Hall (1795-?) and Charity (1802-?)

51. Thomas S. Herron (Dec. 29, 1812-July 19, 1899) and Arminda Hall (March 17, 1823-1915)

52. John Hall (Oct. 1, 1824-Aug. 3, 1898) and Nancy Hamilton (april 3, 1828-March 6, 1914)

53. James Thompson (March 3, 1870-?) and Parthena Hall (1848-?)

54. William R. Day and Parthena Hall (1848-?)

55. G. B. Brown and Parthena Hall (1848-?)

56. Robert Jefferson Hall (March 25, 1850-June 15, 1944) and Sara Jane Brewer (Oct. 2, 1856-June 1, 1940)

57. Paris Cotton and Mary Anice Hall

58. Wellington C. Hall (1879-1964) and Laura (1883-1963)

59. Thomas Cleveland Hall (Dec. 9, 1894-Oct. 13, 1965) and Margie Rena Roberts (Oct. 20, 1889-Oct. 26, 1961)

60. Darien C. Hall (March 1, 1887-Jan. 22, 1922) and Jessie (Oct. 7, 1889-May 2, 1964.

61. Voyd Hall (July 9, 1894-Dec. 9, 1968) and Mary P. (Sept. 24, 1895-Oct. 28, 1970)

62. Carlos Mentril Hall (Sept. 28, 1909-Aug. 20, 1964) and Winnifred Lorena Rogers (Oct. 11, 1917-?)

63. Therman Clemet Hall and Mary Virginia Rogers (Aug. 2, 1915-)

64. Victor Leon Hall (Oct. 16, 1928-Oct. 18, 1952) and Phyllis

65. Theodore Carlos Hall (april 7, 1937-Nov. 13, 1962) and Beverly Daniels

66. Roger Evan Hall (Dec. 12, 1939-) and Sharron Lynn Holland

67. John Knuckles (April 6, 1963-) and Janette Arlene Hall (Dec. 12, 1941-)

68. Floyd Johnson (1961-) and Marjorie Evelyn Hall (June 14, 1943-)

69. Charles Bradley Pearson (Oct. 16, 1940-) and Barbara Joy Hall (Feb. 20, 1945-)

70. Danny Anderson (June 10) and Winnifred Eileen Hall (Nov. 17, 1946-)

71. Dennis Hendric and Marilyn Kaye Hall (June 7, 1949-)

72. Jeffery Royce Hanson (Set. 3, 1964-) and Pamela Ann Pearson (May 4, 1964)

73. Charles Bradley Pearson (Feb. 18, 1969-) and Judy Lynn Housekeeper (May 24, 1970-)

74. Glenn Shane Prestwich (Jan 12, 1966-) and Rena Lyn Pearson (March 25, 1970)

75. Michael Royce allred (May 23, 1964-) and Lorena Ruth Pearson (Oct. 12, 1966-)

76. Richard Gregory Van Wagoner (March 14, 1958-) and Tricia Danette Pearson (June 10, 1971-)

77. Green Berry Hall (1805-) and Charity (1815-)

78. William Newton Hall (1831-ca. 1921) and Darcas (1836-)

79. William Newton Hall (1831-ca. 1921) and Susan Elizabeth Woods (1851-1918)

80. Tyre Hall (1838-) and Arcina N. Merett (1838-)

81. Tyre Hall (1838-) and Annie Cox (May, 1875-)

82. Green Berry Hall (Aug. 12, 1842-Jan 5, 1930)

83. Greeley Teeman Hall (1877-1925 [sic] and Mallie Rue Karr (1872-1971)

The following FGR was submitted by Bertha Joan Hall Davis:

84. Ephraim Riley Hall (Feb. 12, 1870-July 9, 1942) and Mary Ellen McChristian (Aug. 4, 1874-Dec. 14, 1945)

The following FGR was submitted by Robert K. Rainey, 875 E. Stuart St., Bartow, FL 33830

85. Logan Sisemore (June 10, 1887-Dec. 10, 1975) and Delia Hall (March 15, 1891 [sic])

The following FGR's were prepared and submitted by Mark A. Terrill, 913 Burgandy Ln., Modesto, CA 95351:

86. William Newton Hall (1841 [sic] - 1923) and Susan Elizabeth Woods (1851-1918)

87. Green Berry Hall (1905-1815) and Charity (1815-)

88. Greeley Teeman "Horace Greel" Hall (Aug. 23, 1877-March 5, 1965) and Mallie Rue Karr (Nov. 15, 1882-July 12, 1971)

89. Clifford Cleborn Hall (June 3, 1912-Dec. 29, 1974) and Georgia Marie Sage (Sept. 28, 1916-Oct. 30, 1976)

90. William Dean Terrill (June 25, 1935-May 27, 1993) and Shirley Ann Hall (Sept. 26, 1937-Feb. 16, 1989)

91. David Philip Terrill (Oct. 28, 1955-) and Karen Sue Bonds (Jan. 2, 1951-)

92. Arnold Ulloa and Kathleen Marie Terrill (Aug. 29, 1958-)

93. Frank Rock and Merry Susan Terrill (March 4, 1960-)

94. Les Burns and Cara Lee Terrill (May 25, 1962-)

95. Perry Vierra and Cara Lee Terrill (May 25, 1962-)

96. John Richard Sheppard (Jan. 21, 1937-) and Mary Jo Hall (Dec. 27, 1939)

97. Jesse Kilborn Holmes (June 3, 1940-) and Nancy June Hall (June, 1943-)

The following FGR's were repared and submitted by Newton H. Scoggins, 4617 NW 32nd St., Okla. City, OK 73122:

98. Earl Hall (Dec. 19, 1903-March 7, 1993) and Stella Mae Scoggins (Oct. 20, 1906-March 7, 1993)

99. Durward Jack Hall (April 13, 1927-) and Sarah Gladys Slentz (Sept. 27, 1931-May 5, 1981)

100. Val Gene Hall (Sept. 23, 1928-) and Louise Elms (Dec. 25, 1930-)

101. Andrew J. (Mike) Domyan (July 12, 1925-) and Velta Lee Hall (Oct. 5, 1930)

102. Bobby Ray (Bob) Hall (Nov. 24, 1932-) and Anita Marquez (Dec. 20, 1935)

103. William Charley Helton (Nov. 21, 1932-) and Barbara Louise Hall (July 13, 1935)

104. Edward S. Browne (Nov. 17, 1960-) and Joyce Oteka Hall (Dec. 21, 1938-)

105. Larry Wayne Hall (Aug. 27, 1955-) and Christie Mason (Dec. 9, 1956-) [Larry is Durward Jack's son.]

106. Chuck Hoenshell and Tracy Kay Hall (March 12, 1957-) [Tracy is Durward Jack's daughter.]

107. Ronald Hall (Aug. 23, 1951-) and Liz [Ronald is Val Gene's son.]

108. Ronald Hall (Aug. 23, 1951-) Dahlia Josephina Ortiz (May 4, 1954-)

109. Milton Kenneth Hendrickson (Aug. 21, 1971-) and Phyllis Jean Hall (May 30, 1950-)

110. ? Nelson and Debbie Ann Hall (April 27, 1957-)

111. ? Liles and Diana Lynn Hall (July 27, 1958-)

112. ? Smith and Denise Hall (Aug. 27, 1962-)

113. Ezra Marion Hall (Sept. 29, 1902-July 25, 1986) and Florence Viola Scoggins (April 25, 1905-Oct. 9, 1997)

114. Alton Lee Hall (March 10, 1928-Oct. 11, 1989) and Jeanetta Ramsey (Dec. 2, 1932-)

115. David Landers (April 21, 1945-) and Ginger Kaye Hall (June 24, 1949-)

116. Gary Ramsey (June 4, 1947-) and Ginger Kaye Hall (June 24, 1949-)

117. Randall Jones and Marcella Diane Ramsey (June 24,1968-)

118. Tina Lynn Ramsey (Oct. 23, 1970-) and (?)

119. Marlin Joe (Mack) Schornick (Jan. 18, 1926-Aug. 7, 1980)

120. Neil Hugentober and Terrye Lee Schornick (Sept. 25, 1951-)

121. Mickey Joe Schornick (Jan. 9, 1957-) and Cynthia Sue Coder (Sept. 11, 1959-)

The following FGR's were prepared and submitted by Walter Sizemore, 274 Redbud Lane, Tahlequah, OK 74464:

122. James Sisemore (1816-1896) and Mary Ball (March, 1819-ca. 1904)

123. ? and Mary Ball (March, 1819-ca. 1904)

124. John Sisemore, Sr. (Jan. 17, 1839-Jan. 25, 1924) and Sarah Neal (July 16, 1843-Nov. 3, 1929)

125. Aaron Richard Pennington (July 24, 1842-April 10, 1926) and Mary Sizemore (Jan. 29, 1845-Sept. 17, 1926)

126. James Sisemore (July 7, 1861-Oct. 31, 1915) and Sarah Whitehead (1864-1882)

127. Walter Sisemore (Aug. 10, 1882-March 14, 1974) and Alice L. Ritchie (April 15, 1891-Dec. 14, 1913)

128. Ezra Sizemore (Nov. 10, 1910-Jan. 5, 1988) and Billy Burke Hensley (Dec. 12, 1914-Dec. 30, 1998) [Walter Leland Sizemore's parents]

129. Logan Sisemore (June 10, 1887-Dec. 14, 1973) and Cordelia Mae Hall (March 15, 1890 [sic] - Dec. 12, 1982)

TOMBSTONES AND CEMETERY RECORDS

Ledbetter Cemetery, Drakes Creek (Madison County), Arkansas:
Green Berry Hall (August 12, 1842-January 5, 1930/Sarah E. Bradley Hall (January 12, 1850-July 23, 1911)
Ules S. Cowan (born 1890; died 1962)
[Another example of a Southern family naming a child after the great Northern general who led the Yankees to victory over the South; and, ironically, *Cowan* was one spelling of my maternal family name: *Keown*.]

FAMILY PICTURES

These pictures, for the most part old black-and-whites, have been entrusted to me for safe-keeping and for sharing with the family. Send me a SASE and limit each request to five (of whatever size). I will respond on a first-come, first-served basis.

If you have a picture of some member of the family that you would like to share, mail it to me at 1463 Hwy 7 N, Holly Springs, MS 38635; or email it t me as an attachment at <wehall@dixie-net.com>. Be sure to label it and give as much information about it as possible.

1. William N. Hall and Susan Elizabeth Woods, taken in Oklahoma about 1915. This is an old black-and-white 6X9, the only extant picture of these two. There is some dispute about whether the woman in this picture is, indeed, Susan Elizabeth Woods. Marti Hyder sent me a 5X7 copy of it with the caption "Wm. Hall - Susan Owens."

2. Ulysses Grant Hall, holding a small dog. 6X11 b&w

3. Ulysses Grant Hall, wearing suspenders. 4X6 b&w

4. Ulysses Grant and daughter Mary, March, 1959 6X8 b&w

5. Grant and Sylvania (Pennington) and family, ca. 1904, 7X10 b&w

6. Greel and Mallie Rue Hall, 1900 (wedding picture), 6X9 (colorized)

7. Mallie Rue (Karr) Hall, ca. 1928, 5X7 b&w

8. Mallie Rue (Karr) Hall, ca. 1940, 4X6 (colorized)

9. Mallie and Greel Hall family, ca. 1924 5X7 b&w

10. Mallie and Greel Hall, ca. 1942 3X5, b&w (fading)

11. Mallie and Greel Hall, taken in the 'Thirties in California.

12. Delia (Hall) Sisemore, 8X10 b&w (Seated on a divan, ca. 1966)

13. Green T. Hall, ca. 1940's 6X9 b&w

14. Green T. and Nanny (Eversole) Hall, ca. late 1930's, 6X9 b&w

15. Green T. Hall and Zack Hall ca. 1940's, 6X9 b&w

16. Group picture of Green T.'s family, ca. 1920's, 8X9 b&w (fading)

17. The six sons of Greel & Mallie Hall, ca.1947, 7X9 b&w

18. Birtha and Ed Gragg, 5X7 b&w
19. Robert Jefferson Hall, 6X9 b&w
20. Earl and his daughter Jewel, 1997 4X6 b&w
21. Patricia Hatcher and a friend, 3X5 b&w
22. Lucy Dawson (Grant's daughter), 4X6 b&w
23. Delsie, Mallie, Gradie, Mable Hall, ca. 1942 5X6 b&w
24. Ollie Ida Hall, ca. 1930 5X7 b&w
25. Ruth (Hall) Potter and Delsie (Hall) Bernard , 9-69 5X5 color
26. Wanda Hall (Grade School photo, Spiro) b&w
27. Kenneth Murl Hall, 6-26-69 b&w
28. Archie and Nancy Hall, ca. 1952 3X4 b&w
29. Jessie Newton and Finnis Etter Hall, ca. 1950 3X5 b&w
30. Jessie Newton and Finnis Etter, ca. 1960 3X5 color
31. Jessie Newton and daughter Helen Orchid, 9-01 3X5 color
32. Jackie (Jessie Mae Hall) and Gene Heckathorn, 6-99 4X6 color
33. Mallie (Carr) Hall, ca. mid-'20's, 5X8 b&w
34. Group picture of Mallie Hall's 'girls' , 4X4 b&w
35. Gradie (Goff) Hall and Zack Hall, ca. late '30's, 3X4 b&w
36. Mallie (Carr) Hall, ca. 1940, 5X4 b&w
37. Myrna (Bernard) Ceccarelli, 1946 4X4 b&w
38. Ezra and Gradie (Goff) Hall, 1972 4X4 color (Drakes Creek Baptist Ch.)
39. Ezra and Florence (Scoggins) , Terry & Ginger, ca. 1940's 5X5 b&w
40. Zack Hall in the Navy (2 views), 2X2 b&w
41. Ruth (Hall) Potter and Mallie (Carr) Hall (WW2 memorial) 2X3 b&w
42. Forence (Scoggins) and Ezra Hall, 1980 4X5 color
43. Gradie (Hall) Goff, ca. 1980 3X5 color
44. Lou Smith and Ollie (Hall), ca. 1925 7X9 b&w
45. Bud and L. A. Smith (1999), 4X6 color
46. Flora (Putler) Smith, ca. mid-1940's 4X5 b&w
47. Roy Joe Smith, ca. 1964 2X3 b&w

48. L. A. Smith, 1942 5X7 b&w
49. L. A. Smith, 1935 3X5 b&w
50. Bud Smith, 1935 3/x5 b&w
51. Flora Eveline Smith, 1935 b&w
52. Avo (Rincon) Smith, 1943 (school picture) 3X5 b&w
53. L. A. Smith, Oct. 1946 (age 17), 7X9 b&w
54. Avo Smith, ca. 1944 (age 18), 8X10 color
55. The Smith family, including Lou, ca. early '50's, 5X5 b&w
56. Trudy Tobias, 1998 (age 45), 2X3 color
57 Green T. Hall's headstone in Woodbridge Masonic Cemetery
58. Grant Hall funeral, July 1964
59. Grant's headstone
60. Nanny Hall's headstone and casket
61. Logan's and Delia's (Sisemore) headstones
62. A small tintype of Alice (Howard) Carr, Mallie Hall's mother

MISCELLANEOUS DOCUMENTS

1. Facsimile copy of letter written by William Newton Hall to his Commanding General on December 17, 1863. In this letter William mentioned that his father would be in Bullock County, not far from Camp Rose, where his unit was at that time bivouacked, during Christmas and that he wanted to "make arrangements" to dispose of his Negroes the following year.

2. *Hall's Original County Map of Georgia*, by Hall Brothers, civil and marine engineers, Atlanta, Georgia (1895) "Showing present and original counties and land districts." Compiled from state records. [30" X 33 1/2"]

3. *A New Map of Georgia with Its Roads and Distances* [dated 1846].

4. *Map Showing the March Routes [of General Sherman] During the Campaign of Georgia.*

5. *Map Showing the March Routes of the 2nd Division of 15th Army Corps from November 12 to December 21, 1864.*

6. Homestead Claim of Arch B. Hall for 39.65 acres in Arkansas, dated August 12, 1901 (Certificate issued from the Land Office, Harrison.)

7. Ancestor Chart for Ephriam Riley Hall (Prepared by Lillian Davis Newman, 2230 N. Arden, Santa Ana, CA 92706 0 July 16, 1985)

8. Pedigree Chart for Debra Sue (Hall) Shamblin (gg-granddaughter of Archie Booklyn Hall)

9. The Hunter Genealogy, including the shipping list of the *Two Brothers*, which arrived in Philadelphia on September 14, 1749.

10. Ulysses Grant Family Records, Madison County, Arkansas:

Ules Grant Hall (Mar 3, 1880-July 9, 1964, was born in Waldron, Ark.

Wife:	Sylvania Pennington (Feb. 25, 1880-March 11, 1936).
	Children: Viola Helen Hall (1900-1982) (m. Ralph Cannon,1917)
	Willy (Willie) Hall (Oct. 3, 1901-Dec. 6, 1906)
	Albert Hall (May 26, 1903-April 19, 1916) was born in Sallisaw, Oklahoma, and buried at Mt. Comfort Cemetery, Oklahoma.
	Maggie Lee Hall (Feb. 14, 1905-Feb. 27, 1935) married man named Harris. She was born in Madison County, Arkansas, and died in Blaine Bottoms, Star, Oklahoma. She had five children: one boy and one girl died when they were babies. Lowell and Fay Clifton were raised by Ella and Clyde Crisler, and Charles was raised by Mary Elizabeth (Hall) Hyder.
	Mary Elizabeth Hall (Sept. 19, 1906-Oct. 6, 1989) was born in Madison County, Arkansas and died in California. She married Toy Elmo Hyder and later a man named Cole.
	James Arnold (June 8, 1908) married Bessie Crumm on Sept.10, 1932.

Ellar Zona Hall (May 9, 1911-May 10-1990) was born in Japton, Arkansas, and is buried in Woodville Cemetery. She married a man named Crisler.

Goldie May Hall (Dec. 10, 1913-April 20, 1916) died of measles at B. A. Rudolph's Place and is buried in Mt. Comfort Cemetery.

Lucy Florence Hall (March 6, 1915) lives in Arizona (1995). She married Davis Dawson.

Eva Alice Hall (May 2, 1916-Aug 15, 1921) died of measles in Wesley, Arkansas, at Aaron and Mary Pennington's place. She is buried in Duncan Cemetery, Georgetown, Arkansas.

John Theron Hall (April 2, 1919-Sept. 2, 1993)

Aaron Pennington (57) (July, 1892, Ky.) father, N. C.; mother, Ky.

Wife:	Mary (56) (Jan. 1844, Ky.) father, Tnn., mother, Ky.
Children:	John (18) (April, 1882, Ky.)
	Silvania (Vane) (20) (Feb., 1880, Ky.)
Other:	Thomas McChristian (12) (nephew) Feb. 1888, Ark.
Other:	Grant Hall (20) (son-in-law) (Mar., 1880, Ark.) father, Ga., mother, Ga.
Other:	Hiram Sisemore (94) (father-in-law) May, 1806, Tnn.
	James Counts (41) (May, 1859, Ark.) father, Ark., mother, Tnn.
Wife:	Elizabeth Counts (39), b. Mar, 1861, Ark.
Children:	Norman (16), Edward (15), Cordelia (11), Annie E. (8),
	Iva E. (5), Eva E. (3)

CIVIL WAR SERVICE RECORDS
General Services Administration
National Archives and Records Service
Washington, D. C.

Three members of our branch of the Hall family fought in the Civil War: William Newton, Tyre, and Green Berry (the Younger). William Newton Hall enlisted on October 10, 1861, as a second lieutenant with Company E, 5th Georgia Cavalry, C. S. A., Bullock County, Georgia. Tyre and Green B. were conscripted in Haralson County the following year. Tyre became a part of Company G., 40th Georgia Infantry Regiment (called the Haralson Defenders) on April 10, 1862, but sometime later deserted and was captured on October 24, 1864, near Dallas, Georgia. He was released on May 12, 1865. Green B. was drafted a month later and assigned to the same company. He was captured at Vicksburg, Mississippi, on July 4, 1863, but was released shortly after that and went back to his company. In *A Roster of Confederate Soldiers of Bulloch County, Georgia 1861-1865*, by Smith Callaway Banks (1991), there is a brief summary of the action experienced by the Bullock Troops.

William Newton Hall's regiment engaged in picket duty along the coast of Georgia and South Carolina during the first year of the war, until it was ordered south to fight at Olustee, in Florida. They arrived too late for that engagement, however, because of a breakdown in railway transportation. They returned to Georgia just in time to meet General Johnston and his Yankees at Kennesaw Mountain. It was a bloody fight and the Commanding Officer of Company E, Captain George B. Best, was killed at Waynesboro. William N. was promoted to Captain and replaced him as C. O. This position he held until the surrender at Company Shops, North Carolina, in the last year of the war.

1. Green B. Hall Enlistment - July 14, 1863 (for 6 months) - Private, Company C - 11th Battallioon, Confederate State Guards - Capt. Samuel

Harben's Company, Dawson Infantry, Georgia - Dawsonville, Dawson County, Georgia. [Green B. the Elder]

2. William N. Hall - Enlisted October 10, 1861 - Savannah, Georgia (Enlisted by Lt. Col. W. S. Rockwell (12 mos.) - Company Muster Roll - Oct 10 to Nov 1, 1861 (Doc. #1) - Present - Second lieutenant, 2nd Battallion, Confederate Cavalry - Capt. Hendry"s Company, Bullock Troop [This company subsequently became Company C, 2nd Battallion, Georgia Cavalry. On January 20, 1863 it was consolidated with the 1st Battallion, Georgia Cavalry by S. O. No. 20, Headquarters District of Georgia, South Carolina, and Florida to form the 5th Regiment, Georgia Cavalry.]

3. William N. Hall - Company Muster Roll (Doc. #2) - Nov. & Dec., 1861 - Present - Stationed at Camp Rose, Savannah, Georgia - Last paid by Maj. S. J. Smith (to Nov. 1861).

4. William N. Hall - 2nd Lt., Bullock Troop, 2 Battalion Georgia Cavalry - Officers Pay Account: Dec. 1 - Dec. 31 (one month) - $90.

[I hereby certify that the foregoing account is accurate and just; that I have not been absent without leave during any part of the time charged for; that I have not received pay, forage, or received money in lieu of any part thereof, for any part of the time therein charged; that the horses were actually kept in service and were mustered for the whole of the time charged; that for the whole of the time charged for my staff appointment, I actually and legally held the appointment and did duty in the department; that I have been a commissioned officer for the number of years stated in the charge for every additional five years service; that I am not in arrears with the Confederate States on any account whatsoever; and that the last payment I received from (in handwriting: Maj. S. J. Smith, AGM, CSA) and to the (thirtieth) day of (November) 1861. I, at the same time, acknowledge that I have received of (Maj. S. J. Smith AGM CSA) this (Fourth) day of (January) 186(2) the sum of (Ninety) dollars, being the amount in full of said account.]

5. William N. Hall - 2nd Lt., Co. C, 2nd Btt'n., Ga. Cavalry - Company Muster Roll - January and February, 1862 - Present or absent - not stated (Recapitulation shows the 2nd Lt. present).

6. William N. Hall - 2nd Lt., Co. C, 2nd Bttn., Ga. Cavalry - Company Muster Roll - March and April, 1862 - Last paid by S. J. Smith to April - Present.

7. William N. Hall, 2nd Lieut., Co. C, 2nd Bal Ga Cavallry - Officers Pay Account: April 1, 1862, to April 30, 1862 - $90 [Acknowledgement of payment made by Capt. W. M. Davenport, Brigade Paymaster & A.G.M. on May 1, 1862, and that he had last been paid by Maj. S. J. Smith, AGM on March 31, 1862.]

8. William N. Hall - 2nd Lt., Co. C, 2nd Bttn., Ga. Cavalry - Company Muster Roll - May and June, 1862 -Present

9. William N. Hall, 2nd Lt., Co. C, 2nd Batt'n, Georgia Cavalry - Officers pay account for two months: from May 1, 1862, to June 20, 1862: $180.

10. William N. Hall - 2nd Lt., Co. C, 2nd Bttn., Ga. Cavalry - Company Muster Roll - July and August, 1862 -Present or absent - not stated -(Recapitulation shows Btn. 2nd Lt. absent with leave).

11. William N. Hall, 2nd Lt., Co. C., 2nd Batt'n, Ga. Cavalry - Officers Pay Account - August 1 to August 31, 1862 [Acknowledgement of $90 (July pay) from Maj. S. W. Smith at Charleston and that the August pay was given to him on October 10, 1862.]

12. William N. Hall - 2nd Lt., Co. C, 2nd Bttn., Ga. Cavalry - Regimental Return of Company C, 2nd Battallion, Georgia Cavalry - Camp Rose, Savannah, Georgia - June, 1862.

13. William N. Hall - 2nd Lt., Co. C., 2nd Bttn., Ga. Cavalry Register: W. N. Hall, 2nd Lt., Co. C, 2nd Battn., Ga. Cavalry appears on register containing Rosters of Commissioned Officers, Provisional Army Confederate States. Date of appointment: Oct. 10, 1861.

14. William N. Hall - 2nd Lt., Co. C, 2nd Bttn., Ga. Cavalry - Company Muster Roll - September and October, 1862 -Present.

15. William N. Hall - 2nd Lt., Co. C. 2nd Bttn., Ga. Cavalry - List: W. N. Hall, 2nd Lt., Co. C, 2nd Batt'n, Ga. Cavlary (not dated) - From what state appointed: Ga. Where born: Ga.

16. William N. Hall - 2nd Lt. Sr., Co. E, 5th Reg't., Ga. Cavlary - Company Muster Roll - January and February, 1863 - Present.

17. William N. Hall - 2nd. Lt. Sr., Co. E, 5th Regt., Georgia Cavalry - Company Muster Roll - March and April, 1863 - Present.

18. William N. Hall - 2nd. Lt. Sr., Co. E, 5th Reg't., Ga. Cavalry - Company Muster Roll - May and June, 1863 - Present.

19. William N. Hall - 2nd Lt., Co. G, 5th Ret't., Ga. Cavalry - Register: W. N. Hall, 2nd Lieut., Co. G, 5 Regt., Ga. Cav. appears on register containing Rosters of Commissioned Officers, Provisional Army Confederate States. Date of promotion 1st Lieut [In pencil on Register.]

20. William N. Hall - 1st Lt., Co. E, 5th Reg't., Ga. Cavlary - Company Muster Roll - July and August, 1863 - Present. [Remarks: Promoted to 1st Lt., August 10, 1863].

21. William N. Hall - 1st Lt., Co. E, 5th Reg't, Ga. Cavalry - W. N. Hall, 1st Lt., Co., C, 5th Ga. Cav., appears on List of Officers absent from Military District of Georgia. Absent on Sept. 26,1863. Absent from Sept. 25 to Sept. 26 by authority of Brig. Gen. Mercer. Reason for leave: with leave 8 days.

22. William N. Hall - 1st Lt., Co. E, 5th Reg't, Ga. Cavalry* - Company Muster Roll - September and October, 1863 - Present [*Name appears in column of names present as Wm. N. Hall]

23. William N. Hall - 1st Lt. Commanding Co. 3, 5th Reg't, Ga. Cavalry - Requisition for Fuel for Camp Davant (1 Capt., 3 subalterns, 91 men) On October 1, 1863.

24. William N. Hall - 1st Lt., Co. E, 5 Reg't, Georgia Cavalry - Company Muster Roll - November and December, 1863 - Absent on furlough.

25. William N. Hall - 1st Lt., Co. E, 5 Reg't, Georgia Cavalry - Company Muster Roll - December 31, 1863, to April 30, 1864 - Present.

26. William N. Hall - 1st Lt., Co. E, 5 Reg't, Georgia Cavalry - Company Muster Roll - May and June, 1864 - Present.

27. William N. Hall - 1st Lt., Co. E., 5 Reg't, Georgia Cavalry - Regimental Return: Stationed Pocotaligo. Commissioned officers present and absent: Present.

28. William N. Hall - Capt., Co. E, 5 Reg't, Georgia Cavalry - Company Muster Roll - June 30 to December 31, 1864 -Absent with leave. Remarks: Absent with leave. Promoted to Captain from 1st Lieut. December 4, 1864. Capt. Best killed.

29. William N. Hall, 1st Lt., Commanding Officer, Co. E, 5 Reg't, Ga. Cavalry - Requisition for Forage for 97 horses: 30,070 pounds of corn, 20,079 pounds of fodder from Camp Davant on October 31, 1863.

[Apparently, when the Civil War ended April 9, 1865, Capt. William Newton Hall was Commanding Officer of Company E, 2nd Battallion, 5th Regiment, Georgia Cavalry. It would appear from this service record that he did not desert from the Confederate Cavalry as his daughter Cordelia maintained.]

30. Order and Creation of Georgia's 159 Counties, Dept. of Archives & History, Atlanta, Georgia 30334.

THE FAMILY DIRECTORY

Jewel Beard (daughter of Earl and Stella Hall), 1361 E. Academy Way, Dinuba, CA -591-4119

Sandra Bellamy (daughter of Clara Potter Swann) P. O. Box 1403, Murphys, CA 95247 <Lakie33@aol.com>

Sadie and Chuck Berry (mother and stepfather of Sharon Hall) 3759 Sycamore Road, Coldwater, MS 38618.

Lauren Brown (daughter of Leslie Brown, granddaughter of Wesley Hall) 1225 N. Cherokee Ave. #209, Hollywood, CA 90038 - 323 871 4240 - cell phone: 323-683-1639 <santalucia@earthlink.net>

Leslie and Alan Brown (daughter and son-in-law of Wesley Hall) 1304 E. Cherry, Springfield, MO 65807 - (417-831-4390) <alan@fatpanda.com>

Matt Brown (son of Leslie and Alan Brown, grandson of Wesley Hall) 1220 N. June St. #504, Hollywood, CA 90038 - 323 463 1008 - cell phone: 213 948 6316 <matt@fatpanda.com>

Myrna Ceccarelli (daughter of Delsie and Lucy Bernard) 3838 N. Channing Way, Fresno, CA 93705<jorue@concintric.net>

Melford & Floy Cecil (Sharon Hall's aunt and uncle) 428 North Point Drive, Mountain Home, AR Katherine Diebert (daughter of Faye and Steve Kandarian) 2570 W. Palo W. Alto, Fresno, CA 93710

Velta Lee Domyan (daughter of Earl and Stella Hall) 1723 Ivy Road, Oceanside, CA 92054-5640

Jean Finley (daughter of Ruth and Ben Potter) 701 Imperial Way #11, Salmon, ID 83467-4042

Holly FitzPatrick (daughter of Wesley Hall) 501 W. Center, Lebanon, Illinois 62254 <seanfitzpatrick@sapphire.jcn1.com>

Frant Gragg (Nelson Jr's uncle, Birtha and Ed Gragg's son, m. to Aunt Thelma) 313 W. Central, Anadarko, OK 73005 - 1-405-247-5603

Hank Gragg (another uncle of Nelson Jr., also Birtha and Ed's son) 22243 Lone Mountain Road, Whittman, AZ 85361

Nelson Lee Gragg Jr. (grandson of Birtha Hall, great-grandson of Archie and Nancy Hall) 911 E. 3rd, Emmett, Idaho 83617

James Olen Gragg (Nelson Jr.'s first cousin, grandson of Archie Brooklyn Hall) 1-623-972-6874 - 18007 N. 88th Ave., Peoria, AZ 85382 <jgragg2@msn.com>

David and Christy (Heard) Grimes (David is Wesley Hall's grandson) 1555 Barber Rd., Chadwick, MO 65629 <Crsty583@cs.com>

Carl W. Hall (grandson of Dock and Kate Hall) 1053 N. Leslie, Ridgecrest, CA 93555 Chris Hall (son of Wesley Hall) PO Box 42, Union, MO 63084 636-629-9958 <rchrish@yhti.net>

Jack Hall (son of Earl and Stella Hall) 405-946-8094 - Oklahoma City

Leola Hall (wife of James Oliver Hall, who was Arch Hall's grandson) 311 N. 14th St., Broken Arrow, Oklahoma 74455

Luke and Debbie Hall (Luke is the son of Luther and Christine Hall) P. O. Box 156, Milfay, OK (918-968-4270)

Phyllis Hall (wife of Victor Leon Hall, who is the grandson of Robert Jefferson Hall), P.O. Box 45, Cahone, Co 81320

Wesley and Sharon Hall (son of Greel and Mallie Hall), 1463 Hwy 7 N, Holly Springs, MS 38635 - 662-551-2059 <sharonjhall@hot-mail.com><wehall@dixie-net.com>   URL<http://ww2.dixie-net.com/~wehall>

Barbara L. Helton (daughter of Earl and Stella Hall), 2446 Stanford Ave., Clovis, CA 93611-0433 <thorn@cybergate.com>

Terry Hugentober (daughter of Dorothy and Mack Schornick), Rt. 3, Box 233, Bloomfield, Indiana

Marti and Jessie Ray Hyder (Ray is Grant Hall's grandson), P. O. Box 103, Tipton, CA 93272 - 559-752-4464 - 209-752-4460 <RMVID3@aol.com>

Faye Kandarian (daughter of Gradie and Arthur Goff), 7274 N. Dante, Fresno, CA 93722-209-276-7442

Nancy Kay Kemp (daughter of Flora and Jim Putler), 40640 High Street #710, Fremont, CA 94038 <NJPKEMP@cs.com>

Joey Lamanuzzi (son of June (Goff) Lamanucci), 3838 West Beachwood, Fresno, CA 93711

June Lamanuzzi (daughter of Gradie and Arthur Goff), 1846 S. Price Ave., Fresno, CA 93702

Linda Lamanuzzi (daughter of June (Goff) Lamanuzzi), 3252 W. Barstow, Fresno, California 93711

Darcy Langston (daughter of Jean (Potter) Finley), 311 Stevens, Salmon, ID 83467-4038

Nia Clarice Langston (daughter of Jean (Potter) Finley), 309 Lombard, Salmon, ID 83467

Patricia Ann Lehman (daughter of Faye and Steve Kandarian), 433 East Cole, Fresno, CA 93720

Sydney McKay (daughter of Zack and Edith Hall), 3404 Heatherwood, Lufkin, Texas 75905 sydmckay@hotmail.com

Susan McKee (Sharon Hall's sister) Route 3, Box 306B, Coldwater, MS 38618 Billie Ann Minugh (daughter of Annie Dona Hall), 7 Applegate Drive, Apt. C, Springdale, AR 72764

Adrien Lee Murphy (son of Katie Hartness, brother of Mrs. Joe Murphy), 305 W. 3rd, Bristow, OK 74010

Willa (Mrs. Joe) Murphy (daughter of Katie Hartness, granddaughter of Zora (Carr) Hartness, Mallie Hall's sister), 2145 Main, Bristow, OK 74010

Connie Palmer (sister of Sharon Hall), 6010 Sandhurst, Horn Lake, MS 38367 - 601-393-7072

Oma (Hall) Payne (daughter of Green T. and Nanny Hall), 345 California Ave., Dinuba, Calif. 591-5737

Flossie (Long) Potter (Ben Potter's second wife), 422 N Maple, Konawa, OK 74849 (405) 925-3334

Mitchel Potter (son of Ruth and Ben Potter), P. O. Box 168, Newalla, OK 74857 - 405-391-4798

Flora Putler (daughter of Ollie and Lou Smith), 1898 Olive Ave., Fremont, CA 94538

Robert K. Rainey (son of Lucille and Willie Rainey), 875 E. Stuart St., Bartow, FL 33830

Avo Rincon (daughter of Ollie and Lou Smith) 1918 Cougar Ave., Clovis, CA 93612 -209-297-4316

Joyce Robinson (daughter of Delsie and Lucy Bernard), 4262 E. Dayten, Apt. K, Fresno, CA 93726 (559-228-0715)

Grace Rogers (daughter of Charity and Lee Rogers), 8051 E. 8th St., Buena Park, CA 90621(714-523-3847)

Searles Rogers (son of Charity and Lee Rogers), 1472 W. Valencia, Fullerton, CA 92633

Walter Sizemore (distant cousin of Logan and Delia Sisemore), 274 Redbud Lane, Tahlequah, OK 74464 (918-456-3087)

Alma Smith (Roy Joe Smith's widow), 11403 Sage Hollow Rd., Houston, TX 77034 (713) 481-2488

Bridget E. Smith (daughter of L. A. and Lucille Smith) 7342 N. Alma, Portland, OR 97203

Gary Smith (son of L. A. and Lucille Smith), 871 Willys Dr, Arnold, MD 21012

Greg Smith (son of L. A. and Lucille Smith, married to Pebbles), 506 Southeast 46th St., Okla. City, OK 73129

L. A. Smith (son of Ollie and Lou Smith), 9501 SE 29th St., Oklahoma City, OK 73130 - 405-732-7251

Cleo Mae Stubblefield (daughter of Zora Hartness, Mallie Hall's niece), 200 W. Park, Monett, MO 65708 (417-235-7349)

Clara D. Swann (daughter of Ruth and Ben Potter), 7508 NW 12th St., Oklahoma City, OK 73127-4119 -405-495-3536

David Terrill (son of Shirley and Bill Terrill) 11841 Tunnel Hill Way, Gold River, CA 95670 - 916-635-5228

Kathy Ulloa (daughter of Shirley and Bill Terrill), 5913 Newbrook Dr., Riverbank, CA 95367 - 209-869-4947

Floyd Upperman (son of Ethel and Ben Upperman), 5609 Ethel Way, Sacramento, CA.

Richard Van Wagoner (Son-in-law of Barbara (Hall) Pearson, the great-granddaughter of Robert Jefferson Hall), P. O. Box 1232, Huntington, UT 84528

Kathy Ann Wright (great-granddaughter of Rachel Jane Hall) 16116 Cindy Lane, Broken Arrow, OK 74014 - 918-486-2828)

RELATED FAMILY TREES

1. THE DESCENDANTS OF EPHRIAM AARON PENNINGTON

[The link to the Halls: Ulysses S. Grant Hall (1880-1964), the second son of William Newton Hall and Susan Elizabeth Woods, married Sylvania Pennington (1880-1936).]

Aaron Richard Pennington was the son of Ephriam Aaron Pennington and Matilda Fields. He was born July 24, 1842, in Whitesburg (Letcher Co.), Kentucky, and died April 10, 1926, in Georgetown (Madison Co.). He married Mary Sizemore on December 4, 1862. Mary was born January 29, 1845, in Clay County, Kentucky, and died September 17, 1926, in Georgetown (Madison Co.), Arkansas. She was the daughter of Harmon Sizemore and Susan Sizemore. There were ten children by this marriage:

1. Susan Pennington (b. Nov. 8, 1863, Clay County, Kentucky; d. June 10, 1936, Grady County, Oklahoma; m. William Monroe Wood in 1883 in Madison Co., Arkansas.)

2. Harmon Pennington (b. Aug. 4, 1866, Clay County, Kentucky; d. 1867 in Clay County, Kentucky)

3. Nancy Pennington (b. March 26, 1867, Clay Co., Ky.; d. Oct. 4, 1940, in Roland (Sequoyah Co.), Okla.; m. Alvin Calloway Gage Dec. 28, 1888)

4. Martha Jane Pennington (b. Sept. 11, 1869, Clay Co., Ky.; d. Nov. 26, 1939, in Ft. Smith (Sebastian Co.), Ark.; m. Elijah Kenneth Lasiter ca. 1900, in Madison Co., Ark.)

5. Levi Pennington (b. May 22, 1871, Clay Co., Ky.; d. in 1928 in Madison Co., Ark.; m. Alice Ann Gabbard ca. 1890 inMadison Co., Ark.)

6. Smith Pennington (b. April 29, 1872, Louisville (Jefferson Co.), Ky.; d. Dec. 3, 1958, in Buena Park (Orange Co.,) Calif.; m. Anna Arizona Gage April 21, 1893, in Drakes Creek, Ark.)

7. Beverly Pennington (b. March 26, 1874, Clay Co., Ky.; d. 1899; m. Hilah Mae Counts Jan. 6, 1898, in Madison Co., Ark.)

8. Mary Ellen Pennington (b. Sept. 11, 1877, Clay Co., Ky.; d. 1912; m. Henry \Gage ca. 1893 in Muldrow (Sequoyah Co.), Okla.)

9. **Sylvania Pennington** (b. Feb. 25, 1888, Clay Co., Ky.; d. March 11, 1936, in Buckeye (Maricopa Co.), Arizona; m. Ulysses S. Grant Hall on Oct. 12, 1899, in Georgetown (Madison Co.), Ark.

10. John Bristow Pennington (b. April 14, 1882, Clay Co., Ky.; d. July 8, 1969, in Fayetteville (Washington Co.), Ark; m. Rosa Myrtle Howard on Aug. 14, 1913, in Georgetown (Madison Co.), Ark.)

2. THE DESCENDANTS OF JAMES SISEMORE (1816-1896)

[The link: Cordelia Mae Hall (1884-1982), a daughter of William Newton Hall and Susan Elizabeth Woods, married Logan Sisemore (1887-1973).]

The First Generation

James Sisemore's parents' names are not known. He was born in 1816 in Tennessee and died in 1896 in Madison Co., Ark. On March 4, 1835, he married Mary Ball in Harlan Co., Ky. Mary was born in March, 1819, in Harlan Co., Ky.; and died ca.
1904 on Panther Creek,* Madison Co., Ark. Her father was Bennett Ball and her mother was Nancy Bailey. There were nine children by this marriage:

1. Elizabeth Sisemore (b. 1836 in Harlan Co., Ky.; d. 1899 in Japton (Madison Co.), Ark.; m. James Casselman on Aug. 18, 1852, in Japton)

2. John Sisemore (Sr.) (b. Jan. 17, 1839, on Panther Creek, Madison Co., Arkansas; d. Jan. 25, 1924, Ball Creek (Madison Co.), Ark.; m. Sarah Neal on July 6, 1859, in Japton (Madison Co.) Arkansas.

3. Rebecca Sisemore (b. 1841 on Panther Creek (Madison Co.), Ark.; d. ca. 1853 on Panther Creek)

4. Sarah Ann Sisemore (b. June 6, 1843, on Panther Creek (Madison Co.), Ark.; d. April 5, 1863, on Panther Creek; m. James T. Forister (Foster) in 1860, in Japton (Madison Co.), Ark.)

5. Nancy Sisemore (b. 1846 on Panther Creek (Madison Co.), Ark.; d. ca. 1865 on Panther Creek)

6. Mary Frances Sisemore (b. Jan 8, 1850, on Panther Creek Madison Co.) Ark.; d. Nov. 20, 1934, on Ball Creek (Madison Co.), Ark.; m. George Washington Ledbetter Jan. 20, 1867, at Drakes Creek (Madison Co.), Ark.)

7. Joanna Sisemore (b. 1851 on Panther Creek (Madison Co.), Ark.; d. ca. 1865 on Panther Creek)

8. James Coleman Sisemore (b. Jan 9, 1856, in Rawles Township (Mills Co.), Iowa; d. August 28, 1952, in Johnson (Washington Co.), Ark.; m. Louisa Neal on Aug. 9, 1873, in Japton (Madison Co.), Ark.)

9. Abigail Sisemore (b. Jan. 18, 1858, on Panther Creek (Madison Co.) Ark.; d. Dec. 17, 1924, in Asher (Madison Co.), Ark.; m. Reuben Lloyd Lollar in 1879 in Asher)

[*This creek, popularly known as *Panter Crik*, was named for an incident involving William Newton Hall. The story goes that he killed a black panther at a road-crossing on this creek, saving a young girl's life. Cf. *A Visit to Japton and Drakes Creek, Arkansas* in the STORIES AND LEGENDS chapter.]

The Second Generation

John Sisemore (Sr.) was born January 17, 1839, on Panther Creek, Madison County, Arkansas. He died January 25, 1924, on Ball Creek (Madison Co.), Ark. On July 6, 1859, he married Mary Ball in Japton (Madison Co.), Ark. Mary's parents were Peter Neal and Mary Ann

McCarver. She died Nov. 3, 1929, in Huntsville (Madison Co.), Ark. She and John had fifteen children:

1. ? Sisemore (b. and d. on April 3, 1860, on Ball Creek (Madison Co.)

2. James Sisemore (b. July 7, 1861, on Ball Creek (Madison Co.), Ark.; d. Oct. 31, 1915, in Japton (Madison Co.), Ark.; m. Sarah Whitehead in 1881. His second wife was Bethena Louisa Dennis)

3. Mary Elizabeth Sisemore (b. Dec. 15, 1863, on Ball Creek (Madison Co.), Ark.; d. 1864 on Ball Creek)

4. ? Sisemore (b. and d. June 6, 1865, on Ball Creek)

5. Peter Pierson Sisemore (b. July 16. 1865, on Ball Creek (Madison Co.), Ark.; d. July 4, 1948, in Superior (Pinal Co.), Arizona; m. Louisa Tennessee Lewis ca. 1885, in Japton (Madison Co.), Ark.)

6. Enoch Pleasant Sisemore (b. June 13, 1868, on Ball Creek (Madison Co.), Ark.; d. Jan. 24, 1948, in Fayetteville (Washington Co.), Ark.; M. Margaret Ann Drake in1893 in Georgetown (Madison Co.), Ark.)

7. Martha Jane Sisemore (b. June 29, 1870, on Ball Creek (Madison Co.), Ark.; d. June 21, 1928, in Madison Co., Ark.; m. Jefferson Davis Groseclos Dec. 30, 1886, in Drakes Creek (Madison Co.), Ark.)

8. William Sisemore (b. July 16, 1872, on Ball Creek (Madison Co.), Ark.; d. in August, 1872, on Ball Creek)

9. George Washington Sisemore (b. Jan. 23, 1874, on Ball Creek (Madison Co.), Ark.; d. Nov. 22, 1961, in Huntsville (Madison Co.), Ark.; m. Sarah Frances Drake July 8, 1893, in Madison, Co., Ark.)

10. John Sisemore, Jr. (b. Aug. 4, 1876, on Ball Creek (Madison Co.), Ark.; d. Sept. 15, 1909, in Bartlesville (Washington Co.), Okla.; m. Mary Prudence Scott on May 12, 1895, in Madison Co., Ark.)

11. Nancy Abigail Sisemore (b. Oct. 4. 1878, on Ball Creek (Madison Co.), Ark.; d. Nov. 25, 1979, in Rusk (Cherokee Co.), Texas; m. Charles Henry Scott in 1892, in Japton (Madison Co.), Ark.)

12. Smith Sisemore (b. April 13, 1880, on Ball Creek (Madison Co.), Ark.; d. in May, 1880, on Ball Creek)

13. Sarah Ellen Sisemore (b. Nov. 27, 1882, on Ball Creek (Madison Co.), Ark.; d. July 28, 1943, in Huntsville (Madison Co.), Ark.; m. Jacob Franklin Drake Aug. 9, 1900, in Madison Co., Ark.)

14. **Logan Sisemore** (b. June 10, 1887, in Japton (Madison Co.), Ark.; d. December 14, 1973, Stockton (San Joaquin Co.), Calif.; m. Cordelia Mae Hall)

15. Rhoda Ann Sisemore (b. June 20, 1889, in Japton, Ball Creek (Madison Co.), Ark.; d. July 22, 1976, in Fayetteville (Washington Co.), Ark.; m. (1) Minter Sylvester Ball on Feb. 6, 1910; and (2) Green Scott Rogers)

The Third Generation

James Sisemore, the son of John Sisemore, Sr., and Sarah Neal, was born July 7, 1861, near Japton, Arkansas; and died October 31, 1915, in Japton. He married Sarah Whitehead in 1881, in Japton (Madison Co.), Arkansas. Sarah's parents were Joshua Whitehead and Nancy Sisemore. There was one child by this marriage:

1. Walter Sisemore (b. Aug.10, 1882, in Japton (Madison County), Ark.; d. March 14, 1974, in Muskogee (Muskogee Co.), Okla.; m. Alice L. Ritchie on Sept. 25, 1904, in Texanna (McIntosh Co.), Okla.)

The Fourth Generation

Walter Sisemore, the son of James Sisemore and Sarah Whitehead, was born August 10, 1882, in Japton (Madison Co.), Arkansas, and died March 14, 1974, in Muskogee (Muskogee Co.), Arkansas. He married Alice L. Ritchie on Sept. 25, 1904, in Texanna (McIntosh Co.), Oklahoma. Alice was born April 15, 1891, in Texanna (McIntosh Co.), Oklahoma, and died December 14, 1913, in Lindsey Chapel, McIntosh Co., Oklahoma. Her parents were George A. Pettijohn and Mary Alice Stansell. Alice and Walter had four children:

1. Ira Sisemore (b. May 4, 1906, in McIntosh Co., Okla; d. April 9,1978, in Wasco (Kern Co.), Calif.; m. Rennie Mae Ogle on August 24, 1924, in Texanna (McIntosh Co.), Okla.)

2. LaVina Lee Sisemore (b. Aug. 31, 1907, in Lindsey Chapel (McIntosh Co.), Okla.; d. Dec. 15, 1999, in Muskogee (Muskogee Co.), Okla.; m. Taylor Sizemore, Sr. in Eufaula (McIntosh Co.), Okla.)

3. Ezra Sizemore (sic?) (b. Nov. 10, 1910, in Texanna (McIntosh Co.), Okla.; d. Jan. 5, 1988, Tahlequah (Cherokee Co.), Okla.; m. Billy Burke Hensley Nov. 13, 1938, in Union (Franklin Co.), Missouri)

4. Dyton Sisemore (b. Feb. 14, 1913, in Lindsey Chapel (McIntosh Co.), Okla.; d. Feb. 19, 1974, in Bakersfield (Kern County), California; m. Clemie Audean Hamby on April 30, 1933, in Texanna (McIntosh Co.), Okla.)

The Fifth Generatiion

Ezra Sizemore, the son of Walter Sisemore and Alice Ritchie, was born November 10, 1910, in Texanna (McIntosh Co.), Oklahoma, and died January 5, 1988, in Union (Franklin Co.), Missouri. He married Billy Burke Hensley on November 13, 1938, in Union (Franklin Co.), Missouri. Billy Burke was the daughter of Adam Marcus Hensley and Virginia Gertrude Young. She and Ezra had two children:

1. Roger Lee Sizemore (b. Jan. 2, 1940, in Vandalia (Fayette Co.), Ill.); d. June 5, 1940, in Centralia (Marion Co.), Ill.)

2. Walter Leland Sizemore (b. June 19, 1944, in Princeton (Gibson Co.), Indiana; m. Melinda Lew Lynn on November 21, 1964. His second wife is Andrea Janette Sawatzky)

3. THE KARRS AND THE KEOWNS

[The link: Mallie Rue Carr married Greeley Teeman Hall, William Newton Hall's third son. This is the maternal side of my family, that began with a lady named Elizabeth Keown (1790-1890), of South Carolina.]

Sometime before 1810, when Elizabeth was twenty, she moved to Cherokee County, Georgia and married 'to a member of another Scottish family by the name of *Karr*. In that year their first child, Temperance, was born. Apparently, she had made the trip from South Carolina with an older brother, Andrew, born in 1783 in South Carolina, and his wife, Rachel, and who had two children, a girl named Catherino (sometimes spelled *Katherino*) and a boy named Noah E. In the 1850 census for Seminole County, Georgia, Elizabeth and her children were living in the home of a William Carr [In Scotland this name was spelled *Kerr*, but in America it became *Karr*, *Carr*, and sometimes *Car*] and Catherino, the daughter of Andrew. Her husband had either left her or was dead; and in the years that followed she went back to her maiden name. At least two of her older sons, William Jefferson and Jeptha, occasionally went by the name of *Karr*; but when the Civil War came they gave the name Karr (and Carr) as their last name.

The First Generation

Andrew Keown (1783-?), of South Carolina, married a woman named Rachel and they had two children: Catherino, who was born in South Carolina in 1835, and Noah E.

Elizabeth Keown (1790-1890), Andrew's sister, was born in South Carolina and died in Cherokee County, Georgia, at the age of 100.

The Second Generation

Elizabeth Keown (1790-1890), who was born in South Carolina and died in Cherokee County, Georgia, married a man named Karr (Carr), and they had seven children:

1. Temperance Karr (1810-?) (b. S. C., d. Cherokee Co., GA)

2. William Jefferson Karr (1812-1906) (b. S. C., d. Shawnee, OK)

3. Sylvestus Karr (1818-?) (b. S. C., d. Madison County, AR)

4. Jeptha P. Karr (1825-?) (b. S. C., d. Madison County, AR)

5. Thomas Riley Karr (1833-?) (b. Cherokee Co., GA, d. Madison County, AR)

6. Pleasant Karr (1840-?) (b. Cherokee Co., GA. Temperance may have been his mother)

7. Emit W. Karr (1847-?) (b. Cherokee Co., GA. Temperance may have been his mother)

The Third Generation

William Jefferson Karr (Carr) (1812-1906) (b. S. C., d. in Shawnee, OK, m. Sarah Jane Doss in 1825 (?); Sarah was the sister of Narcissa Malissa Doss, who was Jeptha Karr's wife)

1. William Riley Karr (1848-?) (b. Cherokee Co., GA, m. Louisa Temperance)

2. Sylvestus N. Karr (1850-?) (b. Cherokee Co, GA)

3. Henry Allan Karr (1852-1940) (b. Cherokee Co., GA, m. Alice Howard)

4. Rachel Elizabeth Karr (1854-?) (b. Cherokee Co., GA, m. Lum Johnson)

5. Mahaley Eviline Karr (1856-?) (b. Cherokee Co., Ga)

6. Thomas J. Karr (1857-1877) (b. Sep. 25, 1857, in Cherokee Co., GA, d. Sep. 30, 1877, in Madison Co., Arkansas)

7. Sarah E. Karr (1859-?) (b. Cherokee Co., GA)

8. Emeline Irene Karr 1862-?) (b. Cherokee Co., m. George Lee)

9. John Calvin Karr (1863-1950) (b. Cherokee Co., GA, July 18, 1863, d. Feb. 1, 1950, in Shawnee, OK, m. Margarette Irene Nichols, b. Cherokee County, GA, 1881)

Sylvestus Karr (1818-) (b. S. C., m. Dorcas M., b. 1821, Cherokee County, GA)

1. J. Karr (a son) (1841-?)

2. Toliver M. Karr (1843-?)

3. G. E. Karr (a daughter) (1841-?)

4. W. C. Karr (a daughter) (1844-?)

5. Nancy Karr (1846-?)

6. Mary A. Karr (1847-?)

7. Martin T. Karr (1848-?)

8. Enoch S. Karr (1850-?)

9. Margaret Karr (1852-?)

10. (Little) Dorcas Karr (1854-?)

11. Deborah Karr (1858-?)

Jeptha P. Karr (1825-?) (b. S. C., m. Narcissa Malissa Doss in Canton, Cherokee County, Georgia, on September 7, 1848)

1. John Calvin Karr (1850-?)

2. George W. Karr (1853-?)

3. Malissa Karr (1855-?)

4. Malinda E. Karr (1858-?)

5. Lucenia Karr (1862-?)

6. James T. Karr (1866-?)

7. Silvester Karr (1868-?)

The Fourth Generation

Riley Karr (1848-?) (b. Cherokee Co., GA., m. Louisa Temperance (?), who was born in Arkansas)

1. Mary M. Karr (1872-?)

2. A boy (born in Madison County, Arkansas, in 1969))

Henry Allan Karr (1852-1941) (b. Dec. 6 in Cherokee Co., GA; d. Shawnee, OK, m. Alice Howard)

1. Hubert T. Karr (1876-1966)

2. Mallie Rue Karr (1882-1971)

3. Myrtle Karr (?-?)

4. Zora Angeline Karr (1885-?)

5. Ethel Henretta Karr (1889-1976)

6. Edith Mae Karr (?-1941)

7. Elizabeth (Lissie) (?-?)

John Calvin Karr (1863-1950) (b. Cherokee Co., GA, July 18, 1863, d. February 1, 1950, in Shawnee, OK, m. Margarette Irene Nichols, b. Cherokee County, GA, 1881)

1. Lee Jackson Karr (?-?)

2. Jennie Maude Karr (?-?)

3. Edith Mae Karr (?-?)

4. William Harvey Karr (?-?)

5. Elsie Cleo Karr (?-?)

6. Lenna (Linna) Karr

7. James Arnold Karr (?-ca.1917)

8. Gertrude Karr (?-?)

9. Otto Karr (?-?)

10. Hattie Karr (?-?)

11. Orville Karr (?-?)

The Fifth Generation

Hubert T. Karr (1876-1966). He always spelled his name *Carr*, as did his siblings. He was the son of Alice (Howard) and Henry Allan Karr. He was born in Huntsville, Madison County, Arkansas, on August 6, 1876, and died in the Baptist Hospital at Raymondville, Texas, on March 8, 1966. He married Ida Forbes on December 23, 1896, who died in Raymondville, Texas, on January 17, 1959. From Arkansas they moved to Seminole, Oklahoma, where Hubert managed to buy twenty-seven worthless acres of weeds. In 1930 an oil company gave him twenty-seven million dollars for it, and he immediately moved to Raymondville, Texas, where he could find something to spend it on. He and Ida farmed in Willacy County, near Raymondville, Texas, from 1930 to 1966. They had ten grandchildren, sixteen great-grandchildren, and two great-great-grandchildren. Hubert was a member of the Nazarene Church, and his funeral services were conducted by two Nazarene preachers. He is buried in Raymondville Cemetery, Raymondville, Texas. He and Ida had seven children, all of whom but Omer survived them. Children by this marriage:

1. Laurence Karr (?-?)

2. Clarence Karr (?-?)

3. Odie Karr (?-?)

4. Omer Karr (?-?)

5. Carl Karr (?-?)

6. Birchie Karr (?-?)

7. Ruby Karr (?-?)

Mallie Rue Karr (1882-1971). Mallie was the daughter of Alice and Henry Allan Karr. She was born in Harrison, Arkansas, on November 15, 1882, but moved to Wesley, in Madison County, Arkansas, while she was a girl. She married Greeley Teeman (Horace Greel) Hall in 1900 on Barron Fork Creek in Indian Territory (near Tahlequah). She died July 12, 1971, in Fresno, California, and was buried beside Greel in Memorial Gardens. She and Greel had eleven children:

[The descendants of Mallie and Greel will be found in *The Hall Tree* above.]

1. Ezra Marion Hall (1902-1986)

2. Grady Hall (1904-1990)

3. Ollie Ida Hall (1906-1934)

4. Ruth Hall (1908-1976)

5. Clara Mabel Hall (1910-1964)

6. Clifford Cleborn Hall (1912-1974)

7. Delsie Dale Hall (1914-1998)

8. Luther Leonard Hall (1917-1972)

9. Vernon Hall (1920-1974)

10. Zack Oberon Hall (1923-1969)

11. Wesley Elmo Hall (1925-)

Myrtle Karr (1880-). Myrtle was the daughter of Alice and Henry Allan Karr. She was born in Madison County, Arkansas, around 1880. She married Carter Hood, and they had one son:

1. Watie Hood (?-?)

Zora Angeline Karr (1885-). Zora was the daughter of Alice and Henry Allan Karr. She was born February 27, 1885, in Huntsville, Arkansas. She married John Hartness, born April 15, 1882, in Tahlequah, Oklahoma. John was half-Cherokee. They had seven children:

1. Katie Hartness (1906-?)

2. Dave Hartness (1908-1934)

3. Clara Hartness (1909-?)

4. J. B. Hartness (1910-1938)

5. Dolly Lea Hartness (1915-)

6. Gladys Marie Hartness (1918-)

7. Reba Leota Hartness (1919-1963)

8. Cleo Mae Hartness (1922-)

9. Jackie Hartness (1923-1924)

10. Laura Bea Hartness (1927-)

Ethel Henretta Karr (1889-1976). Ethel was the daughter of Alice and Henry Allan Karr. She was born January 3, 1889, in Huntsville, Arkansas, and died June 9, 1976, in Phoenix, Arizona. She married Benjamin Harrison Upperman, of Kansas, who was born January 22, 1883, and died June 9, 1976. They lived in Phoenix for many years (until their deaths). Ben worked for the Coca Cola bottling company of Phoenix. They had two boys:

1. Ben Henry Upperman (?-)

2. Floyd Edward Upperman (?-)

Edith May Karr (?-1941). Edith was the daughter of Alice and Henry Allan Karr. She was born in Huntsville, Arkansas, date unknown. She married Claude Cowan (Keown?) and they had four children:

1. Everette Cowan (?-)

2. Bessie Cowan (?-)

3. Opal Cowan (?-)

4. Mary Cowan (?-)

The Sixth Generation

Katie Hartness (1906-). Katie was the daughter of Zora (Karr) and John Hartness. She was born October 14, 1906, in Tahlequah, Oklahoma.

She married a man named Kuykendall but divorced him on October 15, 1947. In the 1960's and 1970's she and her children and grandchildren were living in Monett, Missouri. They had seven children:

1. Mildred Jean Kuykendall (?-)

2. Boyd Kuykendall (?-)

3. Loyd Kuykendall (?-) (a twin)

4. Donald Dane Kuykendall (?-)

5. Dale Edwin Kuykendall (?-)

6. Willa Mae Kuykendall (?-)

7. Adrien Lee Kuykendall (?-)

Dolly Lea Hartness (1915-). Dolly was the daughter of Zora (Karr) and John Hartness. She was born August 2, 1915, in Tahlequah, Oklahoma. She married Aurell Bounous and they had three children:

1. Fred Hubert Bounous (?-)

2. Howard Dane Bounous (?-)

3. Darrel Ray Bounous (?-)

Gladys Marie Hartness (1918-). Gladys was the daughter of Zora (Karr) and John Hartness. She was born October 9, 1918, in Tahlequah, Oklahoma. She married Ralph L.Holbrook, who was born January 30, 1911, and they had one child:

Elizabeth Laverne Holbrook (?-)

Reba Leota Hartness (1919-1963). Reba was the daughter of Zora (Karr) and John Hartness. She was born on June 10, 1919, in Tahlequah, Oklahoma, and died October 22, 1963. She married a man named Pruitt, first name unavailable, whom she divorced in 1961. She is buried in the Monett I. O. O. F. Cemetery. Her pallbearers were Calvin Bounous, Derrel Bounous, Fred Bounous, Bob Bounous, Bill Burton, and Aurrell Bounous. She had one child:

Connie Jo Pruitt (?-)

Cleo Mae Hartness (1922-). Cleo is a daughter of Zora (Karr) and John Hartness. She was born September 24, 1922, in Tahlequah, Oklahoma. She married Leland A. Stubblefield, and they live at 200 W. Park, Monett, MO 65708.

Laura Bea Hartness (1927-). Laura Bea was a daughter of Zora (Karr) and John Hartness. She was born August 10, 1927, in Tahlequah, Oklahoma. She married Clarence Lester Burton and they had three children:

1. Laura Lea Burton (?-)

2. Carol Ann Burton (?-)

3. Jerry Lester Burton (?-)

Ben Henry Upperman (1916-). Ben Henry was the first son of Ethel and Benjamin Harrison Upperman, of Phoenix, Arisona. He was born August 21, 1916, in Perry, Oklahoma, and married Marjorie Maxine

Bell, who was born January 17, 1917, somewhere in Ohio. They had two children:

1. Ben Michel Upperman (1951-)   •

2. John Wesley Upperman (1955-)

Floyd Edward Upperman (1919-). Floyd is the second son of Ethel and Ben Upperman, of
Phoenix, Arizona. He was born April 12, 1919, in Perry, Oklahoma. He married,
but the wife's name is unavailable. They had four children:

1. Aloha Upperman (1946-)

2. Anna Upperman (1951-)

3. Rebecca Upperman (1952-)

4. Loyd Upperman (1954-)

4. THE HUNTERS AND THE SMITHS

[The link: Ollie Ida Hall, the daughter of Mallie Rue (Carr) and Greeley Teeman Hall, married Lou Albin Smith, who was a Seventh Generation Hunter.]

[In the *Family Archives* is a copy of the passenger list of the ship *Two Brothers*, which sailed from Rotterdam to Philadelphia, arriving in that port on september 14, 1749, carrying 312 *foreigners* (Germans). One of these *Pennsylvania German Pioneers* was Johan Wilhelm Jager, the Paternal Ancestor of the Hunters and Smiths of this genealogical study.]

The First Generation

Johan Wilhelm Jager was born in Germany. He came to America with his family aboard the ship Two Brothers, arriving in Philadelphia on September 14, 1749. Johan's wife died on the ship while in route to America and was buried at sea. They had three children:

1. John Hunter (Johan Jager): born in 1736 in Germany, died on June 7, 1823, in Cherokee Creek, Washington County, Tennessee, married in 1761 in Frederick County, Maryland to Barbara Bowman.

2. Henry Hunter (Heinrich Jager) was born in Germany, married on October 5, 1771, to Susan Beyerix in Frederick county, Maryland.

3. Elizabeth Hunter (Jager) married on June 6, 1773, to Adam Huber in Frederick County, Maryland.

The Second Generation

John Hunter (Johan Jager), the son of Johan Wilheim Jager, was born in 1736 in Germany and died on June 7, 1823, in Cherokee Creek, Washington County, Tennessee. He married Barbara Bowman in 1761 in Frederick County, Maryland. She was born in Pennsylvania in 1747. Her parents were Jacob and Sophronia Bowman. John and Barbara are buried in the Cherokee Creek Cemetery in Cherokee Creek, Tennessee. John was a blacksmith by trade. They had ten children:

1. John Hunter was born November 27, 1762, in Hagerstown, Frederick County, Maryland. He married Elizabeth Dzman in May 1781 in Rockingham County, Virginia.

2. Elizabeth Hunter was born in 1764 in Frederick County, Maryland. She married David Robinson in 1780 in Rockingham County, Virginia.

3. Jacob Hunter was born March 16, 1766, in Hagerstown, Frederick County, Maryland, and died on June 19, 1836, in Cherokee Creek, Washington County, Tennessee. He married Ann Clark in 1788.

4. Henry Hunter was born in 1768 in Rockingham County, Virginia, and died in August 1876, in Speedwell, Claiborne County, Tennessee. In 1789 he married Barbara Bolinger , who was born in 1769 in York County, Pennsylvania, and died on December 3, 1846, in Speedwell, Claiborne County, Tennessee.

5. Abraham Hunter was born September 2, 1771, in Frederick County, Maryland, and died on March 11, 1841, in Cole County, Missouri. He married Mary Marks in 1790 in Pendleton, South Carolina.

6. Christian Hunter was born in 1773 in Frederick County, Maryland. She married Robert Fryer on July 14, 1792, in Washington County, Tennessee.

7. Catherine Hunter was born October 27, 1776, in Rockingham County, Virginia, and died March 11, 1858, in Brighton, Polk County, Missouri. She married John G. Bewley in 1798.

8. Joseph Hunter was born february 22, 1779, in Rockingham County, Virginia, and died May 2, 1869, in Washington County, Tennessee. He married Sarah Linille .

9. Barbara Hunter was born in 1783 in Washington County, Tennessee. She married Henry Rubie.

10. Isaac Hunter was born in 1786 in Washington County, Tennessee. On October 15, 1812, he married Elizabeth Kizer.

The Third Generation

Henry Hunter, the son of John and Barbara Bowman Hunter, was born in 1768 in Rockingham County, Virginia, and died in August, 1826, in Speedwell, Clariborne County, Tennessee. In 1789 he married Barbara Bolinger, who was born in 1769 in York County, Pennsylvania, and died on December 3, 1846, in Speedwell, Claiborne County, Tennessee. She was the daughter of Isaac and Chaterina Bolinger. Henry and Barbara are buried in the Hunter Cemetery in Speedwell, Clairborne County, Tennessee. They had ten children:

1. Joseph Hunter was born March 15, 1791, in Pendleton, Anderson County, South Carolina, and died July 4, 1879, in Claiborne County, Tennessee. He married Elizabeth Moyer on March 7, 1813, in Speedwell, Claiborne County, Tennessee.

2. Rachel Hunter was born in 1792 in Pendleton, Anderson County, South Carolina, and died in Lincoln County, Tennessee. She married William Hamilton.

3. Catherine Hunter was born in 1794 in Pendleton, Anderson County, South Carolina, and died in Sevier, Arkansas. She married John Stinnett.

4. Henry Hunter was born in 1795 in Pendleton, Anderson County, South Carolina. He married Sarah Davis on July 2, 1858.

5. Jesse Hunter was born in 1796 in Speedwell, Claiborne County, Tennessee, and died on July 28, 1856, in Berlin, LaFayette County, Missouri. He married Ursula Stinnett.

6. Barbara Hunter was born October 19, 1798, in Speedwell, Claiborne County., Tennessee, and died on August 6, 1838, in Macoupin County, Illinois. She married William Sharp.

7. Elizabeth Hunter was born in 1802 in Speedwell, Claiborne County, Tennessee. She married James Cain.

8. Mary (Polly) Hunter was born June 18, 1804, in Speedwell, Claiborne County, Tennessee, and died July 3, 1866, in Madison County, Arkansas. She married Frederick Bolinger.

9. Abraham Hunter was born in 1806 in Speedwell, Claiborne County, Tennessee, and died in 1888 in Knox County, Tennessee. He married Patience McFadden on February 5, 1825, in Laurel County, Kentucky.

10. Frederick Bolinger Hunter ws born January 11, 1808, in Speedwell, Claiborne County, Tennessee, and died July 20, 1888, in Decaturville, Camden County, Missouri. He married twice.

Frederick Bolinger Hunter, the son of Henry and Barbara Bolinger Hunter, was born January 11, 1808, in Speedwell, Claiborne County, Tennessee, and died July 20, 1888, in Decaturville, Camden County, Missouri. He married (1) Martha Louise Parker, born in 1808 in South Carolina, and (2 Calpurnia Carter. By Martha Louise he had ten children:

1. Henry S. Hunter was born August 15, 1828, in London, Laurel County, Kentucky, and died on January 25, 1886, in Cabin Creek, Johnson County, Arkansas. On September 7, 1852, in Fincastle,

Campbell County, Tennessee, he married Susan Goins, who was born on April 20, 1837, in Campbell County, Tennessee.

2. John Hunter was born in 1830 in Speedwell, Claiborne County, Tennessee. He married Nancy E. (last name not available).

3. Abraham Hunter was born in 1833 in Speedwell, Claiborne County, Tennessee. He married Lucinda (last name not available).

4. Isaac Franklin Hunter was born February 14, 1837, in Speedwell, Claiborne County, Tennessee, and died on September 27, 1915, in Ozark, Christian County, Missouri. He married Minerva E. (last name unavailable).

5. David C. Hunter was born on May 22, 1838, in Speedwell, Claiborne County, Tennessee, and died November 19, 1910, in Hardeman County, Texas. He married Amanda Fullbright on July 27, 1865, in Laclede County, Missouri.

6. Martha Jane Hunter was born in 1840 in Speedwell, Claiborne County, Tennessee.

7. Mary Ann Hunter was born in 1843 in Speedwell, Claiborne County, Tennessee. On December 15, 1864, she married Harry H. Williams in Laclede
County, Missouri.

8. Catherine E. Hunter was born in 1845 in Speedwell, Claiborne County, Tennessee.

9. Emily Hunter was born in 1848 in Speedwell, Claiborne County, Tennessee.

10. Patrick Frederick Hunter was born in 1850 in Speedwell, Claiborne County, Tennessee.

The Fifth Generation

Henry S. Hunter, son of Frederick B. and Martha Louise Parker Hunter, was born on August 15, 1828, in London, Laurel County, Kentucky, and died on January 25, 1886, in Cabin Creek, Johnson County, Arkansas. On September 7, 1852, in Fincastle, Campbell County, Texas, he married Susan Goins, who was born in Campbell County, Texas, on April 20, 1827, and died on February 20, 1915, in Lead Hill, Boone County, Arkansas. She was the daughter of Preston and Delphia A. (King) Goins. Henry is buried at Cabin Creek, Johnson County, Arkansas, and Susan is buried at Lead Hill, Boone County, Arkansas. They had nine children:

1. Nancy Jane Hunter was born December 20, 1853, in Jacksboro, Campbell County, Tennessee, and died October 4, 1924, in Cushing, Payne County, Oklahoma. She married Albin McVay on March 7, 1872, in Laclede County, Misouri. Nancy is buried in Brown Cemetery in Taney County, Missouri.

2. William H. Hunter was born August 22, 1856, in Penton County, Arkansas, and died May 27, 1940. He is buried in Protem Cemetery, Taney County, Missouri. He married Sara Phillips.

3. Martha F. (Molly) Hunter was born November 23, 1859, in Webster County, Missouri, and died December 15, 1928. She is buried in Lead Hill, Boone County, Arkansas. She married J. Newt Justus.

4. Charles Hunter was born July 27, 1864, in Laclede County, Missouri, and died November 5, 1956. He is buried in Lead Hill, Boone County, Arkansas.

5. Ella Hunter was born in May, 1865, in Laclede County, Missouri. She died September 22, 1865, in Laclede County, Missouri.

6. John M. Hunter was born February 16, 1867, in Laclede County, Missouri, and died May 3, 1941, in Mulberry, Crawford County, Arkansas. He married Vera Wagner.

7. Laura E. Hunter (a twin) was born March 8, 1872, in Lebanon, Laclede County, Missouri, and died on February 1, 1973, in Lead Hill, Boone County, Arkansas, where she is buried.

8. Flora Mae Hunter (a twin) was born March 8, 1872, in Lebanon, Laclede County, Missouri, and died October 2, 1955, in Konawa, Seminole County, Oklahoma. She married **Patrick Looney Smith**.

9. Lou Albon Hunter was born August 12, 1874, in Laclede County, Missouri, and died on June 5, 1938, in Lead Hill, Boone county, Arkansas. He married (1) Jeanie Augten and (2) Ruth Riddle.

The Sixth Generation

Flora Mae Hunter, the daughter of Henry S. and Susan Goins Hunter, was born March 8, 1872, in Lebanon, Leclede County, Missouri, and died October 2, 1955, in Konawa, Seminole County, Oklahoma. On September 8, 1889, in Boone County, Arkansas, she married **Patrick Looney Smith**, who was born January 26, 1869, in Warsaw, Benton County, Missouri, and died on August 12, 1944, in Konawa, Seminole County, Oklahoma. Patrick was the son of Isaac and Orleand (JoAnn)

(Kidwell) Smith. He and Flora are buried in the Konawa City Cemetery. They had nine children:

1. Laura Elizabeth Smith was born August 28, 1890, near Lead Hill, Boone County, Arkansas, and died December 28, 1986, in Conway, Arkansas. She married Bul Trimble.

2. Charles Smith was born in August, 1892, in Arkansas. He married Hannah Ford.

3. Susan Smith was born in August, 1894, in Arkansas. She married George Casey.

4. Gordon Smith was born in July, 1896, in Arkansas. He married Ara Farhus.

5. Lou Albin Smith was born July 16, 1898, in Lead Hill, Boone County, Arkansas. He married (1) Mollie [**Ollie Ida**] **Hall** and (2) Josie [Flossie] Long.

6. Delphia Smith was born January 26, 1901, in Lead Hill, Boone County, Arkansas, and died December 24, 1984. She married Hubert Grady and they had three children. [They adopted Roy Joe Smith, Ollie and Lou's fifth child, after Ollie died in childbirth.]

7. Fannie Smith was born September 22, 1904, in Lead Hill, Boone County, Arkansas. She married Clarence McGrew.

8. Johnnie Smith was born January 26, 1907, in Lead Hill, Boone County, Arkansas. She married Henry Keener. They had at least one child, who was named *Ishmael*. [Our paths crossed in Pleasanton,

California, in September, 1943, when we were in transcient at Shoemaker Naval Distribution Center on our wat to the Pacific.]

9. Troy (Brooks) Smith was born November 6, 1911, in Lead Hill, Boone County, Arkansas. He married Verdy Rogers.

The Ancestors of Lou Smith

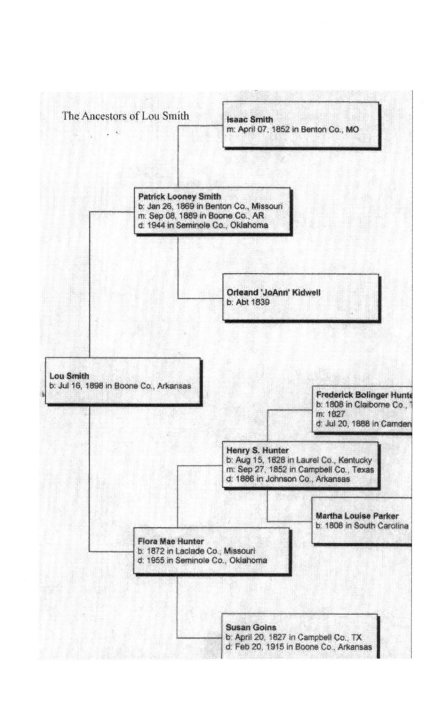

Isaac Smith
m: April 07, 1852 in Benton Co., MO

Patrick Looney Smith
b: Jan 26, 1869 in Benton Co., Missouri
m: Sep 08, 1889 in Boone Co., AR
d: 1944 in Seminole Co., Oklahoma

Orleand 'JoAnn' Kidwell
b: Abt 1839

Lou Smith
b: Jul 16, 1898 in Boone Co., Arkansas

Frederick Bolinger Hunte
b: 1808 in Claiborne Co., T
m: 1827
d: Jul 20, 1888 in Camden

Henry S. Hunter
b: Aug 15, 1828 in Laurel Co., Kentucky
m: Sep 27, 1852 in Campbell Co., Texas
d: 1886 in Johnson Co., Arkansas

Martha Louise Parker
b: 1808 in South Carolina

Flora Mae Hunter
b: 1872 in Laclade Co., Missouri
d: 1955 in Seminole Co., Oklahoma

Susan Goins
b: April 20, 1827 in Campbell Co., TX
d: Feb 20, 1915 in Boone Co., Arkansas

THE MASTER INDEX OF HALLS

1. John Hall (1769-?) and Mary (?) (1770-?)
2. Hiram Hall (1795-?) and Charity (?) (1802-?)
3. Arminda Hall (1823-1915) + Thomas S. Herron (1812-1899)
    4. James Herron (1848-1935)
    4. Hiram Herron (1850-1909) + Martha Guttery (?-?)
        5. Elijah Isham Herron (1873-1875)
        5. Newman Herron (1876-1893)
        5. James Thomas Herron (1879-1966) + Mintie Cheatham (?-)
            6. Mamie Ethel Herron (1900-1972)
            6. Walter James Herron Sr. (1902-1970) + Ceatrice Jenkins (?-)
                7. Walter James Herron, Jr. (1929-)
                    8. Dennis James Herron (1951-)
                    8. William Allen Herron (1953-)
                7. Jerry Edward Herron (?-)
                7. Larry Ray Herron (?-)
                7. Norma Jean Herron (?-)
                7. Douglas Wayne Herron (?-)
                7. Glenda Gail Herron (?-)
            6. Clarence Herron (1904-1986) + Meatrice Odom (?-)
                7. J. W. Herron (?-)
                7. Opal Jean Herron (?-)
                7. Billy Ray Herron (?-)
                7. Bobby Joe Herron (?-)
                7. Carl Dean Herron (?-)

> 7. Raymond D. Herron (?-)
>
> 7. Violet Mae Herron (?-)
>
> 7. Harvey Lee Herron (?-)
>
> 7. Mary Lou Herron (?-)
>
> 7. Jerry Don Herron (?-)
>
> 7. George Edward Herron (?-)

6. Flossie Herron (1906-1996)

6. Edgar Herron (1908-?)

6. Donnie Mae Herron (1910-1995)

6. Grady Herron (1912-)

6. Esther Louise Herron (1915-)

6. Earl Herron (1918-1977)

6. Earnest Herron (1920-1971)

5. Arminda Elvira Herron (1881-?)

5. Cora Ann Herron (1883-1960)

5. Julia Frances Herron (1886-1965)

5. Savannah Silvany Herron (1888-?)

5. Lunceford Osro Herron (1891-1977)

4. Charity Herron (1852-1857)

4. D. F. Herron (1854-1857)

4. Jane Herron (1857)

4. Pierce Herron (1860-1902)

4. Green Herron (1862-1925)

4. Missouria Herron (1864-1945)

3. John Hall (1824-1898) + Nancy Hamilton (1828-1914)

4. Delilah Emeline Hall (1848)

4. Robert Jefferson Hall (1850-1944) + Sara Jane Brewer (1856-1940)

5. Wellington Columbus Hall (1879-1964) + Laura A. Sitton (1883-1963)

5. Thomas Cleveland Hall (1884-1965) + Margie Rena Roberts (1889-1961)

6. Wayne Ambrose Hall (1907-1929)

6. Carlos Mentril Hall (1909-1965) + Winnifred Lorena Rogers (1917-)
    7. Virginia June Hall (1936-1945)
    7. Theodore Carlos Hall (1937-1962) + Beverly Daniels (?-)
        8. Wendy Lee Hall (1960-)
        8. Thea Joy Hall (1961-)
    7. Roger Evan Hall (1939-) + Sharron Lynn Holland (?-)
        8. Jeffrey Evan Hall (1967-)
        8. David Theodore Hall (1970-)
    7. Janette Arlene Hall (1941-) + John Knuckles (?-)
        8. Valorie June Knuckles (1964) (?-)
        8. John Roger Knuckles (1968) (?-)
    7. Marjorie Evelyn Hall (1943) + Floyd Johnson (?-)
        8. William Troy Johnson (?-)
        8. Raymond Kent Johnson (?-)
    7. Barbara Joy Hall (1945-) + Charles Bradley Pearson (1940-)
        8. Pamela Ann Pearson (1964-) + Jeffrey Royce Hanson (1964-)
            9. Emily Louise Hanson (1991-)
            9. Jared Ryan Hanson (1993-)
        8. Lorena Ruth Pearson (1966-) + Michael Allred (1964-)
            9. Tana Elaine Allred (1983-)
            9. Kena May Allred (1993-)
        8. Charles Bradley Pearson (1969-)+Judy Housekeeper (1970-)
            9. Charles Garrett Pearson (1991-)
            9. Paige Kay Pearson (1994-)
        8. Rena Lynn Pearson (1970-)+Glenn Shane Prestwich (1966-)

> 9. Kamie Lyn Prestwich (1994-)

8. Tricia Danette Pearson (1971-)+Richard Van Wagoner (1958-)

>> 9. Lacey Shay Van Wagoner (1992-)
>> 9. Tia Chantel Van Wagoner (1993-)
>> 9. Rondee Leah Van Wagoner (1997-)
>> 9. Shalae Dacy Van Wagoner (2001-)

7. Winnifred Eileen Hall (1946-) + Danny Anderson (?-)

> 8. Danny Carlos Anderson (1967-)
> 8. Steven Terry Anderson (1969-)

7. Marilyn Kaye Hall (1949-) + Dennis Hendric (?-)

> 8. Austin Reed Hendric (1979-)
> 8. Arin Hendric (1981-)

6. Therman Clement Hall (1914-2001) + Mary Virginia Rogers (1915-)

> 7. Allie Jane Hall (?-)
> 7. Richard Wayne Hall (?-)
> 7. Robert Lynn Hall (?-)

6. Thomas Richard Hall (1916-1920)

6. Lloyd Evan Hall (1920-1994) + Frieda Irene Wiederman + Eliz. Davis (?-)

6. Mary Lenore Hall (1923-1991) + Marion Lee Neely (?-)

6. Victor Leon Hall (1928-) + Phyllis Maurine Rice (1952-)

> 7. Steven Blane Hall (1954-) + Connie Corrine Taylor (?-)
> 7. Vickie Lynn Hall (1956-) + Robert Eugene Cooke (?-)
> 7. Timothy Wayne Hall (1959-) + Lori Ann Turner + Janet Gardner
> 7. Derek Duane Hall (1968-) + Kim Denise Weiler (?-)

5. Darien C. Hall (1887-1922) + Jessie (1889-1964) + Lillie Taylor (?-)

5. Marien Hall (1887-1889) twin

5. Cara Ethel Hall (1892-1893)

5. Voyd Hall (1894-1968) + Mary P. Meyers (1895-1970)

5. Earnest Thurman Hall (1891-1982) + Roma Pritchard (1900-1971)

5. Larry Wise Hall (1898-) + Helen Jenkins (1924-)

5. Mary Anice Hall (1899-?) + Paris Cotton (1872-1928)

4. Madison Monroe Hall (1852-1928)

    5. Ida Lenora Hall (1876-?)

    5. Violet May Hall (1879-?)

    5. Harriet Lillian Hall (1881-?)

    5. Josephine Pearl Hall (1883-1926)

    5. Ernest Edward Hall (1886-?)

    5. Raynand Lafayette Hall (1888-?)

    5. Ethel Hall (1890-?)

    5. Anita Gertrude Hall (1895-?)

    5. Rosamond Del Hall (1895-?)

4. Richard Lafayette Hall (1854-?)

4. Janette Ardelia Hall (1856-?)

4. Nancy Lanore Hall (1859-?)

4. Margret Charity Hall (1861-?)

4. Mary (Maty) Ann Hall (1866-?)

3. Nancy Hall (1829-?) + Jefferson Dean (?)

    Susan Dean (?)

    Loucinda Dean (?)

    Charity M. Dean (?)

    Martha Joe Dean (?)

    Vianna Dean (?)

    Jefferson Savannah Dean (?)

3. William Newton Hall (1831-1923) + Susan Elizabeth Woods (1851-1918)

4. Archie Brooklyn Hall (1871-1955 .+ Nancy Caroline McDougal (1876-1955)

    5. Minnie Aloony Hall (1894-1910)

5. Annie Dona Hall (1896-1956) + J. W. Swafford (?-?)+ Irons (1896-?)
    6. Christopher David Swafford (1920-1983) + Edna Marie Pettit (1918-)
        7. Billie Ann Swafford (1953-) + (?) Minugh (?-)
        7. Shirley Flo Swafford (1955-)
        7. Judy Aline Swafford (1957-) + (?)
5. Jesse Newton Hall (1899-1994) +Dora Bell Lawson (1904-1947) + Finise Etter
    6. Oliver Newton Hall (?-)
    6. Roy Hall (?-)
    6. Jerry Hall (?-)
    6. Jim Hall (?-)
    6. Imogene Hall (?-)
    6. Jessie Mae Hall (1930-) + Kenneth E. Holinsworth (?-)
        7. Michael Eugne Holinsworth (1949-1997)
        7. Danny Ray Holinsworth (1950-) + (?)
            8. John Holinsworth (?-)
        7. Valerie Ann Holinsworth (1952-) + (?)
            8. Michelle Holinsworth (?-)
        7. Rodney Lee Holinsworth (1956-1976)
    6. Helen Hall (?-)
    6. Dorothy Hall (?-)
    6. Judy Hall (?-)
5. Carl (Bud) Tyre Hall (1901-1965) + Carrie Melissa Taylor (1902-1982)
    6. Gladys Marie Hall (1922-1986) + Vinnis Bervine Phillips (?-)
        7. Nancy Olene Phillips (?-)
        7. Frankie Lee Phillips (?-)
        7. Shirley Delores Phillips (?-)
        7. Peggy Joyce Phillips (?-)
        7. Richard Dwayne Phillips (?-)

    7. Vinnis Leon Phillips, Jr. (?-)

    7. Dianna Gail Phillips (?-)

    7. Debra Marie Phillips (?-)

    7. Kenneth Lee Phillips (?-)

    7. Candy Phillips (?-)

6. Iva Lorene Hall (1924-) + Charles Edward Smith (?-1944) + Blackwood

    7. Charles Henry Smith (?-)

6. Sadie Lee Hall (1926-) + Calvin Rock + Elmer Shamblin, Jr. (?-)

    7. Ervin Lee Rock (?-)

    7. Calvin Ray Rock, Jr. (?-)

    7. Janis Kaye Rock (?-)

    7. Robbie Dale Rock (?-)

    7. Janie Faye Rock (?-)

6. James Oliver Hall (1928-) + Leola Naomi Ezelle (1930-) + Andrew (?-)

    7.Judy Gail Hall (1949-) + Michael Merrill Lloyd (1951-)

        8. Gwendolyn Lloyd (1975-) + (?) Lopez (?-)

            9. Celina Renee Lopez (1992-)

        8. Carrie Anne Lloyd (1977-)

        8. Rachel Leona Lloyd (1979-)

        8. Brett Lloyd (?-)

    7. James Larry Hall (1974-)+ Paula J. Parfumorse (1954-1989)

        8. Melanie Ann Hall (?-)

    7. Kathy Ann Hall (1951-)+Duke+McCormick+David Wright

        8. Steven Bruce Wright (1966-)

        8. William Floyd Wright (1967-)

        8. Angela Michelle Wright (1973-)

8. Robert Daryl Wright (1976-)
7. Mark Stephen Hall (1953-)+Robin Hirschi (1954-)
8. Marcus Oliver Hall (1985-)
8. Greta June Hall (1992-)
7. David Lee Hall (1959-)+Paula Kay Eakin (?-)
8. Corey Douglas Hall (?-)
8. Amber Brooke Hall (?-)
6. Tyre Roland Hall (1929-)+Ruby Benton (?-)
7. Anna Mae Hall (?-)
7. Debra Sue Hall (?-)
7. Lillian Lou Hall (?-)
7. Bessie Jean Hall (?-)
7. Maye Belle Hall (?-)
7. Jackie Lee Hall (?-)
5. Carl (Bud) Tyre Hall (1901-1965) + Nora May Howell (1913-)
6. Virginia Ruth Hall (1937-1954) + Nieto + Ronning + Klaus + Ohl + Henderson
6. Carl Watson Hall (1940-) + Linda Marie Tolboe (?-)
6. Kenneth Franklin Hall (1943-) + Erlene Endfinger (?-)
6. Richard Douglas Hall (1945-) + Kathleen Meyer+Valerie Hewitt (?-)
5. Pearl Ellen Hall (1903-1985) + James Olin Gragg (1900-1972)
6. James Benjamin Gragg (?-)
5. Birtha Elizabeth Hall (1905-?) + Ed Gragg (?-?)
6. Archie Gragg (?-)
6. Rose Michelle Gragg (?-)
6. Flossie (Gragg) + Edward Duncan (?-)
7. Tommie Duncan (?-)
6. Elizabeth (Gragg) Gray (?-)
7. Eugene Gragg (?-)
7. Johnny Gragg (?-)
7. Curtie Gragg (?-)

7. Ricky Gragg (?-)
7. Calvin Gragg (?-)
7. Doris Jean Gragg (?-)
7. Lulu Gragg (?-)
7. Martha Gragg (?-)
7. Mitchell Paul Gragg (?-)
6. Betty Gragg (?-) + Billy Bob Williams (?-) + K. C. Brorder (?-)
7. Debbie Williams (?-)
7. Linda Williams (?-)
7. Steve Williams (?-)
7. Sonny Williams (?-)
6. Mabel Gragg + Billy Hales (?-)
7. Utah Hales + Sandy (?-)
8. Billy Hales Jr. (?-)
7. Carl Hales (?-)
7. Clifford Hales (?-)
7. Buck Hales (?-)
7. Marty Hales (?-)
7. Tex Hales (?-)
7. Lena Hales (?-)
7. Cherry Hales (?-)
7. June Hales (?-)
7. Nita Hales (?-)
7. Brazil Hales (?-)
7. Tim Hales (?-)
6. Frant and Gragg + Thelma (?-)
7. Joseph Frant Gragg (?-)
7. Rachel Gragg (?-)
7. Neva Gragg (?-)
7. Kelly Gragg (?-)
7. Tracy Gragg (?-)
7. Josh Gragg (?-)

7. Jeremy Gragg (?-)
6. Nelson Lee Gragg Sr. (1940-) + (?)
    7. Tylene Gragg (?-)
6. Nelson Lee Gragg Sr. (1940-) + Marion Bacon (1941-)
    7. Nelson Lee Gragg Jr (1960-) + Wendi Leigh Noland (?-)
        8. Gideon Gragg (1982-)
        8. Seth Gragg (1983-)
        8. Amanda Gragg (1987-)
        8. Jesse Paul Gragg (1988-)
        8. Caleb Gragg (1991-)
    7. Brian Lynn Gragg (1961-)+(?-)
    7. Andrea Marion (Gragg) Schocher (1963-) + (?-)
6. Hank Gragg + Billie (?-)
    7. Richard Gragg (?-)
    7. Thomas Gragg (?-)
    7. Eddie Gragg (?-)
    7. Polly Gragg (?-)
6. Paul Gragg + (?) (?-1974)
    7. Brenda Gragg (?-)
    7. Paula Gragg (?-)
    7. Sandi Gragg (?-)
    7. Tammi Gragg (?-)
    7. Donita Gragg (?-)
5. Aaron Granville Hall (1907-1964)
4. Dock Walter Hall (1873-1951) + Kate K. Elsey (1883-1977)
    5. Arthur Hall (1902-1995) + Vernie V. Tyler (1925-1995)
        6. LaVonna Hall (?-)
        6. Johnnie Clifton (J. C.) Hall (?-)
        6. LeRoy Hall (?-)
    5. Earl Hall (1903-1999) + Stella (-1993)
        6. Durward Jack Hall (1927-) + Sarah Gladys Slentz (1931-)

7. Larry Wayne Hall (1955-) + Christie Mason (1956-)
    8. Justin Wayne Hall (1975-)
    8. Bryan David Hall (1979-)
    8. Matthew Reid Hall (1981-)
7. Tracy Kay Hall (1957-) + Chuck Hoenshell (?-)
    8. Kari Dawn Hoenshell (1980-)
    8. Eric Ryan Hoenshell (1983-)
6. Val Gene Hall (1928-) + Louise Elms (1930-)
    7. Phyllis Jean Hall (1950-) + Milton Kenneth Hendrickson (?-)
        8. Robert Earl Hendrickson (1978-1996)
    7. Ronald Hall (1951-)+Dahlia Josephina Ortiz (1954-) + Espinoza
        8. Aaron Lee Hall (1982-)
6. Velta Lee Hall (1930-) + Andrew J. (Mike) Domyan (1925-)
    7. Nathan Domyan (1958-)
6. Bobby Ray (Bob) Hall (1932-) + Anita Marquez
7. Robert James Hall (1956-)
    7. Debra Ann Hall (1957-) + David Robert Nelson (1954) + Robert E.Stafford (1948-)
        8. Lee David Nelson (1980-)
        8. Donny Ray Nelson (1982-)
    7. Dianna Lynn Hall (1958-) + Jay Dee Liles (1957-)
        8. Jason Dee Liles (1978-)
        8. Amy Christine Liles (1981-)
    7. Denise Hall (1962-) + Donald Michael Smith (1956-)
        8. Nicole Marie Smith (1985-)
        8. Kathrine Ray Smith (1987-)
        8. Daniel Miles Smith (1988-)
6. Barbara Louise Hall (1935-) + William Charley Helton (1932-)

7. William Charles Helton (1960-)
6. Joyce Oteka Hall (1938-) + Edward S. Browne (?-)
7. Rochelle Candine Browne (1961-)
7. Lindsay Edward Hall Browne (1963-)
5. Cecile Hall (1908-1957) + William Lanphear (?-)
6. Doyle Lanphear (?-) + Joy + (?)
6. Leon Lanphear (?-)
6. Suevella Lanphear (?-1978)
6. Drucella Lanphear (?-)
5. Jewel Hall (1915-) + Connie Lee (Bud) Beard (1909-1957)
6. Billy Ray Beard (1939-)+Cathy Stucky (-ca.1990)
7. Gregory Beard (1961-)
7. Keith Beard (1963-)
5. Dovie Hall (1918-)+Lou Peak + James Braun (?-)
6. Darrell Dean Peak (?-) + (?)
5. Oma Hall (1922-)+Johnny Beard + C. L. Payne (?-)
6. Judy Beard (?-)
6. Janet Beard (?-)
6. Brenda Payne (?-)
6. Linda Payne (?-)
4. Greeley Teeman Hall (Horace Greel) (1877-1965) + Mallie Rue Karr (1882-1971)
5. Ezra Marion Hall (1902-1986) + Florence Viola Scoggins (1905-1997)
6. Alton Lee Hall (1928-1989) + Jeanetta Ramsey (1932-)
7. Ginger Kaye Hall (1949-) + David Landers (1945-)
8. Lavina Ruth Landers (1963-) + Ronald Cardona (?-)
9. Christopher Lee Cardona (?-)
9. Andrew DeWayne Cardona (?-)
9. Aaron Raymond Cardona (?-)
7. Ginger Kaye Hall (1949-) + Gary Ramsey (1947-)

8. Marcella Diane Ramsey (?-) + Randall Jones (1947-)

    9. Brandi Jo Jones (1989-)

    9. Beth Marie Jones (1991-)

8. Tina Lynn Ramsey (1970-) + (?)

    9. Justin Davis Ramsey (1988-)

    9. Felisha Marie Diane Ramsey (1990-)

6. Dorotha Faye Hall (1931-2000) + Marlin Joe Schornick (1948-1980)

    7. Terrye Lee Schornick (1951-) + Neil Hugentober (?-)

    7. Mickey Joe Schornick (1957-) + Cynthia Sue Coder (1959-)

        8. Sarah Schornick (?-)

        8. Katelyn JoAnn Schornick (1988-)

5. Grady Hall (1904-1990) + Arthur Lee Goff (1907-1981)

    6. Inas Faye Goff (1926-) + Steve Kandarian (1918-2001)

        7. Katherine Louise Kandarian (1944-) + Steve Diebert (?-)

            8. Stephanie Leann Diebert (1971-)+Kenneth Jeffrey Price (1968-)

            8. Melissa Ann Diebert (1975-)+Layne Bartley Lev (1973-)

        7. Patricia Ann Kandarian (?-)

    6. Maudie June Goff (1929-) + Joseph Lamanucci, Jr. (1930-)

        7. Joseph Arthur Lamanuzzi (1953-)

        7. Linda Faye Lamanuzzi (1955-)

    6. Annie Jo Goff (1930-1995) + Angelo Papagni (1928-1981)

        7. Sandra Elizabeth Papagni (1953-) + James Ray (?-1988)

            8. Kristina Ray (1973-)

            8. James Ray (1975-)

7. Judith Ann Papagni (1956-)+John Biggs (-1976)+Danny Akins

    8. Jodi Angela Papagni (1991-)

7. Carlo Nicholas Papagni (1960-) + Teri Laplaca (?-)

    8. Gianna Maria Papagni (1992-)

5. Ollie Ida Hall (1906-1934) + Lou Albin Smith (1898-)

6. Flora E. Smith (1925-) + Nuckells (-1950) + James Putler (1930-)

7. Nancy Kay Putler (1961-) + James Robert Kemp II (1963-)

    8. James Robert Kemp III (1991-)

    8. Patrick Owen Kemp (1993-)

7. David Allen Putler (1961-1961)

6. Muriel Eston (Bud) Smith (1927-2000) + Florene (?)

6. Lou Albin (L. A.) Smith (1929-) + Lucille Cleveland (1929-2000)

7. Gary Smith (1949-) + Cinderella (Cindy) Meismer (1948-)

    8. Ries Nathaniel Smith (1978-)

    8. Katy Nina Smith (1979-)

7. Bridget Evelyn Smith (1953-) + Michael Thomas O'Leary (?-)

    8. Heather Marie Smith O'Leary (1971-) + John (?-)

        9. Patrick O'Leary (1998-)

7. Bridget Evelyn Smith (1953-) + Charles Patrick Antis (?-)

    8. Crystal Katherine Freedom Antis (1975-)

7. Gregory Paul Smith (1959-) + Pebbles A. McDonald (1965-)

    8. Jessica Lynn Smith (1987-)

    8. Geoffrey Paul Smith (1990-)

8. Megan Elizabeth Smith (1994-)
8. Catherine Michelle Smith (1996-)
8. Patricia Lucille Smith (1999-)
6. Mallie Avo Smith (1931-) + Frank Rincon (1925-)
    7. Mark Anthony Rincon (1951-) + Sherry Rene Hoffman (1953-)
        8. Trenton Mark Rincon (1977-)
        8. Troy Anthony Rincon (1979-)
    7. Debra Ann Rincon (1953-) + David Scott Beach (1956-)
        8. Jonathan David Beach (1992-)
        8. Justan Scott Beach (1993-)
    7. Robert Harlan Rincon (1954-) + Ada Karen Lohne (1955-)
        8. Melissa Anne Rincon (1976-)
        8. Robert Neal Rincon (1978-)
    7. Kelley Maria Rincon (1957-) + Steven F. Brizeondine (1954-)
        8. Erica Allison Brizeondine (1980-)
        8. Jillian Morgan Brizeondine (1983-)
6. Roy Joe Smith (1934-1996) + Alma (?)
    7. Michael Smith (?-)
    7. Donna Smith (?-)
    7. Douglas Smith (?-)
5. Ruth Hall (1908-1976) + Joseph Benjamin Potter (1907-1996)
6. Clara Dale Potter (1935-) + Carl Swann (?-)
    7. Steve Nolan Swann (1956-) + Jan Durelle Greenwood (?-)
        8. Kristyn Durelle Swann (1981-)
        8. Jessica Leanne Swann (1984-)
    7. Gary Alan Swann (1957-) + Becky (?)
        8. Erika Swann (?-)

8. Melissa Rae Swann (1982-)
7. Sandra Gail Swann (1963-) + Mike Bellamy (?-)
8. Erica Nicole Bellamy (1983-)
8. Brandon Michael Bellamy (1985-)
6. David Mitchel Potter (1937-) + Martha Ann Hinson + Mixon
7. Joel Austin Potter (1970-)
7. Timothy Mark Potter (1971-)
6. Beulah Jean Potter (1940-) + Jack Finley (?-)
7. Darcy Marlane Finley (1964-) + Danial Jefferson Langston (?-)
8. Danita Jasmine Langston (1987-)
8. David Mitchel Langston (?-)
8. Dillon James Langston (?-)
7. Nia Clarice Finley (1966-) + Phillip (P.J.) Langston, Jr. (?-)
8. Renae Charise Langston (?-)
8. Chistow (Keestow) Langston (?-)
8. Bowdrie Langston (?-)
8. Jude Alonzo Langston (1998-)
5. Clara Mabel Hall (1910-1964) + James F. Holderby + Melvin Merrill (?-)
5. Clifford Cleborn Hall (1912-1974) + Imogene White (?-)
6. Frances Carol Hall (?-)
5. Cliifford Cleborn Hall (1912-1974) + Georgia Marie Sage (1916-1976)
6. Shirley Ann Hall (1937-1989) + William Dean Terrill (1935-1993)
7. David Philip Terrill (1955-) + Karen Sue Bonds (1951-)
7. Kathleen Marie Terrill (1958-) + Arnold Ulloa (?-)
8. Jacquelyn Renee Ulloa (1982-)

    8. Audrey Lynn Ulloa (1985-)

    8. Olivia Ulloa (1988-)

   7. Merry Susan Terrill (1960-) + Francis (Frank) Rock (?-)

   7. Cara Lee Terrill (1962-) + Les Burns + Perry Vierra (?-)

    8. Kyle Burns (1983-)

    8. Elise Burns (1987-)

   7. Mark Allen Terrill (1964-) + Gerilyn Silva (?-)

  6. Mary Jo Hall (1939-1992) + John R. Sheppard (?-) + Robt. Musgraves

   7. John Richard Sheppard, Jr. (1957-)

  6. Nancy June Hall (1943-) + Jesse Kilborn Holmes (1940-)

   7. Jesse Kilborn Holmes, Jr. (1965-)

   7. Michelle Holmes (?-)

   7. Kimberly Holmes (?-)

5. Delsie Dale Hall (1914-1998) + William Clifford Bernard (1915-1988)

  6. Myrna Jo Barnard (1939-) + Anthony (Tony) Ceccarelli (-2001)

   7. Adam Rocco Ceccarelli (1961-)

   7. Matthew Christopher Ceccarelli (1962-) + Lisa Buckley (1964-)

    8. Alissa Ceccarelli (1986-)

    8. Shannon Ceccarelli Fitzpatric (1984-)

   7. Michael John Ceccarelli (1967-1988) + Lee Ann Turner

    8. (?) Ceccarelli (1988-)

   7. Anna Rue Ceccarelli (1967-) (twin)

  6. Sylvia Ann Barnard (1940-) + Neil AllenWilliams (1940-) + Jerry Cole (?-) = Ted (Theo) Stathakis (?-)

   7. Richard Allen Williams (1957-)

7. Cheryle Ann Williams (1958-) + Randal Mello (?-)
8. Randy Mello (1977-)
7. Cheryle Ann Williams (1958-) + Tom Patterson (?-)
8. Amber Patterson (1984-)
8. Thomas Patterson (1986-)
7. Jack Wesley Williams (1959-1967)
6. Sylvia Ann Barnard (1940-) + Randy Allen Mello (?-)
7. Randy Allen Mello, Jr. (1977-)
6. Joyce Dean Barnard (1942-) + Steve Manning Birdman (?-) +
David Crockett Robinson (?-)
7. Margo Janeen Birdman (1962-) + Steven Boone (?-)
8. Amanda Summer Boone (1980-) + Marco
Manfredo
8. Ashley Dawn Boone (1988-)
7. Margo Janeen Birdman (1962-) + Rick Randolph (?-)
8. Jessica Randolph (?-)
6. Joyce Dean Barnard (1942-) + David Crockett Robinson (?-))
7. April Dawn Robinson (1963-)
5. Luther Leonard Hall (1917-1972) + Christine Clark (-1997)
6. Luther Ray Hall (1942-) + Norma Jean Maddie (?-)
7. Luther Ray Hall, Jr. (1957-) + Rebecca Smith (?-)
8. Rosalie Jean Smith (1977-)
8. Amanda Yvonne Smith (1980-) + (?)
9. Zackary Tyler Smith (1998-)
7. Richard Allen Hall (1958-)
6. Luther Ray Hall (1942-) + Connie Beth Rorabaugh (?-)
7. Angela Rae Hall (1966-) + Jose R. Ramirez Corona
Aquilar (?-)
8. John Ross Hall (1991-)
8. Michael Dewayne Hall (1993-)
7. Darrin Dwayne Hall (1967-2001) + Mary Eliz.
Harmon (?-)

8. Zachary Thomas Hall (1991-)

8. Matthew Luke Hall (1997-)

7. Debra Dawn Hall (1972-) + Johnny Dewayne Bell (1968-)

8. Lyndsey Renee Bell (1991-)

8 Darrin James Hockett (2001-)

5. Vernon Hall (1920-1974)

5. Zack Oberon Hall (1923-1969) + Edith Coonrod (?-)

6. Karen Hall (?-) + R. C. Lawyer

7. Terri Jo Lawyer (?-)

7. Michael (Butch) Dewayne Lawyer (?-)

6. Jim Hall (?-1996) + Gale + Trecias Jo (?)

7. Trecias Hall (?-)

5. Zack Oberon Hall (1923-1974)+Katherine (?-)

6. Sydney Lee Hall(1953-) + Ken Mckay (?-)

7. Regina Mckay (1983-)

7. Kristel Mckay (1984-)

5. Wesley Elmo Hall (1925-) + Bonita Pursiville (1929-1987)

6. Leslie Jeanne Hall (1952-) + John Gott + Alan H. Brown (1942-)

7. Matthew Alan Brown (1975-)

7. Lauren Elizabeth Brown (1977-)

6. Robert Christopher Hall (1959-) + Valorie Chase (?-)

7. Chase Wesley Hall (1989-)

7. Tyler Cody Hall (1992-)

6. Holly Denise Hall (1960-) +David Melton + Katona + Sean FitzPatrick

7. Nicholas Michael FitzPatrick (1995-)

7. Brendan Miles FitzPatrick (1997-)

7. Patrick Stephen FitzPatrick (1999-)

6. John Jeffrey Hall (1962-1982) + Ronda Grimes (?-)

7. David Jeffrey Grimes (1980-) + Christy Heard (?)

8. Courtney Lea Grimes (2001-)
7. Latisha Marie Hall (1981-)
4. Ulysses S. Grant Hall (1880-1964) + Vane Pennington (1880-1936)
5. Viola Helen Hall (1900-1982) + Ralph Cunningham Cannon (?-)
6. Ralph Cunningham Cannon, Jr. (ca. 1918-)
5. Willie Hall (1901-1906)
5. Albert Hall (1903-1916)
5. Maggie Lee Hall (1905-1935) + Floyd Harris (?-)
6. Lowell Harris (?-)
6. Fay Harris (?-)
6. Charles Harris (?-)
5. Mary Elizabeth Hall (1906-1989) + Toy Elmo Hyder (?-?) + Everett Cole
6. Jessie Raymond Hyder (?-) + (?)
7. Michael Ray Hyder (1950-)
7. Pamela Elaine Hyder (1953-)
6. Jessie Raymond Hyder (?-) + Marti (?)
7. David Hyder (1982-)
6. Jerry Albert Hyder (?-)
5. James Arnold Hall (1908-1993) + Bessie Crumm (1915-)
6. Kenneth Murl Hall (1934-) + Rena Irene Walker (1937-)
7. Kathy Irene Hall (1955-) + (?) Burney (?-)
8. Allen Joseph Burney (1976-)
8. Aaron Joshua Burney (1979-)
6. Cecil Ferrell Hall (1942-) + Patricia Bolt (?)
7. Rebecca Jane Hall (?-)
6. Wanda Hall (1940-) + William Dale Smith (1938-)
7. Larry Dale Smith (1960-1983)
8. Jeremy Don Smith (1978-)
8. Misty Dawn Smith (1980-)
7. Tawnya Danita Smith (1961-)
8. James David Daugherty II (1980-)

8. Andrea Nicole Kelley (1984-)

8. Bridgett Leann Kelley (1986-)

7. Tammy Denise Smith (1962-1963)

5. Ella Zona Hall (1910-1990) + Clyde Theron Crisler (?-)

6. Theron Crisler, Jr. (?-) + Trudy Tobias (Trudy Ellen Smith) (-1999)

5. Goldie Mae Hall (1913-1916)

5. Lucy Florence Hall (1915-) + John Davis + Guy Dawson (1916-)

6. Sylvia Dawson (1940-) + Dean Parker + Sisto Benevidez

6. Alma Dawson (1941-) + Alois Schmidt + Loy Fulbright

6. Janet Dawson (1943-) + Darrell Belcher + David Weekley

6. Phyllis Dawson (1952-) + Donnie Price + Leon Ellison

5. Iva Alice Hall (1916-1921)

4. Sidney William Hall (1882-1972) + Cordelia Eubanks

5. Melvin (Red) Hall (?-)

5. Clint Hall (?-)

5. Nadine Hall (?-)

5. Orville Hall (?-1940)

4. Cordelia Mae Hall (1884-1982) + Logan Sisemore (1887-1973)

5. Coleman Sisemore (1909-1991) + Argie Ewing (?-)

5. Theodore Sisemore (1911-1981) + Pearl Miller (?-)

6. Leon Sisemore (?-)

6. Lawrence Sisemore (?-)

5. Jack Sisemore (1914-1989) + Helen (?-)

6. Francis Sisemore (?-)

5. Lucille Sisemore (1915-1977) + Willie Kendrick Rainey (?-) + Tom Bratten

6. Robert K. Rainey (?-) + Marion (?)

7. Robert K. Rainey, Jr. (?-)

7. Evelyn Rainey (?-)

7. Karen Rainey (?-)

6. Betty Jean Rainey (?-)

5. Buena Patricia Sisemore (1917-) + Orville Rainey (1932-1995) + J. Hatcher
  6. Tommy Aubrey Rainey (1938-)+ (?)
   7. Thomas Rainey ((1956-1982)
   7. Jack Rainey (?-)
   7. William Rainey (?-)
  6. Jackie Ray Rainey (1934-)
   7. Mitzi Rainey (?-) + (?)
    8. Sage Rainey (?) (1995-)
   7. Brenda Rainey (?-)
   7. Esta Rainey (?-)
   7. Christine Rainey (?-)
5. Thelma (Tommie) Sisemore (1922-1990) + Richard Hines + Rhoads
  6. Beverly Hines (?-)
5. Carl Sisemore (1926-1996) + Vickey (?)
4. Charity Hall (1885-1964) + Lee Rogers (1886-1964)
 5. Grace Rogers (?-) + Thomas
  6. Thomas(?) Thomas (1936-)
  6. Ginger Sue Thomas (1940-)
  6. Dewey Thomas (1944-)
 5. Searls Rogers (1906-) + (?)
  6. Kenneth Rogers (?-)
  6. Twila Rogers (?-)
  6. Wayne Rogers (?-)
  6. Brenda Rogers (?-)
  6. Rick Rogers (?-)
  6. Vickie Rogers (?-)
4. Green T. (Tyree) Hall (1887-1967) + Nancy (Nanny) Eversole (1888-1945)
 5. Ernest Clifford Hall (1911-)
 5. Olen Hall (?-)

    5. Pearl Zenia Hall (1914-1981) + Belser + Morrison + Leroy Earl Tobias (?-) + Sukut

        6. Trudy Tobias (?-1999) Also Trudy Ellen Smith)

    5. Arizona (Marge) Lee Hall (1916-) + Fletcher + Lee

    5. Delphi (Pat) Hall (1919-) + Hays + Avegio + Kenneth Kodabaugh

    5. Irene Hall (1923-) + Brooks Bryant + Geidt

    5. Imogene (Bonnie) Hall (1928-) + Russell Burrow (?-)

    5. Robert Hall (Kirk, adopted (1931-) + Ella Coffee (?-)

3. Emeline Hall (1836-?)

3. Tyre (Tyree) Hall (1838-) + Arcina N. Merett (1838-?)

    4. David (Davis?) Hall (1860-?)

    4. Lenoria (Lenorah) Hall (1862-?)

    4. Charity E. Hall (1867-?)

    4. Mary A. Hall (1870-?)

    4. James W. Hall (1871-?)

    4. Lucy A. Hall (1872-?)

    4. Margaret (Maggie) Hall (1875-?)

    4. Arcina Hall (1878-?)

    4. George W. Hall (1879-?)

3. Green Berry Hall, Jr. (1842-1930) + Sarah Elvira Bradley (1866-1911)

    4. William Hall (1867-?)

    4. Mary E. Hall (1869-?)

    4. Elizabeth A. Hall (1873-?)

    4. Jessica Hall (1878-?)

    4. Rena Hall (1887-?)

    4. Green M. Hall (1888-?)

    4. Hyram Hall (1892-?)

    4. Olga Hall (1895-?)

3. Elander (Ailey) Hall (1843-?)

3. Clarency (Charity) Hall (1847-?)

3. Parthena Hall (1848-?) + James Thompson (1870) + G. B. Brown + William R. Day

Conclusions

As families go, this branch of the Halls had relatively few skeletons in their closets. On the basis of my research, William Newton Hall did not desert from the Georgia Cavalry, and he did not commit adultery by marrying Susan Elizabeth Woods. We have only the word of Cordelia Mae (Delia), his daughter, that he disguised himself like a woman and sat out the last year of the war, that he attempted more than once to join the Yankee army, and, years later, after the family was in Arkansas, he returned to Georgia to search for *his long-lost Sid.* I am not disputing Aunt Delia's stories; but, to me, without one shred tangible evidence to substantiate them, they seem like the wild imaginings of an impressionable young girl (In later years my dear old aunt embellished a lot and told different versions of her childhood stories).

Our family today is quite diverse, which is to say *typical American.* In Georgia more than one Hall male tied the knot with a Cherokee maiden; and during our trek across the western half of the continent to California some of our women, as well as our men, found lifelong partners in other ethnic minorities. I think this is just as it should be. To those who would bemoan the fact that we have changed a great deal since the time of our early ancestors, I say, "We are Americans now more than we have ever been. America was once the land of the Red Man; then for awhile it was the land of the White Man; and now it is the land of Diversity and Originality. And although we are not entirely unique in this, we are the world's leader in it. Whatever the rest of the world has to offer, we already have in abundance.

APPENDIX
THE NUMBERS INDEX

The Number System used here is one that I developed in the 1960's, when it became clear to me that I was never going to be able to keep all of the Johns and Marys separated (Even then the list of family names was quite long). Since I wanted to make sure that everyone would have his/her own special number, I decided to use dots (decimal points) to separate generations and the order of birth within a nuclear family; that way no two people could possibly have the same number. For example, our farthest-back ancestor would be given the number <1>. Numero Uno. His children would be listed in the order of their birth in the family. This way each child would have an arbitrary number at birth. For example, the first child of this Paternal Ancestor would be identified as 1.1[.] My number is 1.1.4.3.11, which says that I am Fifth Generation (There are five sets of digits), that I descend directly from John Hall of South Carolina (the first 1), Hiram Hall of Georgia (who was the first son of the PA), William Newton Hall (the fourth child of Hiram Hall), and Greeley Teeman Hall (the third child of William Newton). The last digit, 11, is my rank in the Greel Hall family (How much lower can one get?). We are now into the Ninth Generation, and as far as I know the last descendant of John and Hiram Hall is 1.1.2.2.2.2.6.5.4 Shalae Dacy Van Wagoner (August 30, 2001-), the daughter of Tricia Danette (Pearson) and Richard Van Wagoner. The highest number goest to Zack Taylor Smith, who was born in 1998 (1.1.4.3.8.1.1.2.1).

Can you trace Zack's ancestry by this number?

1 John Hall
1.1 Hiram Hall
1.1.4 William Newton Hall
1.1.4.3 Teeman Hall
1.1.4.3.8 Luther Leonard Hall
1.1.4.3.8.1 Luther Ray Hall, Sr.
1.1.4.3.8.1.1 Luther Ray Hall, Jr. (who legally changed his name to *Smith*)
1.1.4.3.8.1.1.2 Amanda Yvonne Smith (second child of Luke Jr.)

He is, then, the first child of Amanda Yvonne Smith (who gave him her maiden name).

First Generation

1.O   John Hall (1769-) and Mary (1770-)

Second Generation

The children of John and Mary Hall:

1.1   Hiram Hall (1795-) and Charity (1802-)
1.2.   Green Berry Hall (1805-) and Charity (1815-)

Third Generation

The children of Hiram and Charity Hall:

1.1.1   Arminda (1823-1915, Carroll County, Georgia)
1.1.2   John Hall (1824, Carroll County, Georgia)
1.1.3   Nancy Hall (1829, Carroll County, Georgia)
1.1.4   William Newton Hall (1831, Carroll County, Georgia)
1.1.5   Emeline Hall (1836, Carroll County, Georgia)
1.1.6   Tyre Hall (1838, Carroll County, Georgia)
1.1.7   Elander Hall (1839, Carroll County, Georgia)

1.1.8	Green (1842, Carroll County, Georgia)
1.1.9	Ailey Hall (1843, Carroll County, Georgia)
1.1.10	Claracy (Clarency) Hall (1847, Carroll County, Georgia)
1.1.11	Parthena Hall (1848, Carroll County, Georgia)
1.1.12	Delila (1859, Carroll County, Georgia)

[In the 1870 Haralson County, Georgia, census Charity was 68, Parthena 23 and still at home, and a child of two named Electious was listed as Charity's grandchild. In the 1880 Haralson County census Charity gave her age as 83 and listed John Thompson as her grandson. He was probably Parthena's son. It is quite likely that Delila and Electious were Parthena's children.]

The children of Green Berry and Charity Hall:

1.2.1	Nancy Hall (1843-?)
1.2.2	John Wesley Hall (1844-?)
1.2.3	James Hall (1846-?)
1.2.4	Mary Anne Hall (1848-?)
1.2.5	Charity Hall (1849-?)
1.2.6	Froni R. Hall (1852-?)

Fourth Generation

The children of Arminda (Hall) and Thomas S. Herron:

1.1.1.1	James Herron (1848-1935)
1.1.1.2	Hiram Herron (1850-1909)
1.1.1.3	Charity Herron (1852-1857)
1.1.1.4	D. F. Herron (1854-1857)
1.1.1.5	Jane Herron (1857-)
1.1.1.6	Pierce Herron (1860-1902)

1.1.1.7	Green Herron (1862-1925)
1.1.1.8	Missouria Herron (1864-1945)

The children of John and Nancy (Hamilton) Hall:

1.1.2.1	Delilah Emeline Hall (1848-)
1.1.2.2	Robert Jefferson Hall (1850-1944)
1.1.2.3	Madison Monroe Hall (1852-1928)
1.1.2.4	Richard Lafayette Hall (1854-)
1.1.2.5	Janette Ardelia Hall (1856-)
1.1.2.6	Nancy Lanore Hall (1859-)
1.1.2.7	Margret Charity Hall (1861-)
1.1.2.8	Mary (Maty) Ann Hall (1866-)

The children of William N. and Susan Elizabeth (Woods) Hall:

1.1.4.1	Archie Brooklyn Hall (1871-1955)
1.1.4.2	Dock Walter Hall (1873-1951)
1.1.4.3	Greeley Teeman Hall (1877-1965)
1.1.4.4	Ulysses Grant Hall (1880-1964)
1.1.4.5	Sidney William Hall (1882-1972)
1.1.4.6	Cordelia (Delia, Deely) Hall (1884-1982)
1.1.4.7	Charity Hall (1885-1964)
1.1.4.8	Green Tyre Hall (1887-1967)

The children of Tyre and Arcenia (Merett) Hall:

1.1.6.1	Davis (David?) Hall (1860-?)
1.1.6.2	Lenoria (Lenorah) Hall (1862-?)
1.1.6.3	Charity E. Hall (1867-?)
1.1.6.4	Mary A. Hall (1870-?)
1.1.6.5	James W. Hall (1871-?)
1.1.6.6	Luca A. (Lucy) Hall (1872-?)
1.1.6.7	Margaret (Maggie) Hall (1875-?)

1.1.6.8	Arcina Hall (1878-?)
1.1.6.9	George W. Hall (1879-?)

The children of Green Berry (Jr.) and Sarah (Bradley) Hall:

1.1.8.1	William Hall (1867-?)
1.1.8.2	Mary E. Hall (1869-?)
1.1.8.3	Elizabeth A. Hall (1873-?)
1.1.8.4	Jessica Hall (1878-?)
1.1.8.5	Rena Hall (1887-?)
1.1.8.6	Green M. Hall (1888-?)
1.1.8.7	Hyram Hall (1892-?)
1.1.8.8	Olga Hall (1895-?)

Fifth Generation

The children of Hiram and Martha (Guttery) Herron:

1.1.1.2.1	Elijah Isham Herron (1873-1875)
1.1.1.2.2	Newman Herron (1876-1893)
1.1.1.2.3	James Thomas Herron (1879-1966)
1.1.1.2.4	Arminda Elvira Herron (1881-)
1.1.1.2.5	Cora Ann Herron (1883-1960)
1.1.1.2.6	Julia Francis Herron (1886-1965)
1.1.1.2.7	Savannah Silvany Herron (1888-)
1.1.1.2.8	Lunceford Osro Herron (1891-1977)

The children of Robert Jefferson Hall and Sara Jane Brewer:

1.1.2.3.1	Wellington Columbus Hall (1879-1964)
1.1.2.3.2	Thomas Cleveland Hall (1884-1965)
1.1.2.3.3	Darien C. Hall (1887-1922)
1.1.2.3.4	Marien Hall (1887-1889) (twin)
1.1.2.3.5	Cara Ethel Hall (1892-1893)
1.1.2.3.6	Voyd Hall (1894-1968)

1.1.2.3.7	Earnest Thurman Hall (1891-1982)
1.1.2.3.8	Larry Wise Hall (1898-)
1.1.2.3.9	Mary Anice Hall (1899-)

The children of Madison Monroe Hall and ?

1.1.2.4.1	Ida Lenora Hall (1876-)
1.1.2.4.2	Violet May Hall (1879-)
1.1.2.4.3	Harriet Lillian Hall (1881-)
1.1.2.4.4	Josephine Pearl Hall (1883-1926)
1.1.2.4.5	Ernest Edward Hall (1886-)
1.1.2.4.6	Raynand Lafayette Hall (1888-)
1.1.2.4.7	Ethel Hall (1890-)
1.1.2.4.8	Anita Gertrude Hall (1895-)
1.1.2.4.9	Rosamond Del Hall (1895-)

The children of Archie Brooklyn and Nancy Hall:

1.1.4.1.1	Minnie Aloony Hall (1894-1910)
1.1.4.1.2	Annie Dona Hall (1896-1956)
1.1.4.1.3	Jessie Newton Hall (1899-1994)
1.1.4.1.4	Carl (Bud) Tyre Hall (1901-1965)
1.1.4.1.5	Pearl Ellen Hall (1903-1985)
1.1.4.1.6	Birtha Elizabeth Hall (1905-?)
1.1.4.1.7	Aaron Granville Hall (1907-1964)
1.1.4.1.8	Cecil Hall (1912-1912)

The children of Dock Walter and Kate (Elsey) Hall:

1.1.4.2.1	Arthur H. Hall (1902-1995)
1.1.4.2.2	Earl Hall (1903-)
1.1.4.2.3	Cecile Hall 1908-1957)
1.1.4.2.4	Jewel Hall (1915-)
1.1.4.2.5	Dovie Hall (?-)
1.1.4.2.6	Oma Hall (1922-)

The children of Greely Teeman (Horace Greel) and Mallie (Carr) Hall:

1.1.4.3.1	Ezra Marion Hall (1902-1986)
1.1.4.3.2	Grady Hall (1904-1990)
1.1.4.3.3	Ollie Ida Hall (1906-1934)
1.1.4.3.4	Ruth Hall (1908-1976)
1.1.4.3.5	Clara Mabel Hall (1910-1964)
1.1.4.3.6	Clifford Cleborn Hall (1912-1974)
1.1.4.3.7	Delsie Dale Hall (1914-1998)
1.1.4.3.8	Luther Leonard Hall (1917-1972)
1.1.4.3.9	Vernon Hall (1920-1974)
1.1.4.3.10	Zack Oberon Hall (1923-1969)
1.1.4.3.11	Wesley Elmo Hall (1925-)

The children of Ulysses Grant and Sylvania (Pennington) Hall:

1.1.4.4.1	Viola Helen Hall (1900-1982)
1.1.4.4.2	Willie Hall (1901-1906)
1.1.4.4.3	Albert Hall (1903-1916)
1.1.4.4.4	Maggie Lee Hall (1905-1935)
1.1.4.4.5	Mary Elizabeth Hall (1906-1989)
1.1.4.4.6	James Arnold Hall (1908-1993)
1.1.4.4.7	Ella Zona Hall (1910-1990)
1.1.4.4.8	Goldie Mae Hall (1913-1916)
1.1.4.4.9	Lucy Florence Hall (1915-)
1.1.4.4.10	Iva Alice Hall (1916—1921)
1.1.4.4.11	Johnnie Theron Hall (1919-1993)

The children of William Sidney and Cordelia (Eubanks) Hall:

1.1.4.5.1	Melvin (Red) Hall (?-)
1.1.4.5.2	Clint Hall (?-)
1.1.4.5.3	Nadine Hall (?-)
1.1.4.5.4	Orville Hall (?-1940)

The children of Cordelia (Delia) Mae (Hall) and Logan Sisemore:

1.1.4.6.1	Coleman Sisemore (1909-?)
1.1.4.6.2	Theodore Sisemore (1911-1981)
1.1.4.6.3	Jack Sisemore (1914-1989)
1.1.4.6.4	Lucille Sisemore (1915-1977)
1.1.4.6.5	Patricia (Bunah) Sisemore (1917-)
1.1.4.6.6	Thelma (Tommie) Sisemore (1922-1990)
1.1.4.6.7	Carl Sisemore (1926-)

The children of Charity (Hall) and Lee Rogers:

1.1.4.7.1	Grace Rogers (?-)
1.1.4.7.2	Searls Rogers (1906-?)

The children of Green T. and Nanny (Eversole) Hall:

1.1.4.8.1	Ernest Clifford Hall (1911-)
1.1.4.8.2	Pearl Zenia Hall (1914-1981)
1.1.4.8.3	Arizona (Marge) Lee Hall (1916-)
1.1.4.8.4	Delphi (Pat) Hall (1919-)
1.1.4.8.5	Irene Hall (1923-)
1.1.4.8.6	Imogene (Bonnie) Hall (1928-)
1.1.4.8.7	Robert (Bob) (Hall) Kirk, adopted (1931-)

Sixth Generation

The children of James Thomas Herron and Mintie Cheatham:

1.1.1.2.3.1	Mamie Ethel Herron (1900-1972)
1.1.1.2.3.2	Walter James Herron, Sr. (1902-1970)
1.1.1.2.3.3	Clarence Herron (1904-1986)
1.1.1.2.3.4	Flossie Herron (1906-1996)
1.1.1.2.3.5	Edgar Herron (1908-)
1.1.1.2.3.6	Donnie Mae Herron (1910-1996)
1.1.1.2.3.7	Grady Herron (1912-)

1.1.1.2.3.8	Esther Louise Herron (1915-)
1.1.1.2.3.9	Earl Herron Herron (1918-1977)
1.1.1.2.3.10	Earnest Herron (1920-1971)

The children of Thomas Cleveland Hall and Margie Rena Roberts:

1.1.2.2.2.1	Wayne Ambrose Hall (1907-1929)
1.1.2.2.2.2	Carlos Mentril Hall (1909-1965)
1.1.2.2.2.3	Therman Clement Hall (1914-2001)
1.1.2.2.2.4	Thomas Richard Hall (1916-1920)
1.1.2.2.2.5	Lloyd Evan Hall (1920-1994)
1.1.2.2.2.6	Mary Lenore Hall (1923-1991)
1.1.2.2.2.7	Victor Leon Hall (1928-)

The children of Annie Dona (Hall) and J. W. Swafford;

1.1.4.1.2.1	Christopher David Swafford (1920-1983)

The children of Jessie Newton and Dora Bell (Lawson) Hall:

1.1.4.1.3.1	Oliver Newton Hall (b. in Norwalk, California)
1.1.4.1.3.2	Roy Hall (b. in Vinita, Oklahoma)
1.1.4.1.3.3	Jerry Hall (b. in Artesia, California)
1.1.4.1.3.4	Jim Hall (b. in Coffeeville, Kansas)
1.1.4.1.3.5	Imogene (Hall) Horn (b. in Afton, Oklahoma)
1.1.4.1.3.6	Jessie Mae Hall (1930-)(b. in Chelsea, Oklahoma)
1.1.4.1.3.7	Helen (Hall) Orchid (b. in Lakewood, California)
1.1.4.1.3.8	Dorothy (Hall) Holinsworth (b. in Nowata, Oklahoma)
1.1.4.1.3.9	Judy (Hall) Boyd (b. in Nowata, Oklahoma)

The children of Carl (Bud) and Carrie (Taylor) Hall:

1.1.4.1.4.1	Gladys Marie Hall (1922-1986)
1.1.4.1.4.2	Iva Loreen Hall (1926-)

1.1.4.1.4.3	Sadie Lee Hall (1926-)
1.1.4.1.4.4	James Oliver Hall (1928-)
1.1.4.1.4.5	Tyre Roland Hall (1929-)

The children of Carl (Bud) and Nor May (Howell) Hall:

1.1.4.1.4.6	Virginia Ruth Hall (1937-1954)
1.1.4.1.4.7	Carl Watson Hall (1940-)
1.1.4.1.4.8	Kenneth Franklin Hall (1943-)
1.1.4.1.4.9	Richard Douglas Hall (1945-)

The children of Arthur and Vernie Hall:

1.1.4.2.1.1	LaVonna Hall (?-)
1.1.4.2.1.2	Johnnie Clifton Hall (?-)
1.1.4.2.1.3	LeRoy Hall (?-)

The children of Earl and Stella Hall:

1.1.4.2.2.1	Durward Jack Hall (1927-)
1.1.4.2.2.2	Val Gene Hall (1928-)
1.1.4.2.2.3	Velta Lee Hall 1930-)
1.1.4.2.2.4	Bobby Ray (Bob) Hall (1932-)
1.1.4.2.2.5	Barbara Louise Hall (1935-)
1.1.4.2.2.6	Joyce Oteka Hall (1938-)

The children of Cecile (Hall) and Bill Lanphear:

1.1.4.2.3.1	Doyle Lanphear (?-)
1.1.4.2.3.2	Leon Lanphear (?-)
1.1.4.2.3.3	Suevella Lanphear (?-1978)
1.1.4.2.3.4	Drucella Lanphear (?-)

The children of Jewel (Hall) and Connie Lee Beard:

1.1.4.2.4.1	Billy Ray Beard (1939-)

The children of Dovie (Hall) and Lou Peak:
1.1.4.2.5.1   Darrell Dean Peak (?-)

The children of Oma (Hall) and Johnny Beard:
1.1.4.2.6.1   Judy Beard (?-)
1.1.4.2.6.2   Janet Beard (?-)

The children of Oma (Hall) and C. L. Payne:
1.1.4.2.6.3   Brenda Payne (?-)
1.1.4.2.6.4   Linda Payne (?-)

The children of Ezra and Florence (Scoggins) Hall:
1.1.4.3.1.1   Alton Lee Hall (1928-1989)
1.1.4.3.1.2   Dorotha Faye Hall (1931-)

The children of Gradie (Hall) and Arthur Lee Goff:
1.1.4.3.2.1   Inas Faye Goff (1926-)
1.1.4.3.2.2   Maudie June Goff (1929-)
1.1.4.3.2.3   Annie Jo Goff (1930-1995)

The children of Ollie (Hall) and Lou Smith:
1.1.4.3.3.1   Flora Evaline Smith (1925-)
1.1.4.3.3.2   Merle Eston (Bud) Smith (1927-)
1.1.4.3.3.3   Lou Albin (L. A.) Smith (1929-)
1.1.4.3.3.4   Mallie Avo Smith (1931-)
1.1.4.3.3.5   Roy Joe Smith (1934-1996)

The children of Ruth (Hall) and Ben Potter:
1.1.4.3.4.1   Clara Dale Potter (1935-)
1.1.4.3.4.2   David Mitchel Potter (1937-)
1.1.4.3.4.3   Beulah Jean Potter (1940-)

The children of Clifford and Imogene (White) Hall:

1.1.4.3.6.1	Frances Carol Hall (?-)

The children of Clifford and Georgia (Sage) Hall:

1.1.4.3.6.2	Shirley Ann Hall (1937-1989)
1.1.4.3.6.3	Mary Jo Hall (1939-1992)
1.1.4.3.6.4	Nancy June Hall (1943-)

The children of Delsie (Hall) and Clifford (Lucy) Bernard:

1.1.4.3.7.1	Myrna Jo Bernard (1939-)
1.1.4.3.7.2	Sylvia Ann Bernard (1940-)
1.1.4.3.7.3	Joyce Dean Bernard (1942-)

The children of Luther and Christine (Clark) Hall:

1.1.4.3.8.1	Luther Ray Hall (1942-)

The children of Zack and Edith (Coonrod) Hall:

1.1.4.3.10.1	Karen Hall (?-)
1.1.4.3.10.2	Jim Hall (?-1996)

The children of Zack and Kaye (?) Hall:

1.1.4.3.10.3	Sydney Lee Hall (1953-)

The children of Wesley and Bonita (Pursiville) Hall

1.1.4.3.11.1	Leslie Jeanne Hall (1952-)
1.1.4.3.11.2	Robert Christopher Hall (1959-)
1.1.4.3.11.3	Holly Denise Hall (1960-)
1.1.4.3.11.4	John Jeffrey Hall (1962-1982)

The children of James A. and Bessie (Crumm) Hall:

1.1.4.4.6.1	Kenneth Murl Hall (1934-)
1.1.4.4.6.2	Cecil Ferrell Hall (1942-)
1.1.4.4.6.3	Wanda Hall (1940-)

The children of Ella Zona (Hall) and Clyde T. Crisler:

1.1.4.4.7.1   Clyde Theron Crisler, Jr. (?-)

The children of Lucy (Hall) and Guy Dawson:

1.1.4.4.9.1   Sylvia Dawson (1940-)
1.1.4.4.9.2   Alma Dawson (1941-)
1.1.4.4.9.3   Janet Dawson (1943-)
1.1.4.4.9.4   Phyllis Dawson (1952-)

The children of Theodore and Pearl (Miller) Sisemore:

1.1.4.6.2.1   Leon Sisemore (?-)
1.1.4.6.2.2   Lawrence Sisemore (?-)

The children of Jack and Eula (Gutten) Sisemore:

1.1.4.6.3.1   Francis (Sisemore) and Willie Rainey

The children of Lucille (Sisemore) and Willie Rainey:

1.1.4.6.4.1   Robert K. Rainey (?-)
1.1.4.6.4.2   Betty Jean Rainey (?-)

The children of Pat Buena (Sisemore) and Orville Rainey:

1.1.4.6.5.1   Tommy Aubrey Rainey (1938-)
1.1.4.6.5.2   Jackie Ray Rainey (1934-)

The children of Thelma (Sisemore) and Richard Hines:

1.1.4.6.6.1   Beverly Hines (?-)

The children of Grace (Rogers) and (?) Thomas:

1.1.4.7.1.1   Thomas(?) Thomas (1936-)
1.1.4.7.1.2   Ginger Sue Thomas (1940-)
1.1.4.7.1.3   Dewey Thomas (1944-)

The children of Searls Rogers:

1.1.4.7.2.1	Kenneth Rogers (?-)
1.1.4.7.2.2	Twila Rogers (?-)
1.1.4.7.2.3	Wayne Rogers (?-)
1.1.4.7.2.4	Brenda Rogers (?-)
1.1.4.7.2.5	Rick Rogers (?-)
1.1.4.7.2.6	Vickie Rogers (?-)

The children of Pearl (Hall) and Leroy Earl Tobias:

1.1.4.8.2.1	Trudy Tobias (?-1999)

Seventh Generation

The children of Walter James Herron, Sr. and Ceatrice Jenkins:

1.1.1.2.3.2.1	Walter James Herron, Jr. (1929-)
1.1.1.2.3.2.2	Jerry Edward Herron (?-)
1.1.1.2.3.2.3	Larry Ray Herron (?-)
1.1.1.2.3.2.4	Norma Jean Herron (?-)
1.1.1.2.3.2.5	Douglas Wayne Herron (?-)
1.1.1.2.3.2.6	Glenda Gail Herron (?-)

The children of Clarence Herron and Meatrice Odom:

1.1.1.2.3.3.1	J. W. Herron (?-)
1.1.1.2.3.3.2	Opal Jean Herron (?-)
1.1.1.2.3.3.3	Billy Ray Herron (?-)
1.1.1.2.3.3.4	Bobby Joe Herron (?-)
1.1.1.2.3.3.5	Carl Dean Herron (?-)
1.1.1.2.3.3.6	Raymond D. Herron (?-)
1.1.1.2.3.3.7	Violet Mae Herron (?-)
1.1.1.2.3.3.8	Harvey Lee Herron (?-)
1.1.1.2.3.3.9	Mary Lou Herron (?-)

1.1.1.2.3.3.10   Jerry Don Herron (?-)
1.1.1.2.3.3.11   George Edward Herron (?-)

The children of Carlos Mentril Hall and Winnifred Lorena Rogers:
1.1.2.2.2.2.1   Virginia June Hall (1936-1945)
1.1.2.2.2.2.2   Theodore Carlos Hall (1937-1962)
1.1.2.2.2.2.3   Roger Evan Hall (1939-)
1.1.2.2.2.2.4   Janette Arlene Hall (1941-)
1.1.2.2.2.2.5   Marjorie Evelyn Hall (1943-)
1.1.2.2.2.2.6   Barbara Joh Hall (1945-)
1.1.2.2.2.2.7   Winnifred Eileen Hall (1946-)
1.1.2.2.2.2.8   Marilyn Kaye Hall (1949-)

The Children of Therman Clement Hall and Mary Virginia Rogers;
1.1.2.2.2.3.1   Allie Jane Hall (?-)
1.1.2.2.2.3.2   Richard Wayne Hall (?-)
1.1.2.2.2.3.3   Robert Lynn Hall (?-)

The children of Victor Leon Hall Phyllis Maurine Rice:
1.1.2.2.2.4.1   Steven Blane Hall (1954-)
1.1.2.2.2.4.2   Vickie Lynn Hall (1956-)
1.1.2.2.2.4.3   Timothy Wayne Hall (1959-)
1.1.2.2.2.4.4   Derek Duane Hall (1968-)

The children of Christopher David and Edna Swafford:
1.1.4.1.2.1.1   Billie Ann Swafford (1953-)
1.1.4.1.2.1.2   Shirley Flo Swafford (1955-)
1.1.4.1.2.1.3   Judy Aline Swafford (1957-)

The children of Jessie Mae (Hall) and Kenneth E. Holinsworth:
1.1.4.1.3.1.1   Michael Eugene Holinsworth (1949-1997)
1.1.4.1.3.1.2   Danny Ray Holinsworth (1950-)

1.1.4.1.3.1.3	Valerie Ann Holinsworth (1952-)
1.1.4.1.3.1.4	Rodney Lee Holinsworth (1956-1976)

The children of Gladys (Hall) and Vinnis Phillips:

1.1.4.1.4.1.1	Nancy Olene Phillips (?-)
1.1.4.1.4.1.2	Frankie Lee Phillips (?-)
1.1.4.1.4.1.3	Shirley Delores Phillips (?-)
1.1.4.1.4.1.4	Peggy Joyce Phillips (?-)
1.1.4.1.4.1.5	Richard Dwayne Phillips (?-)
1.1.4.1.4.1.6	Vinnis Leon Phillips, Jr. (?-)
1.1.4.1.4.1.7	Dianna Gail Phillips (?-)
1.1.4.1.4.1.8	Debra Marie Phillips (?-)
1.1.4.1.4.1.9	Kenneth Lee Phillips (?-)
1.1.4.1.4.1.10	Candy Phillips (?-)

The children of Iva Lorene (Hall) and Charles E. Smith:

1.1.4.1.4.2.1	Charles Henry Smith (?-)

The children of Sadie Lee (Hall) and Calvin Rock:

1.1.4.1.4.3.1	Ervin Lee Rock (?-)
1.1.4.1.4.3.2	Calvin Ray Rock, Jr. (?-)
1.1.4.1.4.3.3	Janis Kaye Rock (?-)
1.1.4.1.4.3.4	Robbie Dale Rock (?-)
1.1.4.1.4.3.5	Janie Faye Rock (?-)

The children of James Oliver and Leola Hall:

1.1.4.1.4.4.1	Judy Gail Hall (1949-)
1.1.4.1.4.4.2	James Larry Hall (1974-)
1.1.4.1.4.4.3	Kathy Ann Hall (1951-)
1.1.4.1.4.4.4	Mark Stephen Hall (1953-)
1.1.4.1.4.4.5	David Lee Hall (1959-)

The children of Tyre Roland and Ruby (Benton) Hall:

1.1.4.1.4.5.1	Anna Mae Hall (?-)
1.1.4.1.4.5.2	Debra Sue Hall (?-)
1.1.4.1.4.5.3	Lillian Lou Hall (?-)
1.1.4.1.4.5.4	Bessie Jean Hall (?-)
1.1.4.1.4.5.5	Maye Belle Hall (?-)
1.1.4.1.4.5.6	Jackie Lee Hall (?-)

The children of Jack and Sarah (Slentz) Hall:

1.1.4.2.2.1.1	Larry Wayne Hall (1955-)
1.1.4.2.2.1.2	Tracy Kay Hall (1957-)

The children of Val Gene and Louise (Elms) Hall:

1.1.4.2.2.2.1	Phyllis Jean Hall (1950-)
1.1.4.2.2.2.2	Ronald Hall (1951-)

The children of Velta (Hall) and Mike Domyan:

1.1.4.2.2.3.1	Nathan Domyan (1958-)

The children of Bob and Anita (Marquez) Hall:

1.1.4.2.2.4.1	Robert James Hall (1956-)
1.1.4.2.2.4.2	Debra Ann Hall (1957-)
1.1.4.2.2.4.3	Dianna Lynn Hall (1958-)
1.1.4.2.2.4.4	Denise Hall (1962-)

The children of Barbara (Hall) and Charley Helton:

1.1.4.2.2.5.1	William Charles Helton (1960-)

The children of Joyce Oteka (Hall) and E. S. Browne:

1.1.4.2.2.6.1	Rochelle Candine Browne (1961-)
1.1.4.2.2.6.2	Lindsay Edward Hall Browne (1963-)

The children of Billie Ray and Cathy (Stucky) Beard:

1.1.4.2.4.1.1	Gregory Beard (1961-)
1.1.4.2.4.1.2	Keith Beard (1963-)

The children of Alton and Jeanetta (Ramsey) Hall:

1.1.4.3.1.1.1	Ginger Kaye Hall (1949-)

The children of Dorotha (Hall) and Mack Schornick:

1.1.4.3.1.2.1	Terrye Lee Schornick (1951-)
1.1.4.3.1.2.2	Mickey Joe Schornick (1957-)

The children of Faye (Goff) and Steve Kandarian:

1.1.4.3.2.1.1	Katherine Louise Kandarian (?-)
1.1.4.3.2.1.2	Patricia Ann Kandarian (?-)

The children of June (Goff) and Joseph Lamanuzzi, Jr.:

1.1.4.3.2.2.1	Joseph Arthur Lamanuzzi (1953-)
1.1.4.3.2.2.2	Linda Faye Lamanuzzi (1955-)

The children of Annie Jo (Goff) and Angelo Papagni:

1.1.4.3.2.3.1	Sandra Elizabeth Papagni (1953-)
1.1.4.3.2.3.2	Judith Anne Papagni (1956-)
1.1.4.3.2.3.3	Carlo Nicholas Papagni (?-)

The children of Flora (Smith) and Jim Putler:

1.1.4.3.3.1.1	Nancy Kay Putler (1961-)
1.1.4.3.3.1.2	David Allen Putler (1961-1961)

The children of L. A. and Lucille Smith:

1.1.4.3.3.3.1	Gary Smith (1949-)
1.1.4.3.3.3.2	Bridget Evelyn Smith (1953-)
1.1.4.3.3.3.3	Gregory Paul Smith (1959-)

The children of Avo (Smith) and Frank Rincon:

1.1.4.3.3.4.1	Mark Anthony Rincon (1951-)
1.1.4.3.3.4.2	Debra Ann Rincon (1953-)
1.1.4.3.3.4.3	Robert Harlan Rincon (1954-)
1.1.4.3.3.4.4	Kelley Maria Rincon (1957-)

The children of Roy Joe and Alma (?) Smith:

1.1.4.3.3.5.1	Michael Smith (?-)
1.1.4.3.3.5.2	Donna Smith (?-)
1.1.4.3.3.5.3	Douglas Smith (?-)

The children of Clara (Potter) and Carl Swann:

1.1.4.3.4.1.1	Steve Nolan Swann (1956-)
1.1.4.3.4.1.2	Gary Alan Swann (1957-)
1.1.4.3.4.1.3	Sandra Gail Swann (1963-)

The children of Mitchel and Martha (Hinson) Potter:

1.1.4.3.4.2.1	Joel Austin Potter (1970-)
1.1.4.3.4.2.2	Timothy Mark Potter (1971-)

The children of Jean (Potter) and Jack Finley:

1.1.4.3.4.3.1	Darcy Marlane Finley (1964-)
1.1.4.3.4.3.2	Nia Clarice Finley (1966-)

The children of Shirley (Hall) and William Terrill:

1.1.4.3.6.2.1	David Philip Terrill (1955-)
1.1.4.3.6.2.2	Kathleen Marie Terrill (1958-)
1.1.4.3.6.2.3	Merry Susan Terrill (1960-)
1.1.4.3.6.2.4	Cara Lee Terrill (1962-)
1.1.4.3.6.2.5	Mark Allen Terrill (1964-)

The children of Mary Jo (Hall) and J. R. Sheppard:
1.1.4.3.6.3.1 John Richard Sheppard, Jr. (1957-)

The children of Nancy (Hall) and Jesse Kilborn Holmes:
1.1.4.3.6.4.1   Jesse Kilborn Holmes, Jr. (1965-)
1.1.4.3.6.4.2   Michelle Holmes (?-)
1.1.4.3.6.4.3   Kimberly Holmes (?-)

The children of Myrna (Bernard) and Tony Ceccarelli:
1.1.4.3.7.1.1   Adam Rocco Ceccarelli (1961-)
1.1.4.3.7.1.2   Matthew Christopher Ceccarelli (1962-)
1.1.4.3.7.1.3   Michael John Ceccarelli (1967-1988) (twin)
1.1.4.3.7.1.4   Anna Rue Ceccarelli (1967-) (twin)

The children of Sylvia (Bernard) and Neil Allen Williams:
1.1.4.3.7.2.1   Richard Allen Williams (1957-) [Adopted by Jerry Cole]
1.1.4.3.7.2.2   Cheryle Ann Williams (1958-) [Adopted by Jerry Cole]
1.1.4.3.7.2.3   Jack Wesley Williams (1959-1974) [Adopted by Jerry Cole]

The children of Sylvia (Bernard) and Randal Allen Mello:
1.1.4.3.7.2.4   Randy Allen Mello, Jr. (1977-)

The children of Joyce (Bernard) and Steve Manning Birdman:
1.1.4.3.7.3.1   Margo Janeen Birdman (1962-)

The children of Joyce (Bernard) and Dave Robinson:
1.1.4.3.7.3.2   April Dawn Robinson (1963-)

The children of Luther Ray (Luke) and Norma Jean (Maddy) Hall:
1.1.4.3.8.1.1   Luther Ray (Luke) Hall, Jr. (1957-)
1.1.4.3.8.1.2   Richard Allen Hall (1958-)

The children of Luther Ray and Connie (Rorabaugh) Hall:
1.1.4.3.8.1.3   Angela Rae Hall (1966-)
1.1.4.3.8.1.4   Darrin Dwayne Hall (1967-)
1.1.4.3.8.1.5   Debra Dawn Hall (1972-)

The children of Karen (Hall) and (?) R. C. Lawyer:
1.1.4.3.10.1.1   Terri Jo Lawyer (?-)
1.1.4.3.10.1.2   Michael (Butch) Dewayne Lawyer (?-)

The children of Jim and Trecias Jo (?) Hall:
1.1.4.3.10.2.1   (A daughter) (?-)

The children of Leslie (Hall) and Alan Brown:
1.1.4.3.11.1.1   Matthew Alan Brown (1975-)
1.1.4.3.11.1.2   Lauren Elizabeth Brown (1977-)

The children of Chris and Valorie (Chase) Hall:
1.1.4.3.11.2.1   Chase Wesley Hall (1989-)
1.1.4.3.11.2.2   Tyler Cody Hall (1992-)

The children of Holly (Hall) and Sean Fitzpatrick:
1.1.4.3.11.3.1   Nicholas Michael Fitzpatrick (1995-)
1.1.4.3.11.3.2   Brendan Miles Fitzpatrick (1997-)
1.1.4.3.11.3.3   Patrick Stephen Fitzpatrick (1999-)

The children of Jeff and Ronda (Grimes) Hall:
1.1.4.3.11.4.1   David Jeffrey Grimes (1980-)
1.1.4.3.11.4.2   Latisha Marie Hall (1981-)

The children of Ray Hyder and (?):

1.1.4.4.5.1.1	Michael Ray Hyder (1950-)
1.1.4.4.5.1.2	Pamela Elaine Hyder (1953-)

The children of Ray and Marti Hyder:

1.1.4.4.5.1.3	David Hyder (1982-)

The children of Kenneth Murl and Rena (Walker) Hall:

1.1.4.4.6.1.1	Kathy Irene Hall (1955-)
1.1.4.4.6.1.2	Ricky Murl Hall (1957-)

The children of Cecil and Patricia (Bolt) Hall:

1.1.4.4.6.2.1	Rebecca Jane Hall (?-)

The children of Wanda (Hall) and William Dale Smith:

1.1.4.4.6.3.1	Larry Dale Smith (1960-1983)
1.1.4.4.6.3.2	Tawnya Danita Smith (1961-)
1.1.4.4.6.3.3	Tammy Denise Smith (1962-1963)

The children of Robert K. and Marion Rainey:

1.1.4.6.4.1.1	Robert K. Rainey, Jr. (?-)
1.1.4.6.4.1.2	Evelyn Rainey (?-)
1.1.4.6.4.1.3	Karen Rainey (?-)

The children of Tommy Aubrey Rainey and (?):

1.1.4.6.5.1.1	Thomas Rainey ((1956-1982)
1.1.4.6.5.1.2	Jack Rainey (?-)
1.1.4.6.5.1.3	William Rainey (?-)

The children of Jackie Ray and Helen Rainey:

1.1.4.6.5.2.1	Mitzi Rainey (?-)
1.1.4.6.5.2.2	Brenda Rainey (?-)

1.1.4.6.5.2.3   Esta Rainey (?-)
1.1.4.6.5.2.4   Christine Rainey (?-)

Eighth Generation

The children of Theodore Carlos Hall and Beverly Daniels:
1.1.2.2.2.2.2.1   Wendy Lee Hall (1960-)
1.1.2.2.2.2.2.2   Thea Joy Hall (1961-)

The children of Roger Evan Hall and Sharon Lynn Holland:
1.1.2.2.2.2.3.1   Jeffrey Evan Hall (1967-)
1.1.2.2.2.2.3.2   David Theodore Hall (1970-)

The children of Janette Arlene Hall and John Knuckles:
1.1.2.2.2.2.4.1   Valorie June Knuckles (1964-)
1.1.2.2.2.2.4.2   John Roger Knuckles (1968-)

The children of Marjorie Evelyn Hall and Floyd Johnson:
1.1.2.2.2.2.5.1   William Troy Johnson (?-)
1.1.2.2.2.2.5.2   Raymond Kent Johnson (?-)

The children of Barbara Joy Hall (1945-) and Charles Bradley Pearson:
1.1.2.2.2.2.6.1   Pamela Ann Pearson (1964-)
1.1.2.2.2.2.6.2   Lorena Ruth Pearson (1966-)
1.1.2.2.2.2.6.3   Charles Bradley Pearson (1969-)
1.1.2.2.2.2.6.4   Rena Lynn pearson (1970-)
1.1.2.2.2.2.6.5   Tricia Danette Pearson (1971-)

The children of Winnifred Eileen Hall and Danny Anderson:
1.1.2.2.2.2.7.1   Danny Carlos Anderson (1967-)
1.1.2.2.2.2.7.2   Steven Terry anderson (1969-)

The children of Marilyn Kaye Hall and Dennis Hendric:

1.1.2.2.2.2.9.1	Austin Reed Hendric (1979-)
1.1.2.2.2.2.9.2	Arin Hendric (1981-)

The children of Judy Gail (Hall) and Michael M. Lloyd:

1.1.4.1.4.4.1.1	Gwendolyn Lloyd (1975-)
1.1.4.1.4.4.1.2	Carrie Anne Lloyd (1977-)
1.1.4.1.4.4.1.3	Rachel Leona Lloyd (1979-)
1.1.4.1.4.4.1.4	Brett Lloyd (?-)

The children of James Larry and Paula Hall:

1.1.4.1.4.4.2.1	Melanie Ann Hall (?-)

The children of Kathy Ann (Hall) and David Wright:

1.1.4.1.4.4.3.1	Angela Michelle Wright (?-)
1.1.4.1.4.4.3.2	Robert Daryl Wright (?-)

The children of Mark and Robin Hall:

1.1.4.1.4.4.4.1	Marcus Oliver Hall (1985-)
1.1.4.1.4.4.4.2	Greta June (Gracie) Hall (1992-)

The children of David Lee and Paula Kay Hall:

1.1.4.1.4.4.5.1	Corey Douglas Hall (?-)
1.1.4.1.4.4.5.2	Amber Brooke Hall (?-)

The children of Larry Wayne and Christie (Mason) Hall:

1.1.4.2.2.1.1.1	Justin Wayne Hall (1975-)
1.1.4.2.2.1.1.2	Bryan David Hall (1979-)
1.1.4.2.2.1.1.3	Matthew Reid Hall (1981-)

The children of Tracy Kay (Hall) and Chuck Hoenshell:
1.1.4.2.2.1.2.1   Kari Dawn Hoenshell (1980-)
1.1.4.2.2.1.2.2   Eric Ryan Hoenshell (1983-)

The children of Phyllis (Hall) and Kenneth Hendrickson:
1.1.4.2.2.2.1.1   Robert Earl Hendrickson (1978-)

The children of Ronald and Dahlia (Ortiz) Hall:
1.1.4.2.2.2.2.1   Aaron Lee Hall (1983-)

The children of Debra (Hall) and David Robert Nelson:
1.1.4.2.2.4.2.1   Lee David Nelson (1980-)
1.1.4.2.2.4.2.2   Donny Ray Nelson (1982-)

The children of Dianna Lynn (Hall) and Jay Dee Liles:
1.1.4.2.2.4.3.1   Jason Dee Liles (1978-)
1.1.4.2.2.4.3.2   Amy Christine Liles (1981-)

The children of Denise (Hall) and Donald M. Smith:
1.1.4.2.2.4.4.1   Nicole Marie Smith (1985-)
1.1.4.2.2.4.4.2   Kathrine Ray Smith (1987-)
1.1.4.2.2.4.4.3   Daniel Miles Smith (1988-)

The children of Ginger Kaye (Hall) and David Landers:
1.1.4.3.1.1.1.1   Lavina Ruth Landers (1963-)

The children of Ginger Kaye (Hall) and Gary Ramsey:
1.1.4.3.1.1.1.2   Marcella Diane Ramsey (?-)
1.1.4.3.1.1.1.3   Tina Lynn Ramsey (1970)

The children of Mickey and Cynthia Schornick:

1.1.4.3.1.2.2.1	Sarah Schornick (?-)
1.1.4.3.1.2.2.2	Katelyn JoAnn Schornick (1988-)

The children of Kathy (Kandarian) and Steve Diebert:

1.1.4.3.2.1.1.1	Stephanie Leann Diebert (1971-)
1.1.4.3.2.1.1.2	Melissa Ann Diebert (1975-)

The children of Sandra (Papagni) and James Ray:

1.1.4.3.2.3.1.1	Kristina Ray (?-)
1.1.4.3.2.3.1.2	James Ray (?-)

The children of Nancy (Putler) and J. R. Kemp II:

1.1.4.3.3.1.1.1	James Robert Kemp III (1991-)
1.1.4.3.3.1.1.2	Patrick Owen Kemp (1993-)

The children of Gary Lynn and Cindy Smith:

1.1.4.3.3.3.1.1	Ries Nathaniel Smith (1978-)
1.1.4.3.3.3.1.2	Katy Nina Smith (1979-)

The children of Bridget (Smith) and Michael Thomas O'Leary:

1.1.4.3.3.3.2.1`	Heather O'Leary (1971-)

The children of Bridget (Smith) and Charles Patrick Antis:

1.1.4.3.3.3.2.2	Crystal Antis (1975-)

The children of Gregory and Pebbles Smith:

1.1.4.3.3.3.3.1	Jessica Lynn Smith (1987-)
1.1.4.3.3.3.3.2	Geoffrey Paul Smith (1990-)
1.1.4.3.3.3.3.3	Megan Elizabeth Smith (1994-)
1.1.4.3.3.3.3.4	Catherine Michelle Smith (1996-)
1.1.4.3.3.3.3.5	Patricia Lucille Smith (1999-)

The children of Mark and Sherry (?) Rincon:

1.1.4.3.3.4.1.1   Trent Rincon (1977?-)
1.1.4.3.3.4.1.2   Troy Rincon (1979?-)

The children of Debra Ann (Rincon) and David Beach:

1.1,4.3.3.4.2.1   Jonathan Beach (1992?-)
1.1.4.3.3.4.2.2   Justan Beach (1994?-)

The children of Harlan and Ada Harlan:

1.1.4.3.3.4.3.1   Melissa Rincon (1977?-)
1.1.4.3.3.4.3.2   Robbie Rincon (1979?-)

The children of Kelly (Rincon) and Steve Brizeondine:

1.1.4.3.3.4.4.1   Erica Brizeondine (1981?-)
1.1.4.3.3.4.4.2   Jillian Brizeondine (1984?-)

The children of Steve and Jan Swann:

1.1.4.3.4.1.1.1   Kristyn Durelle Swann (1981-)
1.1.4.3.4.1.1.2   Jessica Leanne Swann (1984-)

The children of Gary Alan and Becky Swann:

1.1.4.3.4.1.2.1   Erika Swann (?-)
1.1.4.3.4.1.2.2   Melissa Rae Swann (1982-)

The children of Sandra (Swann) and Mike Bellamy:

1.1.4.3.4.1.3.1   Erica Nicole Bellamy (1983-)
1.1.4.3.4.1.3.2   Brandon Michael Bellamy (1985-)

The children of Darcy (Finley) and Danial Langston:

1.1.4.3.4.3.1.1   Danita Jasmine Langston (1987-)
1.1.4.3.4.3.1.2   David Mitchel Langston (?)
1.1.4.3.4.3.1.3   Dillon James Langston (?)

The children of Nia (Finley) and P. J. Langston, Jr.:

1.1.4.3.4.3.2.1	Renae Charise Langston (?-)
1.1.4.3.4.3.2.2	Chistow Langston (?-)
1.1.4.3.4.3.2.3	Bowdrie Langston (?-)

The children of Kathleen (Terrill) and Arnold Ulloa:

1.1.4.3.6.2.2.1	Jacquelyn Renee Ulloa (1982-)
1.1.4.3.6.2.2.2	Audrey Lynn Ulloa (1985-)
1.1.4.3.6.2.2.3	Olivia Ulloa (1988-)

The children of Cara Lee (Terrill) and Les Burns:

1.1.4.3.6.2.4.1	Kyle Burns(1983-)
1.1.4.3.6.2.4.2	Elise Burns (1987-)

The children of Matthew and Lisa Ceccarelli:

1.1.4.3.7.1.1.1	Alissa Ceccarelli (1987-)
1.1.4.3.7.1.1.2	Shannon Fitzpatric Ceccarelli (?-)

The children of Cheryl (Williams) and Jim French:

1.1.4.3.7.2.4.1	Randy French (?-)

The children of Cheryl (Williams) and (?) Patterson:

1.1.4.3.7.2.2.2	Amber Patterson (?-)

The children of Janeen (Birdman) and Rick Randolph:

1.1.4.3.7.3.1.1	Amanda Randolph (?-)
1.1.4.3.7.1.1.2	Ashley Boone Randolph (?-)
1.1.4.3.7.1.1.3	Jessica Randolph (?-)

The children of Luther Ray (Luke), Jr. (Hall) and Rebecca Smith:

1.1.4.3.8.1.1.1	Rosalie Jean Smith (1977-)
1.1.4.3.8.1.1.2	Amanda Yvonne Smith (1980-)

The children of Angela Rae (Hall) and Jose Refuigeo Ramirez Corona Aquilar:

1.1.4.3.8.1.3.1   John Ross Hall (1991-)
1.1.4.3.8.1.3.2   Michael Dewayne Hall (1993-)

The children of Darrin Dwayne and Mary (Harmon) Hall:

1.1.4.3.8.1.4.1   Zachary Thomas Hall (1991-)
1.1.4.3.8.1.4.2   Matthew Luke Hall (1997-)

The children of Debra Dawn (Hall) and Johnny Bell:

1.1.4.3.8.1.5.1   Lyndey Renee Bell (1991-)

The children of Debra Dawn (Hall) and (?) Miller:

1.1.4.3.8.1.5.2   Mashayla Nicole Miller (Oct. 5, 1999)

The children of David-Hall Grimes and Christy (Herd):

1.1.4.3.11.4.1.1   Courtney Lea Grimes (August 19, 2001-)

The children of Mitsi Rainey and (?):

1.1.4.6.6.2.1.1   Sage Rainey (?) (1995-)

Ninth Generation

The children of Pamela Ann Pearson and Jeffrey Royce Hanson:

1.1.2.2.2.2.6.1.1   Emily Louise Hanson (1991-)
1.1.2.2.2.2.6.1.2   Jared Ryan Hanson (1993-)

The children of Lorena Ruth Pearson and Michael Allred:

1.1.2.2.2.2.6.2.1   Tana Elaine Allred (1983-)
1.1.2.2.2.2.6.2.2   Kena May Allred (1993-)

The children of Charles Bradley Pearson and Judy L. Housekeeper:

1.1.2.2.2.2.6.3.1 Charles Garrett Pearson (1991-)
1.1.2.2.2.2.6.3.2 Paige Kay Pearson (1994-)

The children of Rena Lynn Pearson and Glenn Shane Prestwich:

1.1.2.2.2.2.6.4.1 Kamie Lyn Prestwich (1994-)

The children of Tricia Danette Pearson and Richard Van Wagoner:

1.1.2.2.2.2.6.5.1 Lacey Shay Van Wagoner (February 2, 1992-)
1.1.2.2.2.2.6.5.2 Tia Chantel Van Wagoner (November 18, 1993-)
1.1.2.2.2.2.6.5.3 Rondee Leah Van Wagoner (Agust 22, 1997-)
1.1.2.2.2.2.6.5.4 Shalae Dacy Van Wagoner (August 30, 2001-)

The children of Gwendolyn Lloyd and (?) Lopez:

1.1.4.1.4.4.1.1.1 Celina Renee (Lloyd) Lopez (1992-)

The children of Lavina Landers and Ronald Cardona:

1.1.4.3.1.1.1.1.1 Christopher Lee Cardona (1984-)
1.1.4.3.1.1.1.1.2 Andrew DeWayne Cardona (1987-)
1.1.4.3.1.1.1.1.3 Aaron Raymond Cardona (1987-)

The children of Marcella Ramsey and Randall Jones:

1.1.4.3.1.1.1.2.1 Brandi Jo Jones (1989-)
1.1.4.3.1.1.1.2.2 Beth Marie Jones (1991-)

The children of Tina Lynn Ramsey and (?):

1.1.4.3.1.1.1.3.1 Justin Davis Ramsey (1988-)
1.1.4.3.1.1.1.3.2 Felisha Marie Diane Ramsey (1990-)

The children of Amanda Hall Smith and (?):

1.1.4.3.8.1.1.2.1 Zackary Taylor Smith (December 20, 1998-)

REFERENCES

Banks, Smith Callaway. A ROSTER OF CONFEDERATE SOLDIERS OF BULLOCH COUNTY, GEORGIA 1861-1865 (1991).

UNITED STATES CENSUS OF BULLOCH COUNTY, GEORGIA 1820, transcribed and indexed by Mrs. Alvaretta Kenan, Register, 307-A College Blvd., Statesboro, Georgia 30458.

UNITED STATES CENSUS OF BULLOCH COUNTY, GEORGIA 1840, transcribed and indexed by Mrs. Alvaretta Kenan, Register, 307-A College Blvd., Statesboro, Georgia 30458.

THE FIFTH CENSUS OF THE UNITED STATES 1930 - Bulloch County, Georgia, transcribed and indexed by Mrs. Alvaretta Kenan, Register, 307-A College Blvd., Statesboro, Georgia 30458.

THE SEVENTH CENSUS OF THE UNITED STATES 19350 - Bulloch County, Georgia, transcribed and indexed by Mrs. Alvaretta Kenan, Register, 307-A College Blvd., Statesboro, Georgia 30458.

THE 1960 CENSUS OF BULLOCH COUNTY, GEORGIA, transcribed and indexed by Mrs. Alvaretta Kenan, Register, 307-A College Blvd., Statesboro, Georgia 30458.

THE WORLD BOOK OF HALLS. Volumes 1, 2. Published by Halbert's Family Heritage.

SURNAME SEARCH

[The following is a chronological index of surnames that became a part of the Hall family during the Third, Fourth, Fifth, Sixth, and Seventh Generations.]

G3
Herron, Hamilton, Dean, Woods, Eaves, Merett, Bradley, Sandford, Thompson, Brown, Day

G4
Guttery, Whitehead, Abraham, Miller, Ingle, Brewer, Frey, McDougal, Elsey, Carr, Pennington, Eubanks, Sisemore, Rogers, Eversole, Maner, Patrick

G5
Cheatham, Ferguson, Sitton, Roberts, Prichard, Meyers, Jenkins, Cotton, Algood, Edmondson, Bryan, Tillman, Turner, Robinson, Robb, Swafford, Irons, Lawson, Etter, Gougler, Zinn, Pogue, Manier, Taylor, Howell, Gragg, Huckaby, Tyler, Scoggins, Lanphear, Beard, Payne, Goff, Smith, Potter, White, Sage, Bernard, Holderby, Merrill, Clark, Coonrod, Pursiville, Wright, Cannon, Harris, Hyder, Cole, Crumm, Crisler, Dawson, King, McKissick, Ewing, Miller, Rainey, Hines, Rogers, Thomas, Belser, Morrison, Tobias, Fletcher, Lee, Hays, Avegio, Kodabaugh, Bryant, Geidt, Burrow, Coffee

G6

Jenkins, Wiederman, Neely, Rice, Pettit, Reed, Williams, Horne, Cochran, Zinn, Hollinsworth, Hillis, Heckathorn, Ames, Orchid, Dixon, Pagent, Moyer, Phillips, Smith, Blackwood, Rock, Shamblin, Ezell, Benton, Nieto, Ronning, Klaus, Henderson, Ohl, Tolboe, Endfinger, Meyer, Hewett, Whinery, Carrillo, Gragg, Hales, Duncan, Tatharow, Felther, Williams, Broder, Bacon, Crotcher, Slentz, Elms, Domyan, Marquez, Helton, Browne, Stucky, Ramsey, Schornick, Kandarian, Papagni, Lamanucci, Ceccarelli, Putler, Nuckells, Cleveland, Rincon, Swann, Hinson, Mixon, Finley, Terrill, Sheppard, Musgraves, Holmes, Cole, Mello, Stathakis, Birdman, Robinson, Maddie, Rorabaugh, Lancaster, Lawyer, McKay, Brown, Gott, Chase, Grimes, FitzPatrick, Melton, Katona, Walker, Bolt, Smith, Tobias, Parker, Benevidez, Belcher, Weekley, Price, Ellison, Thomas

G7

Heaton, Daniels, Holland, Knuckles, Johnson, Pearson, Anderson, Hendric, Taylor, Cooke, Turner, Shelley, Weiler, Minugh, Dodgin, Donato, Springer, Robards, Morton, Stewart, Kennedy, Jones, Priola, Lloyd, Parfumorse, Andrew, Duke, McCormick, Wright, Hirschi, Eakin, Noland, Grantham, Schocher, Mason, Hoenshell, Hendrickson, Ortiz, Espinoza, Nelson, Stafford, Liles, Smith, Landers, Ramsey, Hugentober, Coder, Diebert, Lehman, Rice, Ray, Biggs, Akins, Laplaca, Kemp, Meismer, O'Leary, Antis, McDonald, Hoffman, Beach, Lohne, Brizendine, Greenwood, Bellamy, Langston, Bonds, Ulloa, Rock, Burns, Vierra, Parker, Dewitt, Barkley, Patterson, Boone, Randolph, Aquilar, Harmon, Bell, Hockett, McKay, Heard, Burney, Daugherty, Kelley Hanson, Allred, Housekeeper, Prestwich, Van Wagoner, Lopez, Cardona, Jones, Price, Lev

0-595-21750-8

Made in the USA
Columbia, SC
26 April 2025

57173785R00271